"SO HAS YOUR LITTLE GAME ENDED, MA CHERIE?"

Philippe's drawl was contemptuous. "You have what is called a 'dual personality'? On one hand, the innocent; on the other, the tramp?" he accused her, casting magnetic gray eyes down the shivering slopes of her breasts.

"Please, Philippe, listen to me. You don't understand," Daye cried pleadingly, reaching out her arms to him.

"I understand only too well. Both personalities lie in one very alluring woman," he murmured as he moved slowly to embrace her, nuzzling her hair and neck until her senses swam drunkenly. His feverish lips met hers, igniting flames of desire within her, and he whispered bitterly, "I just wish I didn't know all that you are...."

AND NOW…

SUPERROMANCES

Worldwide Library is proud to present a
sensational new series of modern love stories —
SUPERROMANCES

Written by masters of the genre, these longer,
sensuous and dramatic novels are truly in keeping
with today's changing life-styles. Full of intriguing
conflicts, the heartaches and delights of true love,
SUPERROMANCES are absorbing stories —
satisfying and sophisticated reading that lovers
of romance fiction have long been waiting for.

SUPERROMANCES
Contemporary love stories for the woman of today!

Daphne Hamilton

PRELUDE TO PARADISE

A SUPERROMANCE FROM
WORLDWIDE

TORONTO · NEW YORK · LOS ANGELES · LONDON

Published January 1983

First printing November 1982

ISBN 0-373-70048-2

CHAPTER ONE

THE YOUNG WOMAN framed within the television screen was exquisitely beautiful. Fine, richly golden hair tumbled to her shoulders. She had large dark green eyes and a delicately boned face with perfect features. She wore a shimmering golden gown fitted to reveal a slender yet curvaceous body, and when she spoke her voice possessed a lilting quality pleasing to the ear. "I'm Gloria Day," she told her unseen audience, "and *this* is Golden Dreams perfume from Max Lucan." A smile curved her lovely mouth as she indicated a small pear-shaped bottle balanced on her upturned palm. Without haste she removed the golden stopper and touched the perfume wand to her graceful throat. "Wear Golden Dreams, ladies," she huskily advised, "and all his dreams will be of you."

With an impatient movement, Daye Hollister flicked the television's off switch and then gazed for a moment at the blank screen. Well, at least she no longer felt embarrassed, she thought. Now she felt only intense irritation. She gave a small resigned sigh and turned to face the man who was sprawled comfortably in her largest armchair. "Well, Reg, that was Gloria's latest endeavor. Satisfied?"

If Reg Parker noticed the sarcasm in her voice, he chose to ignore it. "Terrific! Another winner, Daye, luv."

She smiled slightly. "As far as you're concerned, everything Gloria does is terrific."

Reg grinned amiably. "Can I help it if I'm mad about the girl? You must admit, luv, Gloria is an absolutely ravishing female."

"She was wearing false eyelashes."

"But we both know she doesn't really need them; the girl is a *genuine* beauty. Besides which—" he rolled his blue eyes appreciatively "—she radiates enough sex appeal to sizzle an iceberg."

"Amazing, isn't it? Particularly when she is in fact a chilly virgin." Daye moved with restless grace to the window and stared absently into the quiet cul-de-sac below.

"Now, I wouldn't say that. . . ." His tone was light, teasing. "That she's chilly, I mean. I'd say that our Gloria's fires are banked. When the right male comes along—*whoosh!* Talk about infernos."

"You make it sound devastating." She smiled over her shoulder.

"I've heard love often is." There was something different in his voice now, and he got to his feet rather abruptly. "What I need is a drink."

"I'll make it, Reg," she said, and moved quickly to the sideboard on which an assortment of decanters and drinking glasses was arranged.

"Scotch and a dash of soda," she said, feeling the need to keep on talking. "There you are, darling, just as you like it."

Reg took the glass and raised it in a silent salute before he drank. Over the rim he watched her steadily until she uttered a protesting murmur and turned her head away. But she looked back almost immediately and said, "Did you suppose I would change my mind after watching myself just now?"

He lifted his shoulders. "Actually, luv, I refuse to believe you are really serious."

"Oh, I am, I assure you. I have no intention of signing the new Lucan contract. Reg, I'm fed up with Gloria Day, really fed up! I simply can't go on."

His brow creased. "All right, so you're fed up. We all get fed up at times. But, Daye, do you realize exactly *what* you are doing? There's a great deal of money involved here, and for your own good...." He swallowed the remainder of his drink before adding, "You're already famous, luv, but there's no telling how far you could go if you stay with Lucan for another year or so."

"But I don't want to go any further! I don't like being where I am now!" Daye spoke vehemently. "Reg, you know me so well you must know I'm speaking the truth." And when he didn't answer, she flung herself onto the padded velvet love seat and stared at him half angrily, half anxiously. "Oh, darling, don't you see how I seethe with resentment because I've let myself be molded into someone I'm not?"

He grinned. "Come on, now, aren't you exaggerating? You're still the same old Daye inside."

She nodded. "That's the problem, I suppose. Had I changed along with my outer image I'd most likely be quite happy and contented. As it is, I'm definitely not."

He studied her a moment, his long fingers tapping against his empty glass. "Okay, then, you're chucking Gloria in. So what will you do when this contract is up? Do you want to work as a photo model again? The money won't be nearly as much as you've made with Lucan, but you can pick and choose your assignments. And there are bound to be plenty of those once word gets around that you're leaving Lucan.''

Daye didn't answer immediately. She was wondering rather nervously what Reg would say when she told him. She twisted her fingers together and looked at them with concentration. ''Well, here goes,'' she said, and looked up to meet his eyes. ''I...I won't be taking any assignments, Reg.''

''Hmm?'' He frowned.

''No. You see, I'm going to—'' she forced a laugh ''—retire. Well, for a long time, at any rate. I have quite a bit of money saved, and if I'm careful it will last me a few years.''

''Let me get this straight,'' Reg said slowly. ''You, Daye, are giving up your career. Completely?''

''Yes.''

The silence was long and intensely uncomfortable. Then Reg said uneasily, ''It's a man, isn't it? You've met someone, Daye.''

''No!'' Daye blurted the word and then bit her lip. That wasn't true; she *had* met someone. Only it wasn't the way Reg thought. ''If...if you mean have I fallen in love—no, I have not,'' she said decisively and for some inexplicable reason rather irritably.

''But your career....'' Reg shook his head. ''Is it Max? Do you feel this is the only way you'll ever get rid of him? Daye, luv, short of moving to the moon—or getting married to someone else—you won't get rid of Max so easily.''

''You're barking up the wrong tree, Reg, although I will admit Max is rather a problem.'' Daye was unable to suppress an uneasy shudder. For all his wealth and power and dark good looks, Max Lucan, the president of Lucan Cosmetics, was not a man she could admire or even like. He was far too ruthless and domineering, and in a black temper he could be unspeakably rude to his employees. For the past two years Max had pursued her, evidently assuming that she would eventually give in and agree to marry him. Often his attentions had left her with her nerves frayed to the breaking point. Still, she couldn't blame Max for her decision. She told this to Reg, adding, "I can't blame any particular person or thing. It's me, Reg. I'd like to be free to do as I choose, to go where I please."

"Wouldn't we all?" Reg uttered a short laugh and crossed to the sideboard. Daye watched him, feeling a surge of affection. He was a tall man and rather thin. His thick light hair was touched with gray and there were deep laughter lines about his eyes and mouth. Not a handsome man, she thought, but very dear.

Presently he came back to her and handed her a glass of white wine. Then he lowered himself into a chair opposite her and drank from his own replenished glass before saying, "Your mother's been dead almost a year now—have you been planning this career break since then?"

"No, I haven't. At least, not consciously." Daye swallowed. The death of her gentle, beautiful mother still caused her anguish. "Of course, if mother were still alive I would certainly have stayed with Lucan."

Reg asked idly, "How long have you been planning to do this?"

She stared at her pink fingernails. She could have

told him four months and two days exactly, but she did not. "A few months," she answered vaguely, raising her eyes.

He sat there staring at her, hunched forward, his elbows on his knees and his glass of Scotch clasped in both hands. Suddenly he said, "You're twenty-two, Daye, and at your peak in this business, I'd say. You ought to take advantage while you can." He grinned, but she knew it was forced. "After all, in a few years you might have sagged and wrinkled, and have no alternative but to retire."

"What a comforting thought," she retorted.

His eyes moved over her face. "In my professional capacity, I'd say the chances are highly unlikely," he amended softly. "You, Daye, will be beautiful when you're eighty."

She looked at him silently, feeling a compelling desire to weep. To prevent herself from doing so, she raised the glass of wine to her lips. After a few moments she felt better and flashed Reg a smile. "You know, darling, I'm not denying you're right," she said gently. "I *am* only twenty-two, and if I had any sense I *would* take advantage of the next few years. Why, I could become rich, couldn't I?" She gave a little laugh. "I'm almost rich now. I own a house in the country and a super sports car—which, incidentally, I've driven only three times—and all this." Her eyes roamed about the living room of her small but delightful Mayfair flat. Without regard to cost she had chosen darkly gleaming mahogany furniture and luxurious pile carpeting. Two fine original paintings graced the walls, and behind the glass doors of the china cabinet were several exquisite antique figurines. Her bedroom, too, was beautifully furnished, and her wardrobe housed a costly selection of clothing that included two fur coats. One of these she'd bought herself, and she'd worn it often. The other, a far more expensive fur, was a birthday present; so far she had not been able to bring herself to wear it. . . .

"Pleasant, the things money can buy." Reg's voice broke into her thoughts.

She laughed. "You read my mind. Yes, I agree, it's extremely pleasant, but I wonder. . . ." She hesitated. "In my case it hasn't brought happiness, has it?"

"Don't be trite, luv."

"I mean it! Oh, I suppose it has in at least one way. I was able to take care of my mother, to keep her out of that sanatorium, and that was all I ever wanted. But I could have done that if I'd stayed with you, couldn't I? We'd become a successful team in four years." Unconsciously her tone had become wistful. "And then I signed with Lucan."

Reg swallowed his Scotch and put the empty glass on the table beside him. "Look here, Daye, I advised you to accept Max Lucan's offer because I wanted you to have a chance to be something more than a photographer's model. I'm damn sorry you've been so miserable, but I meant well and most girls would be grateful. . . ." He drew in his breath, his eyes glinting angrily. "Damn it, your mother spent her last months in a lovely country house that Lucan money bought. And that's Lucan money in your bank account. You have all that beautiful security because you work for Lucan."

"And I work hard for it! Beastly hard!" Daye's hand trembled, threatening to spill the wine in the glass she held. Reaching forward she placed it on the low table in front of the love seat, and sat up straight and glared at Reg. "I haven't had a proper rest for the past two years! Sometimes it seems I'm living in a weird dream, I'm so exhausted. Filming, photo sessions, personal appearances—do you have any idea what those personal appearances are like?" The tone of her voice rose, taking on a shrill, desperate note. "I have to stand for hours in that uncomfortable gown and answer foolish questions. I have to smile and remain sweetly charming no matter what the circumstances, no matter how I feel. Sometimes a woman in the crowd will be openly hostile, and *always* there's at least one man who will do his best to paw me as if I were a...a piece of merchandise." Her voice shaking, she broke off, then covered her face with her hands and began to cry.

Reg was beside her instantly, taking her in his arms and holding her tightly. He let her cry for a time, then he gently began mopping her cheeks with his handkerchief. "Don't cry," he begged, "I can't bear it. You know I didn't mean to be so disagreeable, but I'm worried about you and I'm upset because I feel that you're slipping away from me. Plus—" he paused to kiss her cheek "—I'm damn mad at myself for not noticing you were unhappy. What a friend I am! My poor little luv, you're right, you have worked hard. And not only for Lucan. When you were a kid of sixteen you were working at a shop in the morning and for Milo and me in the afternoon. And you spent the weekend taking care of your mother. Hey!" He tilted her chin and smiled into her reddened eyes. "You'd better give up being Gloria. If I caught some chap pawing you, I might commit murder."

"Oh, Reg!" Daye put her arms around his neck and hugged him. "I do appreciate you and all you've done for me. Sometimes I feel I don't deserve you." She sighed, feeling emotional again. "You would make a marvelous husband. If I weren't such a silly fool I would—" She stopped rather abruptly, lowering her arms and eyeing him tentatively.

"Love me enough to marry me?" Reg laughed without humor. "Never mind. Can't be helped and all that. Just look upon old Reg as one of the crowd of lovesick males who pant after you."

"But you are special," she said, distressed by his bitter tone.

"I know I am! Now stop looking so tragic, luv." He kissed her abruptly and stood up. "By the way, we have an anniversary in three days. Had you forgotten?"

She shook her head. "Do I ever forget?"

"No, can't say you do. So it will be our sixth, won't it? Six years since you walked into Sam Milo's studio and asked for the job. Only you said 'position' in a very prim little voice." Reg's expression was almost dreamy. "I remember I couldn't take my eyes off you. You were so damn beautiful, I was already photographing you in my mind."

"You were so sweet to me, but when I had to tell you I was only sixteen, you said I was too young," Daye recalled. "I almost hated you because the advertisement had said 'excellent wages,' and I so badly wanted the job—position." She laughed. "Oh, how I pleaded!"

"And won! I wasn't to know it then, but that turned out to be my lucky break. I've had the nerve to suggest *you* should be grateful when all the time it's I who should be." He reached out to briefly touch her hair. "Because of you I've become successful. I've got my own studio and more assignments than I can keep up with. What a lot I have to thank you for."

"You would have been a success without me. Reg, you're a superb photographer."

"Agreed," he said smugly. Then, "Daye, remember my first sale as a free-lancer? There you were in black and white, with no makeup and your hair as straight as a pick. The offers came flying in after that for both of us." He paused and gave her a thoughtful glance. "I suppose that's why I advised you to take the Lucan offer. I always knew you could have earned three times as much if you hadn't elected to stay with me."

"I loved working with you," she said warmly. "You were everything to me: teacher, adviser, comforter...." She hesitated, but met his eyes frankly. "I'll never forget the risk you took for me. No! Don't turn away, darling, I must say it. You took a terrible risk. Sam Milo had some brutal friends, and when you destroyed those negatives I was desperately afraid for your safety." The memory caused her to feel agitated, and she fiddled nervously with the buttons on her blue silk blouse.

He looked down at her moodily. "Luv, you know damn well I would have deserved it if he had sent someone after me. I wasn't unaware of Sam's little sideline; I'd even helped him. Can't say it ever bothered me, either. Not until he tried to drag you into it."

They stared at each other a moment, then Daye said, "I shouldn't have brought it up. Now I've made us both miserable. Oh, Reg, why can't we remember only pleasant things?''

He grinned faintly. ''Don't you know it's the unpleasant things that build one's character? And speaking of unpleasant things—'' he grimaced ''—I suppose you'd like me to tell Max the bad news? Of course you would! Well, don't worry about it, luv, although I don't think my telling him will be the end of it. Max won't let you off too easily.''

Her face shadowed. ''I know that. But my contract has only two weeks to run, and then I can leave London.'' She noticed his frown and added quickly, ''I'll go to the Isle of Skye. You remember Flora Evans, my mother's nurse, don't you? Well, she moved to Skye three months ago, and I promised to visit the first chance I got.''

His brow cleared and he nodded approvingly. Then he glanced at his wristwatch and declared he must be off. As much as she enjoyed his company, Daye was relieved when he promptly left. Had he stayed longer he undoubtedly would have questioned her about her plans after leaving Skye, and this she wanted to avoid. Daye tried to imagine looking her friend in the eye and saying, ''A man I met in Paris has invited me to stay on his island. It's in the South Pacific, Reg, near Tahiti, I believe. Now, you mustn't worry, dear, because Charles Chavot is a sweet, good man and quite old enough to be my father....''

''Oh, heavens, no!'' she said aloud and got to her feet. Reg would explode if she told him that. He would accuse Charles of being a lecherous scoundrel and her of being bewitched, or else a little mad. Restlessly Daye paced back and forth. She wouldn't write to Reg until she was settled in her new environment, she thought. After all, she couldn't expect Reg or anyone else to understand about Charles. She herself had, at times, marveled at the relationship that had developed between two perfect strangers in the space of a few hours—a relationship, moreover, having nothing to do with sexual attraction. Charles Chavot was a handsome widower, it was true, but to Daye he was like a father. Her own father had died when she was seven and she realized she might subconsciously have missed him and have longed for someone to take his place. In Charles's case, she felt sure he saw in her a daughter. For his own daughter, Claudette, had died five years earlier. Had she lived, she would have been exactly Daye's age.

This odd coincidence—Daye's sharing his daughter's birthday—had sparked Charles's sympathetic interest in her into something more personal and caused him to declare that Madame Fate had directed his footsteps to the garden where he'd encountered her. "Why else would I suddenly desire a stroll in the moonlight?" he asked. "The night is cool, and my blood longs for my tropical home." Charles had a beautiful voice, Daye remembered, and he spoke English with an attractive French accent.

Daye stopped pacing, and a muffled sound escaped her as another voice echoed in the silent room, another face slipped into her mind. She did not want to think of *him*, but it was impossible not to, for in a way he and Charles were connected. It was because of *him*, the other Frenchman, that she'd met Charles in the first place. Quite unintentionally, that man had done her a great favor—a favor she deserved after the bitterly cruel and insulting words he had directed at her shocked ears. Daye shuddered, thrusting the memory of his voice and hard, handsome face away from her. True, he had done her a favor but she could feel nothing but hatred for him. Hatred . . . and a disturbing desire for revenge.

Her legs were trembling, and she felt rather sick. She was hungry, she told herself, trying to ignore the fact that she felt this way every time that other Frenchman's image came back to haunt her. Swiftly she left the room and went into the small, beautifully efficient kitchen. In the refrigerator was a tempting-looking chicken salad that Millie, her daily maid, had left for her, but she regarded it without enthusiasm. It seemed, sometimes, that she survived on salads; she was only too aware that the camera ruthlessly added extra pounds. She was, however, more appropriate for her role than a high-fashion model would be, since the Golden Dream Girl was supposed to be curvaceous. Daye couldn't have been in high fashion had she wanted to; she possessed neither the height nor the exaggerated bone structure fashion designers seemed to prefer.

Although it was August, the evening was growing chilly and Daye moved about the flat closing windows. She would eat her salad, she told herself, and afterward would watch a little television before going to bed early. She was still a working girl with a contract to honor—but not for much longer. Such glorious relief swept through her that she wondered if she *could* be just a little mad. Many girls would give anything to be in her shoes.

After she had eaten, she made a mug of instant coffee and carried it into the living room. The program on television was a comedy, one of her favorites, but she found herself completely unable to concentrate, and after a while she gave up trying. She knew, of course, what the problem was, and she realized there was not much use fighting it. Why not indulge those memories, she thought. Perhaps she would feel better for doing so. Leaning her head back, she closed her eyes and allowed her mind to drift back four months, to Paris and the evening of her twenty-second birthday

CHAPTER TWO

SHE HAD BEEN IN PARIS for three days promoting the Lucan products at several exclusive boutiques. A photographer and two other members of Max Lucan's staff had accompanied her, and that afternoon Reg had flown in to help her celebrate her birthday. She was not much in the mood for celebration by the time she arrived back at her hotel, however. What she really wanted to do was slip out of her golden gown, cream off her makeup and soak for ages in a tub of scented water. But Reg wouldn't hear of it. An aggravating little grin on his face, he firmly urged her through the hotel's vast lobby and down a long corridor to a private dining room. There, to her surprise, Daye found about thirty of her friends and co-workers assembled to give her a birthday party. "Courtesy of dear old Max," Reg had murmured. "Everyone flown over at his expense. I'll say this, Daye, where *you* are concerned Max can be extremely thoughtful and generous."

She pulled a face, then said hopefully, "I wouldn't imagine Max will be able to get here."

"Wishful thinking? Sorry, luv. Although Max has been in Spain on business, his pilot will bring him to Paris so that he can wish his Dream Girl a happy birthday." Reg slipped his arm about her. "He probably won't stay more than an hour or so—you know how Max hates parties. So come on, luv, have some champagne and *smile*, for God's sake!''

The party was well under way by the time Max arrived, and Daye was glad she had drunk two or three glasses of wine. She could then more easily tolerate Max's rather excessive embrace, and the manner in which his bold dark eyes roamed possessively over her. But when he began to propel her away from her friends and toward the door, she drew back in protest.

Max Lucan was quick-tempered, and it showed in his expression. ''Relax, little girl, I have a present for you,'' he snapped irritably, but when Daye still held back, his expression and his voice softened. ''I want to give it to you in private. It's a present from my board of directors, Gloria.''

Stifling a sigh, Daye gave in and allowed Max to lead her to a small anteroom at the end of the corridor. One of the hotel's porters waited there, obviously standing guard over a large beribboned box. She had suspected what it contained, but still she was unable to prevent a gasp of pleasure and admiration from escaping her lips. ''It's absolutely beautiful!'' she breathed, tentatively reaching out to touch the pale, luxurious mink. ''But I can't accept it, Max. You know I can't.''

''You can and you will.'' Max spoke smoothly. ''It's a present from the board, as I told you, Gloria. We all appreciate our Dream Girl.'' He removed the coat from its bed of tissue and tucked it about her shoulders, holding it there as he bent his head to kiss her unresponsive mouth. ''Next time it will be ermine, sweetheart.''

Considerably startled by such a promise, Daye

said, "Oh, really, Max. . . ." and went no further. The awareness that swept over her was as shocking as it was sudden, and she turned her head to gaze uneasily toward the doorway.

A man was standing there: a tall, strikingly attractive man dressed in evening clothes. He stood very still, watching them with curious intensity. Daye thought she had never before seen such incredible eyes, so light in color and so unusually clear. But perhaps they only appeared to be because he was extremely tanned, and his hair looked as black as night. She shivered, experiencing an emotion that was inexplicably tormenting. Not understanding exactly why, she slipped out of Max's arms and moved slowly away, her eyes never leaving the tall stranger's face.

Her movement appeared to break the stranger's concentration. *"Pardonnez-moi!"* he muttered. His clear eyes darted quickly to Max, then returned to linger on her face.

Max, who evidently had been unaware of the man's presence until he spoke, glowered. "What the devil do you want?" he demanded truculently.

The tall man looked surprised. Daye saw anger flare in his expression. "It appears I intrude, *monsieur.*" His voice, with its slight French accent, was cold.

"You certainly do! And now that you know it, will you kindly leave?"

Daye gasped. Accustomed as she was to Max's autocratic, often insufferable behavior toward his staff, she was unprepared for him to be so blatantly rude to a perfect stranger. Shaken by sudden temper, she glared at Max before returning her gaze to the

Frenchman. "I'm sorry," she said faintly, taking it upon herself to apologize.

He smiled, his teeth flashing pure white against his tan. "*Je vous en pris*, do not concern yourself," he answered in an almost lazy tone and moved into the room, pausing only a few feet away from her. "I was here earlier, *madame*, and carelessly left something." He spoke directly to her, ignoring Max completely.

"Yes, of course. Please, do look. This isn't a private room, after all." Daye wondered if her voice sounded as strange to him as it did to her.

"*Merci.*" He inclined his dark head and moved over to a small table standing against the wall. "*Voilà!*" He held up a gold lighter before slipping it into the pocket of his superbly tailored jacket. "And now *madame*, I will intrude upon you and your husband no longer. *Bonsoir.*" He glanced briefly at Max. "*Bonsoir, monsieur,*" he said, and there was the hint of insolence in his tone.

"No!" The denial burst suddenly from her lips, and the tall Frenchman looked mildly intrigued. "I mean, I'm not *madame*," she went on distractedly. "We—" she gestured vaguely toward Max "—are not married." She stopped, pressing her fingers against her mouth. What on earth was the matter with her? Why was she explaining all this to a perfect stranger?

Evidently Max wondered the same for he said explosively, "This is ridiculous!" He strode over to her and thrust his arm about her shoulders and held her firmly. Daye wanted to protest, to move away, but she did neither. She had already made an enormous fool of herself, she thought miserably. Better now if she simply kept quiet.

But almost against her will her eyes were drawn once more to the Frenchman's face. He was looking at the two of them, no doubt seeing Max's jealously possessive embrace. Then his beautiful mouth curved in a brief, slightly wry smile, and with grace he turned and strolled out of the room. Daye watched him go, not understanding the sensation of desolation that crept over her. Or was it, she wondered, that she didn't want to understand? The possibility of this was provocative, and she was relieved when Max suggested they return to her birthday party. She was also relieved, and surprised, that Max refrained from mentioning the Frenchman and the fact that she had more or less sided with the stranger. But perhaps even Max was aware when he was in the wrong and considered it prudent to keep silent.

Max stayed for nearly an hour, and after he left everyone relaxed visibly and began to enjoy the party—everyone but Daye, who though exhausted, was restless. She was, consequently, extremely relieved when Reg, who had shown signs of drinking himself into oblivion, suddenly decided he needed to sleep. "I'll go up with him," she told the others, and after protesting a trifle halfheartedly they all returned to their fun. Daye hastily retrieved her new fur coat and handbag and left with her bleary-eyed friend.

In the elevator, Reg tipsily insisted on draping the coat around his own shoulders, and when she laughed at him he put his arms around her and proceeded to nibble at her ear. Since they were alone, Daye tolerated this familiarity with affectionate amusement, but when the elevator stopped at Reg's floor, and the doors began to slide apart, she tried to extricate herself from his embrace. "We're here, Reg—behave yourself!" she scolded laughingly. "Now do stop it, darling, that hurt!"

"You are having difficulty, *mademoiselle*?" The male voice was familiar.

Daye turned her head quickly. The tall Frenchman was standing just outside the elevator, one hand on the edge of the door to prevent it from closing. The dark stranger, she realized, had been with her in thought the entire evening but she had not expected ever to see him again! Her heart flipped crazily and she felt warm color touch her cheeks. "Oh, it's you!" she declared breathlessly and took a step toward him, stopping when she noticed what she was doing. "It's you, isn't it?" This time she spoke lamely.

"C'est moi!" he agreed. His eyes roved over her face almost thoughtfully before looking beyond her to Reg. "Your...companion appears to need assistance," he added dryly.

Daye turned to Reg. He was leaning against the wall of the elevator, his chin on his chest. He looked pathetic and a little foolish with the fur coat still around his shoulders. Daye's heart went out to him. "Oh, darling, come along, don't go to sleep here," she coaxed.

Reg raised his head and grinned foolishly. "Lead me to bed then, luv." He put his arm around her. "Give us a kiss, first, Dream Girl."

"Reg!" she protested, knowing the Frenchman was watching. "Come *on*! Someone wants to use the elevator." At her urging Reg moved obediently, saluting the Frenchman as he passed and then ruining his exit by stumbling and almost falling. The Frenchman steadied him with his free hand, and Reg said gravely, "Thanks, old man."

"De rien." He spoke just as gravely, his face expressionless. *Oh, but he's terribly good-looking,* Daye thought. She who had been quite unaffected by many handsome men, was unable to prevent herself from staring at him. His dark hair was thick and inclined to waviness, his face well shaped, and his firm chin had just the slightest hint of a cleft. He turned his head suddenly, and she saw that his eyes were, as she had first thought, the purest light gray. Confused because she was caught staring, she gave him a hesitant smile. But he made no attempt to return it. Instead his lips pressed into a grim line, and his eyes became as cold and bleak as ice. Daye shivered, unaccustomed to being viewed with such hostility by a member of the opposite sex.

Her lips parted, but before she could speak, he said in a low angry voice, "Do you consider it fair to take advantage of this gentleman in his condition? Has your evening not been profitable enough?"

She stared at him in absolute bewilderment. "What?" she asked faintly.

"Such innocence!" His laugh was short, mirthless. Then he turned to Reg who stood smiling inanely. *"Mon ami, mon pauvre ami*, I wish you luck! You will, I fear, have difficulty competing with *mademoiselle*'s earlier admirer," he said, as he derisively motioned toward the fur coat now hanging carelessly from one of Reg's shoulders. He cast a brilliantly scornful glance at Daye, stepped swiftly into the elevator and allowed the doors to slide shut.

Feeling curiously numb, Daye stared at the closed doors and listened to the low hum of the elevator as it descended. What on earth did the Frenchman mean by those words, she wondered. She asked herself the question several times, until she finally accepted the fact that she knew quite well what he meant. She felt suddenly ill. After coming upon her earlier in Max's embrace and moments ago in Reg's, the Frenchman had formed his own opinion of her morals. And what an opinion!

It was Reg's rather plaintive voice that jerked her back to his plight. Even so, she went with him to his room feeling as if she was sleepwalking. It wasn't until he was snoring contentedly into his pillow that she realized her mind was clear, and the emotion that now filled her was a cold, resentful anger toward the Frenchman.

How dare he, she thought as she left Reg's room and turned down the corridor toward the elevator. How dare he! It was bad enough that he should have formed a completely erroneous opinion of her, but it was worse by far that he should take it upon himself to chastise and insult her. She reached the elevator and pressed the button. Well, she would have to find him, she thought, impatiently tapping one foot in its lacy gold sandal. She would not be able to rest until she had told him exactly what was on her mind.

But when she left the elevator and stepped into the huge hotel lobby, she hesitated. There were still many people around—people of all nationalities—but so far there was no sign of the tall Frenchman. However, she thought with resignation, it was unlikely that he would be here, wandering about the lobby. Perhaps he had left the hotel, or perhaps he was in one of the cocktail bars or lounges. She gave a frustrated sigh. For the past few years she had seldom gone anywhere unescorted, particularly into cocktail bars and such, and she knew now she had not the courage to begin making that sort of round. A small group of brown-skinned, black-eyed men passed her, their glances filled with admiration and curiosity. With a vague sense of embarrassment, Daye remembered she still wore the golden gown. Designed especially for her, it was one of several identical ones she wore as Lucan's Golden Dream Girl. It was undeniably a beautiful creation, though it was deliberately ostentatious and at the moment quite out of place. Which rather settled it, she thought, turning to go back to the elevator. She could only hope the Frenchman was staying in the hotel and that she would meet him again....

"Gloria!"

Daye turned, automatically acknowledging the name Max Lucan had given her two years ago. Bruce Janis, the photographer who had accompanied her to Paris, was crossing the lobby toward her. "Where are you off to?" he asked in his somewhat slow voice. "Well, no matter, you are coming with me, aren't you? I'm joining a few of the others in the downstairs lounge. It seems a French chanteuse is appearing and they say she is absolutely super!" He took her hand, tucking it under his arm and talking all the while. Daye allowed him to lead her into the ultraplush downstairs lounge, feeling as she did so an uncanny sense of inevitability.

The lights were blazing and on a small dais at one end of the room Daye saw a black-haired woman in a sequined gown smiling and blowing kisses at her loudly applauding audience. Evidently the chanteuse had just finished a number, but Daye wasn't really interested. Almost instinctively she turned her head and saw him. He was standing near the bar, one hand resting on the red padded surface, the other holding a glass. He was listening, his dark head slightly tilted, to the plump woman who stood in front of him, and as Daye watched he laughed as though really amused. Then he saw Daye, and his amusement seemed to fade. Quite deliberately he stared at her and she could see how coldly his eyes glittered.

"Gloria, wake up, darling! The others are over there." Bruce tugged at her arm, and before Daye turned to him she knew the Frenchman had noticed.

Oh, dear heavens, she thought, as she followed Bruce to the small table around which half a dozen of their friends were crowded. *This is the third time tonight, and each time I've been with a different man.* A desperate urgency swept through her as she realized what the Frenchman must be thinking, and she knew she had to go to him at once—not to give him the intended, angry piece of her mind, but to explain, to clear herself.

Mumbling some vague excuse, she left her friends and began to make her way toward the bar at the other end of the room. The Frenchman's back was turned, and he now appeared to be in conversation with a middle-aged man whose bald head gleamed under the lights. As she approached, Daye saw the man watching her rather avidly and when she paused, reaching out a tentative hand to touch the tall Frenchman's sleeve, he said in hearty British tones, "You Frenchmen have all the luck! Well, old boy, I shouldn't imagine you'll be a bachelor much longer; this one is a *beauty*!"

The Frenchman seemed to stiffen, then he turned

slowly and stared down at her. *"Que désirez-vous?"* he asked tersely, and when she looked confused, he repeated, "What do you want?" Spoken in English, the question sounded more than terse—it sounded rude.

Wishing she felt less intimidated, Daye forced a smile. "I should like to speak to you in private, if you wouldn't mind."

"Pourquoi?"

Daye knew he had asked why. Fighting the desire to be rude in turn, she answered with quiet patience, "Because I do *not* want to say what I have to say in front of others."

The Frenchman looked down at her with narrowed eyes. "I can well understand why you would not wish to do so. However, *mademoiselle*, I must refuse your request." His tone was sarcastic.

Daye's temper rose but before she could say anything, the bald Englishman asked jovially, "Will I do, miss? I should love to speak to you in private."

Daye cast him a harried glance and he shrugged his shoulders and moved a little farther away.

"Well?" The Frenchman spoke softly. "*Will* he do, *mademoiselle*?"

Her cheeks felt hot. "You are extremely rude!" she said distinctly. "I don't know why I'm putting myself out like this. It's becoming quite obvious to me that you would not be interested. . . ." She broke off without finishing the sentence. A lump had formed in her throat. As she turned to leave the Frenchman caught her wrist in a firm grip, and she gazed at him in surprise.

He spoke clearly but softly. "You are correct, *mademoiselle*, I am *not* interested. And if I were—"

he paused, his clear eyes darting over her in an almost insulting manner ''—I should feel compelled to inform you that I have never in the past purchased the favors of *la femme* and I do not expect to do so in the future.''

Still holding her wrist, he raised his other arm and swallowed the contents of the glass he held. Then he looked at her, a cruel little smile on his mouth. ''But do not despair, *petite Anglaise*, for I am certain there are men in this room who are not, shall we say, as fortunate as I?'' He released her arm as if it had suddenly scorched him. ''Go, then! The evening is still young for a lady of the night.''

If she had been shocked earlier, it was nothing compared to the way she felt now. All the blood seemed to have drained from her body, leaving her rigid and chilled to the bone. And although her mind was completely alert, she was unable to speak because her throat felt as though a heavy cord was inexorably tightening around it. But she could see quite clearly, could see that the Frenchman's eyes were on her face and that he looked patently disturbed. She was wondering if she looked as dreadful as she felt when he said savagely, ''Do not look at me so! I refuse, *mademoiselle*, to believe that you can be so shattered because you are told the truth. *Mon Dieu!*'' He turned swiftly and put his empty glass on the bar.

There was a dull throbbing in Daye's head as she stared fixedly at the Frenchman's straight, rather broad back. She wondered absently if she could bring herself to plunge a knife into it—if she had a knife and the ability to move. Oh, God, but she had to move! She had to get out of here, away from the laughter and conversation, away from the curious onlookers who must be watching and wondering about the woman who was so obviously being humiliated. She must get away from this hateful man before she found her voice and *screamed*.

He swung around in a swift, unexpected movement. "I imagine, *mademoiselle*, you are convinced I am *très*...I am extremely narrow-minded, *n'est-ce pas?*" His voice was soft but still the note of savagery remained. "However, I am not. Indeed, I can understand and respect a woman who is mistress to one particular lover. What I cannot tolerate is a woman who is mistress to many. A woman such as yourself, *petite Anglaise*, who sells her beauty...."

In that moment Daye had the most certain impression he was inviting her to slap him. They glared at each other, he with contempt, she with white-hot hatred. Her hands clenched, then all at once her fury abated leaving her weak and shivering and dangerously close to tears. Desperately, she forced herself to recall everything she had been taught about the art of appearing composed in the most trying circumstances, and, blessedly, she was able to do so. Raising her head, she moistened her dry lips and allowed the corners to tilt into a vague little smile. Then, while silently praying Bruce and the others would not notice her and call out, she turned slowly and gracefully walked toward the exit.

It was not until she found herself at the top of a flight of stairs that she realized she had come the wrong way. After leaving the lounge, she had thought only to escape as quickly as possible and had blindly turned right instead of left. But she would not for anything retrace her steps. Almost in a panic, she pushed open the first door she came to, and when cool air enveloped her, she was relieved to know it led outside.

The moon was at its peak, and she had no trouble seeing the gardens stretched out below her. She recalled a postcard in the hotel's gift shop, a colorful portrait of the hotel gardens basking beneath a summer sun. Now the early spring night would soon become quite cold. She knew she was unwise to be outside dressed as she was, but she automatically descended to the pathway and began to walk. As the coolness bit into her, she thought longingly of the fur coat lying uselessly at the foot of Reg's bed. She should not have left it there, but then she remembered she would never be able to look at the coat without feeling humiliated and miserable.

There was a mist before her eyes, and she stumbled against something hard. It was a wrought-iron seat and she sat down, drawing up her knees and wrapping her arms around them. Almost immediately the tears began flowing so profusely that soon a great wet patch had marked the skirt of her gold gown.

She had no idea how long it was before she heard the voice. It was a male voice, speaking in French, and for a dreadful moment she thought it was *him*. She raised her head defensively and stared at the darkly clad figure before her. But although he was tall, the clear moonlight showed that he wore a neat beard and appeared to be some years older. With a sigh of relief, she said huskily, "I'm afraid I understand very little French."

"Then it is fortunate I understand your language, *n'est-ce pas, mademoiselle*? Or is it *madame*? Ah, I thought not." He began to remove his overcoat and before she could wonder why, it had encircled her, giving her the most wonderful sensation of warm security. "You are desolate, *mademoiselle*, perhaps I can be of service? Ah, but first I must introduce myself. I am Charles Chavot...."

Daye opened her eyes and stared for a time at the flickering stars in the sky. She could not remember exactly when she had started to talk but she knew she had begun by telling him about the man—the other Frenchman. After that, it seemed, there was no stopping her. He was so easy to talk to, so understanding. Later, sitting in one of the hotel's smaller lounges, he had told her about Anani, his island, and had invited her to come to stay for as long as she wished. "Tomorrow I must leave Paris," he told her, "but I will not forget you. I will write and so will you, *mon enfant*, and one day you will come to Anani."

SHE HAD NOT DREAMED that she would really do so—not then. But the seed had been planted and within days it had grown into an obsession. And now it was to become reality. In a month she would fly to Tahiti, and after spending a few days sight-seeing she would contact Charles and he would come to fetch her and take her with him to Anani.

That night Daye dreamed of hot sun and silver sands and palm trees. And for a change her dreams were not disturbed by brilliant gray eyes and a beautiful but cruel male mouth.

CHAPTER THREE

FROM TAHITI, Daye gazed across the Sea of Moons to where the mountains of Mooréa loomed darkly, their craggy peaks softened by a shrouding mist. Aeons ago Mooréa had been a massive volcano and now, or so Daye had heard, it was one of the most exotic of the Polynesian islands, a place of mystery and enchantment, where the ruins of ancient *marae* lay beneath ever thickening layers of rich vegetation, and spirits roamed. Be it superstition or fact, Daye thought the folklore fascinating and began to wonder if Anani was enchanted and if spirits roamed there, too. She laughed softly, feeling excited. Soon she would know about Anani for herself. Less than two hours ago she had spoken to Charles, and tomorrow morning at nine he would arrive to take her to his island.

This was her fifth day in Tahiti, and although her room was booked for a week, she had not believed she would actually stay that long. However, after taking a guided tour of the island on the second day, she had discovered she wanted to see more. Tahiti was gloriously beautiful, a place of verdant mountains, shimmering waterfalls, deep, steamy valleys and some black-lava sand beaches. And everywhere—or so it seemed to Daye's bemused eyes—there were trees weighed down with fruit, and bushes heavy with exotic, highly perfumed blossoms.

Since she had always been fascinated by stories of Captain James Cook, another day, Daye had joined a tour to Point Venus. It was here, in 1769, that the famous navigator-explorer had observed the transit of Venus across the disk of an eclipsed sun. Point Venus jutted into Matavai Bay, and Daye learned that Samuel Wallis had sailed into this body of water and discovered Tahiti and Mooréa. Here, too, Fletcher Christian and the *Bounty* mutineers had anchored before sailing off to Pitcairn Island.

And then, of course, there was Papeete. Tahiti's capital was a thriving city, densely populated, bustling with traffic and inundated with restaurants, small shops and souvenir stalls. There was also a modern shopping center, and Daye had spent several hours purchasing casual clothes: sundresses, colorful halter tops, brief shorts and swimsuits. Another purchase was a wide-brimmed straw hat with a multicolored ribbon. This she felt to be a necessity, for although she wanted a tan, there were times when the sun's rays became too fierce.

But how she loved the sun! It was a tonic she savored as she roamed Papeete's narrow streets, or lingered at the waterfront where brisk trade winds freshened the air, and where numerous and varied seagoing vessels shared a crowded tenancy. The waterfront was her favorite spot, but she found another place to be the most fascinating. This was the marketplace where stalls laden with bananas, taro, papayas, mangoes and large gleaming fish were crowded closely together. Between these stalls, dusky skinned Tahitians, dressed in brightly patterned shirts or pareus, mingled with inscrutable Chinese in their traditionally drab tunics and baggy trousers.

They all seemed unhurried as they inspected and selected the proffered goods, storing their purchases in the large woven baskets they invariably carried. Here, as in British cities and towns, the marketplace was a meeting place, with small groups of people pausing to chat. Only here the language was melodic Tahitian or French, and more often than not the conversers stood directly in the path of the traffic that patiently threaded its way along the narrow thoroughfare. Children, it often seemed, were everywhere. They ran about freely, apparently accepted by all.

Surprisingly, even though she was alone in this crowded city, she never felt lonely or self-conscious as she might have elsewhere. She was, in fact, inordinately happy and relaxed, and for the first time in two years she did not tense resentfully when men attempted to make her acquaintance. She was actually flattered because it was Daye Hollister they wanted to know, not sexy Gloria Day.

A last look at distant Mooréa, and Daye turned away. Her hotel was closer, but she decided to walk the short distance to Papeete and have lunch at the restaurant she had noticed earlier. It was tucked away on a side street, away from the traffic noises, a cozy-looking place with flower-filled blue vases in the window. Somewhat to her dismay, the interior of the restaurant turned out to be more opulent than the exterior indicated, and she hoped her plain, lime-green dress was smart enough.

Obviously it was, for the headwaiter, a rotund Frenchman, ran a noticeably appreciative eye over her and, with some ceremony, ushered her to a table near a wide window. The food she ordered at the waiter's suggestion was delicious, and afterward she felt guilty because she had indulged herself. If she kept this up she would put on a great deal of weight, she told herself ruefully.

She was drinking her coffee, dreamily gazing at the glorious flower garden beyond the window, when she became aware of men's voices close by. They were speaking French, and when she casually glanced around she saw that the waiter had escorted two well-dressed men to the next table. One was Polynesian, the other a European. Dark-haired, darkly tanned, he had a tall lithe body that was clothed in a beautifully cut cream sports jacket and tan trousers. His shirt, too, was tan, only a shade or so darker than his skin. Carefully, Daye lowered her coffee cup to its saucer. She was aware that she stared at him, but she felt unable to tear her gaze away. *Perhaps,* she thought desperately, *I'm mistaken. Perhaps it's just someone who looks like him!* But then he paused in the act of lighting a cigarette and looked directly into her eyes.

And of course it *was* him! No two people could have such eyes, could they? Daye felt as if all strength had left her limbs. She had not seen him since that frightful evening in Paris, she had not expected ever to set eyes on him again. Yet here he was! By some diabolical quirk of fate he, the *other* Frenchman, was here in Tahiti.

Sudden panic gripped her, and she swiftly lowered her eyes. She must get away from here at once, back to the safety of her hotel room. Oh, thank heavens she was leaving Tahiti tomorrow. It would be intolerable if she had to remain here knowing she might bump into him at any moment. She felt the sting of frustrated tears. This wasn't fair! She had felt so happy! With blind haste she groped for her white shoulder bag, which lay on the table, and her hand brushed a wineglass, knocking it over.

Fortunately, the empty glass did not shatter, but the minor accident jerked Daye to her senses. She was being stupid, almost going to pieces like this. True, it was rather a shock to suddenly see him again, nevertheless she mustn't behave as though she was afraid or had something to be ashamed of. Anger stabbed her sharply. If anyone should feel ashamed it was the Frenchman. Even if Gloria Day had been a woman of loose morals it was certainly not his right to moralize, to insult and humiliate her. All the bitter, furious speeches she had once rehearsed danced about in her brain. She should be glad he was here because now she could tell him what she thought of him.

With a sense of shock Daye realized she was staring at him again, and that he was reciprocating. But while she knew her hostility must be quite apparent, his expression held no hostility at all. He was, in fact, eyeing her in much the same manner as did other men. Even, she mused, with that unmistakable suggestion of lust—which seemed to suggest he did not recognize her. Instinctively she raised her hand to tuck strands of hair behind her ears. She did, of course, look quite different from the girl he had treated so shockingly. Her hair was much longer, and it hung very straight from the center part; her only makeup was a pale coral lipstick, and her light golden tan gave her a distinctly outdoor-girl appearance. And as for her dress, it did not bear the slightest resemblance to a sexy golden gown. No, it wasn't at all likely that he would recognize her as she looked today, she told herself, and then wondered if he had perhaps forgotten that night in Paris or simply had cold-bloodedly put it out of his mind.

She gave a small start as she noticed the Frenchman's mouth curve slightly while one dark eyebrow raised inquiringly. Did he respond this way because her hostility showed so blatantly? Or did he assume she was interested in him? It could be the latter, she thought, for she was openly staring, and he had to be aware of his attractiveness. Most likely women fell over themselves to get his attention. Daye sighed, and the depression she felt was so acute all other emotion faded rapidly.

It seemed imperative, once again, that she leave the restaurant immediately. Judging from the way he was looking at her, she saw he might very well decide to come over to talk to her. And she wasn't at all prepared. She scooped up her bag and fumbled inside for some money, then she got to her feet and without so much as a glance at the Frenchman, hurried toward the exit. Her waiter met her halfway, and she thrust the money at him. "*Mais non, mademoiselle*, it is too much," he protested, but she made a vague gesture and kept going. Once outside in the brilliant sunlight, she paused to collect her breath and her wits. A taxi. . . she must find a taxi and get back to her hotel.

Daye closed her eyes. She was not surprised but shaken to the core. Drawing in her breath she opened her eyes again. The Frenchman was standing right in front of her, his clear, light eyes seeming to penetrate her being. Then he spoke to her in French. It sounded like a question.

"I don't understand," she answered faintly.

"You are English." He nodded slowly. "*Mais oui,* indubitably! *Mademoiselle* has the look of the Anglo-Saxon."

Daye searched her mind for a witty comeback to that remark, but, failing, she heard herself saying, "Thank you. I accept that as a compliment."

"It was meant as such." His eyes roved over her face as though memorizing it. She felt disturbed, oddly vulnerable, and stifling a gasp she turned away. But before she could take more than a step or two, his hand was on her arm. Rather wildly she looked down at it, remembering the other time he had touched her.

"Let go of me," she ordered, her voice rising.

He removed his hand immediately. "You are not a prisoner, *mademoiselle*," he said softly.

She felt foolish and annoyed. "I realize that. But I...well, really! Do you make it a habit to accost strange females in this manner?"

He raised his eyebrows. "Surely you do not consider yourself a 'strange' female, *mademoiselle*?" he asked solemnly.

She gazed at him with suspicion. "You are deliberately misunderstanding me, I think."

He looked amused, but when Daye merely stared gravely up at him he said quickly, "I was, of course, teasing. Do not be offended, *mademoiselle*."

"Oh, I'm not," she said coolly, and looked away from him. "Well, it is awfully hot standing here, so...goodbye." She gave him a sidelong glance, irritated because he could make her feel so uncomfortable.

"Do not leave, *s'il vous plaît*," he said, a hint of urgency in his voice. "I would like to speak to you further."

Daye tensed. "Why?" she demanded.

Again he looked amused, but only briefly. "Perhaps I am curious. The glances you cast at me in the restaurant were somewhat antagonistic. Or perhaps...." He looked at her intently. "You are *très belle*, very beautiful, *mademoiselle*; it is not unnatural that I should wish to know you." Unexpectedly he reached for her left hand and lifted it. "No ring. So you are neither married nor betrothed. Amazing. And immensely satisfying."

For a moment she was stunned. Then, recovering, she snatched her hand away and said breathlessly, "Don't be too sure of that. I might not choose to wear a ring."

He looked down at her, his mouth curved in a lazy smile. "If you were mine you would wear a ring," he said with almost arrogant assurance.

His statement evoked images that were distracting, but she managed to retort, "Through my nose, I suspect."

This time he gave her the full benefit of his undeniably devastating smile. "*Mademoiselle*, I protest," he said reproachfully. "How could you have formed such an opinion of me in so short a time?"

"Am I wrong, then?"

He shrugged, the gesture purely Gallic. "Frankly, I have never found it necessary to 'dominate' your sex, *mademoiselle*! Persuade, perhaps...." He stopped, his expression devilish.

"You are awfully conceited, aren't you?" Daye challenged coldly. She did not wait for his answer to that but added quickly, "Please excuse me. This conversation is quite pointless."

Before she could take a step, however, he said, "Will you dine with me? Tonight?"

She gazed up at him blankly, then, as his words fully sunk in she felt a wild desire to laugh. This was the man who had not hesitated to express his contempt for what he, albeit wrongly, thought of her morals. He had looked at her that night in Paris as though he despised her, and now he had just asked her to have dinner with him. What would he say if he knew she and Gloria Day were the same woman, she wondered, and was immediately tempted to tell him. But the desire to prolong these incredibly satisfying moments was even more tempting. "Why, *monsieur*, how do I know you haven't a wife? Or at least a sweetheart?" she asked in a deliberately provocative voice.

"If I had either, I should not have invited you, *mademoiselle*." He spoke softly.

"Surely you don't expect me to believe you are the faithful sort," she answered with scorn. "You certainly don't look as if you are. You look...." She swallowed, lowering her eyes to his chin.

"I look...?" he prompted.

She made the mistake of meeting his eyes again and immediately her thoughts became confused. Dear heaven, she could be hypnotized if she stared into those eyes for too long, she told herself, taking an instinctive step backward.

"*Mademoiselle* intended an unflattering description?" the Frenchman asked pointedly.

Daye could not remember what she had intended to say, and feeling irritated and unsettled, she blurted the first thing that came to mind. "I suppose you would be crushed had I done so."

His laugh had a low attractive sound. "*Au contraire, mademoiselle*. Sometimes a lady will use unflattering remarks and antagonistic glances in an effort to conceal her interest.''

Daye felt her grace growing warm. "Do you mean...? Well, I can assure you that most definitely does not apply in my case!" Shaking with rage she began walking swiftly along the narrow pavement.

The Frenchman fell into step beside her, his height and potent masculinity causing her to feel intimidated. "Forgive me, it was not my intention to offend you." He was trying to placate her, but when she ignored him he made a sound of exasperation and stepped directly in front of her. Daye halted in time to prevent herself from colliding with him—although he was still uncomfortably close. "*Mademoiselle*, do me the courtesy of at least acknowledging my apology," he said tersely.

She sighed. "Very well, I acknowledge it. Now, please...."

"And you will have dinner with me?" He asked the question as though he fully expected her to accept.

"No. I can't!" Daye shook her head vehemently.

"*Pourquoi?* Why, *mademoiselle*? Because I have not introduced myself? That, of course, is easily rectified. I am Philippe—"

"No, don't! I don't want to know who you are," Daye interrupted, curiously upset because she did, now, know his first name. "Now, please! I really must go. And...and don't stop me anymore." She put out her hand with some vague notion of keeping him at a distance, which was another mistake since he caught it and held it tightly. Torn between annoyance and inexplicable fear, Daye gazed into his face.

"*Mon Dieu!* Why do you look at me so?" Again

he sounded exasperated. "You seem to view me with either antagonism or fear, and I cannot believe I have said or done anything to cause such emotions. But if I have, *mademoiselle*, I wish you would tell me." His voice trailed off, and he looked thoughtfully down at her, his dark lashes almost covering his clear gray eyes. "There! It has happened once again! *Mademoiselle*, I feel certain that somewhere we have met before. When first I saw you it seemed there was a familiar...." He broke off, his eyes, sharp now, roving over her face. Then he smiled slightly and said, "*Mais non*, it could not be so! Had we met, I should not have forgotten you."

Daye had been holding her breath, and now she exhaled slowly. She had expected him to recognize her; had almost willed him to do so. Yet now she was relieved that he had not. She was a coward, she told herself bitterly. She lacked the courage to say what must be said. Or was it that she feared her words would not come fast enough? That he would manage to outwit her and demoralize her with brutally scornful remarks? Daye stared almost unseeingly down at the darkly tanned fingers entwining her own. She must tell him, get it over with now! After today she would never see him again. An unpleasant chill shivered through her body, and she said stiffly, "Possibly I resemble someone you know."

"*Non!*" He laughed softly. "I know no one who looks remotely like you. But it is possible that somewhere I have caught a glimpse of you. Not here in Tahiti, I think, but Sydney? Rome? London would, of course, be the logical city; however, I have not visited there for two years, so...." Daye sensed that he shrugged.

She drew in her breath, raising her eyes to meet his and willing herself to remain cool. "What about Paris? I have been there, and so, I imagine, have you. Perhaps you even live there?"

"*Non*, Paris is not my home, although I do know it well." He smiled that altogether too intriguing smile and quickly raised her hand to his lips. "But it is not important, *mademoiselle*. It is only important that I know you now. Tell me, *petite Anglaise*, what is your name?"

His voice was soft, almost like a caress, and his masculine appeal shatteringly potent. It was all Daye could do to shake her head and try to draw her hand from his. Then, without a word, he released her and began to fumble in the pocket of his cream sports coat. Presently he pulled out a gold cigarette case, and when Daye shook her head as he offered her a cigarette, he put one between his own lips and flicked a gold lighter at the tip. She stared at the lighter, a strange sensation in the pit of her stomach. Was it the same lighter he had left in the hotel anteroom that night in Paris? The question burned on the tip of her tongue, but when she saw that he was eyeing the small object with what could only be termed a moody expression, she felt certain she had her answer. She was also certain that he had remembered, that he knew she was the girl he had seen—and judged—that awful night.

But when his gaze returned to her face, he merely smiled faintly and said, "*Mademoiselle* is partly correct. You do resemble someone." He drew deeply on his cigarette.

Again she realized she had been holding her breath. "Someone you know?" she asked, wondering why she didn't let well enough alone.

"Non! Merely someone I met briefly and unpleasantly." He drew again on his cigarette before he dropped it distastefully to the street and ground it beneath his heel. "She is...was someone of absolutely no importance," he said derisively.

Stung to anger, Daye gasped, "You are cruel to dismiss her like that! Everyone is important."

"Mais certainement! I should have said she is of no importance to me." He reached out to briefly touch her cheek. "You are hasty with your criticism as far as I am concerned, *petite.* Or could I be mistaken? Are you critical and antagonistic toward everyone?"

"No, I am not!"

"So. It is only this desolate male who sparks such feelings? How can I help but wonder why?"

"Just so you don't imagine I'm covering up an intense interest," she returned shortly.

"I am becoming quite convinced you are not," he answered wryly. "In fact, I am inclined to believe you dislike me enormously. Tell me, do you?"

She gazed at him helplessly. *I've disliked you, hated you, for months,* she wanted to say, but the words were caught in her throat. All at once she felt drained and a little sick. If only she had not left her hat in her hotel room she thought, realizing the heat of the sun was getting to be a little too much for her. To her relief, at that moment, a taxi entered the narrow street and cruised slowly toward them. Quickly Daye raised her hand and moved toward the curb. She knew she was giving up her chance to make the Frenchman squirm but she did not care. She had to get away. Desperately she made herself concentrate on Charles. And on Anani—her refuge.

"A taxi will not be necessary. I will drive you wherever you wish." The Frenchman spoke from just behind her, his tone arrogant.

She wanted suddenly to weep. Oh, why didn't he just give up? "You flatter yourself if you think I'd go anywhere with you," she said bitterly, forcing herself to be angry to keep back the tears. "Besides, have you forgotten your friend is still inside the restaurant?"

"*Mon ami* will understand," he said quietly.

Still she did not turn to look at him. "Yes, I expect he will. I imagine you do this sort of thing rather often." She spoke disparagingly, keeping her eyes on the taxi. It slid to a stop a few feet away and the youthful Tahitian driver climbed out. Eager to get away, Daye started toward the driver, but the Frenchman caught her shoulder in a firm grip and she was swung around to face him.

That he was angry was obvious, for his eyes blazed down into hers. But when he spoke his voice was perfectly controlled. "You have an exquisite face and body, *mademoiselle*. What a great pity it is that you should have such a disagreeable and unfriendly nature."

The state of her emotions would not permit Daye to accept this. "Disagreeable? Unfriendly? Because I am not groveling in gratitude for the attention you've given me? What would you have preferred, *monsieur*? Coy receptiveness?" She tilted her head and raised her eyebrows then continued recklessly, "Had I been...receptive, *monsieur*, would you, perhaps, have judged me to be a woman of easy virtue?"

He frowned deeply. *"Mademoiselle?"*

Daye ignored the question in his voice. "You

might even have decided I was a lady of the night, I
suppose," she said contemplatively. "Of course then
you would have felt compelled to lecture me, insult
me, humiliate me, wouldn't you? No!" she put up
her hand to stop him from interrupting. "You don't
have to answer, because I already know. Five months
ago, in Paris, I received your insults...your vile,
cruel insults." In spite of herself, Daye's voice
faltered. "I was completely innocent, but you...
dared to judge me. You wouldn't even listen when I
tried to explain; you actually assumed I was...pro-
positioning you. Well, I think you should know how
wrong you were in your arrogant, hasty judgment.
The fur coat was a birthday present from the firm I
worked for. The man in the elevator was Reg, my
best friend. A *platonic* friendship, I might add,
monsieur." She paused, swallowing and blinking her
eyes rapidly to keep the tears away. "In any case, you
had no right! Even if Gloria Day had been a...what
you said, you had no reason to be so horribly cruel.
You must be the most hardhearted man...." She
broke off again and this time turned hastily away and
ran to the waiting taxi.

As it sped off, she cast one brief glance out of the
window. The Frenchman was standing quite still, his
handsome face devoid of expression, his eyes—even
at a distance she could see his eyes—as blank and
cold as ice.

CHAPTER FOUR

DESPITE A RESTLESS, MISERABLE NIGHT, Daye was awake before seven, and after ordering a pot of tea to be brought to her room, she lay back against the pillows and tried rather desperately to capture the delight and excitement she should have been feeling at this time. In a little over two hours Charles would arrive and together they would go to Anani. She had longed for this day, and now that it was finally here something had happened to spoil it. No! *Someone* had happened to spoil it. Tears that were only too ready brimmed in her eyes. Why, oh, why, had he, the other Frenchman, come back into her life now? True, she had at last been able to speak her mind about that night in Paris, but it had not helped at all. Certainly it had not given her the satisfaction and peace of mind she had expected. She was in fact more restless and nervous than she had been in months. The Frenchman had completely monopolized her thoughts. The Frenchman. Philippe. Ironic that a man she so despised should have a name she'd always liked.

Irritably she threw back the covers and slipped out of bed. Brushing at her wet cheeks with her palms, she went to the dressing-table mirror and gazed into it. She looked awful, she thought, positively haggard! And her hair! Almost masochistically she dragged a hairbrush through the tangles, and when she winced she said aloud, "Now you've got something to cry about, Daye Hollister!" Then she flung the brush down and closed her eyes. "You've got to buck up," she said, still aloud. "You might as well stop brooding about him because you'll probably never see him again."

Her eyes flew open, and she stared at her reflection in dawning horror. She had not meant to say that—not, at least, in that bitterly unhappy tone of voice. Oh, God, what was the matter with her? She wanted never to see him again...or did she? Hardly daring to even think about this, Daye went to sit on the edge of the bed. She would *not* cry anymore, she told herself. But it took a great deal of self-control not to do so.

Presently her tea arrived, and after drinking two unusually sweet cups of the hot liquid she felt a little better. Vowing to think only of Charles and the forthcoming trip to his island, she went into the delightful pink-tiled bathroom and took a cool shower, shampooing her long hair thoroughly. She was toweling herself dry when someone rapped smartly on the door and, thinking it must be one of the hotel maids, she pulled on a short bathrobe and wound a towel about her wet hair. "Coming," she called sharply, as the impatient rapping sounded again. Vaguely surprised because the hotel employees were not usually so demanding, Daye opened the door. "What is...?" she began, and her voice faltered to a stop. No hotel employee stood on the other side of the door—it was the Frenchman.

Her first reaction was shocked surprise, but almost immediately it was overshadowed by an intense, heart-stopping pleasure she did not attempt to analyze. Silently she gazed at him, noticing that he looked different. Of course, it was his clothes. He was dressed very casually in dark blue Levi's and a V-necked blue knit shirt. His hair, too, was more ruffled than she had ever seen it, and although his eyes were still devastatingly clear, the lids looked heavy, as if he needed sleep. She was so disturbed, looking at him, that her legs felt weak. "Hello. What do you want?" she managed to say huskily.

He gave an audible start and Daye was aware he had been staring at her as if he found her unbelievable. Hadn't he expected to see her, she wondered. Who had he expected would be here, and why had he come? Her pleasure at seeing him faded and she felt chilled. Why didn't he say something instead of staring at her so strangely?

Then he did speak. "*You* are Mademoiselle Hollister?" His lips barely moved but Daye heard the throb of anger in his voice.

She nodded, stepping back and wrapping her arms about herself in a protective manner.

"So!" The gray eyes blazed. "Now I can understand why it was impossible to find you. Do you always use an alias, Mademoiselle Hollister? If *that* is your correct name," he finished in a hard voice.

She was too puzzled to be annoyed. "Of course it's my correct name. And I don't know what you are talking about when you accuse me of using an alias."

He gave her a cynical look. "You do not recall mentioning your name yesterday, Mademoiselle Gloria Day?"

"But I never mentioned Glori.... Oh!" Daye chewed her lip, recalling that she had from force of habit called herself Gloria Day. But she had no intention of explaining Gloria to this man. "I did *not* tell you that was my name," she snapped defensively. "You merely assumed that it was." Before he could argue the point, she added, "Anyway, I really don't know why you should have tried to find me."

The look he gave her was oddly bitter. "At the time it seemed imperative. Now, however, I can only say I am relieved that I did not find you."

"You are confusing me," Daye said, trying to sound cool. "Shall we get to your reason for being here now? I mean, it's an unusual hour to be calling, and as you can see I'm not...." She paused abruptly.

His eyes roved in insolent appraisal. "*Mais, oui*, my vision is excellent."

Instinctively Daye moved to tighten the loosely tied robe. "I think..." she began and then stopped abruptly as the towel, wrapped turban-style about her head, chose this moment to come loose. Her hair fell, tangled and damp, to her shoulders, and the towel slid uselessly to the floor. Thoroughly disconcerted she half turned, wondering if her legs would carry her to the bathroom where she could regain her composure behind a locked door. And then she told herself she was being a fool, because all she needed to do was close this door in his face.

As if he read her mind, he stepped swiftly across the threshold and pushed the door shut behind him.

She could not help the small gasp of fright that escaped her. "What do you imagine you're doing?"

He gave her a cold look. "Do not concern yourself, I have no plan to seduce you. Unless, of course—'' he smiled grimly ''—that is what you wish.''

Daye's face grew warm with panic. ''You must be mad! Get out or I'll call for the manager.''

''I am terrified!'' he said shortly, bending down to pick up the towel. He held it out and Daye snatched it quickly, one hand still clutching her bathrobe tie. ''It would appear I have arrived at an inconvenient moment,'' he finished rather mockingly.

''Have you only just come to that conclusion?'' she asked tartly, and not waiting for his answer, she flung the damp towel over the back of a nearby chair and went to the bedside table.

''Well?'' She put her hand on the telephone.

''Well...what, *mademoiselle*?'' he asked, teasingly innocent.

She drew in a sharp breath. ''Are you going to leave?''

''Without explaining why I am here?''

Daye's temper flared. ''You are being deliberately annoying. And as far as I'm concerned it doesn't matter why you're here, only that you go.'' She turned her back on him and lifted the receiver. But before she could dial, he was there, his hand covering hers without gentleness. Helpless and frustrated she choked, ''How dare you!'' and the hand holding the telephone receiver swung around instinctively.

He was quick, which was fortunate for him. And for her, Daye realized, as he removed the receiver from her unresisting fingers. She was not prone to physical violence, and if the blow had landed she would never have forgiven herself. She closed her eyes, shaking with emotion. She felt remorse for what she had almost done, but also a simmering anger because he had caused her to lose her self-control. Her eyes flew open and she rasped accusingly, "It's all *your* fault! You started this!"

"Your eyes are spitting green fire," he drawled, ignoring her accusation.

"I'm very upset and angry," she retorted unnecessarily. "And...and it would have served you right if I'd hit you."

"*Peut-être.* But I would not have been at all pleasant had you done so."

He was too close for comfort and Daye backed away. But her legs touched the bed and she stopped. "I suppose you are the sort of man who would hit a woman back," she said scornfully.

His mouth tightened.

He closed the gap between them and slid his hands up her arms, under the short loose sleeves of her bathrobe, to her shoulders. "You are uncommonly desirable, *petite Anglaise.*" His fingers tightened and he jerked her roughly toward him.

She was confused because he was holding her tightly, and she felt no anger, no desire to push him away. Held against his chest, her hands caught between them, she could feel the steady beat of his heart and the penetrating warmth of his body. She could smell his subtle male scent pleasantly mingled with some spicy cologne and cigarette tobacco. A heady excitement pulsated through her veins and her heart pounded unbearably. From somewhere she grasped a little common sense. "Please, let me go," she said huskily, moving her body in protest.

Immediately he stiffened, drawing in his breath sharply. His hands eased their pressure and slid farther beneath the robe to caress her back. The intimacy of his touch was inordinately seductive, making her dizzy and weak. She closed her eyes, fighting the overwhelming urge to slide her arms around him. "Oh, no! No!" she said in a whisper, having no idea if she was protesting against his desires or hers. Shame filled her, and she opened her eyes and looked up at him. "This is—" she began, but without hesitation he lowered his head and his mouth covered hers.

It was a gentle, tentative kiss, quite out of character with the grim expression he had worn, and later Daye was to feel certain he would have let her go had she resisted. But as his lips touched hers, she felt as though a fire had suddenly flamed within her, a fire that had waited only for this moment to be kindled. Her response was eager, and the Frenchman reacted accordingly. His kiss deepened and without knowing exactly when it had happened, Daye found her arms wrapped around his neck and his arms encircling her in a close embrace. It was a long kiss, and when he finally raised his head her senses were swimming drunkenly. Softly he spoke to her in French, the unfamiliar words sounding as seductive to Daye as his caresses had felt. Then he began to kiss her again with different, more demanding kisses, while his hand pushed aside her robe and slid insistently over her body.

It was when his hand lingered on her breast that her drugged senses suddenly rebelled. Gasping a frenzied, "Stop it! No, stop it!" she struggled fiercely, pushing away his hands as if they were contaminated. As he let her go, he turned away from her, raking his hands through his hair. Trembling from head to toe, she watched him, praying he would keep his back to her until she could regain her composure.

But he did not. He turned slowly, meeting her horrified eyes with an oddly bleak expression. Silently they stood there facing each other, and although Daye wanted to move she felt totally unable to. Then the Frenchman rubbed his chin almost uneasily and said, "*Mademoiselle*, your... robe."

For a moment she did not comprehend. "My...?" Hot color rushed into her face and she pulled her robe tightly around her. "Please, please, will you just *go*?" she begged tremulously. She turned unsteadily and walked to the window, tears of self-disgust rolling down her cheeks. She must have gone completely mad. She had actually *encouraged* him. Knowing he was still there, behind her, she repeated, "Please, will you go?"

She heard him sigh before he said huskily, "At this moment I can only wish it were that simple, *mademoiselle*. Unfortunately for us both, I came here to escort you to Anani."

Daye stiffened, hardly believing she had heard him correctly. Forgetting her tearstained cheeks she spun to face him. "What? Anani? You... are lying!" she blurted out.

"What would be the point?" He shrugged.

"But I don't understand! Charles said he would come... and besides, why *you*?" She felt confused and frightened. "Did Charles ask you to come for me?" She realized as soon as she had asked the question that it was unnecessary. Why else would he be here if Charles had not asked him?

"His message was waiting when I arrived at my *appartement* earlier today," the Frenchman said. He rubbed his forehead frowning in a weary manner. "Apparently *l'avion*—the plane—is in use and I....'' He hesitated. "I have a launch," he finished shortly.

"You...Charles *hired* you to take me to Anani?" Daye asked apprehensively.

"Non, mademoiselle."

She was almost afraid to ask, but she did. "Then why are you...? I mean...is Charles a...your employer or...?" She stopped abruptly, her hands nervously twisting the tie of her robe.

His clear eyes watched her intently. "Charles Chavot is a *bon ami, mademoiselle.* You understand? He is a close friend."

She nodded without speaking and turned back to stare almost blindly out the window. Too much was happening, and she doubted she could cope. Oh, God, wasn't it bad enough that the Frenchman had come back into her life, that she had permitted him to start to make love to her as no man had ever done? Did he have to be a friend of Charles's? Daye bit her lower lip to stop it from quivering. Oh, dear heaven, she had complained to Charles about this man and by a frightful coincidence the two were friends. Why— she pressed her hand to her stomach—the Frenchman probably lived in Tahiti.

Without turning she asked, "I suppose you live here?"

"Oui, I live in Polynesia."

"I see." She spoke coolly but her mind was in turmoil. She needed badly to think, but it was impossible while he was here. She swung to face him, momentarily distracted when she found his eyes steadily watching her. "I'm afraid I wasn't at all prepared for this.'' Her hand fluttered to her mouth and then fell to her side. ''It's still so early and yet, for me, there has been one shock after another.''

''I am somewhat shocked myself,'' he admitted, adding dryly, ''In more ways than you can imagine.''

She flushed, positive he referred to what had happened between them only minutes ago. But she wanted to forget that—if she could. ''I suppose you visit Anani sometimes,'' she said miserably.

''As often as is possible.''

She pressed her lips together, hating him for ruining all these months of planning. How could she go to Anani now, knowing that he could at any time turn up and shatter her peace of mind? For that he could do and without even trying. With frustration and misery, she admitted she ran the gamut of emotions where this man was concerned. She hated him—he made her angry, uncomfortable and very depressed. And yet in his arms she had felt other emotions. She had even been happy. She was quite badly attracted to him, of course. She didn't want to be, but she simply couldn't help herself. She realized now she had been attracted to him from the very beginning. Under different circumstances, she would very likely have fallen in love with him.... Daye pushed back her damp hair with trembling hands. ''If you wouldn't mind leaving, I'd be grateful,'' she said. ''There is rather a lot that I have to think about.''

''You are, perhaps, indecisive about visiting Anani, now, *mademoiselle*?''

Something in his tone caused her to look at him searchingly. But his expression gave nothing away.

"You don't want me to go to Anani, do you?" she asked in surprise.

He eyed her and said, "No, Mademoiselle Hollister. I do not."

She bit her lip. "May I ask why?"

"Mais certainement!" He paused and groped in his back pocket. "Does *mademoiselle* mind if I smoke?" And when she shook her head he lit a cigarette, inhaling deeply and closing his eyes. He *was* tired, Daye thought, her immediate reaction one of sympathy. Then she told herself irritably that he did not deserve sympathy. More than likely he had spent half the night making merry in some bawdy nightclub—or some woman's bed. Her nerves tingled and she made an impatient sound. Slowly his eyes opened but remained lazily narrowed. Then he said, as if he had not paused at all, "Frankly, Mademoiselle Hollister, I believe your presence on Anani can cause only...problems."

She stared at him, mystified. "What problems, for goodness' sake?"

His eyes opened fully and swept over her. *"Mademoiselle*, does the way you look never become a problem?"

"I don't believe I know what you mean." Her eyelashes flickered.

"Of course you know what I mean!" He spoke impatiently, looked about him then strode toward her. Daye stiffened involuntarily, feeling relieved but a little foolish when he paused at the small table near the window, grinding his cigarette into the ashtray lying there. That he had noticed her reaction was obvious but he only smiled a trifle cynically and said, "Anani is not a large island, *mademoiselle*. A few

French families reside there and one Australian. The majority of the population is, naturally, Polynesian.'' He drummed his fingers on the tabletop, his brilliant gaze never leaving her face. "Aside from the Polynesians, there are more males on Anani than there are females. And—although they are most delightful females—there is not one as young and tempting as yourself.'' He stopped drumming his fingers and crossed his arms over his chest. "Have I made myself clear, Mademoiselle Hollister?''

"Oh, yes. But tell me, *monsieur*, are you concerned for me or for Anani's male population?'' she asked softly.

"Perhaps for both.'' He spoke deliberately.

Daye forced a smile. "Actually you have made the island sound wildly attractive. And I was assuming I would spend my days wallowing in boredom. Peace and quiet—that's what Charles promised I'd find on Anani. He said nothing about men lining up to ravish me.''

"*Mademoiselle* is being sarcastic,'' he stated blandly.

"Yes, *mademoiselle* is,'' Daye answered coldly. "Well, you haven't put me off, *monsieur*. I'll definitely go to Anani.'' As, of course, she would, she told herself. She had wondered if she could, but only for a moment. How could she allow this man to destroy her plans, her relationship with Charles? "Do you realize Charles is looking forward to my visit?'' she couldn't help asking.

"I did not speak to him personally. There was, as I said, a message waiting.'' He uncrossed his arms. "Have you been acquainted with Charles a long time?'' he asked casually.

"No, I haven't." She gave him a curious look. "Has Charles never mentioned me? If you are friends, as you say you are, I'd think he would've."

"One week ago, when I returned from a business trip, he mentioned that a *jeune fille*, a young lady, would soon be visiting Anani. That is all. He was... reticent." He spoke casually but Daye was certain he was resentful. She was puzzling over this when she heard him say, "Are you not at all concerned that I will speak to Charles about how we met?"

"Why should I be? Oh!" She gave him a wary glance. "Do you mean, *your* version?"

"Mais, oui." He showed his teeth in a brief, hard smile.

"Do you think Charles would believe you?" She sighed. "I would tell him my side of the story, too, you know."

"Certainement. But a seed of doubt would be planted, would it not?"

"You would really stoop so low?" Daye queried in a disgusted tone of voice.

"If necessary to protect *mon ami*."

"Protect? Against me? What in heaven's name do you think I'm going to do to Charles?" she asked in bewilderment.

"I dread to consider it." He spoke bluntly.

She was trembling again. "This is ridiculous! What on earth do you have against me? And please don't insult my intelligence by repeating that story you told only minutes ago." She tried to keep her voice steady. "You don't...you can't still believe I'm a...." She found she was unable to say the words. She pushed her hands through her hair. "Oh, God, I let you kiss me!" Frantic, she glanced toward the bed. "If I had let you go on, you would have thought—"

"Mademoiselle Hollister, you came dangerously close to allowing it," he said harshly.

"Yes, I did, didn't I?" Daye felt like bursting into tears. "I don't know why. I don't even like you!"

He said very softly, "And I do not like you."

Their eyes met, and the awareness between them was practically tangible. Then he said blandly, "Which seems to prove that sexual attraction can exist between two people who have no liking or respect for each other."

Daye expelled her breath. "But such an attraction should be easy enough to resist. Particularly if the people involved are seldom together."

"Seldom?" He raised a mocking eyebrow. "Does *mademoiselle* assume I visit Anani infrequently?"

"You said, as often as possible. Surely you don't...I mean, you must have work to do. Or something," she finished lamely.

"Perhaps my work gives me plenty of leisure time." His eyes were watchful.

"You are deliberately trying to put me off, aren't you?" she asked angrily. "Well, forewarned is forearmed, as they say, and whenever you turn up I shall make myself scarce."

"And how will you explain your behavior to *mon ami* Charles?"

"He will understand. I won't have to explain myself to Charles." Daye spoke confidently, feeling oddly pleased when the Frenchman's mouth tightened. "Now before you say anything else, I think I ought to tell you that Charles knows all about you and the way we met. I told him, you see." She gave him a challenging look. "He was mortified to know a countryman of his could behave so outrageously. He would be even more mortified and shocked if he knew that man was his. . . *bon ami*. Of course—" she paused deliberately "—I wouldn't dream of telling him. Not unless I was forced to."

He was looking at her as though he hated her and Daye noticed his hands were clenched into fists. But when he finally spoke, the cool control was in his voice. "May I inquire where and when you met Charles, Mademoiselle Hollister?"

Her hesitation was brief. "It isn't your business, really, but I'll tell you. We met in Paris. On the same night I met you. It was *after* that frightful scene in the lounge, I might add." The memory of that evening caused her distress and her voice faltered.

If he was surprised it did not show. "Was it not late by then, *mademoiselle*? Where could you have met Charles at such an hour?"

But Daye ignored his question. Something had, surprisingly, only just occurred to her. "You and Charles were in Paris at the same time. Did you travel there together?"

"We did. We shared the same suite."

For a moment she thought she might have a fit of hysterics. "How strange. And neither of you discussed meeting. . . me?"

He frowned, gazing at her for a long silent moment. At last he said, *"Non!"* in a decisive tone, and added, "Where did you meet *mon ami*, Mademoiselle Hollister?"

How persistent he was, Daye thought, feeling irritated. "If Charles had wanted you to know that he would have told you," she snapped. "Look here, I really must get dressed. Do you think you could go?"

He seemed about to argue but after glancing at the wide-banded gold watch on his wrist, he nodded. "*Très bien*, I will leave." He seemed about to turn and then hesitated. "Is there nothing I can say to make you change your mind?"

"About Anani? Nothing! Only one person could prevent me from going there and that would be Charles himself."

His expression was grim. "So be it! If you find yourself unpleasantly surprised, you have yourself to blame."

"What do you mean?" Daye swallowed nervously. "You're trying to...worry me."

"Am I?" Again he looked at his watch.

"Will half an hour be sufficient, *mademoiselle*?" As he spoke he strolled indolently to the door.

"For what? Oh! Don't bother about me. I'll find my own transportation to Anani." She spoke hastily.

He just looked at her. "That will not be necessary. It is all arranged. Be ready in half an hour, *s'il vous plaît*."

"I will not! I told you I would find my own way." Daye spoke stubbornly.

His well-shaped mouth became a hard line. "Do not be difficult, Mademoiselle Hollister. Charles will be concerned if I do not escort you."

"Really? And what if I'd decided not to go at all? How would Charles have felt then? Or wouldn't you have minded, in that case?" Daye knew she was being aggravating.

"If you are determined to go to Anani, I am equally determined to take you. Now I repeat: in half an hour. You will be ready, *n'est-ce pas?*"

She met his cold gray gaze for as long as she was able. "Very well," she murmured, lowering her eyes.

"A bientôt."

Daye heard the door open, and on a sudden impulse she called, "Wait!" Raising her eyes, she saw that he was looking at her over his shoulder and for a moment her pride rebelled. But she thrust it aside, knowing she had to tell him. "I'm not, you know. I swear to you I'm not . . . that sort of woman."

His expression was oddly disinterested. "It hardly matters, *mademoiselle*. However, whether you speak the truth or not, I would still prefer you did not go to Anani." He inclined his head very slightly, and the next moment the door closed behind him.

CHAPTER FIVE

THEY DROVE TO THE HARBOR in a sleek, cream-and-maroon-colored American car. A young Chinese man, whose name was James, was the chauffeur, and the Frenchman sat beside him. Although nothing was said, Daye felt sure the luxurious automobile belonged to the Frenchman and that James was in his employ. What did this man, this Philippe whoever-he-was, do for a living, she wondered, her gaze drawn to the dark head directly in front of her. It was a well-shaped head, and she found herself fascinated at the way the hair twisted and curled on his tanned neck. Swiftly she turned her head to stare out the window. She was becoming far too fascinated by this man, she thought despairingly.

She had been waiting for him in her hotel foyer when he had returned for her a short time later, and when she saw him coming toward her she had felt again that burst of heart-stopping pleasure. He moved with an easy, almost feline grace. His dark unruly hair and rather moody expression only added to his ordinate physical appeal. As early as it was, the hotel foyer was crowded, but it seemed to Daye that everyone except this man faded into insignificance.

She had been unable to speak when he reached her but she was aware of his eyes moving slowly over her. She was wearing a sleeveless pink blouse and tailored pink slacks, and had secured her fine flyaway hair with a pink-and-lilac scarf. Suddenly it seemed terribly important that he liked the way she looked, and before she realized it she had spoken, "Will I do?" She felt color rush into her face immediately, and she could have bitten her tongue in embarrassment. "I mean," she amended, rising to her feet and carefully adjusting her shoulder bag, "Am I properly dressed for a sea trip?"

He had been eyeing her intently, but now his thick black lashes flickered, and he said, "Quite properly dressed. And you have a hat, I see. *Bon!* Now, if *mademoiselle* will excuse me I will settle her hotel *note*."

"My what?"

"Your account, *mademoiselle*."

"I paid my bill," she said in an offended tone.

"Pardon." He inclined his head. "And your luggage is with the bell captain?"

She said it was, and he nodded and left her. When he returned he took her arm in a light grip, and as they moved toward the door he said almost grimly, "The man you marry will be mad if he ever allows you out of his sight." He looked down at her, and when she gazed back in bewilderment, said, "Do you not notice how men stare at you? Come, *mademoiselle*, I cannot...." He stopped, but when they were outside in the warm Tahitian sunlight he said unexpectedly, *"Je regrette,* Mademoiselle Hollister. I should not have spoken as I did."

His apology left Daye even more bewildered. However, she said nothing and presently he was courteously helping her into the back seat of the car.

It took only a short time to reach the harbor, and

while a smiling, stoutly built Polynesian removed her luggage from the trunk, the Frenchman led Daye toward a handsome vessel painted gleaming white with a vivid red trim. If this, too, belonged to Philippe, Daye thought, as she navigated the narrow ramp, he must be far from impoverished. But then, everything about him suggested wealth. And not only wealth but also breeding—his arrogance, perhaps, made him seem aristocratic. Daye caught her breath as he grasped her waist and swung her up to the deck.

He held her no longer than was necessary to steady her. Moving away he paused at the companionway and called in a questioning voice, "Audrey, *ma chère*?"

"Yes, I'm aboard," a female voice answered, and the woman emerged from the cabin. She was, Daye thought, in her early forties, a tallish woman with a slender figure, an attractive freckled face and short reddish brown hair. Her eyes, too, were brown and they held a mischievous sparkle. She was wearing a white cotton shirt, navy blue shorts and nothing at all on her feet. "Hello," she smiled warmly at Daye. "I'm Audrey Edwards. Welcome, Miss...did Philippe say your name is Hollister?"

Daye took her proffered hand, knowing instinctively she would like this woman. "That's right, but call me Daye." She smiled. "It's spelled with an *e* on the end."

"How delightful and unusual. Somehow it suits you," Audrey said with obvious sincerity.

"Daye." Philippe spoke her name softly, thoughtfully.

Daye flashed him a quick look before asking Audrey, "Are you going to Anani, too?"

"I live on Anani. I'm one-half of the only Australian family on the island. The other half is my brother Derek who will undoubtedly fall in love with you on sight. But I suppose most men do, don't they?" And while Daye was still blinking at her directness, Audrey put her hand on Philippe's arm and pleaded, "Why don't you run along and give Hiro a hand, my dear? We women can't talk with a distracting fellow like you breathing down our necks."

Philippe, apparently, was used to Audrey. *"Très bien, ma chère,"* he agreed lazily. Then his clear eyes moved to Daye's face. "If you have any secrets, be warned, *mademoiselle.* Audrey is a most inquisitive female."

"You beast!" Audrey laughed.

But Daye, oddly on the defensive, snapped, "I have nothing to hide."

"Then you are most fortunate." The Frenchman raised a mocking eyebrow and moved away.

"Philippe was teasing you," Audrey spoke gently.

Half ashamed, half irritated, Daye tried to smile. "I suppose he was. But, you see...." She shrugged casually. "I can tell you this, Audrey, there goes one man who clearly did not fall in love with me on sight."

Audrey frowned, "Oh, dear, he hasn't been unpleasant to you, has he? Charles would be furious if he had."

Wishing she had kept quiet, Daye assured Audrey that Philippe had not been unpleasant at all. Then, hastily changing the subject, she asked, "You're not married, Audrey?"

"I'm a widow. My husband, bless him, died six years ago. I spent a year in Sydney by myself and then decided to go to Anani and keep house for Derek.'' Her face softened. "We get along famously. Of course, he's ten years my junior and I am inclined to fuss over him a bit. But I believe he likes it. I think all men enjoy being fussed over, don't you?''

Daye did not answer. Reg was the only man she had ever been close to, and it seemed he had always fussed over *her*. She suddenly wondered what it would be like, looking after a man. Not a brother, but a husband.... Involuntarily, her eyes drifted in the direction Philippe had taken, and a curious warmth stole over her. Flustered, she turned her attention to Audrey. "Er, your brother works on Anani, I suppose.''

"Derek is an artist and a truly excellent one.'' Audrey sounded proud. "I'm a terrible braggart when it comes to Derek's work, Daye, but he could become quite famous. However, the dear man refuses to devote himself to painting. He's a super engineer—just as Philippe is—and he works for the Chavots on a more or less part-time basis. In fact, he's just gone to New South Wales to supervise the installation of new machines in one of their fruit-canning factories. And that's why I happen to be here. Derek flew from Anani to Tahiti and I hitched a ride, as they say.'' She smiled. "I've spent two lovely days shopping and visiting a friend who's ill. I intended staying longer, but when Philippe phoned and—'' she hesitated briefly "—and said he was taking a young woman to Anani, I made a mad dash for the waterfront.'' She grinned. "Oh, dear! I suppose that does mean I'm inquisitive. I wanted to meet Charles's guest right away.''

"I'm glad you did," Daye spoke impulsively. "It will be pleasant having you to talk to."

"Thank you, dear. And I hope you will come to see me often while you're visiting Anani. Will your stay be a long one, do you think?" She asked the question casually.

"I don't know. I've always intended it would be, but now...I don't know." Daye's eyes drifted once again to Philippe, who was talking to Hiro, and then back to Audrey. "I've looked forward to this for a long time. Ever since I met Charles, in fact."

"Oh." A slight shadow crossed Audrey's face, but she brightened almost immediately. "Well, you'll love Anani, I'm sure." She took Daye's arm, and in her friendly manner drew her to the rail. "You can watch as we leave Tahiti—it's quite a sight."

The boat's engines were roaring now, and presently they were pulling away from the harbor. Daye watched as the vessels bobbing gently in the crystal water became mere specks, and the red roofs and tall church spires disappeared into the trees. Before long Tahiti became a large, uneven olive-green hump on the horizon, and there was nothing around them but the endless blue of sea and sky. It was glorious! Daye raised her face to the sun and pulled the scarf from her hair. Immediately the breeze caught it, playing wildly with the long, fine strands. She looked at Audrey and laughed. "My hair can be a problem. It isn't thick enough."

"Dear, dear! Do you mean to tell me you're not perfect?" Audrey shook her head in mock sympathy then ran her hand through her short wavy hair. "And this mop of mine is so thick I have to keep it short for comfort. But to get back to Anani, Daye, did you know the island belongs to the Chavots? It's quite an interesting story—how they acquired it, I mean. Something to do with an old deed that dates back almost two hundred years—before the Society Islands became a French protectorate in 1843, of course, although I imagine the fact that the Chavots are dyed-in-the-wool French helped in the original fight to keep it their property."

"I didn't know all that," Daye confessed. "Charles merely spoke of Anani as his island. We really had only a short time together, you see, and I did most of the talking. Oh, we've written to each other but our letters were simply a means of keeping in touch until I could come to Polynesia."

"I see. You...don't know each other very well, then?" Audrey spoke slowly.

"I suppose not. But...well, I believe there are some people you could know for years and still not know them really well. And then you meet someone you instantly understand and love. When I met Charles I...." She hesitated, sensing another presence, knowing who it was.

There was an odd little silence before Audrey said quickly, "There you are, Philippe! Any chance of coffee? And croissants, if possible. Your early phone call caused me to miss breakfast." She gave him a critical look. "You'd better swallow a few cups yourself, my dear. You look terrible! I suppose you were out all night chasing *les femmes*?"

Philippe laughed without humor. "That I will not reveal, *ma chère*." He moved into Daye's line of vision, and she saw that the lines of his handsome face were set stiffly. He looked straight at her as if about to speak, then he turned quickly away and disappeared below deck. Daye watched him go, hardly aware that she did so until Audrey said softly, "Handsome devil, isn't he?"

"Yes, I suppose he is," Daye agreed reluctantly.

Audrey gave her a quizzical glance as though she expected Daye to ask questions about the "handsome devil." But Daye merely smiled and turned to look out at the ocean.

Conversation between them lagged a little after that, but perked up when Hiro brought them coffee and a plate of tempting-looking rolls. "I think we were both half starved," Audrey laughed as they devoured the food. And Daye could only nod in agreement, because her mouth was too full to speak.

They sat in canopied deck chairs as they ate, and afterward they stayed there, stretched out lazily. Philippe did not reappear, and during a lull in their conversation Audrey remarked that the "poor lamb" was probably having a doze. There were moments when Daye wished she could doze herself, especially when the launch swerved or dipped a little too readily. She couldn't help uttering a sigh of relief when, almost two hours after leaving Tahiti, Hiro shouted something in French, and Audrey told her Anani was in sight.

It was still little more than a blot on the horizon but as they speedily drew near it took on shape, rising from the ocean like a great black forest. Then Daye saw the coral reef against which the persistent ocean lashed itself into foam, and beyond that a gleaming, curving band of white that she knew must be sand. All at once the dark vegetation was vividly green and on the beach small specks of color—people—moved.

The launch slowed, and suddenly the water was still and clear as they headed toward the jetty that seemed to be filled with people. Daye felt a stirring of anticipation. She was here at last. Anani. And Charles—where was Charles? Her eyes searched the jetty and the shoreline, but she saw only colorfully clothed, happily smiling natives, young and old, male and female.

Audrey said into her ear, "They do this every time a boat arrives. And every time the plane lands, too."

"And I thought it only happened in films," Daye answered. Then she gave a delightful laugh as a young girl in a red-and-white pareu leaped into the boat and slipped a wreath of fragrant white flowers about her neck. "Oh, thank you," she said, and the girl spoke in her own language, touching Daye's long windblown hair with tentative fingers.

"She welcomes you, Daye," Audrey said. "That's all I could understand, I'm afraid."

"She also said *mademoiselle* is more beautiful than moonlight," Philippe said from behind them. He swung himself to the jetty in a swift, lithe movement, then reached over to assist them. Actually, Audrey needed very little assistance, and Daye knew that if Philippe had not been there, his lean dark face looking into her own, she would have been able to manage quite adequately, as well. As it was, she felt nervous and clumsy, and she had to rely on him or fall flat on her face. He did not let her go as quickly as he had when lifting her on board, but held her lightly, an enigmatic expression on his face. Her head swam dizzily, but she told herself it was the seductive sweetness of the flowers about her neck and not his nearness that affected her so. Then he said in a resigned voice, "Well, *mademoiselle*, you are here." Abruptly he released her and bent down to speak to Hiro who was still in the launch.

"The car is just across the beach." Audrey took Daye's arm.

"We drive to the house?" Daye laughed lightly. "Do you know, Audrey, I rather expected to step out of the boat and into Charles's front hall."

"Anani isn't all that tiny," Audrey explained as they walked along the jetty. "There are several cars on the island as well as a truck used when supplies arrive. And, of course, the aircraft is kept here, which means we have a landing strip. I must admit, though, we seldom drive on the island. There are always shortcuts if one is walking, and Charles has several horses that we're welcome to ride." She gave a sudden spurt of laughter. "Good heavens! You're causing a sensation, Daye. If these were the old days, you would probably be set up as a goddess."

The islanders were gathered on the beach. Their expressions were openly curious but friendly, their dark eyes warmly admiring. They were very quiet, even the children, but when Daye and Audrey moved across the sand they all followed. Then Audrey began pointing them out, telling Daye their names, and soon they were all chattering and laughing, with the braver ones coming close to reach out and touch Daye's hair. *How odd,* she told herself, *I don't mind in the least.*

The car, a station wagon, was in a small clearing surrounded by bushes of pink frangipani whose lovely perfume filled the air about them. Daye and Audrey settled themselves in the back seat while Philippe directed the loading of Daye's luggage and several large boxes into the back of the car. This accomplished, he climbed behind the wheel, and after waving a casual but friendly goodbye to the hovering islanders, started the engine. It struck Daye then, with some force, that Philippe was entirely at home here. It was evident from his manner, his easy familiarity with the islanders and now in the way he'd taken over this car. *Almost as though it belonged to him,* she thought uneasily, and decided she must face the fact that the Frenchman was, indeed, a frequent visitor to Anani.

They drove along a winding, primitive road fringed with mango and breadfruit trees, passed through a lush grove of coconut palms and entered a small forest, where the road was even more primitive, and where dense, moist vegetation enveloped the car in a mantle of green. The effect, Daye thought, was eerily claustrophobic, and she was relieved the drive through it was brief.

Out in the sunlight once more they climbed to higher ground, and as the idyllic tropical scenery unfolded before her delighted eyes, Daye said with spontaneous warmth, "I don't think I could ever grow tired of all this!"

"Mademoiselle...."

Daye turned her head and in the rearview mirror she caught the icy glitter of Philippe's eyes. But before he could say more, Audrey laughed. "Let's hope you don't then, Daye. It would be nice having someone like you living on Anani." She touched Daye's arm and pointed. "I'm almost home."

They passed three neat, almost British-style bungalows set in their own tropical gardens before stopping. "This is where Derek and I live." Audrey smiled her warm smile. "It isn't far from Charles's home, so I will not accept any excuse if you don't come to visit." She stepped out of the car and took her small suitcase from Philippe. "Bye, bye, dear," she said, and reached to kiss his cheek. He muttered something in French, but she only laughed again and hurried toward her front door. When she had waved and disappeared inside the house, Philippe got back into the car and without a word jerked it into gear. Daye stared out the window, sensing his hostility, but refusing to let herself dwell on it. Soon she would be with Charles, and this man would be gone. She hoped he would be gone, anyway. The thought that he might stay for a time made her squirm.

"We have arrived." He spoke curtly.

They were turning onto a narrow path bordered on each side with huge bushes of white and pink frangipani, wild orchids and scarlet hibiscus. Then the path widened into a smooth driveway curving between carpetlike green lawns. Ahead of them—Daye uttered a startled gasp of surprise—was a house, a large, gracious house, built of white stone. It was two storied, with a colonnade, balconies and many tall, glistening windows. Broad white steps led to the massive front door, and as Philippe halted the car at the foot of these, the door opened and a tall man came out and hurried to meet them. Daye sat quite still, watching him, wondering why she was again experiencing a queer unease. Then the car door opened and the man held out his arms, a smile of welcome on his handsome face. "*Ma chère! Ma chère* Mademoiselle Daye."

"Charles?" Daye slid from the car, regarding the man tentatively. "Oh, Charles, you've shaved off your lovely beard!'' She gave a tremulous laugh. ''For a moment I didn't recognize you.''

He put his hands on her shoulders and kissed both her cheeks. ''At last you are here! Ah, but I am so happy!'' He tucked his arm securely about her shoulders. ''But you are early, are you not? I was about to drive to the beach to await you.''

''We were able to start out earlier than expected,'' Philippe explained smoothly from his position just behind Daye.

Charles smiled at him. ''Well? Is *mademoiselle* not as beautiful as an angel?'' He raised his brows quizzically.

Philippe answered him in French and Charles said, ''*Non*, Philippe. We must remember to speak English. Daye does not understand French. As yet,'' he added, as he began to lead her up the steps.

A smiling Chinese man waited by the open door, and Charles told Daye his name was Kao and that Kao was in charge of the household staff. Then she was ushered through a spacious hall from which an elegant stairway curved upward and into a large, high-ceilinged room. The room was elegantly furnished and its predominant colors seemed to be blue and gold. Daye noticed this only vaguely because her eyes were instantly drawn to a portrait that hung over a white marble fireplace. It was the portrait of a young man and she knew without a doubt who it was.

''It is *très bon, n'est-ce pas?* A fine portrait?'' She heard Charles's voice ringing oddly in her ears. ''Philippe was twenty-two when it was painted, the age I was when he was born. And now he is thirty-five, and still he has no son.'' He chuckled. ''Tell me, *mon enfant*, do you notice the likeness between us?''

She turned her head slowly and gazed at him. Her heart pounded and she felt her blood run cold. Likeness? Of course there was! She had noticed it when Charles, minus his beard, had descended the steps toward her. Only she had not realized it was this that had caused her uneasiness. Charles's face was, perhaps, a trifle fuller and his eyes were very dark although Philippe's were not. Otherwise the likeness was quite remarkable. Daye softly expelled a sigh. ''You and Philippe are related.'' It was not a question.

''*Mais, oui*, did you not know? Philippe, you did not tell Mademoiselle Daye?'' Charles seemed puzzled.

''I confess it did not occur to me to do so.'' Philippe's voice was as smooth as before. ''However, since Audrey was on the launch, I am amazed that *mademoiselle* did not learn from her—that I am your son.''

CHAPTER SIX

THE BLUE COCKTAIL DRESS was a favorite of Daye's. Sleeveless, it had a low rounded neckline and a full tiered skirt. She stepped into it with care, and Terii gently eased up the back zipper. "You look much pretty, miss," the girl said, smiling.

Daye smiled back. She liked Terii, the young Polynesian who, Charles had said, would be Daye's personal maid. Not that she needed a personal maid, but Terii happened to be the only person other than Charles and Philippe who spoke English, so she had gratefully accepted.

Terii had helped unpack Daye's suitcases earlier, and now everything was neatly put away in drawers or hanging in the wall-length wardrobe. Daye had had no idea, when packing her clothes, whether she would need formal wear on Anani, but that one meeting with Charles had given her the impression he might adhere to the rule of dressing for dinner. She was relieved now that she had packed one large suitcase with her more lightweight cocktail dresses and two full-length chiffon evening gowns. The rest of her formal wear had gone into storage with her fur coats and heavier clothing. Her furniture, too, had been stored, for the London flat would no longer be hers when the lease was up. She had not wanted to renew it although Reg had begged her to do so. She knew, even if she did not remain on Anani, that she would never again live in London. There was always the small country house she had bought for her mother to live in, and since it was being taken care of by a woman in the nearby village she need only write and it would be made ready.... But she did not want to think about that now. This afternoon she had made up her mind to try not to think too far ahead.

Gazing thoughtfully at her reflection in the tall mirror on one of the wardrobe doors, she found her mind slipping back to that moment when she had learned Philippe was Charles's son. That Philippe had intended shocking her was obvious, for those words: "I am your son," had been uttered deliberately in a tone that was triumphant. Her mind had registered this even as she fought to keep her self-control, and she had wanted to turn on him and demand to know why he had not told her before. But to her relief—and amazement—she'd heard herself saying warmly, "I had no idea you even *had* a son, Charles."

"*Ma chère*, is this possible? Have I never told you of Philippe? But how could I not do so?" Charles had sounded genuinely upset. "I do apologize, *petite*. You will forgive me? You will tell me you are not displeased to learn I have a son?"

She had somehow managed to assure him that she was not displeased, while her whole being had cried out that "displeased" was an insufficient word to describe her feelings. And somehow she had managed to go on behaving normally even though she was uneasily conscious of Philippe in the background, a silent figure, watching and listening as she and Charles talked. Philippe did not leave them alone at all. It was evident to Daye when he appeared for lunch that he'd waited until she was in her suite before he had changed his clothes and shaved.

The meal had been served on a large terrace behind the house, and during it Daye's self-control had been even harder to maintain. They were seated at a round table that was not overly large, and it was practically impossible to avoid all eye contact with Philippe. Fortunately, although at times he joined in the conversation between Charles and herself, he did not address her directly. Had he done so, Daye was sure she would have choked rather than answer him.

She hated him! He was despicable! He had lied to her, deliberately deceived her about his identity and let her travel to Anani knowing it was only a matter of time before she learned who he really was. Of course, he *had* warned her, she reflected, sipping her wine and trying to look as if she was enjoying herself. "If you find yourself unpleasantly surprised you have only yourself to blame," Philippe had said. That she might have received this surprise from Audrey while en route to Anani was, perhaps, immaterial to him. But she felt certain he was entirely satisfied with the way things had turned out.

So it would seem Philippe Chavot derived pleasure from tormenting her. It was a frustrating thought, and not for the first time she asked herself why he should do so. Could he possibly believe, in spite of their conversation this morning, that she was a woman with loose morals? She found herself meeting the chilling gray eyes and looked hurriedly down at her plate. It was all too much for her at the moment. Later on, when she was alone, she would think about it.

Daye was relieved when the meal was over and she could ask to be excused. "You are weary, *petite*," Charles said at once. "Of course you must rest. Tell me—" he put an affectionate arm around her shoulders as he led her into the house "—you are satisfied with your suite?"

"Oh, Charles, it's absolutely lovely. I'm more than satisfied." She smiled up at him. "Everything there looks brand-new. Except for the beautiful little desk, and I'm sure that's an antique."

"*Mais, oui*, it is. It's a family treasure that belonged to my wife. And then when Claudette was fourteen, it became hers." His voice was soft. "You occupy my daughter's suite, *ma chère*. It has been completely redecorated and, as you have guessed, all but the desk is new." He looked down at her as they strolled through the hall to the stairs. "You will not feel uncomfortable in my Claudette's room, *petite*?"

She thought he sounded anxious, so she reassured him, "Of course not, Charles, but you know I would have been quite content with one room." They reached the beautifully curved stairway and Charles gave her a quick warm hug and released her. She walked up two stairs and turned to smile at him, noticing that Philippe was standing a short distance away. He seemed determined not to let them out of his sight, she thought, trying to disregard his presence. "You are far too good to me, Charles," she told him softly. "How can I ever thank you?"

"There is no need, *ma chère*, it is enough for me that you are at last here." Charles reached up to take Daye's hand. "It is important that you are happy. You will be happy here? You will love my island?"

Again his obvious anxiety caused her to reassure

him. "I *am* happy, Charles. And I already love Anani. As for your home, it's truly beautiful. I confess I never dreamed to find such...such luxury on your tropical island...."

Which was the truth. Daye looked around at the large airy bedroom. The walls and carpet were the color of rich cream, and the completely feminine furniture in pale oak was trimmed with gold. Silk curtains in perfectly harmonized shades of green and blue were drawn back from the French windows, and the quilted cover on the bed matched those colors exactly. Several fine watercolors hung on the walls and Daye was sure the scenes depicted were of Anani. The sitting room, by which one entered the suite from the hall, was smaller than the bedroom and decorated in restful shades of green and fawn with touches of dull orange. As well as the small antique writing desk there were a sofa and matching chair, two small, darkly polished tables, a bookcase filled with books printed in English and a cabinet containing a stereo and a generous supply of records. The bathroom was a picture of coolness: pastel-green tiles and accessories, towel racks hung with various sizes of green-and-white patterned towels and a wall-length, marble-topped vanity over which hung a glistening mirror surrounded by small, white-globed electric lights. Charles had done all this for her, and by so doing he told her, as he had told her in his letter, he hoped she would make Anani her home.

Daye sighed contentedly and crossed to the French windows. They were closed against the heat, and she opened them and stepped out onto the balcony. Immediately the exotic island scents enveloped her, and she inhaled deeply as she gazed across the color-splashed landscape to the line of cobalt blue that was the ocean. England was so far away, so remote, that she almost imagined it existed only in a dream. The thought frightened her and she shivered in the radiant warmth of the sun. Suddenly, she wanted to cling desperately to memories of her homeland and of Reg and all the others she liked, as if they might simply slip away forever. Then she chided herself for being fanciful. She was homesick, that was all. And it was perfectly natural for her to be homesick, no matter how beautiful and comfortable her surroundings.

"You wish for Terii to do more?"

The girl's voice broke into Daye's thoughts, and she turned. "Thank you, no, Terii," she said, going back into the bedroom. "I won't need you anymore today, so why don't you go home?" Terii lived in the village, Daye had learned. She came to the house each day to help Pepe, who was her grandmother. Pepe, Terii had proudly stated, had worked for Monsieur Charles for many years and was much loved. Daye had met Pepe and she'd found it difficult to believe the plump, bright-eyed Polynesian woman had a granddaughter of seventeen. Of course, she had most likely married at a very early age, as most Polynesian women did. Or at least as they once did, Daye had silently amended. After all, Terii was seventeen and still unmarried. Daye looked at the ripe young figure in the blue-and-white pareu. If ever a girl looked ready for marriage, Terii certainly did. Almost involuntarily she asked, "Do you have a boyfriend, Terii?"

The girl gave her a totally adult look. "Two, three—more, I think." She shrugged in the French manner. "But I do not want any man. Not in village." She spoke the last three words in an odd little voice, but when Daye gave her a questioning look she flashed her ready smile. "Tomorrow you need?"

"Oh. Well, we'll see. I won't need you a great deal, Terii, so you can still help your grandmother." She thought the girl looked disappointed, so she added, "It will be lovely knowing you are here if I need you, Terii, and I'm so glad you speak English. Who taught you, by the way?"

Terii's face lit up. "Mister Derek teach. He paint me. In picture, you know?"

"Oh, yes." So Derek painted Terii. Shades of Gauguin, she thought and went through the sitting room, Terii at her heels. "I think I'll take a walk in the garden before dark," she said, opening the door to the hall.

"I show you quick cut to garden," Terii offered, closing the sitting-room door behind them.

"Thank you," Daye began and paused, listening. Faintly, from somewhere, she could hear music. "Does someone in the house play the piano, Terii?" she asked.

Terii shook her head. "No one play piano except Mademoiselle Montand. And she not here. Not yet."

"Mademoiselle Montand? Who is she, Terii?"

"She is friend of Monsieur Philippe. Much good friend, I think." Terii lowered her dark lashes and her full mouth pouted. Then she looked up and grinned. "She does not come to Anani much often," she added, with cheerful redundancy.

Daye absorbed this information rather absently, her ears still attuned to the music. It seemed to come from the room opposite her own. Yes, it did. And it was the music of Chopin, she was certain. She looked at Terii but before she could ask the question hovering on her lips the girl said, "You hear recording. Monsieur Philippe has many more."

"Monsieur Philippe?" Daye's lips felt stiff. "He...his room is there?" She raised a trembling hand and pointed.

Terii nodded, her smile warm. "Yes, yes. Monsieur Philippe has suite like you. But different, you know—for man."

Daye chewed her lip. The hall they stood in had only two doors. One was hers, the other Philippe's. "Where does Monsieur Charles sleep?" she asked faintly.

"In other part of house," Terii gestured vaguely. "You want me to show you quick cut now?"

Silently Daye nodded, following Terii but scarcely noticing the direction they took. Then they were in the garden and Daye was watching Terii cross the lawn with swift, natural grace, her long black hair lifting slightly in the breeze. At the trees the girl paused and looked back to wave before disappearing into the mass of greenery.

Daye stood there, unmoving, feeling completely and horribly alone. She wished, with an urgency that made her want to weep, that Reg would come out of those trees and walk toward her; that she would hear his voice, see his warmly affectionate grin. She clenched her hands tightly. This would not do. If she was going to be like this, she might as well give up and go home. But she did not want to go home. She loved Anani, or at least she *could* love Anani, given the chance. The trouble was, too much had occurred to upset her and her nerves were beginning to fray.

She was distraught because she knew she and Philippe Chavot were the only two people in that wing of the house. But there was nothing she could do about it. She could never bring herself to hurt Charles by refusing to use Claudette's suite. She sighed, moving at last, her high heels sinking into the cushion-thick grass. What was the matter with her, anyway? She was not afraid of Philippe Chavot, was she?

The sun's rays seemed weaker, the air a trifle cooler. Daye glanced at her tiny gold wristwatch and knew that before long the sky would be shot with fiery color, and the flaming ball that was the sun would sink out of sight with frustrating speed. Darkness would as speedily follow, so she would not stray far from the house, she told herself, looking back for reassurance. Much of the house could be seen from here, and Daye recognized the terrace on which they had lunched. Raising her eyes to the upper floor she mused over which windows marked her rooms, then realized she was behind the house and her suite was at the front. She felt the color rush into her face and turned swiftly away. Philippe's rooms were opposite her own so it was more than likely his windows overlooked these gardens. Even now he could be up there, looking down at her.

Nevertheless, she walked on, concentrating on the beauty of her surroundings. Flowers bloomed everywhere, splendid, extravagant blossoms that looked as though they were painted onto the green background of bushes. There were scarlet hibiscus and poinsettia, waxy white frangipani, pastel-gold candle flowers and white gardenias. The perfume emanating from the various blossoms was heady, causing Daye to feel rather giddy. The beauty all around her seemed un-

real and overwhelming and she felt as though she
walked in a dream or a fairy tale. *A romantic fairy
tale,* she thought foolishly, and heard herself laugh.
All that was needed now was a prince.

And there he was!

He was standing some distance from her, beyond
the masses of flowers and in the shadow of the trees.
His shirt gleamed in startling contrast to his face,
which appeared even darker than she knew it to be.
The waving palm fronds threw strange shadows
across him, giving him a look that was more satanic
than princely. She stood quite still, watching him as
intently as he watched her, and she thought almost
dispassionately that the mask of the devil sat well on
him. He suddenly moved, leaving the trees and strolling toward her. The look of the devil had disappeared with the frond shadows, and in his dark blue
dinner jacket he was disturbingly handsome. Daye
had gone upstairs after lunch, her heart burning with
dislike for this man. But now her heart was traitor-
ous, thudding so hard she felt breathless. She wanted
to look away from him, yet she wanted to keep on
looking at him. The sensation was unnerving, and for
a timeless moment she thought she would be unable
to cope. Then he paused a short distance from her
and took out his cigarettes. She watched him light
one, managing as she did so to control her beating
heart and her almost painful breathlessness. Still,
she was scarcely prepared when he flicked out the
lighter flame and allowed his clear gaze to sweep over
her.

"*Bonsoir, mademoiselle,*" he said. "Your gown is
très chic, and the color suits you admirably."

She tried not to sound surprised. "Thank you."

He inclined his head very slightly, smoking his cigarette and saying nothing. But he still watched her, and she thought how odd it was that she who was so used to being stared at should find this man's gaze so upsetting. Distractedly she said the first thing that came to her. "You lied to me! You said you were Charles's friend." To her dismay she realized she sounded reproachful instead of accusing.

He rubbed his chin, his expression unreadable. "I did not lie, *mademoiselle.* I am Charles's son and also his friend."

Daye bit her lip. Well, she could not refute that, could she? "I suppose I should consider myself properly squelched." Her tone was sarcastic.

"Je ne sais pas." He shrugged. "Squelched? The word is unfamiliar. It is in your English dictionary?"

She felt annoyed. "I believe it is. Anyway, I'm sure you understand me well enough." She caught the glint of amusement in his eyes and felt even more annoyed. "You are horribly deceitful! Why on earth didn't you tell me who you were from the beginning?"

His eyes narrowed as he drew on his cigarette. "I did not expect to see you, Mademoiselle Hollister. Shall we say the shock caused me to temporarily forget the, er, amenities?" He flipped his cigarette to the grass and ground it beneath his heel. "And later—" he gave her a suggestive little smile "—a man cannot be expected to think clearly when he has just held a desirable woman in his arms."

Daye stared at him, her eyes locked with his. His words had sent her back to those moments in her hotel room, and a shattering excitement took hold of her. She trembled as she forced out her words be-

tween stiff lips. "There was plenty of time after...
afterward. You...I might not have come here if I'd
known who you were."

"You said nothing would make a difference, if I
remember correctly." His tone was chilly.

She swallowed. "And...and then you warned me
that I'd be 'unpleasantly surprised,' didn't you?
Well, it was definitely unpleasant, so you can be
satisfied that I was properly punished. You did intend punishment, didn't you?" She tried to keep the
quaver out of her voice but was unsuccessful.

His face darkened. "Save your tears, *petite
Anglaise*. I assure you I am immune."

"Oh!" Daye shuddered. "I wasn't going to cry; I
wouldn't give you the satisfaction."

She swung about and began to walk away, but he
called, "Wait, *s'il vous plaît*," and she stopped.

"What do you want?" she asked coldly, without
turning around.

"You accused me of deceit, did you not? Tell me,
is the use of an alias not deceitful?"

She faced him defiantly. "You are referring to
Gloria, I suppose. As it happens, I used the name
from force of habit. In my profession I'm known as
Gloria Day."

"And what *is* your profession, Mademoiselle
Hollister?" He made no attempt to disguise his ma-
licious tone.

"Believe it or not, I was in television," she said
sweetly.

"Television?" He frowned. "You are an actress?"

"No. I was never what you could call an actress."

"Was? That is the second time you have used the
past tense. Does this mean you have given up your

profession, *mademoiselle*?'' He sounded only mildly interested.

Daye hesitated. ''Yes, I have.''

''I see. It was not, perhaps, a lucrative profession?'' He spoke almost sympathetically, yet there was a curious hardness to his mouth.

''On the contrary,'' she said stiffly, watching him with suspicion.

''Then may I inquire why *mademoiselle* has given it up?'' The hardness had spread into his voice.

She was immediately defensive. The man was forever asking questions. ''You can inquire all you like, but I don't think I'll tell you.''

His beautiful mouth twisted. ''Perhaps I can guess why,'' he said contemptuously. ''Tell me, Mademoiselle Hollister, does Anani and the home of *mon père* satisfy your expectations?''

She clenched her hands, disliking his tone. ''I'm positive you were listening when I told Charles how I felt,'' she stated pointedly.

He slowly covered the space between them until they were close enough to touch. ''Ah, *oui*, I recall you said you did not expect to find such luxury on his tropical island. Do not tell me you believed Charles Chavot lived in a grass hut?''

She flinched at the derision in his voice. ''I'm telling you no such thing.''

''What, then, did you expect to find, *mademoiselle*?''

She debated ignoring him and walking away. But to her disgust, she heard herself say truthfully, ''A pleasant, comfortable house. Those are Charles's exact words.''

He raised a dark eyebrow. "And he did not, of course, mention his enormous wealth?"

"His...why, no, I...." She broke off, gazing at him in confusion.

"He did not mention the factories owned by the Chavot family? Nor the plantations of vanilla, of pineapple, of tea and coffee?"

His tone was mildly sarcastic. "But perhaps there was no need for him to mention such things. Perhaps *mademoiselle* acquired this information herself."

Daye's confusion had fled. She knew exactly what he meant and she stared at him, insulted and angry. "What a rotten mind you have!" she spluttered, pressing her fingers to her temple. "So you think that I...oh, heavens! If you didn't look so much alike I'd never believe you were Charles's son. He is kind and good, and he's a true gentleman. You...you are...." Words failed her.

"What am I, *mademoiselle*, besides those unflattering adjectives you flung at me in Papeete yesterday?" She flinched again as his voice cut her ruthlessly. "Am I perhaps too inquisitive, too suspicious for your comfort? You would be more at ease if I, too, succumbed to your undeniable charms, *n'est-ce pas? Mon Dieu!* I may find you sexually stimulating, *petite Anglaise*—indeed, I would not hesitate to take you to my bed. But make no mistake, I can resist you. I shall never permit you to beguile *me*. Neither shall I permit you to take advantage of *mon père*'s vulnerability."

The shadows were lengthening, the whisper of wind the only sound in the heavily perfumed garden. Daye looked up into Philippe Chavot's darkly handsome face and saw the bitter dislike stamped on his features. Her anger receded, leaving her feeling thoroughly miserable. So this was the reason for his attitude, the reason he did not want her to remain on Anani. He thought she was a fortune hunter, deliberately worming her way into Charles's affections, using his vulnerability over his dead daughter as a means to gain something for herself. In all likelihood he imagined she would eventually persuade his father to adopt her, make her a legal heir to his fortune. Naturally, Philippe would resent such a thing, as he would also resent her taking his sister's place. Perhaps he was even jealous, afraid that she would take precedence in his father's affections.

Suddenly she wanted desperately to reassure him, tell him that she would never dream of spoiling his relationship with his father. She wanted to convince him she had no ulterior motive for being here, that she was willing, in spite of everything, to try to be friends with him. Instinctively she put out her hand, then hesitated, wondering what would be the most tactful thing to say. After all, she could be wrong, and if she were she would feel embarrassed and foolish. Then again, if she were right, he might resent the fact that she had guessed his fears. Why this should matter one way or the other Daye did not pause to consider.

Choosing her words carefully she said, "Don't you think it would be better—and more fair to me—if you told me straight out what it is you have against me? I think I already know, but I can't be certain, can I? So tell me, tell me now, and afterward...well, I hope I'll be able to convince you how wrong you are." She smiled, deliberately intending to disarm him.

He looked down at her outstretched hand, and raised his heavy lids to stare uncompromisingly into her face. Daye's hand fell to her side and heat rushed into her cheeks. If the ground opened up to swallow her, she felt she would be unspeakably grateful.

"You say you are not an actress, *mademoiselle*?" Philippe spoke softly and with the utmost sarcasm. "I would venture to say you are quite a convincing actress. There was exactly the right amount of pleading, of innocent bewilderment in your voice." He pressed his lips together, took a deep breath and added harshly, "Do you not understand? It is useless to lie to me. It is useless to pretend."

"But I'm not—" she began to protest, pausing as a gust of wind sent her long hair splaying like golden fingers across the Frenchman's broad chest. He stared down at it, a frown creasing his forehead, and before she could brush it away he caught hold of the wayward strands and twisted them around his fingers. She gasped and moved automatically toward him to relieve the pressure on her scalp. "Let go," she insisted.

They were so close she could feel his breath on her upturned face. "You think I am cruel, do you not? *Oui*, you have said as much. And of course you are correct, Mademoiselle Hollister. I am a cruel, heartless man." His teeth glimmered in a mirthless smile. "You would be wise to remember that."

Her lashes flickered. She was so intensely aware of his body close to her own, that she could hardly speak.

"Do you mean that to sound threatening?" she whispered at last.

"Mais certainement." But he spoke absently, and his eyes moved from her face to the hair still entwined in his fingers.

"In this light it glitters like golden thread," he murmured. "It cannot be *naturel*."

Daye cleared her throat. "Oh, but it *is* natural."

His eyes moved quickly to meet hers and for a long moment held her gaze. Then he loosened her hair from his fingers and took a step back. "Long ago, jealous queens would have condemned one as beautiful as you to be destroyed at the stake. *Mon Dieu*, I cannot find it in my heart to blame them!"

He spoke the last sentence in an almost vicious tone, and Daye recoiled instinctively. The vindictive compliment was unpleasant enough but it was his implication that she deserved a brutal fate because she looked as she did that so upset her. He did not merely dislike her, he actually *hated* her. Automatically, she repeated to herself that she detested him, so it did not matter how he felt toward her. But she was aware of a curious little pain somewhere in her breast as she said unsteadily, "Whether it's in Paris or Anani, you are the master when it comes to finding beastly things to say to me."

"And you are not used to men speaking to you in such a manner, *n'est-ce-pas?*" The mockery in his tone was obvious.

The hurt inside her seemed more intense. "No, I'm not. As a matter of fact, I can't remember that any man ever treated me as you do." She had not intended saying that, and she was annoyed with herself for letting it slip out. Forcing a rather brittle laugh, she added, "Oh, well. I expect I'll get used to it." She gave a helpless little shrug and turned to make her way across the shadow-steeped garden.

She did not get far, however. He caught her wrist and then her shoulder, and twisted her around to face him. His back obscured the last vestige of light so that his form became a tall, intimidating shadow. Wearily she asked, "What is it now, Monsieur Chavot? Have you thought of some more unpleasant remarks to make to me?"

"*Mademoiselle*, to be truthful, there are many delightful things I could say to you had we met under different circumstances." His voice was husky and the hand on her shoulder slid down her arm to grasp her other wrist. This time he held her gently so that she could easily have broken away from him. But— while she despised herself for it—she did not want to break away. And when he drew her toward him and held her hands against his chest, she was filled with a heart-shaking emotion.

"*Petite*, you know what I mean, do you not? If we were not who we are, if we were not here on Anani we would not spend our time in enmity. You are as attracted to me as I to you; did we not admit as much only this morning?" His arms moved about her, holding her closely, his hands stilled upon her, taking no liberties, but his lips moved caressingly over her face and paused, hovering above her mouth. She could not see his face but she could feel his breath mingling with hers. "*Ma belle* Daye, how will we be able to bear it? It will be agony for us if you remain here." He touched her mouth gently with his own once, twice, three times. "*Petite*, I believe I have the solution to this... problem."

Dazed by the tantalizing kisses, Daye asked, "Solution? What do you mean?"

"Tahiti, *ma belle*. I have an *appartement* in Papeete; you will go there and I will join you as soon as it is possible. Come put your arms around my neck, *petite*. Let me kiss you—a kiss to last until we can meet again. . . in Papeete."

Daye did not move; her hands remained crushed against his chest. When had she first felt suspicious, she asked herself. Or had she been suspicious all along but blinded, hypnotized by the sheer delight of being in his arms—the one place she wanted to be, of course. He angered, antagonized, hurt and humiliated her, but she could forget all that the moment he held her. A sigh escaped her lips, and she pushed against his chest until his arms fell to his sides. "Daye, what is it, *ma belle*?" he asked in his seductively gentle manner.

"Oh, God!" She raked her hands through her hair, sick at heart because he weakened her so. She made an effort to speak without betraying her emotions. "When do you suggest I leave Anani, then?"

She felt his hand touch her cheek and had to steel herself to remain aloof. "For the sake of *mon père*, it should be soon. Perhaps in a day or two."

"I see. And what will I tell Charles?"

"That I must think about. Do not concern yourself, *petite*." His hand slid across her neck to her shoulder.

She shivered. "I suppose you are satisfied now that you've. . . persuaded me to leave Anani?" She kept her voice low and steady.

She saw the gleam of his teeth as he smiled. "Come, Daye, do not say that. At least, not in that so sad little voice. I am pleased it is true, but only because *I* shall have you. You will not regret it, *ma belle*. We will give each other great pleasure.''

"Oh, stop it!" Daye shuddered away from his touch. "You can't really believe I will leave Anani, and Charles, to become your temporary mistress? You can't possibly be that egotistical."

He drew in his breath sharply. "Egotistical? Mademoiselle Hollister, I am not inexperienced. I know when a woman responds, when she tells me without words that she finds me desirable."

"But I don't! You are wrong!" Daye spoke desperately. "I...perhaps I misled you. Yes. Yes, I did, I deliberately misled you. I...well, you said yourself I was an actress, didn't you?" The last was said defiantly.

"*Oui*, I did. So!" Philippe paused. "It would appear I was mistaken. Would *mademoiselle* care to inform me why she...misled me?"

Daye stared at the dark figure looming before her. "I don't know. Perhaps I wanted, somehow, to hurt you." She feigned indifference. "As if I *could* hurt you, Monsieur Chavot."

"You do not believe I am hurt because you have rejected me?"

She laughed scornfully. "Don't be silly! Oh, perhaps your pride is a bit singed but your delightful proposition was all part of a plan to get me to leave Anani, wasn't it?"

A thought struck her and suddenly she exclaimed, "What if I had been weak and foolish enough to agree to meet you in Papeete? How long would I have waited until you informed me you had no intention of joining me?"

He was silent for so long that Daye was sure he would not answer. Then he said coolly, "Who knows, I might have taken advantage of such a tempting situation and joined you for a brief period. After all, *mademoiselle*, I am a man and you are a most desirable woman."

Daye felt sick. "How disgusting! You despise me, yet you would...." She stopped, unable to go on.

"Make love to you? Sleep with you? *Mais naturellement.*" There was a roughness to his tone. "As I told you, *mademoiselle*, it is possible to be sexually attracted to someone for whom you feel no particular fondness."

"Even someone you dislike." Why, oh, why, did she harp on it so, she wondered angrily. Once more she felt him grip her shoulders.

"Knowing this, *mademoiselle*, are you not a little alarmed?"

"Alarmed?"

"Are you unaware of the fact that my bedroom is not far from your own? That we two are alone in the east wing of the house? Are you not alarmed that one night I might decide to visit you?" He seemed to speak between gritted teeth.

Daye shook off his hands. "I'm not afraid of your threats."

"Are you not? You would, perhaps, welcome a visitor to your bedroom? Even a visitor whom *you* dislike?"

"There you go again!" she uttered the words scornfully. "Listen, *monsieur*, if you keep this up I shall...inform your father." It was an idle threat but she hoped Philippe would not guess.

"You would enjoy causing a situation, a rift, in the

relationship between *mon père* and myself?'' His voice was dangerously soft.

"No, of course not! Oh, I've had enough!'' Daye turned and walked as quickly as possible toward the lighted house. It was not easy; twice she almost stumbled and fell. But as she neared the house, lights suddenly sprung up on the terrace and a tall figure in a dark suit strolled into view.

"Charles!'' Daye uttered a cry of pleasure and relief and hurried toward the terrace steps where Charles waited, his arms outstretched in welcome.

CHAPTER SEVEN

THE SOPORIFIC WARMTH of the sun, the relaxed, peaceful atmosphere that prevailed on Anani, was making Daye shamefully lazy she thought as she languidly stretched her pale gold limbs on the comfortable chaise longue. A week had passed since her arrival, and she felt she ought to involve herself in activities other than strolling in the garden and swimming in the pool. She should go bicycling, find her way about the island, or perhaps take up tennis; there was a beautifully kept court not far from the house. There was also horseback riding; many times she had been photographed perched in the saddle on a horse's back, but she had never learned to ride. Charles and Philippe rode as though born to the saddle. They rode together each morning, and once or twice, when she had risen early, she saw them leave and wished she could have galloped off with them. Well, one of these days she would. She had only to say the word, and Charles would teach her to ride.

The trouble was, she scolded herself, she was enjoying the inactivity, enjoying everything about life on this glorious fairy-tale island. It was marvelous to be able to go to bed when she wanted to because there was no need to get up at a certain time; marvelous to be able to lie in the sun, to read, to spend pleasant hours with Charles, either talking or listening to music. "I'll get horribly fat," she had said to him that morning. "My clothes won't fit and I'll have to go about in a pareu."

Charles's smile was tolerant. "You must give your body the rest it has long needed, and the time to become accustomed to a tropical climate, *ma chère*. And as for growing fat...." He threw up his hands in a dismissive gesture. "However, *petite*, you would look *très charmante* in a pareu. A golden-haired native."

"Mademoiselle Daye would look charming in sackcloth," someone said in a fervent tone, and Daye glanced up to see that Paul Dubois had come onto the terrace. Paul was not yet eighteen, the son of Jean Dubois who was Anani's schoolteacher. Next year Paul would be attending a university in Australia, and when his education was completed he would enter one of the Chavot companies. In the meantime he was spending several hours a day working under the eagle-sharp eye of Monsieur Perrot, Charles's secretary.

Paul was a handsome youth with a pleasing personality and Daye could not help but like him. She had quickly learned, however, that he could easily present a problem. For Paul Dubois had clearly fallen in love—with her.

Had Paul been older, Daye would not have felt so concerned. But an upsetting experience involving a youth who had worked at the television studio in London had taught her that adolescent love, though usually of short duration, could be despairingly traumatic. It had also taught her that a youthful would-be suitor could be more persistent than an adult male and more horrifyingly abusive if rejected.

So for her own sake as well as for Paul's, she hoped his infatuation for her would rapidly fade. Meanwhile, she realized she would need to be careful not to say or do anything Paul could interpret as encouragement. With mild exasperation she told herself it would be so much simpler if she could just keep out of the boy's sight, but since Paul, along with Monsieur Perrot, took lunch with them each weekday, this was impossible.

She wondered how long it would be before Philippe noticed the lovesick glances Paul bestowed on her. Or had those clear, all-seeing eyes of his already noticed? And was he telling himself, with angry triumph, that he had been right to accuse her of being a troublemaker?

Not that Philippe had shown animosity toward her since that first distressing day. He had, in fact, behaved in a polite, cordial manner. Still, she was uneasy. She distrusted him, sensed his behavior was a thin veneer that would crack one day. He was most likely waiting for just the right moment, she told herself ruefully. Until now they had not been alone long enough to indulge in more than brief, idle conversation.

In spite of her uneasiness concerning Philippe, when he was not around she felt mysteriously incomplete, and even when she was relaxed something inside her was tense, as if waiting for the moment he would appear. This was the reason she liked the evenings best of all, because Philippe was present from the time she entered the salon, before dinner, until the time, hours later, when she said good-night and went up to bed. It had become a habit, during those evenings, for her to turn her head occasionally and look at Philippe as he lounged in the armchair he favored. Invariably, he was smoking, his cigarette held between long, tanned fingers, his dark head resting against the high back of the chair. He was always watching her, his eyes brilliant beneath lowered lashes, but he never seemed disconcerted when she caught him looking. Indeed, his mouth would curve in a slight, but sensuous and mocking smile, and it would be she who would flush with embarrassment and turn her head away....

Daye moved restlessly and sat up. The heavily scented breeze was too warm to be refreshing and the sun-drenched landscape so colorful it hurt her eyes. In a week Philippe was leaving, flying to New York on business. He traveled frequently, so Charles had told her, sometimes not returning to Anani for several weeks. "At first, as our interests expanded, it was important that one of us travel, and since—" Charles had hesitated briefly before continuing "—Philippe is younger, to travel thousands of miles means little to him. However, it is no longer necessary for him to do so as frequently as he does. We have extremely capable executives in all parts of the world; it would be a simple matter for any of them to fly to Anani when business matters appear crucial."

"Then why does Philippe keep it up?"

Charles's smile was mischievous. "He grows restless, *ma chère*. He loves his home and his papa, but the world holds so very many attractions that Anani does not."

"I can't imagine what," she said. "Anani is so perfect. Oh!" She felt rather foolish. "I see what you mean." Women, of course. The world's attraction for Philippe would undoubtedly be its women.

Charles's eyes were very bright. "What Philippe needs is a wife, a *famille*. He would not then grow restless. He would travel only when absolutely necessary and then, I think, he would insist his wife accompany him." He smiled again. "And if there were little ones they could stay here to amuse their *grand-père*. Ah!"

His sigh held longing, Daye thought. Charles truly wanted grandchildren. Well, it was only natural that he would.

"It seems strange to me that Philippe isn't already married with a brood of children." Daye kept her tone casual. "He is thirty-five, after all."

"*Ma chère* Daye, do not imagine I have remained silent on this subject." He gave a short laugh, as though remembering. "Philippe will not marry before he is ready merely to satisfy his papa's desire for grandchildren...."

With a muted exclamation, Daye swung her feet to the balcony floor and stood up. There was little doubt in her mind that Philippe Chavot was not the sort of man who could settle down, married or not. Take his wife with him on business trips? Not he! She would stay at home never knowing exactly where he was or whose bed he was sharing. Well, it had nothing to do with her, thank goodness. Daye pressed her hand against her stomach, which had suddenly developed an odd, hollow feeling. Perhaps she was hungry, she thought, going into her suite to ring for Terii. She would have a cup of tea and one of those delicious cakes that Celeste, Charles's superb French cook, concocted.

That evening, as they left the elegant scarlet-and-white chandelier-lighted dining room, Charles said, "Derek, Audrey's brother, returned today, and I have arranged a small dinner party for tomorrow evening. Does it meet with your approval, *ma chère*?"

"Of course. But this is your home, Charles. You know you don't have to ask for my approval." Daye felt embarrassed.

"*Mais, oui*, I do." Charles pressed her arm in an affectionate manner. "It is important to me that you are happy and at ease. So! You will at once inform me if the plans I make do not please you?"

"Yes." But of course she would do no such thing, she thought.

"*Bon!* There are, *naturellement*, other neighbors who will also wish to greet you. But it would be better, I think, to have several small dinner parties over the next few weeks than to have everyone here at once. Do you not agree?"

"Absolutely," she smiled, touched by his anxiousness to please her. They entered a small sitting room evidently furnished with more thought to comfort than to decor. Daye had warmed to this homely room the first time she had set foot in it and was pleased to know they would take their after-dinner coffee and liqueurs in here each evening. Moving to the plump cushioned sofa, she sat down, her eyes wandering as always to the portrait of Claudine, Charles's wife, who had never recovered from the difficult birth of her daughter and had died when the baby was two months old. She had been a lovely, vivacious-looking woman, with a cloud of dark hair and fascinatingly clear gray eyes. Philippe had inherited those eyes, but it was Claudette, she'd noticed from another portrait, who actually resembled her mother though she had Charles's dark eyes. As always, when she thought of Claudette, Daye could not suppress a shudder. The seventeen-year-old girl, on her way home from a Swiss boarding school, had died in the flames of a crashed jet airplane. Poor Charles—life had dealt him some cruel blows. Only a year before his daughter's tragic death, his father, alert and apparently healthy at eighty-three, had been felled by a stroke and died within hours. And that night, in her sleep, his beloved *maman* had joined her husband.

"They were always the truest of lovers," Charles had told Daye, "and I was joyful that they were still together." But his eyes shadowed, and she knew it must have been a severe shock to lose them both at virtually the same time.

She wondered then about Philippe. He was only thirteen when his mother died, which must have been dreadful for him. But when his grandparents died, when his young sister was killed—how had it all affected him? Was he still terribly hurt by the tragedies, or was Philippe the man too cold and hard of heart to feel that sort of pain? A tremor of guilt ran through her. Was she wrong to judge him merely because he had been cruel and unkind to her? After all, he did seem devoted to his father. Her eyes drifted toward Philippe. He was standing at the sideboard pouring brandy into a snifter, and as she watched he turned to speak to his father. He smiled as he spoke, a warm, natural smile that added even more potency to his attractiveness. He was wearing a silver gray roll-collared shirt beneath a jacket of darker gray, and she thought how well the color suited him. The shirt in particular seemed to be a remarkable match for those eyes.... Her own eyes slid quickly away as Philippe's head turned in her direction.

Charles was sitting opposite her, and she concentrated on him as she drank the coffee that Suzy, one of the Polynesian maids, had brought to her. He looked very fit, and his fifty-seven years sat easily on him. The night they met he had looked older, she thought, but he had worn a beard that could have aged him. She'd liked that neat gray beard—it gave him a rakish look. When she told him this he had laughed ruefully.

"And to think, *ma chère*, I removed it to please you. Somehow I assumed you would prefer me to be—how do you say—clean shaven, no?"

Philippe was present at the time, and Daye noticed the sharp almost anxious glance he gave his father. Charles frequently said things that made it appear she was influencing his life, and this made her uncomfortable since she was doing no such thing—at least, not intentionally, as Philippe no doubt thought she was.

"You are pensive, Daye." Charles's voice broke into her thoughts. "You dream of your England, *n'est-ce pas?*"

"Actually, Charles, I was thinking about you."

"That is understandable," he teased, adding cautiously, "You are certain you do not feel the homesickness, as yet?"

"Not yet. I do miss Reg a bit, though," she admitted. Charles knew all about Reg and the part he had played in her life, and soon Reg would know about Charles. Only yesterday she had written him a long letter, and tomorrow it would go with the rest of the island mail to Papeete's post office.

"Reg must one day join you on Anani, *mon enfant*," Charles remarked kindly.

"I'd love that." A smile touched her mouth at the thought. Then she caught Philippe's eye and knew from his expression that he remembered Reg. Embarrassed, she said quickly, "What a nice cozy room this is, Charles. I admire those other elegant rooms, but next to my own this is my favorite."

She spoke truthfully, although she had mentioned the room merely to change the subject. Whether or not Charles guessed her intention was unclear, but with a pleased look he said, "When this house was completed, my wife decided this would be the room for our *famille*, a place where we could truly be ourselves. Philippe was three years old at the time, and we hoped there would be several more *enfants, naturellement*." He sighed. "Philippe was thirteen before Claudette was born." A frown appeared and depression seemed to settle over him; but then he shrugged and smiled. "This room, *petite*, has been kept as close as possible to its original state. Some furnishings have, of necessity, been replaced, but—" he patted the wide arm of the large, old-fashioned chair in which he sat "—this is the chair Claudine used. She would sit here with her needlework and Philippe would play at her feet. *Oui, ma chère*, it is true. My son, who so moodily listens to his papa's reminiscences, was once a small boy who played with his trains and sat upon his mama's knee. Ah, well, if *le bon Dieu* is willing, I will one day see another small boy playing here at his mama's feet."

Daye swallowed. Her mouth felt incredibly dry, so

she picked up her cup again and drank the remaining coffee, not caring that it was quite cold. Of course Charles was talking about a grandchild; only this afternoon she had been thinking how much he wanted a grandchild. She supposed he was tossing out a hint to Philippe and wondered with shocking suddenness if he knew his son had someone special all picked out and was trying to get him to set a wedding date. Something twisted inside her, and she turned her head to give Philippe a questioning look.

He was seated in his usual chair, but now he was not relaxed. He was leaning slightly forward, his eyes brilliant with accusation fixed steadily upon her. Her hand trembled, and she set the cup back on its saucer and returned it to the table. Now what was wrong? What had she said or done to cause him to look at her so? Scarcely knowing what she was doing, she gave Charles an overly bright smile and teased, "Must it be a little boy? Wouldn't a little girl be acceptable?"

"*Mais, certainement!* It would be even more acceptable, even more pleasurable, if there could be one of each sex. A small boy with black curls, and a—" his hesitation was almost imperceptible "—small girl with golden hair and eyes as green as the verdant mountainside."

Philippe's sharply indrawn breath was clearly audible, but Daye made no sound at all. In startled surprise she stared at Charles, who smiled complacently back at her. She wished she had only imagined the words he had just spoken but knew this was not so. What on earth had come over him, she wondered in bewilderment. The remark about the desired granddaughter's hair and eyes had been too obvious to be misconstrued. Oh, God! He had actually been hinting at a relationship between Philippe and herself. He'd more than hinted at it; he'd made it sound as though he desired and approved of such a relationship. Embarrassment filled her. How could Charles have said such a thing in front of Philippe? How could he entertain for a moment the preposterous, ludicrous notion that she and Philippe would *marry*? For she did not doubt that was what he had meant. She bit her lip nervously as the silence in the room increased. Preposterous? Ludicrous? It was perhaps so to her and to Philippe, but to Charles it probably seemed a most feasible proposition, particularly when he was blissfully unaware of the antagonism that existed between his son and herself. He would have to be set straight, of course, before he built his dreams too high. She would talk to him; unless, perhaps, Philippe decided to talk to him first.

She stole a glance at Philippe and saw that he was eyeing the lighted tip of his cigarette in a now-familiar moody fashion. What was he thinking, she asked herself. Was he, too, embarrassed by his father's remark? She watched as he put the cigarette to his lips and drew in deeply, closing his eyes as though he derived sensuous enjoyment from it. Daye wished he would smile at her, or simply look at her for once with friendship in his eyes. But the look in the eyes that turned in her direction was far from friendly; his expression held cold contempt. He blamed *her* for what his father had said. As if he had spoken the words, accusing her, she could not have been more sure. And it was more than likely he thought she was actually plotting with his father's blessing to maneuver him into marriage. Oh, Lord!

Did he think she had lied when she told him she disliked him, or did he imagine she would do anything—even marry without love—for wealth and security?

Not that he had ever come right out and accused her of being a fortune hunter—not in those words, at any rate. She reminded herself he had not needed to use exact words—his insinuations had been clear enough.

At that moment Daye felt the wildest inclination to exclaim how much Philippe had misunderstood her, to defend herself here in front of Charles who would, of course, support her. Philippe would be forced to listen, and she knew he would believe his father. He would believe him, wouldn't he? He would not stubbornly insist that Charles was beguiled and under her influence.... She was holding herself stiffly, gathering her courage together so that she could speak. But she could not bring herself to utter the words; she could not, she knew, cause this quiet room to become the setting for bitter discord. She sank back against the sofa cushions, defeated. No, she could not do that to Charles. Let Philippe think what he liked, let him be the one to speak if his father's remarks perturbed him. Let him tell Charles exactly what he thought of his little English guest.

She became aware that Charles was talking to Philippe, his tone bland, as if he was innocently unaware of the tense discomfort he had caused. Her eyes followed him as he rose and went to a large glass-fronted bookcase. He came back presently, carrying a thick red leather volume. "In here are many photographs of our family and friends. This you will enjoy, *ma chère*," he said, seating himself beside her.

And enjoy she did, so much that the evening passed swiftly, and soon it was well past midnight. But although she felt drowsy, Daye's interest was avid, particularly as she viewed the photographs on the album's last few pages. Philippe was in most of these, and they appeared to have been taken over the past ten years or so. He photographed well; Reg would consider him an ideal subject. She recalled some of the handsome men who had posed with her over the years and realized none had possessed the almost tangible sex appeal of this dark, arrogant Frenchman. Or was it only she who would think that? This possibility was infinitely upsetting until she recalled the girls in some of those photographs, girls who smiled adoringly up at him or clung possessively to his arm. *Women obviously make fools of themselves over him,* she told herself scornfully and almost laughed out loud when she remembered that Philippe thought men behaved that way over her.

"And this is Melisse Montand," Charles said in her ear. He was pointing to the photograph, a large glossy photograph, of a woman who was wearing a cream evening gown that fitted her superb figure to perfection. There was something vaguely familiar about her striking face with its dark eyes and jet black hair, and Daye remembered she had appeared in several earlier snapshots.

"Is she a relative?" she asked casually, although she was now recalling that Terii had mentioned a Mademoiselle Montand who was Philippe's "much good friend."

"*Non, petite*, Melisse is a great family friend. Her

mama and *ma chère* Claudine attended the same
school in Paris, and since she was a child Melisse has
come to Anani to spend her holidays. Melisse is an
accomplished professional pianist, and we are most
proud of her, *n'est-ce pas*, Philippe?'' Charles took
the album which Daye had reluctantly closed. ''There
is a piano in our guesthouse; Melisse prefers to occupy a place where she can practice without disturbing others.'' He glanced at Philippe. ''Has Melisse
not finished her concert tour, Philippe?''

''*Oui*, papa. In a few days I will fly to Papeete to
meet her.''

''And in a week you must leave us? How unfortu-
nate. Melisse will be most disappointed.''

''When we met in Sydney recently, I explained,
and being Melisse, she understood.'' Philippe sounded almost indifferent. Then as Daye was wondering if
this woman had stayed in the same apartment he had
suggested she herself share with him, he continued,
''However, papa, I have decided against the New
York trip. Greenwood is perfectly capable of deciding upon the site of the new factory.'' His pause
was practically infinitesimal. ''There are several matters I must attend to. . . in Tahiti as well as here on
Anani.''

Daye heard the odd little note in his voice, but was
too filled with a sudden rush of pleasure to pay much
attention. He was not leaving. At least, he was not
going to New York. Tahiti was not far; if he went
there he might not be gone for more than a day or
two. Her body tingled with warmth. She should be
dismayed and upset by his decision, she knew; after
all, she wanted peace of mind, the comfort of being

able to move about and talk without the sensation of being constantly watched. Of course she did! So why on earth did she feel so ridiculously happy?

Her happiness fled as Charles said, "Ah, *bon, bon!* This pleases me, Philippe. What delightful evenings we will have together. *Ma chère* Daye, you will be enchanted when Melisse plays Chopin. . . ."

Melisse. The family friend, Philippe's "much good friend!" Of course! Philippe had canceled his trip because Melisse was coming to Anani. She must be very special to him, much more than a friend, Daye decided, and was surprised by an unfamiliar, unpleasant pain deep inside of her. Were they lovers, this woman and Philippe? Did they, perhaps, intend to marry one day? But if this was so, if there was something between Philippe and Melisse, Charles would almost certainly be aware of it. And yet tonight he had intimated he approved of Daye as a daughter-in-law.

Unless—unbidden, Daye's thoughts rambled on— Charles only suspected a romance between the couple. In that case, his reference to a golden-haired, green-eyed child might have been made in a deliberate attempt to provoke Philippe into admitting he had already chosen his future wife.

Somehow the thought of Charles using *her* to achieve this result was inordinately upsetting, even more than the earlier embarrassment he had caused her. Again, she thought, *oh, Charles, how could you!* Then, afraid she might burst into tears this time, she rose and announced she was going to bed.

By the time she reached her suite she was ashamed of herself. She had leaped to conclusions about Philippe and Melisse and, because those conclusions did not appeal to her, she had made Charles the scapegoat for her excited emotions. Unhappily she paced her sitting room, hoping Charles had not noticed the abrupt manner in which she had said good-night. He had not appeared to, but, thinking back, she recalled Philippe had given her a curiously intent look...almost as if he knew something had upset her, she decided. But perhaps he had assumed she was merely nervous because of his father's implication earlier that evening. He might even have assumed she expected him to follow her upstairs to berate her. Come to think of it, it was surprising he had not done exactly that. Of course, he had probably discussed it with his father after she'd left the room. She hoped so, for Charles would assure him she had nothing to do with what he had said.

She stopped pacing and stood quite still, her eyes moving to the door. The hall between the two suites was tiled but Philippe's tread was almost as quiet as an animal's, and it was the sound of his door closing that usually indicated he had retired for the night. It was that sound she had heard now, and she was amazed because Philippe had come up so soon, and anxious because it could mean he had not talked to Charles about this evening's incident.

Oh, well, there was no point in worrying about it, she told herself, going into her bedroom. Sooner or later Philippe would learn the truth. She slipped out of her Qiana shirtwaist frock and flimsy underwear and into a short nylon nightdress before going over to the mirror to stare at her reflection. "And soon you'll learn the truth, Daye Hollister," she said aloud. "You'll learn whether or not Philippe loves Melisse Montand."

Amazingly, her features retained their composure but her dark green eyes seemed suddenly shot with emerald fire. Green for jealousy! Or was it for envy, Daye wondered with a twinge of irritation. Well, it was one and the same for what she was feeling toward Melisse Montand. Melisse...who quite probably occupied the most special of places in Philippe Chavot's heart.

CHAPTER EIGHT

DAYE WAS AWAKE earlier than usual, assailed by a new restlessness. She found she could not lie in bed lazily contemplating the day ahead as she had done on previous mornings.

It was already warm and even more humid today, and she slid the glass over the screened French window and flipped the air-conditioning switch to the on position. She was not overly fond of air conditioning, but she was developing a headache, which the humidity did not help. She would take a bath, she decided, then thought longingly of the island pool. She had always been accompanied by Charles when she swam, and he had suggested she never swim alone. But Charles was almost certainly out riding with Philippe, and she did not feel like waiting.

Quickly she pulled off her short nightdress and put on one of the swimsuits she had purchased in Papeete. It was sky blue in color, a one-piece affair that was nevertheless quite revealing. Daye viewed her reflection, absurdly proud of her pale golden limbs, then pulled on a cheerfully patterned beach coat, took one of the large towels from the bathroom and left her suite. It was very cool and peaceful in the large house, and she met no one as she hurried down the stairs. However, as she crossed the hall, she had the uncanny sensation of being watched. It caused her to hesitate and look swiftly about, but seeing no one she went on her way and soon was outside in the brilliant sunshine. The morning was glorious in spite of the humidity; later on, Daye knew, the sun would sizzle her fair skin if she was not extremely careful.

The comparative formality of the grounds was left behind, and Daye followed a narrow track that meandered between slender palms and dense, leafy foliage. Silken fronds brushed her limbs and small bronze gold lizards slithered lightly across her feet. Butterflies, exquisitely iridescent, flicked delicate wings about her head, and tiny, brightly hued birds darted in swift panic from her alien presence. It was all so beautiful, so extraordinarily enchanting, that Daye laughed aloud, filled with a sudden pure joy.

Presently she came to the end of the track where the ground sloped to a small clearing, and there was the pool, shimmering under the sun like pale blue crystal. Its setting was perfect—one of vivid, intoxicating color combined with the somber splendor of dark volcanic rock. This rock rose on one side of the pool, towering into a jagged cliff over which water tumbled in an effervescent cascade. As always, in this particular spot, the breeze seemed nonexistent, the hot, humid air even heavier, the island scents more cloying. It made the water look so coolly enticing that Daye ran quickly down the slope, pausing only to drop her towel and beach coat to the ground and slip out of her sandals before diving into the blue water. It was deliciously cool and she swam lazily, luxuriously. She loved to swim and considered it to be one of the few things she did really well. Even in London she had managed to swim at least once a week throughout the year. But indoor swimming at a public pool was nothing at all like this, she told herself, lazily turning onto her back and gazing at the fantastic brilliance of the cloudless sky.

She came out of the water at last, her hair hanging long and dripping wet over her bare back. Dropping to her knees on the soft grass she reached for her towel. Her arm was still outstretched when she happened to glance up—and saw Paul Dubois at the top of the slope, watching her.

He had not, apparently, come to swim, for he was wearing a blue-checked shirt and dark blue Levi's, the bottoms of which were tucked into short black boots. He could be wearing swim trunks beneath his Levi's, Daye mused, fighting a surge of irritation and resentment. She had tried to remain aloof with Paul, thinking it was the wisest solution to a sticky problem. But here he was, and since she could not bring herself to ignore him, she waved casually and called, "Going for a swim, Paul? The water feels marvelous."

Slowly Paul descended the slope and stood looking down at her. Daye reacted instinctively, reaching for the towel to cover herself. Paul might as yet be a youth, but the expression in his dark eyes was that of a man. As casually as possible she dabbed at her throat, taking care the towel covered the swell of her breasts. "Well?" she queried, forcing a smile.

"*Non, mademoiselle*, I did not come to swim. I must shortly report to Monsieur Perrot." Paul sat down not far from Daye, and she noticed he was biting his lower lip nervously. "You swim well, *mademoiselle*."

"Thank you. I didn't realize I was being watched."

"Do not be angry, I beg of you. You were so. . . beautiful. Like a golden mermaid." His tone was fervent.

"Flatterer!" Oh, no! Why on earth had she said that? To Paul it must have sounded deliberately provocative. "It's always nice to receive a compliment," she amended, the towel still clutched against her chest.

Paul did not answer. He simply gazed at her ardently. Torn between sympathy and irritation, Daye said, "Well if you didn't come here to swim, why did you come, Paul?"

He swallowed convulsively. "This morning I rode one of Monsieur Chavot's mounts. After I returned him to the stables I went to the house. You were in the hall and I. . . I saw that you intended to swim." He stopped, and again licked his lips nervously.

Daye remembered she had felt she was being watched. "You followed me here, Paul?"

"Not immediately. At first I was undecided, but I wanted. . . Mademoiselle Daye, you are angry, are you not?"

"Not angry, Paul. But why didn't you speak to me at the house?"

He shook his head, looking so unhappy Daye's heart softened. "Let's forget it, shall we? And since you're here we might as well have a chat." Paul's face brightened, and Daye eased herself into a sitting position and adjusted the towel so that it was draped about her shoulders. "Now tell me, Paul, have you always lived on Anani?" She spoke lightly to put him at ease.

"*Oui.* At least, I have lived here since I was three weeks old. That is when my parents adopted me.

Mon père was the schoolmaster then, as he is now."

"And he taught you, I suppose."

Paul nodded and grinned. "Until I was thirteen and went away to boarding school in Australia." He grinned again, and all at once was happily talking about his childhood on Anani and the mischief he and his friends, mostly Polynesian, would get into. Daye found it all very interesting and soon she was laughing with him, completely forgetting her earlier irritation. Then somehow Paul's future was mentioned, and the fact that he would attend a university next year, and Daye noticed a glum expression erasing the happiness on the boy's face.

"What's the matter, Paul?" she asked. "Don't you want to go to the university?"

He pulled a face. "You will laugh if I tell you what I really want to do."

"Of course I won't laugh," she said indignantly.

"*Très bien*, I will tell you. I would much prefer to attend a college of music." He looked at her anxiously.

"Music? You have ambitions to become a singer, Paul?"

He laughed. "*Non*, Mademoiselle Daye, to become a pianist. It is, I think, something I have always desired. Even as a child I would steal into Monsieur Chavot's guesthouse to use the piano that is kept there. But I did not learn to read music until I attended boarding school, and it was there I was given my first piano lessons." Paul's face shadowed. "At that time my parents seemed delighted, and *maman* insisted a piano be installed in our home. Unfortunately, they are no longer delighted. They say they do not approve of my embarking on a musical career and prefer...*non*, insist that I study for a future in one of the Chavot companies.''

He looked and sounded utterly dejected, but although Daye felt sorry for him she felt she had to say, ''I don't claim to know much about the Chavots' business interests, Paul, but I should imagine you are fortunate to be given the chance to work for them.''

''Ah, but I agree, Mademoiselle Daye, and I am not ungrateful. The Chavot enterprises are vast.'' Paul spread his arms in sudden enthusiasm. ''If I did well, I could live anywhere in the world, I could travel as does Philippe.'' He sighed heavily. ''But I would not be happy. Music is...is my life. My parents must understand that this is so.''

''Perhaps they...what I mean to say is, Paul, are you certain you have talent?'' She eyed him anxiously.

''*Mais, oui*, of this I am certain. Melisse... Mademoiselle Montand has said as much. And who would know if she does not?''

''Yes, I see.'' Daye spoke absently, confused by the feelings the woman's name evoked. ''Mademoiselle Montand is a concert pianist, isn't she?''

''A superb *artiste*!'' Paul declared, his expression animated. ''She is also most charming. When I was a child she would give me sweets and small presents, and sometimes she and Philippe would play card games with me.'' He frowned. ''*Maman* did not mind at all and papa often joined in our games. Now, it is all so changed.'' He shook his dark head as if bewildered. ''Mademoiselle Daye, since Melisse—she permits me to use her first name—began encouraging me to study for a career in music, my parents—

maman in particular—have forbidden me to associate with her. Tell me, is this not unreasonable?" Paul's voice held a hint of passion.

"Oh, dear." Daye brushed back strands of drying hair, reluctant to agree with Paul, at least openly. In her heart she did agree, however. Paul's parents were unreasonable. After a moment she said tentatively, "Do your parents understand you have this talent, Paul? Enough talent, I mean, to make a successful career?"

He nodded vigorously. "Melisse told *mon père* over a year ago. They were in the guesthouse and I overheard. It was not my intention to do so," he said rather defiantly. "The windows were open, you understand?" He pulled out thick blades of grass, his young face moody. "*Mon père* was angry, I believe. He told Melisse he could not be expected to accept her opinion of my potential, that he could not trust her. Possibly he said much more, but I saw Philippe approaching and decided it was the moment to leave."

Daye gave him a helpless glance before she said, "Try to cheer up, Paul. Your parents might very well change their minds."

"That I doubt. Mademoiselle Daye, it is so frustrating! I cannot practice at home, for *maman* threatens to have palpitations, and although Monsieur Chavot permits me to use the piano in the guesthouse, I am aware that he does not enjoy this situation."

"It must be an awkward situation for him." Daye was mildly reproachful.

Paul looked ashamed. "*Mais, oui*, I admit it. But, *mademoiselle*, what am I to do? I must play. I must!"

"Of course you must. Oh, Paul, my dear, I wish I could help in some way." It was the truth she spoke, but she felt totally helpless. Instinctively she reached out to cover his hand with her own, a sympathetic gesture that she regretted almost at once for Paul suddenly grasped it tightly.

"You will come to the guesthouse to listen to me play?"

"Yes, yes, I'll come," Daye promised, attempting to draw her hand away.

"Merci, mademoiselle." He raised her hand to his lips, his eyes glowing almost feverishly. *"Ah, mon amour, mon amour—"*

"Bonjour!" The cool voice cut off Paul's impassioned words, and had it been anyone but Philippe Chavot standing there watching them, Daye would have been intensely relieved. As it was she withdrew her hand from Paul's, feeling nothing but embarrassment.

Unlike Paul, Philippe had come to swim. He was wearing black swimming trunks that hung low on his narrow hips and over one shoulder was draped a towel, its whiteness pure against his bronzed skin. Daye had not seen him wearing so little before, and her earlier impression of potent maleness was intensified when she saw his well-shaped muscular legs, his lean hard-looking body and superb shoulders. And when he moved she noticed again his indolent, animallike grace and every feminine nerve in her body tingled in excited response.

He paused only a few feet from where she and Paul sat and for a drawn-out moment he simply looked at them. Then he spoke curtly in his own language and Paul hastily scrambled to his feet. *"Merci, made-*

moiselle, you have been most kind," he said formally and gave her a jerky little bow. *"Au revoir."*

Daye watched Paul leave before letting her gaze slide back to Philippe. "Whatever did you say to make him rush off like that?" she inquired, trying not to let his looks disconcert her.

"I told Paul Monsieur Perrot was growing impatient." His tone remained curt.

"And is he?"

"If he is not, then he should be." He dropped his towel and strolled away, skirting the edge of the pool until he came to the rocks. Without apparent effort he began to climb, and as Daye watched in fear and fascination, he reached one of the high jutting ledges and hoisted himself onto it. At the edge he poised briefly before making an expertly clean dive into the pool below.

Daye sighed with relief and got hastily to her feet. She would go back to the house at once, she thought. It was obvious Philippe was disagreeable and not inclined to talk. Not that they would be able to talk if he was so inclined, she silently acknowledged. They were two people doomed to finish any conversation with argument.

Daye bent to slip on her sandals and pick up her beach coat. Then she turned to stare at the pool. There was no sign of Philippe's dark head or his brown arms cleaving the water. Where was he? Dropping the beach coat she ran to the water's edge and, cold with alarm, she gazed desperately over the smooth crystal water. "Oh, God, no!" she whispered, and prepared to dive into the blue depths.

And then on the far side of the pool a dark head pierced the shimmering surface, and she saw him swimming strongly toward the bank on which she stood.

Once again she experienced relief, but this time it was so intense she felt almost nauseous. Blindly she turned around and walked slowly across the grass. What was the matter with her? Had he really been under long enough for her to become so upset? She should, of course, have known better. He had lived here all of his life, he dived and swam like a native. Her hands trembled as she pushed back her hair. The nausea had disappeared, but she felt confused, disoriented.

"Mademoiselle!"

Daye kept walking. She could not face him. But when he spoke again she stopped immediately. "You are leaving? But I wished to speak to you." He sounded as though he was right behind her.

She turned around, and he was close enough for her to see the water still clinging to his skin and dripping from his hair, running in tiny rivulets down his face. Some drops of water hung from his eyelashes, and it was not until he blinked them away that Daye realized she had been staring, enthralled. The knowledge did nothing to help her already frail composure, and it was all she could do to keep herself from crumpling in a heap at his feet.

"Mademoiselle?" He raised a brow. "Something is wrong, perhaps?"

So he had noticed her discomfort. "No, nothing is wrong. I...yes, I forgot my robe and towel." She had forgotten. Both articles lay where she had dropped them.

But when she would have moved to pick them up, he put up his hand and said quickly, "Since the moment appears convenient, there is something I wish to say to you.''

Although his tone was mild Daye felt wary. "Of course," she murmured.

His eyes were brilliant in the sunlight, and he allowed them to appraise her face and body before he spoke again. "You are aware, are you not, that Paul Dubois is seventeen years old?" His tone was still mild, his eyes held hers.

She stiffened. "I know that."

"You know, also, that the boy is infatuated with you?" And when she did not answer, "*Mademoiselle*, is it your intention to add Paul to what I am certain must be a long list of conquests?" Now his voice was hard.

Daye's temper rose. "I can't help it if Paul imagines he is in love with me! I've done nothing to encourage him!"

"Have you not? What I saw a short time ago appeared to be encouragement."

"Appeared to be! There! You said it yourself." She glared at him. "Obviously you've been waiting for an excuse to find fault with me. I'm only surprised you didn't take it into your head to follow me upstairs last night." And as he frowned, she added, "Oh, I knew you were incensed when your father began talking about children and...marriage, but I couldn't very well say anything in front of him. I mean...." She hesitated. "When I left, you did discuss it, didn't you? It's all straightened out now?"

He did not move but Daye felt as though he had come menacingly close. "*Non, mademoiselle*, it is not—as you say—'straightened out.' *Mon père* did not mention the subject, and I could not bring myself to do so. Even now I am finding it difficult. . . ." He paused, his mouth becoming a straight hard line before he continued, "I was not surprised by his wish—it has been apparent since your arrival. However, I confess to being somewhat surprised that he did not first discuss it with me in private." Daye could have sworn he sounded almost hurt.

"But I was altogether surprised," she said hastily. "He didn't discuss it with me either."

"You deny, *mademoiselle*, that you and *mon père* have ever spoken on the subject of marriage?" He spoke disbelievingly.

Daye hesitated before she answered. Only a day or two ago Charles had spoken so eagerly of a wife and family for his son, and she herself had contributed her opinion. She met Philippe's clear, disconcerting gaze and felt her lashes flicker. "We didn't actually discuss it," she ventured. "Not the way you mean." She lowered her eyes, suddenly tempted to ask him about Melisse Montand, to tell him she suspected Charles might very well prefer this family friend for his daughter-in-law. But she resisted, afraid Philippe would tell her something she did not wish to hear. Besides, she was not at all certain Charles did prefer Melisse, was she? Last night, as she lay sleepless, she had thought, among other things, of Charles's affection for her, and she had realized the intense pleasure he would derive from having her as his daughter-in-law. He wanted her to stay on Anani. He had often told her so, and if she married his son. . . . Daye had a sudden picture of herself playing with children. Charles's grandchildren, Philippe's children. . . . She felt a surge of warmth spreading rapidly through her body. When she raised her eyes to look at the vitally attractive man before her, she thought, *oh, God, what on earth will I do?*

He was looking at her expectantly, and she gave him a bewildered look. "Well, *mademoiselle*, in what way did you discuss it?" he prompted.

She shook her head, wanting only to get away from his distracting presence. But he must have sensed it, because he stepped closer and placed his hands on her upper arms. His touch sent tremors through her body, and it took great effort to meet his eyes without flinching.

"*Mon Dieu!* The more I dwell on it, the more mysterious this situation becomes." He spoke with quiet intensity. "You are exceptionally lovely. There must be many men, wealthy men, who have wished to marry you. So tell me *petite Anglaise*, why did you choose to travel across the world for a wedding ring?"

"But I didn't!" she protested, knowing she should wrench away from his hands and having no desire to do so. "You were right about the men I could have married. It isn't remotely logical that I would come all this way just to get a husband. Unless, of course, I'd met someone and fallen in love. Then, I suppose, I'd travel any...." She broke off in confusion. If he would let her go she could think sensibly, she told herself, but although he remained silent his hands tightened on her bare arms. She swallowed. "I wish I could make you understand how it was, why I felt I had to come to Anani. After I met your father and we became such friends, he told me about his island and somehow I knew it was the perfect place for me. Oh, I told Charles I would think about it and I did, and as soon as I was free I—"

"Free?" His hands tightened.

"Please!" she said, and his grip lessened. "From my contract," she explained, lowering her eyes in case he read in them how much his nearness was upsetting her.

"Ah! There was confusion over this contract, *n'est-ce pas?*"

"Confusion? Of course not. Except that Max...." Daye paused, reluctant to talk about Max Lucan and his anger over her refusal to sign a new contract with his company. She had been afraid before she left England that Max would manage somehow to stop her. She moved restlessly under Philippe's hands, imagining for a moment they belonged to Max.

Philippe's hands fell to his sides and Daye looked up. Under the sun's ever-increasing warmth, his hair was drying into small curls around his ears and over his forehead. There was only the lightest covering of hair on his chest but that, too, was curly....

His voice interrupted her observation. "Why do you not continue, *mademoiselle?*" And when she looked at him in confusion, "Your last words were, 'Except that Max....'"

Daye frowned, wondering why he sounded so belligerent. "There isn't anything more," she answered quickly.

"Is there not? It would seem there is a great deal more. Who is this Max? Ah, *un moment!* Is this not the name of the ill-mannered gentleman with the mink coat and the promises of ermine?"

Daye was startled that he had remembered so well. "He was my employer," she answered shortly.

"And your lover, *n'est-ce pas?*"

"No!" She felt her cheeks flame. "Not that it's your business."

"*Mais, oui, mademoiselle*, it is, I assure you. You have made Anani your haven, *n'est-ce pas?* And it is my belief, no matter how vehemently you deny it, that you desire the Chavot name. Perhaps for reasons other than the most obvious." He scrutinized her face coldly. "You have escaped some...unpleasantness, have you not? And *mon père* is aware of this?"

Daye felt chilled and miserable. He made it sound as though she were some sort of criminal. Of course, in a vague way he had hit the nail on the head. She had escaped a life she considered unpleasant, hadn't she? Too depressed by his antagonism to attempt an explanation, she muttered, "Oh, why don't you leave me alone," and turned to walk away.

She had not gone far when his voice halted her steps. "You must know it has become impossible for me to do that."

It was not so much his words but his voice that made her look back at him. He had spoken in a strange, unsteady tone, and now he was looking at her in a way that made her heart seem to turn over. Paying no heed to the small voice of caution telling her to be wise and continue on her way, Daye said faintly, "I don't know what you mean."

"Do you not?" Philippe uttered a mirthless laugh. "This past week has been hell. I despise myself for my weakness, for wanting you as I do, but there seems to be little I can do about it."

Daye caught her breath, resisting the impulse to cry, *oh, I know, I know how you feel!* Instead, she retorted sarcastically, "And only a week ago you insisted you could resist me. You would never permit me to beguile *you*, remember?"

"I remember. *Mon Dieu*, what a fool I was!" He looked angry, but Daye felt his anger was directed toward himself. "Since then I have lain awake at night, thinking of you, wanting you in my arms, in my bed. I am *obsessed* with you." He began walking toward her, and in sudden panic she swung around. But before she could move a step his arms were around her, pulling her back against him and holding her there tightly. His body was hard and still cool from his swim, yet even as he held her, his skin warmed. Daye felt the warmth radiating from him, flowing into her until her whole body was suffused with heat. "I cannot sleep, I desire you so." Philippe's hoarse whisper was in her ear. "Lovely, lovely Daye, what am I to do?"

She was shaken to her very toes, both by his words and by his nearness, and more than anything she wanted to relax, let herself melt against him, let his beautiful male body absorb her own. But she fought to control her senses, forcing herself to remember that only minutes ago he had been distinctly cold and unfriendly. He had behaved in the same manner in Papeete and on Anani that first night, and afterward, each time, he had almost made love to her. *It's getting to be a habit,* she told herself and had no trouble managing a cool laugh. "I really don't know what to tell you, Monsieur Chavot. As for myself, I've never slept better."

By the tensing of his body, Daye knew he was angered. Still, she was unprepared when he swung her to face him. She moved her head too late to avoid his fast-descending mouth. There was something almost violent in the way he kissed her, and she felt the shock of it piercing her body, affecting every nerve, enervating her so that she stayed passive and unresisting in the iron circle of his arms. As though he sensed her shock, Philippe's kiss gentled, and he moved his lips slowly, seductively over every part of her mouth touching her lips with his own as if savoring the taste, the feel of them. Deep inside Daye, a waiting excitement flared to life and her heartbeat quickened. Almost before she realized it she was returning his kiss with urgency, her arms frantic to hold him as her carefully suppressed emotions broke free.

It was the painful need to regain her breath that caused her to struggle at last. Immediately Philippe released her mouth, his face burrowing into the softness of her hair. Daye could feel his warm breath stirring the fine strands of her hair, and she closed her eyes, absorbed in the tender intimacy of the moment.

"Will you now deny what is between us, *ma belle* Daye?" Philippe's voice was husky in her ear.

Daye's eyes flew open and she wrenched away from him. Wild with suspicion she stared, searching his dark handsome face for a sign of mockery or triumph. But she saw only a raw desire that he made no effort to disguise. Disturbed beyond reason, she lowered her eyes, her teeth catching her lower lip. "I'm neither confirming nor denying," she said in a low voice. "I just...." She looked up, flinging out her hands in distraction. "You mustn't think this sort of thing can go on. You can't insult me one minute and kiss me the next. I won't have it! I'm not made of stone, you know."

"I know." He smiled, his gray eyes narrowing. "*Oui*, I *know* that, Daye."

A pulse in her throat beat rapidly. "You know what I meant. Oh, if you would only listen to me!"

"Perhaps I will listen to you; but not now." Philippe's voice was soft. "Now, I wish only to hold you, *ma petite belle*." He reached for her, murmuring, "*Non, non*, do not fight me," when she would have struggled away. He went on murmuring then, but it was in French, and Daye wondered bemusedly if he knew the effect his fascinating, provocative language was having on her senses.

And because this was so, she said almost irritably, "Why do you speak French? I can't understand you."

He laughed softly. "Perhaps that is why I speak it." He bent his head, his lips brushing across each of her eyelids and over her cheekbones, then slid downward to nuzzle the side of her neck. Still he kept on, his mouth roving over her face and neck, coming tantalizingly near her mouth but never quite touching it. Daye was caught and held somewhere between delight and disquiet, loving the touch of his mouth.

Philippe raised his head to murmur seductively, "You are so lovely, so desirable. I could never tire of looking at you, of holding you. Ah, *mignonne*, this need I have for you is an agony inside me." His arms tightened around her, and she felt his fingers moving against the sides of her breasts.

Daye held herself stiffly. He had admitted he wanted her, but abhorred himself for doing so. Because in his heart he neither liked nor trusted her, she knew. He had not from the beginning, and now it was even worse because he thought she was plotting to marry him. Yet here he was, obviously planning to seduce her if he could. Surely he should be afraid her seduction would compromise him....

A small gasp escaped her lips as the tips of his fingers slid beneath her swimsuit, brushing the bare skin of her breasts. "No!" she said sharply, raising her eyes to meet his.

He said nothing. One arm loosened, and she thought for a moment he was going to let her go. Relief and regret warred, but before either emotion could take control, Philippe's hand had slid to her nape and deftly unhooked the halter strap of her suit. "No!" she cried again, her hands going frantically to her breasts, clutching at the swimsuit before it could fall. "How...how dare you?" She swallowed. "Let me go! Please!" But she made no effort to free herself.

He stared down at her, his mouth curved in a slight smile, his eyes a narrow slash of brilliance between the black lashes. "You do not want to go, *ma belle* Daye," he whispered tauntingly. "You do not wish to leave me." He bent his head and lightly touched her lips with his. "I have seen you watching me and knew you desired me as I desired you. Come, lovely one, admit it." His hand pushed deliberately beneath the swimsuit, finding the soft flesh of her breast. Daye instinctively clutched harder, then gave a low cry as his hand crushed against her, the fingers pressing painfully over her nipple. But it was an exquisite pain, and she felt her breasts respond and a wonderful, slow burning sensation spread through her like wildfire. It was unfamiliar, almost unbearable, and caused her heart to drum tormentedly. But when Philippe's eyes unexpectedly locked with her own, she again begged, "Please, let me go."

"If I do, you will fall," Philippe told her softly, and Daye knew he was right. Her legs were so weak they could not have supported her. Shame swept over her. If he knew this, then he must know the mere touch of his hand on her breast had nearly sent her into shock. Oh, dear God! From this he would either assume she was so quickly aroused she would be an easy conquest, or that she was deathly afraid of sex. Well, perhaps both of those applied to her—at least where he was concerned.

"*Chérie*, will you not loosen your hands? You are only hurting yourself." Philippe's tone was persuasive. "But if you do not mind the discomfort, I shall be delighted to let my hand remain."

Daye felt the color flood her face, but before she could say or do anything Philippe uttered a low exclamation and claimed her mouth.

This time his kiss was different. There was only passion and stunning demand, his beautiful, compelling mouth working a magic that set Daye's senses blazing. She responded, so lost in the mists of passion that she scarcely noticed she had relaxed her hold on her swimsuit, that Philippe had both arms around her and that her hands moved back and forth caressingly over the fine hair covering his chest, then slid upward to his nape. The touch of his heated body against her skin was an intoxicant and she drove restless fingers through his dark hair, fondled his neck and wide muscular shoulders. His skin was warm and smooth, his muscles tensed beneath her eager hands. She had never even guessed that touching a man's body could bring such pleasure.

With evident reluctance Philippe eased his mouth

from hers. Through half-open eyes Daye saw that he wore a drugged expression.

"You are truly a witch, *ma belle* Daye," he said thickly. "My desire for you is maddening." Slowly, but with deliberation, he began to draw her down with him, and Daye, lost in an unfamiliar world of sexual excitement, went willingly.

They lay on the soft, thick grass, their legs intimately entwined, their lips meeting and parting in brief but heady kisses. Daye was trembling and so, she knew, was Philippe—a Philippe who was so passionately aroused that her instincts rose to warn her. Mindlessly she ignored them, excited by his arousal, excited by his hand on her bare breasts. He caressed them gently, fondling the flesh until Daye wanted to cry out her pleasure.

He raised himself to look down at her, his breath heavy and uneven. Neither of them spoke, but when he lowered his head to press his mouth to each nipple Daye shuddered in violent reaction and gave a sharp cry. But Philippe paid no attention, his mouth wandering over her, his tongue teasing, until she twisted her fingers into his hair and moaned softly. She closed her eyes, desire washing over her in waves, shocking and paining her untried body. Her will was slipping away and she could only move her body in languid protest.

"Give me time, *chérie*." Philippe's slurred tones seemed to come from far away. His hands were urgent, pushing at her swimsuit. "This is defeating me. Help me to remove it."

Confused by passion, Daye's first instinct was to obey. Her hands left his head, her eyes fluttered open. The sun's brilliance was temporarily blinding and she began to close them again, turning her head to the side....

With shattering clarity she realized where she was and what she was doing. What *they* were doing. "No! No, Philippe!" she cried in panic, her body twisting beneath his lips and hands. "Please, Philippe, stop! We must stop! Someone might see us!" Through an emotional haze she pictured Charles coming upon them, lying here in broad daylight, herself half-naked.... Panic gave her strength and she pushed at him violently.

His hands stilled, and he raised his head to look at her with eyes that seemed almost opaque. There was a harsh raggedness to his breath and when at last he spoke his voice was very low and husky. "Unfortunately you are right, *ma belle*, this is not the place for us." His eyes wandered over her, lingering on her breasts before he sucked in a sharp breath and, with obvious expertise, drew the swimsuit over her nakedness and fastened the strap. Daye lay passive as he did so, her panic ebbing and a cold, frustrated misery replacing it. There was shame there, too, shame because of the liberties she had permitted, even desired. Had they been somewhere totally private with no fear of intrusion, she knew she would have allowed him to continue making love to her. A shiver racked her body. Never before had she come even remotely close to allowing such a thing. Never before had she felt this way about a man, as if he need only touch her to make her eagerly abandon herself to desire.

"You are trembling, *ma chère*," he said and gave a low laugh. "I tremble also, but inside where it does not show. It is torment, is it not, to rise to such heights of passion and to remain unfulfilled?'' His eyes, still unusually opaque, searched her face, then, curiously, a small muscle twitched at the corner of his mouth and he muttered, *"Tu es belle!* Daye, *ma chérie,* I....'' He bent his head, his mouth taking hers possessively. Daye, her heart racing, had to fight for control. It would never do to throw her arms about his neck and hold him as tightly as she wanted to. If she did, it would all begin again, and next time she was not sure she would be able to call a halt.

But Philippe drew back at last and sighed. *"Non,* I forget, I must not do this. Not here. But—'' he played with a long strand of her golden hair "—there is a tiny atoll not far from Anani; we will go there now? No one will disturb us, I promise you.'' He sat up drawing her to sit beside him. "Come, let us go. I feel....'' His hand brushed back her hair, his touch a caress. *"Ma belle,* I feel I have waited for you for a very long time.''

Daye fought the desire to rest her cheek against his hand. She had to be sensible, she had to maintain control of her emotions. "Philippe, I must go back to the house now. Charles will... will wonder where I am.'' She started to get to her feet but his hand on her arm stopped her.

"Très bien, we will leave, I think, after lunch, when *mon père* rests. I do not enjoy this deception, Daye, but I want you, and I intend to have you.'' There was a determined arrogance in his voice that suddenly softened persuasively. "And you want me, do you not? You would enjoy being quite alone with me?'' His hand slid caressingly up her arm to her shoulder. "You are very beautiful, Daye. I wish....'' He broke off, frowning, then shrugged. "The next few hours

will seem an eternity," he said softly, and raised her hand to his lips.

In a swift movement, Daye pulled her hand away and got to her feet. "Philippe, I can't! I can't go anywhere with you."

He, too, rose swiftly and stood looking down at her. "You do not mean that, of course."

"Yes, yes I do!" Daye's hands fluttered distractedly. "I admit I...I was...I know I led you to think I would let you...make love to me, but I really couldn't simply go with you somewhere...oh, dear!" Her eyes fell before the sudden blaze in his.

"Why not?"

"Because I don't believe in—" she paused, adding in a rush "—promiscuous sex."

He stared, then burst into a laugh, his white teeth flashing. "Promiscuous? Come, come, *petite*, I suppose now you will insist you are a virgin."

"I am!" She was stung by his amusement.

His expression changed, showed irritation. "Come, there is no need to lie to *me*, *ma chère*." The hand on her cheek moved caressingly. "Your eyes are the color of dark jade, so beautiful and so innocent. How easy it would be to believe anything you care to tell me. As many of my sex do believe, *petite*?" His hand fell to his side, his mouth was suddenly hard. "But I am not so gullible, and now I am becoming impatient. So...we will leave as soon as *mon père* retires." He smiled without humor. "Do not be concerned, I shall tell no one, either before or afterward." He lifted his broad shoulders in a shrug. "If we are missed, we will merely say we went for a boat ride."

Daye gazed at him unhappily. How cold-bloodedly

he made these arrangements. Somehow it seemed far more cold-blooded than the time he asked her to go to Papeete to become his mistress. And yet, if she loved him and knew he loved her, it would not seem so, would it? She moved away from him to where her robe and towel lay and picked them up. "I'm sorry, Philippe," she said across the space dividing them, "but I am not going with you."

He covered the space in seconds and caught her by the arm. "Are your passions so easily cooled? How long do you torment a man before you finally give in to him? Does this afford you a perverted pleasure?" He stopped, his arm falling to his side, his eyes blazing.

"Damn! I am a fool to have allowed your pleas to stop me. Another moment or two, and you would not have been able to; it would not have mattered to either of us if we were seen." Furious and frustrated, he pounded a fist into his palm. "Perhaps it would have been as well had we been noticed. If *mon père* learned his adored *petite Anglaise* was capable of making love to his son where an audience could assemble, he might realize she is not fit to bear the Chavot name, give birth to Chavot *enfants*." Philippe seemed to spit out the last few words.

Daye knew her face must be pale. He was wicked to her, cruel and vile! All the dreadful things he had said, how could she begin to defend herself? She felt exhausted suddenly, too exhausted to say anything. And yet she did. Taking him up on his last two sentences, she said, "And I suppose Melisse Montand is."

His brow furrowed. "Melisse? What has she to do with this?"

"Nothing. Nothing, I suppose." Daye stood there in the hot bright sunlight and felt a wave of nausea sweep over her. She needed a drink, some food. She needed to get out of this sun. . . .

"Melisse. Why did you mention Melisse?" Philippe's voice persisted. "Tell me, did Paul. . . ." He broke off and she realized, vaguely, he was eyeing her with concern. "Daye, what is the matter?"

"Nothing. I'm tired and thirsty." She spoke shortly and without more ado turned away from him. He fell into step beside her, taking her arm. But she shook him off. "Let me be!" she said wildly. "Remember, I'm not fit. And don't you ever dare touch me again, Philippe Chavot!"

He said her name once, but when she walked unsteadily away he did not follow, although she could sense that he watched until she reached the path and was hidden from sight.

CHAPTER NINE

By the time Daye reached the house she was shaking uncontrollably and without pausing headed straight for her suite. Terii had been there, for a jug of fruit juice stood on the bedside table. She drank a small amount, cautiously allowing it to settle in her squeamish stomach before swallowing a little more. Then she shed her swimsuit, pulled on her nightdress and crawled, still shivering, into bed. She lay there, huddled and wretched, praying that sleep would soon blot out what had just happened.

It was not long before Charles came to see her, anxiety evident in his dark eyes. He wanted, of course, to send for a doctor, but Daye managed to convince him that she had simply stayed in the sun too long and would soon be well. He finally left after warning her the doctor would be sent for if she were not improved by the afternoon.

When the door had closed behind him, Daye lay back on the pillows and pulled the bed covers up to her chin. She did not doubt the hot sun had much to do with the way she felt, but the primary blame lay with Philippe and what he had said and done. Strangely enough, the cruel words he had spoken before she left him faded insignificantly when compared to what had happened between them. Horrified, she accepted that she had almost given herself to him, and worse, that she would have done so out in the open, in full view of anyone who happened to come by. She felt cheapened, humiliated, and even the knowledge that she had refused to accompany him to some private place to continue their lovemaking, did little to console her. In her heart she knew she had desperately wanted to go with him, and she knew if he should ask her again, she *would* go.

But it was doubtful he would come after her again. Melisse Montand would be here soon, and he would not want her if he had Melisse. Something painful clutched her heart. Melisse was probably his mistress, because Philippe Chavot was definitely a man with lusty sexual urges and he had known the woman for a long time. What was wrong with her? The thought of seeing Philippe and this Melisse together affected her as would a raw gaping wound. Oh, she could never tolerate it! Never! But what choice did she have? Black depression filled her and she rolled onto her stomach and buried her face in the pillow. She could leave Anani, of course, leave this island and Charles...but she didn't want to! Why had this to happen? Why, of all the men she had known, did it have to be Philippe Chavot she wanted? For want him she did and not only in a physical way. She felt now she had always wanted him, even while she hated him.

It was on this disturbing thought that she at last fell asleep. When she awoke it was late afternoon and Terii was beside her, offering a tray. "Monsieur Charles insists you have refreshments," the girl said, arranging the tray over Daye's lap.

There was tea, warm and milky, and toast laden with butter. Hungry, Daye ate and felt immediately better. She was out of bed when Charles arrived and able to smile at his worried expression. "I'm attending your dinner party and nothing will stop me," she laughed, ignoring a flutter of nervousness at the thought of facing Philippe again.

That evening Daye decided to wear the blue cocktail dress she had worn the night of her arrival. She had been pleased to discover this past week that dressing for dinner did not necessarily mean formal attire. Even tonight would be an informal affair, Charles had told her.

As she dressed, with Terii's somewhat unnecessary assistance, Daye remembered she would be meeting Audrey's brother this evening. Derek, she had been told, had lived on Anani for nine years. He had met Philippe at university in New South Wales and the two had become firm friends. Later, when Derek married, Philippe had been his best man. Two and a half years later Derek was divorced and Philippe had persuaded him to come to Anani. Audrey had been reticent about her brother's marriage and divorce but Daye knew Derek had been young, somewhere in his early twenties. She also knew that Audrey was grateful to Philippe for helping Derek through what she termed a difficult time. Derek must have taken the divorce very hard, Daye thought.

Audrey had come to the house several times since Daye's arrival and she had found that her first, favorable impression of the woman was more than confirmed. Audrey was forty-four, old enough to be Daye's mother, but she retained a lighthearted almost youthful outlook that was, nevertheless, combined with a reassuringly mature common sense. Daye derived a great deal of pleasure from Audrey's company. They laughed a lot and told each other stories about their respective lives. Charles, who already knew so much about Daye—and perhaps about Audrey, too—often sat nearby listening, a smile on his face. Once or twice she had caught him staring at Audrey and was surprised and startled to see that he seemed irritated. It had happened at times when Audrey was particularly animated, and Daye could see no earthly reason for his irritation. At those moments Audrey had looked even more attractive than usual.

One thing was certain, Daye told herself, removing her favorite piece of jewelry, a diamond pendant, from her jewel case, Audrey never looked at Charles with irritation. Audrey looked at Charles as though she loved him. It would be a delightful situation if Charles showed any sign of loving her.

Daye fastened the pendant and admired it as it lay glittering against the pale gold of her skin. Reg had given it to her for her twenty-first birthday and she treasured it. She had teardrop earrings to match but these she did not wear unless she put her hair up or drew it back into a plait. She had considered getting Terii to help her with an upswept style but had decided against it. Now her hair hung long and straight, the golden sheen enhanced by silvery highlights she had not seen since she was a child. Thoughtfully she looked into the mirror at the eyes gazing back at her. The color of dark jade, Philippe had said. Were they really? She leaned closer, then flushed as she saw Terii reflected there. "I was wondering if I needed a touch of mascara," she said quickly.

"I do not think so." The girl gave her an unsmiling glance.

Daye frowned. Now that she thought about it, Terii had been unusually quiet this evening. "Is something the matter, Terii?" she inquired.

"No, miss." Terii bent her glossy black head. When she raised it again her mouth drooped sullenly. "Monsieur Philippe think you much beautiful, yes?"

Daye felt suddenly breathless. "Whatever made you ask that, Terii?"

The girl's shrug was as Gallic as any French-woman's. "He...Monsieur Philippe came here while you sleep. He ask is it true you are ill."

"What?" Daye's mouth felt dry.

"He want to see you. I tell him no, you sleep. Still he come in and stand there." Terii pointed to the bedroom door. "He tell me to go away but I will not go. Then he stand and watch you long time."

Daye sensed a coldness in Terii's voice, but her thoughts were so confusing she paid scant attention to that feeling. She was thinking about Philippe, wondering why he had come to her suite, why he had watched her as she slept. It couldn't matter to him whether or not she was ill so he must have come for another reason. Surely he had not intended finishing what they had started there by the pool? Oh, he wouldn't! Not here in his father's house. Heat spread through her body. Or would he? Her response to his lovemaking might have caused him to think she would welcome him.

But she would not welcome him—of course she would not. Still, even though it had not occurred to her to do so before, it now seemed prudent to lock her bedroom door at night.

When she paused at the entrance to the salon a short time later, her eyes were drawn automatically to Philippe who was talking to a man whose back was toward Daye. Philippe was well dressed as always, wearing dark brown slacks, a matching open-necked shirt and a creamy beige, expertly tailored sports coat. He looked so handsome and vital that Daye almost without conscious thought gravitated toward him. But she stopped herself in time, feeling rather horrified. She wasn't behaving like herself at all. Not at all.

She swiftly turned her attention to Charles and Audrey who were seated together on one of the elegant blue velvet sofas. Audrey was laughing about something and Daye thought how attractive she looked in a lemon yellow sleeveless dress. Reluctantly she moved toward them, thinking she wouldn't blame Audrey if she became downright resentful. After all, she was intruding upon the two of them. But Audrey's smile was warm. "Daye, you look very lovely," she said.

Charles rose and kissed her hands and then her cheek. "You are recovered, *ma chère*?" He inspected her closely. "Still there is an unnatural quality to your eyes, and I fear you will tire rapidly. If you do you must go to bed at once." He tucked her hand in the crook of his arm. "You see, *petite*, I have invited Audrey and Derek to come early. Derek is most anxious to meet you."

"That's putting it mildly, Charles," said a new voice, and Daye found herself looking into a pair of deep blue eyes. Derek was of medium height, sturdily built with a good-looking, fair-skinned face and sun-streaked brown hair. "You are Daye, of course," he grinned engagingly. "Audrey warned me you were a knockout, but I'm afraid nothing could have prepared me." Derek reached for Daye's hand and clasped it in both of his. "You are *bewitching*. A regular shock to a vulnerable fellow's system."

"Oh, dear, I'm so sorry," Daye smiled.

"Don't be sorry. You're worth it, I assure you." His eyes roamed her face almost avidly. "I'll have to paint you, you know."

"Ah, yes, you are the resident artist, aren't you?" She laughed. "You don't look like the stereotype of an artist."

"How would you like me to look? Tell me and I'll do my best to please you."

"Well, a long shaggy beard and hair to match; untidy clothes and—" Daye looked at the hands still clasping hers "—paint-stained fingers."

"Done! At least, I'll begin by not shaving tomorrow." He frowned. "By the way, Charles, what happened to *your* beautiful brush?"

Charles's eyes twinkled. "It aged me, do you not agree?"

"No." Derek frowned again, but turned to Daye and said, "I should like to begin a few preliminary sketches of you at once. How about it, beautiful Daye? Charles, may I steal her away?"

"Goodness, I believe you are serious." Daye was surprised.

"He is, *petite*," Charles broke in, and firmly disengaged Derek's hands. "Derek, *mon ami*, control yourself, *s'il vous plaît*. There will be plenty of time for Daye to consider if she wishes to sit for you. Plenty of time, *n'est-ce pas, ma chère*?" He smiled into her face. "However, Derek, if Daye should agree to sit for you, I shall insist the finished portrait become my property."

"Not on your life, old boy! Sorry, *je regrette* and all that stuff, but I'd never part with a portrait of Daye." Derek spoke seriously.

"I suggest you both wait until such a portrait exists before you fight a duel because of it." Philippe had approached silently. Daye gave him a quick, sidelong glance and noticed that his expression was irritated despite the comparative mildness of his tone. She lowered her lashes, raising them again when he said softly, "Your wine, *mademoiselle*."

She took the crystal glass he offered and murmured her thanks. Since that first evening, when she had indicated a preference for this particular wine, he had automatically served it to her. She raised the glass to her lips and sipped the contents, her eyes unable to avoid Philippe's as he softly asked, "You are feeling well again, Daye?"

Carefully she lowered the glass. "Thank you, yes." She felt a brief moment of exhilaration because he sounded concerned and because it might have been concern that had sent him into her suite that afternoon. Then she told herself not to be a fool. He was probably being sarcastic, inquiring after her health like that. An inexplicable disappointment swept over her, and because of it she said with deliberate coolness, "It must have been a touch of the sun. After this I shall be *much* more careful—swimming or otherwise."

She saw the clear gray eyes narrow and the jet lashes flicker. Swinging her head away she favored Derek with a brilliant smile. "Why don't we sit down and have a nice talk?" she suggested, putting a light hand on his arm.

Derek needed no further encouragement to lead

her to a sofa some distance from the others. When they were seated he wasted no time questioning her in a frankly interested manner about her career. Daye answered him without hesitation, feeling the same ease she felt with Charles and her dear Reg, in England. She told Derek about Reg, of course. It was Reg who had started her career, after all. "One wonders why you didn't marry the chap," Derek said bluntly. "I'll bet he is in love with you."

"I don't love Reg. Not *that* way."

"It's amazing someone hasn't captured you before this. You must have met some fascinating chaps, I'm sure." He didn't wait for an answer but said with the candor Daye was becoming accustomed to, "Our Charles is a dark horse, I'd say. To think he's known you for months and told no one. Not even Philippe."

"Did Philippe tell you so?" Daye sipped her wine, her eyes lowered.

Derek grinned. "Audrey mentioned it first. Philippe merely confirmed it when I asked. Confirmed it somewhat abruptly, I may add." He slid one arm along the back of the sofa and began to fiddle with her hair. "Philippe is reticent about you, but I get the impression you were a shock to him."

"No more than he was to me," Daye said emphatically. She tilted her glass and finished its contents quickly before meeting Derek's blue eyes. "Charles and I talked about many things the night we met, but somehow—" she managed a small laugh "—he never did mention having a son."

"Oh, well, it doesn't really make a difference, does it?" Derek spoke casually. "You and Charles still get along as well, don't you?"

"Yes, of course." Her fond gaze strayed to where

Charles sat, deep in conversation with Audrey. Beyond them, near the window, Philippe was standing. He was smoking steadily and in his other hand was a drink. His expression was inscrutable as he stared directly at Daye, and for some reason this threw her into confusion. Quickly she returned her attention to Derek who said almost disinterestedly, "Wonder why Philippe canceled the New York trip? He always seemed to enjoy that particular city."

"Probably he has half a dozen girl friends there," she retorted.

"Most likely he does." Derek laughed.

Unable to leave the subject alone, Daye went on, "Perhaps he's staying because Melisse Montand is coming."

"Or perhaps he's staying because of you."

Daye's eyes widened and she felt warmth in her cheeks. "Because of me? Oh." Then she sighed exasperatedly. "Perhaps so. He's probably afraid to leave me alone with Charles. Afraid I shall influence him in some way, or...." She stopped, reaching to put her empty glass on the table in front of the sofa. Immediately she sensed movement and saw Philippe crossing toward them.

Derek said, "I didn't mean that, Daye," but went no further when Philippe reached them. He grinned up at his friend, however, and asked, "Have I had Daye to myself too long, old pal?"

Philippe's clear eyes glinted. "I merely noticed *mademoiselle*'s wineglass needed replenishing." He picked up the glass and gave Daye a questioning look, but before she could speak Kao ushered in a well-dressed couple who appeared to be in their fifties. Philippe went immediately to greet them and

Derek said, rising to his feet, "Henri and Marguerite Chavot. And Jean and Denise Dubois," he added, as another, younger couple entered.

Henri, who was Charles's cousin, and Marguerite, his wife, were a charming couple. Although their English was limited they did their best and Daye sensed their friendship was genuine. Charles hovered around her, apparently anxious for her reaction to his family, and Daye was glad she could smile at him, indicating honestly that she liked these two people.

She was not immediately as certain about Paul's parents, however. Jean Dubois, the schoolmaster, was a tall man with gray-streaked dark hair and heavily lashed amber brown eyes. He had a thin intelligent face, and although he could not be considered good-looking he possessed a certain something that rated a second, interested look. His voice was decidedly attractive, and Daye felt certain his pupils would hang on to his every soft word as he taught. To Daye he directed a courteous smile, and if an admiring light appeared in his eyes, it did not linger. He put his arm around his wife in an almost protective gesture then, *as if,* Daye thought, *I might want to do her harm.*

Denise Dubois was small and fair with a gentle sort of prettiness: her voice was light and rather sweet. She seemed, Daye mused, the sort of woman who would dote on her children, refusing them nothing and failing even to discipline them when necessary. Yet this woman was Paul's mother, who threatened heart palpitations if he played the piano in his own home and demanded he have nothing to do with the talented woman who encouraged his art. Could Paul have been exaggerating or even deliberately lying?

Daye wondered this as Denise, smiling faintly, said in stilted English, "We have heard of you, *naturelle-ment*. Paul, *mon fils*, is charmed by you, *n'est-ce pas?*"

"I'm sure it's a temporary, er, feeling," Daye answered, disconcerted by the woman's intent blue-eyed stare. She hoped Denise did not think she was encouraging Paul. "Paul is a very nice boy," she said lamely.

"*Merci, mademoiselle*. We are most proud of Paul," Jean said quietly.

"We are indeed!" Denise agreed swiftly. "Next year Paul will attend the university." Her slender hands twisted the tie belt of her green silk dress. "Charles has so generously offered Paul a position in one of his companies." Her tone bordered on defiance, and since the woman's eyes were still on her, Daye wondered if she knew, or suspected, that Paul had confided in her. Suzy appeared at that moment, directing the newcomers' attention to a selection of drinks, and Daye, stifling a sigh of relief, was able to return her own attention to Derek.

At dinner she was seated between Charles and Derek, the latter clearly monopolizing her, keeping her so entertained that she was essentially oblivious to anyone else. It came as something of a shock when she happened to glance toward the other end of the long table to meet, above the gleam and glitter of silver and crystal, Philippe's stormy gaze. Had it been any other man but the arrogant Frenchman, she would have suspected that look held jealousy. As it was, she could only assume he was angry because she was enjoying herself with his friend Derek. Which was too bad, she thought, and unhesitatingly flashed him a provocative smile.

He did not return her smile but his expression changed, and his eyes seemed to send her a message. And all at once the voices, the laughter, the clinking of glass and china faded into the background and she was alone with Philippe, lying with him beneath the hot sun, his long, muscular legs warm against her own. . . .

With difficulty she dragged her eyes away from his, but it was no longer easy to concentrate on Derek. Throughout the remainder of the meal Philippe was disquietingly uppermost in her mind, and she knew she had only to turn her head to find his watchful gaze upon her.

She was relieved when dinner ended and they adjourned to the terrace that was tonight lighted by softly flickering amber-shaded lamps. They sat around in comfortable cane armchairs while Kao deftly served coffee and liqueurs, and for a time the conversation drifted in a pleasant, desultory fashion. Even here, though, Daye's ears were tuned to Philippe's deep attractive voice, and she was despairingly conscious of the quickening beat of her heart when she heard it. He was sitting somewhere to her right, his chair set in the shadows so that his dark face and hair blended into them. She had looked his way only once and then had deliberately kept from doing so again. She admitted that she was becoming more and more aware of him as the minutes passed. She also admitted there was absolutely nothing she could do about it.

"You are not tiring, *ma petite*?" Charles's voice broke into her thoughts. She found him leaning forward in his chair, his dark eyes anxious. She assured him she was not at all tired and, kissing his fingertips in a gesture of affection toward her, he relaxed once more.

Daye smiled and returned the gesture, then her eyes met Audrey's and her smile wavered as she noticed the woman's tormented look. It faded almost immediately and quickly Audrey smiled. But Daye could see it was a strained smile and she felt a flicker of dismay. Dear heaven, was Audrey annoyed, jealous perhaps of the friendship she and Charles shared? Had she, Daye, unintentionally come between Charles and Audrey, taken up time he might have spent with the other woman? But Audrey had never indicated as much; she had always been so warm and friendly. Still, if she was in love with Charles—and Daye suspected she was—she might have been putting on an act, cleverly hiding her resentment. "Oh, dear!" she whispered unintentionally.

Derek who sat in the chair beside her asked, "Problems, my lovely?"

"No. I mean. . . ." She turned to face him, keeping her voice low. "Derek, I haven't broken up something special, have I?"

For a moment he frowned. "You mean between my sister and the boss? As far as I know, they've always been friends and still are. Satisfied?" He grinned cheerfully.

She bit her lip. "I wondered if Audrey was—" her voice became even softer "—in love with Charles."

Momentarily Derek's wide mouth tightened. "Maybe so. But Charles isn't in love with her, is he?" Again he spoke bluntly.

Daye began to tell him she had no idea, when Denise Dubois said in a surprisingly loud voice, "*Mademoiselle*, you were a fashion model, *n'est-ce pas?* But are not models so tall and—what word do I

seek—ah, angular! *Oui*, angular.'' Her laughter
trilled and Daye wondered if she could possibly be a
bit tipsy. ''*You* are not at all angular,'' she finished,
making the statement sound uncomplimentary.

Charles cleared his throat and Derek whispered,
''Stupid cat!'' But Daye smiled coolly and said,
''Thank you, I suppose I'm lucky. As a matter of
fact,'' she continued gently, ''I wasn't a fashion
model. They are, as you thought, usually quite tall
and very slender.''

If Daye hoped Denise would leave the subject now
she was doomed to disappointment. The woman's
fair eyebrows raised, her blue eyes widened. ''Then
you were, perhaps, a....'' She frowned. ''I cannot
recall what you say in English. Ah, *mais, oui*, you
were a model for the...the center pages, yes? One
who poses, er, unclothed?''

In the silence that followed Daye's face blanched
with shock. Not that Denise's question was so terrible, it was more ignorant and rude than terrible. But
it had brought back a memory, something Daye
wanted badly to forget. She closed her eyes, hearing
Charles's voice. He was speaking French and he
sounded angry. She opened her eyes and smiled at
him. ''It's all right,'' she said, then looked at Denise.
The woman was twisting her hands together, looking
as if she wanted to cry.

''No, I didn't pose like that, Madame Dubois.''
She laughed. ''Although sometimes I wore very little.'' Unbidden, her gaze wandered to Philippe and
she felt the color rush back into her face. She could
not see him properly but she knew, nevertheless, that
he was watching her intently.

''I shall paint you wearing something soft and

flowing and blue,'' Derek said thoughtfully, and she forced herself to pay attention. "Not the same color as you are wearing, a more...." He narrowed his eyes dreamily. "Tell you what, you and I will take a trip to Papeete to pick out exactly the right thing. You won't mind, will you, Charles? I swear I'll guard her with my life.''

Before either she or Charles could answer, Philippe said coldly, "I am flying to Papeete in three days. If *mademoiselle* wishes, she may accompany me." He stood up and crossed to the glass-topped table that held brandy and liqueurs. As he poured golden liquid into a large snifter there was something about his stance that suggested anger.

"Oh, good!" Audrey spoke now. "May I beg a lift, Philippe? My friend is still in hospital, poor dear, and I'd love to pay her another visit.''

"*Mais certainement, ma chère* Audrey.'' Philippe's smile when he turned to her was fond. "You are always a most welcome companion.''

"What about me, am I welcome?" Derek grinned. "There is room for four, old chap, you can't refuse.''

"But I can, *mon ami*. There will be a passenger returning with us." He seemed to hesitate, his gaze sliding toward Denise and Jean. "Melisse will return with us." He spoke deliberately.

"Melisse!" Daye jumped slightly at Denise's shrill tone. The woman rose swiftly and, ignoring her husband's restraining hand, crossed to where Philippe was standing. He stared down at her, his handsome face impassive, as she spoke to him in their own language. Daye could not, of course, understand, but it was more than obvious that Denise was upset and not difficult to guess it was because Melisse was coming to Anani. So it appeared that Paul had not lied; his mother did object to Melisse. And Philippe must be aware of it. Daye wondered what his thoughts were behind his impassive facade. If he cared for Melisse he must resent Denise's attitude.

Still he betrayed no emotion not even relief when Jean gently but with a definite firmness led his wife from the terrace. He did, however, raise the glass he was holding and did not lower it until it was empty.

Charles, meanwhile, had hastily followed his guests, but not before casting a frowning glance in the direction of his son.

"Hmm, that was careless of Philippe," Derek remarked sotto voce. "He knows how Denise feels about Melisse."

"Oh?" Daye was listening but her eyes were on Philippe. He was talking to Audrey who had joined him, and now he poured brandy into a glass and gave it to her. She sipped it, then said something that made him laugh. He laughed with his head thrown back, his strong beautiful teeth flashing white, his brilliant eyes crinkling at the corners. "Are you chastising me, *ma chère*?" he asked Audrey.

"Certainly not! I merely asked why you did it." Audrey looked toward Daye and Derek, and when she turned back to Philippe her voice was softer.

He listened, his eyes lowered, and when he turned to refill his glass there was a wry twist to his mouth. Audrey put out her hand, as if to touch him, then drew it back and wandered over to sit near Marguerite and Henri. The warm night air, perfumed and salt-tanged, was heavy with tension. Daye stared at Philippe's tall form, and her slim fingers twisted nervously. She wished Derek would say something, anything. . . .

And he did. "It's time, I think, for you and I to go for a walk, Daye."

She rose automatically, and at that moment Philippe turned and met her eyes with curious deliberation. She stiffened, shock tingling throughout her body, and she thought, with a touch of fear, *am I in love with him? Have I always been in love with him? While I hated him, was I loving him?*

She was conscious of Derek's voice in her ear and the touch of his hand on her arm. But it wasn't until he passed his hand over her eyes, breaking the intangible link with Philippe, that she became fully aware of him. She cast him a stricken look and whispered, "I'm sorry."

"For what? Come on, my dear, don't look so tragic." He tucked her hand beneath his arm as Charles so often did. "Now for that walk in the garden."

"Where are you going?" Philippe asked, but Daye did not look at him. She dared not. Not yet anyway.

"For a moonlit stroll, my friend," Derek mocked.

"There is no moon." Philippe's tone was controlled.

"You don't see it? Ah, but it is there, old chap. You just have to know where to look." Derek squeezed Daye's arm and she forced herself to smile.

"Beware the *tupapau*," Audrey warned, as they walked toward the terrace steps, and Daye asked Derek what she meant.

He laughed. "*Tupapau* is a spirit, a mischievous sort of spirit that leaves no tracks and casts no shadow. Or so the more superstitious of the Polynesians believe. Some of them won't venture out after dark unless they carry a light of some sort. Light, you see, protects them from the *tupapau*. Are you afraid, lovely Daye? Some do claim he is evil.''

"I'm sure I'm safe with you, Derek," she answered absently.

"Hmm. I don't know if I'm flattered by that remark." Derek's tone was dry.

Daye did not answer and for a time they strolled in silence, keeping, in what seemed an unspoken agreement, to the part of the garden lighted by the terrace lamps. Small insects flicked near their heads and the powerful scent of blooming night flowers seemed to be everywhere. But it was very quiet and when Derek spoke, Daye started. "I hope Denise didn't upset you."

"No, no, she didn't. Well—" Daye gave a small laugh "—perhaps she did a bit. She seems to be...a nervous sort," she finished haltingly.

"She wasn't always like that. It's this past couple of years that she seems to have changed."

"It's to do with her son and Mademoiselle Montand, isn't it?" Daye added hastily. "Paul mentioned something to me, but I wouldn't want his parents to know about it."

"They won't from me." Derek seemed to hesitate. "Philippe knew Denise would be upset that Melisse is coming here."

Daye had guessed as much. "I wonder why he mentioned it then?"

"He was angry because she embarrassed you, I imagine."

Daye stopped walking. "You must be mistaken, Derek." Her heart was thudding, and she knew she sounded shaky. "Philippe wouldn't care. He...we don't really hit it off too well."

"Don't you? Those looks you were throwing at

each other were not exactly warlike. Look here, Daye—'' Derek put his hands on her shoulders— ''I don't know exactly what Philippe is up to. I mean, for his father's sake he might behave himself, but then again, Philippe has always had his way if he wanted a woman. You do understand, don't you? Oh, God, but this is difficult! I don't want you to be hurt and that goes for Charles *and* my friend Philippe. And you must see this situation could become explosive.''

Daye, half angry, half bewildered, shook her head. ''What situation? There really isn't one unless...oh, I'm confused, Derek.'' And she was. Confused and exhausted. What Derek was trying to say, she supposed, was that Charles would be upset if his son seduced her. She had an urge to laugh and blurt out that Charles might not be at all upset. He might, instead, feel justified in insisting that she and Philippe get married. She and Philippe...married. The thought was so intensely pleasing Daye had to catch her breath. But to Derek she said lightly, ''Let's go back, shall we? I'm really dreadfully tired.''

The party broke up soon after they reached the terrace, and Daye was thankful when she was at last in her bedroom. The bed, with its turned-down sheets looked inviting, and Daye slid out of her dress and pulled on her short nightdress with a sigh of pleasure. One knee was on the bed when she heard the knock on her sitting-room door and her first thought was one of irritation. Who on earth could it be, she wondered and gasped as the hair on the back of her neck tingled. Oh, no! It couldn't be! But she *had* intended locking the door. On winged feet she moved across the bedroom and stared out at the door leading to the hall. As she watched, the handle turned and the door opened.

Philippe had removed his jacket, and he looked very tall and lithe in his close-fitting pants and matching brown shirt. She stared at him, lips parted, her breathing shallow. Then he spoke her name in a husky voice and took a step forward.

She came to life, slamming the bedroom door and pushing the bolt across. She leaned against the door for what seemed an aeon, listening to Philippe's voice on the other side. Then at last she ran to the bed and climbed in, pulling the pillow over her head so that she could not hear.

When at last she removed it all was silent, and she assumed he must have gone. Still it was a long time before she finally fell into an uneasy sleep.

CHAPTER TEN

"THIS MORNING I must pay a visit to Père Martin," Charles declared when Daye met him on her way downstairs. "I would be delighted if you would accompany me, *ma chère*, and allow our good priest the pleasure of meeting you. Afterward, if you wish, I will show you the village where our Polynesian friends live."

Daye accepted willingly. She was anxious to see the village as well as to meet Père Martin who served not only Anani's primarily Catholic population, but three other islands as well. "Shall we ride there?" she questioned eagerly. "I can change in a few minutes. Oh, Charles, can we? Coco is such a dear and I did very well yesterday, didn't I?"

Yesterday she had been given her first riding lesson, and Coco was the placid little mare Charles had designated to be her own. But now Charles laughed and shook his head. "It is difficult to refuse you anything, *petite*, but our bridle paths do not resemble those you might find in Paris or London parks."

So Charles drove a Peugeot along a road that was narrow, winding and hilly. The scenery was wildly primitive, and when they passed between huge boulders of glossy black lava rock, Daye considered the effect to be rather awesome. They met no one along

the way, and finally Daye asked if this was the only
road to the church and village.

"For the automobile, *oui*, it is. But there are many
rough bridle paths as well as those for walking and
cycling." Charles turned the steering wheel, making
a sharp right turn. "The school is this way. We will
pause there before continuing to the church."

The school turned out to be a low, modern building surrounded by smoothly mowed lawns. Play-
ground and gym equipment were set up nearby, and
beyond the school Daye could see what appeared to
be a games field. "Come, let us go inside," Charles
said, stopping the car.

The school consisted of only two rooms, but each
was spacious and surprisingly cool. Windows took
up one entire wall and these were carefully shuttered
to keep out the heat of the sun while allowing air to
seep in. The smaller of the two rooms was the kinder-
garten, and Daye could tell it was carefully and properly furnished and equipped for little ones of five and
six years old. Madame Larousse, a pleasant, middle-
aged widow, was in charge of these youngsters, while
Jean Dubois taught the older students. There were
twenty-five of them at the moment, their ages rang-
ing from seven to fifteen years. All but half a dozen
of the children were Polynesian, but with the excep-
tion of one or two girls wearing pareus, all were
dressed casually in jeans and brightly patterned shirts
or blouses. There was an atmosphere of happiness
and relaxation in the pleasant room, although it was
perfectly obvious that Jean was in complete control.
He had divided the children into groups, apparently
according to age, and Daye could not help wondering
how he managed to teach such varied grade levels.

"You must be awfully clever," she told him admiringly, and he flushed, before a charming smile flashed across his lean features. Briefly Daye was reminded of Paul, then realized this was a mere coincidence since Paul was an adopted child.

As she and Charles walked to the car a short time later, she said, "The children must be happy to have such a lovely, well-equipped school. And Madame Larousse and Jean are both such pleasant teachers."

"*Mais, oui,* that is true, *ma chère. Madame* is not a qualified teacher, of course, but she is highly intelligent and the small ones adore her. As for Jean—" Charles frowned, and when Daye looked at him questioningly, he continued "—we would find it difficult to replace Jean if he should ever decide to leave us."

"He isn't thinking of that, is he? I thought Anani was his home and he loved it here."

"There is no doubting that." Charles opened the car door and assisted Daye to climb in. "You think we have a fine school?" he said, obviously not caring to discuss Jean any further.

Daye dismissed her curiosity concerning the schoolmaster. "Did you have the school built, Charles?"

"I contributed financially, *naturellement*, as did Philippe and my cousin Henri. It was Philippe, however, who made all arrangements. With Jean's help he planned a school our children would enjoy."

She said, "Oh," in a flat little voice.

Charles paused in the act of turning the ignition key. "You're amazed that my son would do such a thing?"

Daye carefully smoothed the skirt of her pink sundress. "Well, I suppose I am, rather. I...Philippe seems so...too sophisticated to bother with the planning of a school. I mean, I'm sure he would give his money but not his time."

Charles touched her arm and she looked at him quickly. "You do not know Philippe well as yet, *mon enfant*. He is greatly concerned for people, for our employees, for all who live on Anani, especially the children, most of whom are Polynesian." His voice was soft, his expression fond. "Philippe has great rapport with our villagers. As a child he played with their children, attended school with them, dived and swam as one of them. He learned many of their ways, and could scale a coconut palm or spear a fish as well as they." He laughed suddenly, as though at memories. "Ah, *petite*, if you could have seen him then you would have thought he, too, was a native. At least, until you saw his eyes. Such eyes. A gift from his beautiful mama."

Daye scarcely noticed the sad sentiment that had crept into Charles's voice. She was too busy picturing a young boy, darkly tanned and lithely formed, his black hair windblown, his teeth pure white as he laughed with gleeful mischief. Then the boy's image faded and she saw instead a tall, lithe, shatteringly handsome man whose clear gray eyes held passion and planned seduction....

"Oh! What?" She turned startled eyes to Charles, aware that he had spoken. "I was thinking," she explained, her whole body feeling hot and uncomfortable.

His dark eyes seemed to penetrate her thoughts for he said, "What are your feelings toward Philippe, *ma petite* Daye?"

Her lips parted, then pressed together. After a moment she gave an evasive little shrug. "I haven't known him long, Charles."

"You knew me but a short time, *n'est-ce-pas?*"

"Yes, that's true, Charles, but this is different. I mean...." She sighed. "Oh, Charles, you're not hoping Philippe and I will fall in love, are you?"

"*Mais, oui*. It would give me great enjoyment, *ma chère*." He spoke bluntly.

"There's no chance of that happening." Her answer was swift. "Charles, your son really doesn't think much of me."

He scowled. "*Petite idiote!* How can Philippe, who is a perfectly normal man, not be attracted to one as lovely as you?"

"I didn't say he wasn't attracted," Daye pointed out, then could have bitten her tongue when Charles's eyebrows raised. "Don't you know, dear Charles, that attraction and affection do not necessarily go together. Do you understand what I mean?"

Charles reached for one of her hands and raised it to his lips. "I understand, and agree that this may be so in many instances. But, Daye, *mon enfant*, you are not only beautiful to look at, you are warm and affectionate, you are kind and gentle. And—" he kissed her hand again "—you are extremely virtuous. Now, tell me, how can any man not feel affection for one with so much *inner* beauty?"

"Oh, Charles!" Daye could not help the bubble of laughter escaping her. "You are an outrageous flatterer. I shall begin to believe I'm simply too good for any man."

He smiled slyly, releasing her hand and starting the

car engine. "Still you have not answered my question. What are your feelings for my son?"

The smile on her lips faded and she turned her head to stare out of the window. The scenery was so exquisitely beautiful it actually made her heart ache. Or was it the scenery that was responsible? Again she evaded his question, asking her own. "Charles, what about Philippe and Mademoiselle Montand?"

"Do you ask me if they are lovers, *ma chère*?"

Still she stared out the window. "I suppose so."

"I cannot tell you that, *petite*," he said gently, and after a slight hesitation added, "Philippe is thirty-five, Daye, he is certain to have had love affairs. You understand this, do you not?"

Daye's throat was dry. "Yes, of course I do." A procession of vague, unknown women floated through her mind. But she had seen a photograph of Melisse and she was real. She turned to look at Charles's handsome profile. "Would you have liked Philippe and Melisse to marry?"

Again he hesitated before saying carefully, "Had Philippe wished to marry Melisse he would have done so."

It was an evasive answer, just as hers had been when he asked her how she felt about his son. But while Charles had probably guessed she was more than mildly interested in Philippe, she still could not tell whether or not he approved of Melisse. Or was she being obtuse? Only minutes ago Charles had admitted he would be delighted if she, Daye, was loved by his son.

Neither of them spoke for a while, but when the small red-steepled church came into view, Daye said a little desperately, "Charles, you won't say anything to Philippe about our conversation, will you?"

He stopped the car and gave her an innocent look. "What conversation, *petite*?"

For a moment she was puzzled, then she smiled with relief and kissed his cheek.

Since Père Martin was nowhere to be seen, Charles suggested they walk to the village. "It will be easier to leave the car here, as you will see," he declared, taking her arm in a firm grip.

Daye understood what he meant as they started off along a well-trodden path that appeared to wind through a veritable jungle. Besides thick, waist-high bushes, there were inevitable palm and breadfruit trees, the thorny lantana and prickly leafed pandanus with its sickly scented blossoms. And there was a tree she did not recognize that Charles said was the *bourao* whose yellow leaves were used to make native dancing skirts.

As they approached the village they were met by several women wearing brilliant smiles and colorful muumuus. A few carried tiny infants while others had toddlers clinging to their skirts. One of the women was in an advanced stage of pregnancy, yet Daye noticed she still retained the fluid grace peculiar to Polynesian females. "She is the wife of Philippe's *bon ami*, Mari," Charles said, evidently noticing Daye's eyes on the young woman. "Her name is Vairea." He spoke to Vairea in French and she answered in the same language. "It would appear our good priest is here, visiting the old ones of the village," Charles told Daye.

Followed by the softly chattering, giggling women, they continued on their way, Daye gazing with interest at the houses snuggled between the trees. Some were built of wooden planks and resembled, in a rough sort of way, European bungalows. Others— and these were in the majority—had walls and roofs made of woven palm leaves and were built on stilts, several feet above ground. Fishing nets hung from nearby trees, bananas hung in huge bunches beneath shaded verandas; dogs barked, small grunting pigs and squawking chickens ran freely, mingling with children and adults. And as Daye watched, fascinated, a land crab, dragging debris behind it, scuttled in front of them before vanishing into an underground burrow.

Then Charles said in a pleased voice, "Here is Père Martin, Daye, *ma chère*," and she looked up to see a short, slenderly built man hurrying toward them, his hands outstretched in welcome.

"Mon cher ami," he said to Charles when he reached them. Almost at once, however, he turned to Daye. "You are the English *mademoiselle* I have heard about. Ah!" He sighed. "Thank *le bon Dieu* that I am neither too old nor too saintly to appreciate such rare beauty."

Daye smiled, putting her hands into his and feeling them tightly clasped. Père Martin's hair was silver, his eyes a somewhat faded brown. He was obviously getting on in years, yet he gave the impression of possessing wiry strength and boundless energy. "I don't believe I have ever been given a lovelier compliment," she told the priest sincerely.

He beamed, and in his heavily accented English mentioned a visit he had made to London some twenty years earlier. But Daye sensed he really wished to speak to Charles and when, after a polite look of apology, he did so, she was not surprised. He spoke in French and somewhere in the rapid parlance she was certain she heard the name Melisse. But she probably had Melisse on her mind rather too often, she told herself in some irritation.

Presently Charles intimated he wished to speak privately with the priest. "I will accompany Père Martin to the church, Daye," he said. "You will not mind remaining here? The women would be most disappointed were you to leave them so soon."

Daye assured him she did not mind, refusing to admit she felt rather strange and shy at the thought of being left here. But she found she had no need to be, for after Charles and the little priest left, the women fussed over Daye and she found herself being led into various houses where she was given sweet milky coffee or pale coconut milk to drink. The houses were surprisingly cool and Daye saw that most of them were furnished after a fashion. The majority, too, contained oil or gas stoves for cooking, although Charles had told her many natives still cooked over smoldering coconut husks or clung to the ancient method of the earth oven.

Once more out in the sunshine, Daye sat on the soft grass to watch the children who, their curiosity about her apparently satisfied, had returned to their play. They were all so chubby and adorable with their large eyes and silky looking brown skins. She wished she could put her arms around them and feel their warm little bodies close to her. It was the first time she could recall having felt the *need* to actually hold a child in her arms, although she had often casually wondered what it would be like to become a mother.

It wasn't until the few women who were still hovering nearby began to giggle softly among themselves, their coy glances directed at something behind her, that Daye became suspicious, conscious of being watched. Turning her head quickly, she saw Philippe. He was some distance away, on horseback, and he and his mount were very still, like figures carved by a master craftsman. Instantly her heart gave a great leap and then began a rapid pulsation against her breast. She looked away from him, staring almost blindly at the children. She and Philippe had exchanged only a few polite words since the dinner party last night. The fact that he had come to her bedroom door and tried to persuade her to let him in might never have happened, except in Daye's imagination. Still, last night she had locked the door of her suite the moment she entered, but although she had paced fearfully between bed and sitting room until well past midnight, Philippe had not come to her door again.

When at last she climbed exhaustedly into bed she lay wondering why she had been so afraid, safe as she was behind that locked door. The clear morning light, however, brought with it her answer. She had been afraid, had Philippe come to ask admittance, that she would have allowed him to enter her suite. And if she had gone that far she would not have asked him to leave. She shivered now, thinking about it. How she would have despised herself afterward—when it was too late.

From behind her, the object of her traumatic thoughts spoke softly. "It is unexpected, finding you here in the village."

She turned her head and found herself looking at dusty, knee-high riding boots. "I came with Charles." To her own ears her voice sounded stilted.

He moved to sit beside her and called out something to the women who giggled again and slowly went away. "And where is *mon père*?" he asked casually.

"With Père Martin." His nearness bothered her dreadfully and she prayed he was not aware of her state. "He is very nice, your priest."

"You have met him?"

"Oh, yes, Charles wanted me to. That's really why I came. Although I did want to see the village, too." She knew her voice was shaky.

Philippe was silent for so long she was tempted to look at him. Her swift look took in the tense expression he wore. Then he asked suddenly, "You are a Roman Catholic?" And she looked at him again and shook her head.

"You are now to take instructions to become one, I assume." The harshness in his voice startled her.

"You assume wrongly. Why ever should I want to change my religion?"

"To please *mon père, naturellement*."

"To please Charles? What are you talking about? Charles has never suggested such a thing." Daye frowned, an elusive suspicion drifting through her mind. Did he truly think she would go to any length to strengthen her position in his father's heart and home? "I can assure you I've no intention of becoming a Catholic for any reason," she stated in a tight little voice, finding it quite easy to meet his eyes. She scrambled to her feet, smoothing the skirt of her dress automatically.

Philippe rose, too, in a movement swift and graceful for such a tall man. "Do not leave, Daye," he said. "There is...." He paused, a smile lighting his grim expression as a childish voice shrilled his name.

He turned, bending to sweep a small girl into his arms. "This is Mara," he told Daye. "She is the third daughter of Mari and Vairea. Soon they will have another *enfant*—a son, perhaps." He gazed fondly at the child and spoke to her in her own language. She responded by curling her plump arms even tighter about his neck.

Daye's heart appeared to turn completely over. "She seems to like you." Her voice sounded strange and husky to her ears.

"And you find that most surprising, *n'est-ce pas?*" He smiled again, this time at her, and once more her heart somersaulted. "Tomorrow I fly to Papeete. You will go with me?"

His abrupt changing of subjects threw her into confusion, and she began to stammer, "I don't know...I haven't thought...." She willed herself to think now, *Papeete. Of course; he's going there to fetch Melisse Montand.* An arrow-sharp pain shot through her. "No, thank you. If I ever need to go, I'm sure Charles or Derek will take me."

He set the child down and gave Daye a smoldering glance. "So you would go with anyone but me? I may ask why?"

Her lashes flickered and she looked down at her feet.

"You do not trust me; that is the reason, is it not?"

She lifted her shoulders. "Would you be surprised if I didn't? After all, you can't claim you wanted me to come to Anani, can you? And neither can you claim you would like me to stay. You've insulted me, threatened me, tried to...." She stopped, her own guilt would not allow her to accuse him of attempted seduction. "Perhaps I'm afraid you will find a way to leave me in Papeete," she finished lightly.

He gave a short hard laugh. "What would be the point, *mademoiselle*? You could return to Anani once more, could you not?" Unexpectedly his hand reached out to grasp her chin and tilt her face upward. "And you need not fear that I would drop you into the deep blue Pacific. Audrey will be with us, or had you forgotten?"

"I hadn't forgotten." Briefly Daye allowed herself the pleasure of letting her eyes slide over his lean yet strongly boned face, the straight handsome nose and beautifully defined mouth—the mouth that could arouse in her a passion she had not known she possessed. She drew in her breath, her eyes meeting his as he looked at her from beneath his lashes. "Still, I will not be going with you." Her voice was uneven.

He seemed about to say more when they were again interrupted, this time by a fat elderly woman in a red-and-white muumuu. "Philippe, *mon cher bébé*," she cried, waddling toward them, arms outstretched, her wrinkled face split by a wide delighted smile.

Philippe let go of Daye's chin, his eyes lingering for a moment on her face. Then he turned his attention to the old woman who promptly threw her arms around his waist and hugged him with vigor. He winced teasingly, speaking to her in French, and when she released him he bent to kiss her on both cheeks.

"She is Repeta, the child's great-*grand-mère*." He smiled at Daye over the top of the woman's gray head. "I have known Repeta all my life and she is as dear to me as my own *grand-mère* would be." He looked down at Repeta and again spoke to her. Obviously he asked a question, for she nodded, turning to look Daye over with inquisitive black eyes. Presently she nodded again, her hand shooting out to stroke Daye's hair.

"Do not move away from her," he commanded.

"I had no intention of moving away." Daye felt annoyed that he should think she might do so. Did he believe the woman repulsed her?

Repeta's hand left Daye's hair and moved to stroke the side of her cheek. She said something then, a smile flashing in her dark face, her eyes gleaming as though with mischief.

"What did she say?" Daye asked Philippe.

"I am not at all certain I should repeat it." He looked amused.

"Goodness, was it that uncomplimentary?"

"You, *mademoiselle*, might say it was." He shrugged. "Repeta believes you to be my woman. She said we will make beautiful, healthy babies together." He spoke coolly, but the look in his eyes was far from cool and his smile was taunting.

Strangely, his words provoked no feeling of embarrassment. Instead Daye experienced an acute sense of desolation and knew it was because there would never be children belonging to her and Philippe. "I do hope you will set her straight," she said flatly.

"Set her straight?" Philippe raised one dark eyebrow. "Do you mean that I should agree with her?"

"You know very well that isn't what I meant," she said sharply. Her eyes slid away from his vital attractions and rested on Repeta, who was now cuddling her great-grandchild and eyeing Daye in a puzzled manner. "Please, Philippe, tell her the truth. After all, neither of us would want the wrong sort of rumors floating about, would we?" She smiled at Repeta and gently touched little Mara's fat brown arm. "Good-bye. . .no, *au revoir*, Repeta," she said, and walked off in the direction—she hoped—of the church.

Somehow she was not in the least surprised when Philippe caught up to her. "You need have no fear, *mademoiselle*, Repeta has been told the truth."

"That's good. Now you can rest easily, too, can't you?"

"Can I?" His tiny question held a tinge of bitterness, but Daye did not answer. She was so desperately aware that he was striding along at her side that she could not think straight. And she had no idea how fast she was walking until he said in an amused voice, "Is it necessary to hurry so? You are quite breathless."

She slowed, realizing she was, indeed, breathless. "I hope this is the way to the church. I thought I'd go to meet Charles." She paused, catching her breath. "He has been rather a long time."

This time he did not answer, and they walked in silence for what to Daye seemed ages. Then he suddenly caught her arm, startling her so that she stopped, staring up at him apprehensively. "*Mon Dieu!* Do not look at me as though you expected to be instantly devoured," he grated harshly. "I merely wished to keep you on the correct path. In that direction you would walk into a grove of orange trees."

She felt foolish for being so nervously conscious of his nearness. To cover it she said with forced interest, "Orange trees. I don't believe I've seen any on Anani."

"There are not many left. Come, I will show you the grove." He had not released her arm and now he gave it a determined tug, leading her along the path that branched off to the right. It came to an end quite soon, and Daye gazed at the slender-trunked, dark-green-leafed trees, which were loaded with pale orange fruit.

"Are they sweet?" she asked him, and he answered that they were not particularly tasty.

"They are best when made into wine." He laughed. "This the villagers do well and it is a somewhat potent drink. Tell me, *madem*...Daye, did you not know the native word for orange tree is Anani?"

"No, I didn't know that."

"*Mon père* did not tell you? This is surprising."

She gave him a suspicious look but could see no mockery or sarcasm in his expression. "Yes, it is, isn't it?" she answered lightly, smiling up at him. "Who named it? I mean...oh, I don't suppose you know that." She swallowed. The look in his eyes was incredibly disconcerting. "Do you?" she finished weakly.

He did not answer directly and she had the distinct feeling he, too, was rather disconcerted. But if he was, he recovered quickly enough and Daye was left wondering if she had imagined it. "*Mais, oui*, I do know," he said, and began to tell her about his ancestor, Ferdinand Chavot, who had discovered and claimed the island. At that time there had been numerous orange groves growing here. Philippe had spoken in an almost indifferent tone but when he added that Ferdinand had once sailed with Louis Antoine de Bougainville, Daye could detect a note of pride creeping into his voice. "You have, of course, heard of this famous Frenchman?"

Daye was taken by surprise. "Er, yes, I believe so. Was he an explorer, or something?"

He gazed at her solemnly. "Louis de Bougainville led the first French expedition to sail around the world."

"Oh."

"Oh," he mimicked softly. "You are, of course, more familiar with your Captain James Cook?" His voice teased, his smile set her heart racing. She wanted to converse with him in a clever, lighthearted way, but it was impossible. This man affected her as no man had ever done. No man's smile, no matter how attractive, had ever caused her to become witless and tongue-tied. Sometimes, she thought, it seemed she could only talk to him when he made her downright furious....

"*Mademoiselle*. Daye."

She blinked at him. "Oh! Yes?" He was looking at her in a way that did shocking things to her nervous system. "I...I think I'd better look for Charles. We might miss each other and he will worry." She spoke quickly, so quickly her words sounded garbled to her ears. But she made no move to leave, and when he put out his hand and took one of hers she did not stop him.

"You were sensible not to allow me to enter your room."

His words were totally unexpected and for a moment she simply stared up at him. "Sensible?" She felt heat staining her cheeks. "Yes, I was, wasn't I?" Then because she had to know, "Did you expect me to let you in?"

"It seemed probable that you would."

"But that morning I told you how I felt. Didn't

you believe me?'' She did not wait for him to answer but went on rapidly, ''Is that why you came to my room in the afternoon and told Terii to leave? Did you think you could carry on where you left off?'' She tried to pull her hand away but he held on to it tightly.

''In the afternoon I came to see you, that is all. *Mon père* mentioned at luncheon that you were unwell, and I was concerned.''

''Concerned?'' Daye tried to ignore her leaping pulse. ''But of course you were! Oh, don't make me laugh, Philippe.'' Again she tried to tug her hand from his.

''You do not believe me?'' He did not seem surprised. ''That morning we parted in anger. I was unkind, *n'est-ce pas?*''

She felt breathless again. ''You were, rather.''

''I was disappointed, frustrated.'' His mouth curved wryly. ''It is not a sensation I am accustomed to.''

His words provoked her, and with angry strength she twisted her hand away from him. ''No, I don't expect you are,'' she agreed coldly. ''Oh, well, most likely it will do you no harm.''

''Abstinence is good for the soul?''

It occurred to Daye that after tomorrow Melisse would be here and Philippe would have no need to abstain. That is, if they were indeed lovers as she suspected. The jealousy stabbing her was almost debilitating, and she turned blindly away from him. If they were lovers they would share a bed in Philippe's room, a room just across the hall from her own. Or perhaps, out of respect for Charles, they would sleep together in the guesthouse. Daye found herself walking directly into the trunk of a pandanus tree and put out her hands in an attempt to save herself.

But it was Philippe who did so, pulling her back with an exclamation. "What is wrong? Are you ill?" His tone was urgent.

She saw that he did, in fact, look extremely concerned. Possibly he was afraid she might faint at his feet, she thought bitterly, shrugging away from him. "Must you keep on touching me?" she cried, aware that she sounded nearly hysterical.

He looked briefly puzzled before a glint of temper flared in his eyes. "Why are you so unreasonably annoyed?" he asked curtly.

"I'm not!" Daye lowered her eyes. Forcing herself to speak calmly she added, "I must go now. Charles is probably looking everywhere for me."

Without a word he took her arm and this time she made no protest. When they reached the village path, he let her go and when she dared a hasty upward glance, she saw that he was watching her in that strange, indefinable way, as he so often did. It set her heart beating erratically, but she felt quite proud of herself when she said, still calmly, "You're going back to the village, I expect. So if you see your father would you tell him I'll wait near the church? Of course, I might meet him myself...." Her voice trailed into silence as she realized she was beginning to sound nervous. If only he would stop looking at her like that....

"Daye." Philippe spoke her name as if it was a sigh, and he reached out to gently pull her close. But even as her senses reacted and a current of desire whipped through her, he let her go, stepping back and muttering in French. Bewildered, Daye looked at him blankly, then fiery embarrassment overwhelmed her. Oh, what a weak fool she was! Had she no willpower at all? Philippe had only to look at her in a certain way, hold her against his body as if he wanted her there, and she almost threw herself at him.

"Daye," he said again, this time steadily, "yesterday, I vowed I would not attempt to make love to you again. It is, however, a difficult vow to keep. You are beautiful, irresistible, and I am a man who...." He gave her an odd look, as though he had been about to say something, only to change his mind.

"You are obviously a man who can't keep his hands to himself." Daye made herself smile.

He did not smile back. "Before you leave, Daye, may I beg a favor of you?"

"A favor? Well...yes." She was hesitant and vaguely uneasy.

"You have not, as yet, promised to allow Derek to paint you?"

"No."

His clear eyes slid over her. "I would prefer you never do so."

"What? Why not?" She was too puzzled to be annoyed.

"If Derek paints you, he will fall in love with you. I do not care for anything so disastrous to happen to my *bon ami*." He spoke deliberately.

Daye's lips parted. "Oh! Disastrous! How flattering of you!"

He frowned. "Some years ago Derek was devastated by his wife's infidelity. Since then he has taken no woman seriously." Again those eyes slid over her. "You, *mademoiselle*, with your green eyes and sunlit hair, are not an ordinary woman, and *mon pauvre ami* would be a bedazzled wreck long before your portrait was completed.''

Daye stared at him speechlessly, although not for long. ''That's the silliest thing I've ever heard.'' Her voice shook. ''Derek could fall in love with me whether I pose for him or not.''

''And that is what would please you?'' His voice was hard.

Daye bit her lip. ''Naturally. I must keep on adding to my list of admirers, after all.''

Their eyes met and silence hung between them like a palpable thing. Philippe's chest beneath his close-fitting white shirt betrayed his heavy, uneven breathing, but Daye felt as though she were not breathing at all. Then, without warning, Philippe grabbed her roughly and pulled her with him into the shelter of the trees. She would have fallen, but he held her against him, his arms tightening, and as he bent his head she raised her face and slid her arms upward in an involuntary movement.

There was nothing gentle or tender in the meeting of their lips. Behind Philippe's kiss was a crushing urgency, as though he had been thirsting for just this moment and could not easily take his fill. Daye clung with fast-closed eyes, her own fierce hunger naked in its response. She loved him, loved him! Her body throbbed with longing, a longing that had lain dormant, waiting only for him to revive it, since she had left him yesterday morning.

Philippe groaned, dragging his mouth from hers and covering her upturned face with kisses. His behavior held a curious desperation that affected an extremely sensitized Daye in the same manner. Tightening her arms, she fervently returned his kisses, her pliant body curving against him. With a low, tortured murmur, Philippe returned his mouth to hers, his kiss hot, his tongue edging between her lips in tentative exploration. Daye drew in her breath in sharp surprise. No one had ever kissed her in this manner, and she was not certain she liked it. But she parted her lips eagerly, wanting to please him, and when he passionately explored her mouth she shuddered, her insides surging with heat, her pulse leaping frantically. Dear God, but she wanted him! She might never have experienced the ultimate intimacy between male and female, but she knew instinctively that her body craved satisfaction.

Philippe was fully aroused, his strong body shuddering, his groans low in his throat. *Oh, darling, my darling,* she thought. *I'd like to give you what you want—what we both want.* Her hands moved to lovingly caress his dark head, his well-shaped ears, the warm, tanned neck. . . .

Philippe's body stiffened, his mouth left hers abruptly. Reaching up, he dragged her hands away and began to lash out at her in his own language. It sounded, she thought numbly, as though he cursed her. Shaking visibly, she stood there in the leafy coolness, dimly aware of palm fronds brushing her cheek and the heavy scent of hibiscus wafting about her. What had she done to make him so bitterly angry? He had kissed her and she had kissed him back. She had said nothing, done nothing. Dazed and bewildered she gazed up at him, her heart slowly filling with misery.

Philippe still gripped her hands, hurting the slender bones. Daye's lips parted to protest, but he grated in English, "Do not look so innocent. No innocent would kiss as you kissed me, or use her body to arouse as you aroused me. Tell me, *petite Anglaise*, do you do such things deliberately, or can you not help yourself when you are in a man's arms?" His eyes glittered furiously.

Daye's anger rose to meet his. "If you remember, it was you who dragged me here and started the kissing, not the other way around." Her voice was hoarse with anger and misery. "And you seemed to be enjoying yourself for a while. Now. Will you let go of me!"

He let her go at once, his arms falling limply to his sides. "Daye, *je regrette*, I . . . ." He paused, his expression bleak.

"I don't want your apologies!" Daye took a step backward, raising her hand to rub it savagely across her mouth. "You said you vowed never to kiss me again. Well, make sure you stick to it from now on. I'm sick of your taking out your frustrations on me, blaming me, as if I'd walked up to you and started the caressing and the kissing." She had kept control of her voice but now it threatened to break. Before she could make a fool of herself, she turned and found her way through the trees and tangled green growth. Once on the path she walked hurriedly, hoping she did not look as devastated as she felt.

CHAPTER ELEVEN

DAYE WAS NOT SURPRISED when Philippe failed to appear at lunch. She told herself she was relieved, but her gaze drifted frequently to his empty chair. Even the place setting before it looked forlorn, as though it waited for him. Daye was aware she was being foolish, and she did her best to join in the conversation while pretending to enjoy the beautifully cooked food that, to her, tasted flat and dry.

Charles looked at her perceptively once or twice, but he asked no questions. He had not questioned her on the drive home either, although she knew she was unusually quiet and withdrawn. She had met Charles soon after leaving Philippe, and he had apologized profusely for staying away for so long. "Ah, but you were not without company, I see." Charles smiled over her shoulder, and for a moment she thought the villagers had reappeared. This thought was instantly dismissed as Charles continued, "I trust you have intentions of visiting our priest, Philippe. Père Martin grumbles that you have not been to mass since you returned home."

So Philippe was behind her all the while, Daye thought, keeping her eyes fixed steadily on Charles's face. She would not look at Philippe again. She could not!

"You met in the village, *mes enfants*?" Charles

questioned, as they strolled toward the church. Fortunately, Charles walked between Philippe and herself, so Daye was not as uncomfortable as she might have been. Still, she had no desire to talk and was grateful because Charles's conversation was directed toward his son. When they reached the church, Daye could not stifle a sigh of relief and Charles said at once, "*Pauvre petite*, you are exhausted. Come, we will go home." To Philippe he said, chuckling, "You will make your confession, *mon fils*?"

"*Peut-être*, papa. It will depend on how much time Père Martin can afford. As you know, I have *many* sins to confess." He spoke mockingly, and Daye was certain he meant the words for her ears.

Paul had lunch with them as usual and afterward he said, pleadingly, "*Mademoiselle*, you promised you would listen to me play. I am free for two hours this afternoon, and if Monsieur Chavot will allow me to use the guesthouse?" His dark eyes now pleaded with Charles.

"The guesthouse is being readied for Mademoiselle Montand, I believe, Paul." Charles smiled. "There is, however, a very fine instrument in the salon, *n'est-ce pas?*"

Paul's face glowed, apparently at the thought of using the baby grand that sat in one corner of the huge salon. Daye could not help smiling herself at Paul's so obvious pleasure. "Come along then," she said, "I'm looking forward to hearing some of my favorite composers."

"You like the classical music, *mademoiselle*?" Paul asked, as they walked to the salon.

"Yes, I do. But I also enjoy today's music."

"As I do," Paul exclaimed enthusiastically. "In

Papeete there is a club—more than one. Some day, I...." He broke off hastily, casting a look at Charles. Daye wondered if Paul was afraid Charles would object to the club, or if he had intended inviting Daye to go with him and thought better of it. She was sure it was the latter.

Charles stayed, listening to Paul for half an hour before excusing himself. He was going to rest, Daye knew, and for the first time she experienced a vague unease. Charles's rest was extremely important. He never missed it. But, of course, he was up quite early each morning, so it was only natural for him to rest each afternoon. She herself did so at times and she knew the Polynesian staff always had an afternoon nap. Reassured, she turned her attention back to Paul who was playing the exquisite "Clair de lune," by Debussy.

There was no denying Paul was extremely talented, Daye thought, as she sat curled in a comfortable armchair listening to the music come to glowing life beneath Paul's long fingers. Not that she was any true judge. Only an experienced professional could tell if the boy possessed enough ability to guarantee him a successful career in music. And apparently Melisse Montand, who should know, was certain he did.

Paul played for almost an hour and a half before saying reluctantly, "Soon I must return to the office. Mademoiselle Daye, I have given you pleasure?"

"Oh, Paul, such great pleasure!" Daye uncurled her slender legs and got to her feet. "I think I could listen to you for hours."

"*Merci, merci,* Mademoiselle Daye. That is praise indeed!" Paul's eyes shone. He came to stand beside her, looking down at her tenderly. "I will never forget this day. When I become famous I shall remember your rapt expression as I played."

He was so serious she dared not smile. "That's a lovely thing to say, Paul."

"Do you think it is possible that you will attend my concerts?" He looked at her hopefully.

Poor Paul. He was making his plans already. She hoped he would not be disappointed. "Well, of course I will. I'll probably brag about you to my friends, telling them I knew you when you were still. . . ." She paused. She had been about to say "still a boy," but she added quickly, "still an unknown."

He frowned slightly and asked, "You think of me as *un garçon*, a boy, do you not, Mademoiselle Daye?"

She looked at him warily. "I'm twenty-two, five years older than you, Paul."

"What can it matter? Five years is nothing!"

"I suppose not. At least, not if the man was, say, twenty-five and the woman thirty." *Oh, I hope I'm saying the right thing,* Daye thought nervously.

"But the ladies prefer to marry men who are older than they are, *n'est-ce pas?*"

"In most cases, I suppose." Daye laughed. "There is an excellent reason for that, Paul. We women want to *look* years younger than our men."

"You will look young and beautiful forever." Paul spoke earnestly.

"I don't know that I'd want to. Sometimes it can be difficult to. . . well, to look as I do."

"You do not smile when you say that, so you must be serious." Paul gazed at her worriedly. "Has someone made you unhappy, *mademoiselle*? I believe, I truly believe I should want to harm anyone who made you unhappy.'' There was passionate sincerity in those last words.

''Then I must be careful not to let you know if anyone does.'' Daye spoke teasingly although she was genuinely touched by Paul's declaration.

He gazed down at her for a long moment, and Daye wished there was something she could do to ease the pain the boy was so clearly enduring. To tell him this infatuation for her would pass, that he would very likely fall in love several times during the next few years, would be trite and completely useless. But because she wanted to help him she searched her mind for something to say and found it. ''At any rate, Paul, *you* could never be unhappy for long, could you? I mean, you have your music and that would take your mind off anything upsetting, wouldn't it?''

His dark eyes narrowed thoughtfully. ''*Mais, oui*, that is so. I am fortunate, am I not? Always I must remember this.'' He reached for her hand and kissed it as charmingly as would any adult French male. ''You are as kind as you are beautiful,'' he said. ''But it is no use; nothing can stop me from thinking of you.'' He gave her a stiff, courteous little bow and walked swiftly to the door.

But still he was not to leave. Once there he swung around and came back to her. And there was an expression on his face that puzzled her. ''What's the matter, Paul?'' she asked.

He sucked in his breath. ''Mademoiselle Daye, I have heard—do you intend to marry?''

''To marry?'' Oh, heavens, she thought, was Paul going to ask her to wait for him to grow up or something? ''I suppose so, one day,'' she answered.

"*Non, non*, you do not understand." Paul swallowed. "I have heard that you came to Anani to...to capture a wealthy prize." He gazed at her miserably. "I should not have told you!"

She felt chilled and resentful. "In other words, you've heard that I'm a gold digger, a fortune hunter. Is that so, Paul?"

"*Oui, oui*, but I did not believe it. I could not! If you married, if you became Madame Chavot, it would be for love, not for...." He pressed his lips together like a child trying to stop the tears.

Daye's chair was directly behind her and she sank into it. "Who said such a thing about me, Paul?"

"I cannot tell you, I cannot! But she...it is said you will become Madame Chavot before the year is over."

Daye gasped, but before she could say anything a voice asked coldly, "Paul, was it not presumptuous of you to speak to *mademoiselle* as you did?"

Daye's eyes flew to the door. Philippe stood there, hands resting on lean hips, his face dark with anger. But although he had spoken to Paul, Daye had the most uncanny certainty that his anger was directed at her.

As he stepped into the room he did not even glance at her, however. The object of his steely gaze was Paul. He stood in front of the boy, his hands still on his hips, his stance somehow menacing. "Well, Paul?" he asked silkily.

To give Paul credit he met Philippe's stare. "No offense was intended, Philippe; *mademoiselle* knows I would not intentionally offend her."

"That's right!" Daye got up quickly. "Paul has said nothing—"

Philippe did not glance at her as he interrupted, "You will tell me, Paul, who...." He stopped speaking English and continued in rapid French. Paul answered him in the same language, a reluctant expression on his youthful countenance, but from the irritated frown Philippe gave him, Daye thought Paul might not have told him what he wanted to know. Good for Paul if he hadn't, she told herself, realizing she was stung by Philippe's rudeness, ignoring her as he had done.

Philippe was talking to Paul again, and Daye saw that the boy looked uncomfortable. Unhesitatingly she said clearly, "Paul is supposed to be in the office by now. Why don't you let him go, Monsieur Chavot?"

Both man and boy turned to stare at her. "I'm involved in this nasty rumor, whatever it is, but Paul does not have to be questioned about it now." Her voice shook but her expression was determined.

Philippe's eyes narrowed. "*Très bien*, Paul. Later, perhaps, we will talk."

Paul shot Daye a grateful look and headed for the door. Once there he turned and kissed his fingers to her before disappearing. Philippe, whose back was to the door, did not see this affectionate gesture and Daye smiled to herself.

But her smile faded as she recalled what Paul had said. Somewhere, from someone, Paul had heard she was a fortune hunter, that she was determined to marry one of the wealthy Chavots. Philippe, of course. Oh, Lord! No wonder Philippe had looked so angry. He would not want such a rumor floating about, particularly since his precious Melisse would soon be arriving.

"Were you responsible for this incredible nonsense?" Philippe's cold voice cut into her thoughts.

Daye gasped. "Are you mad? It's the last thing I would have a hand in. Besides, you must have heard me ask Paul who was talking about me. You were listening, weren't you?" Her anger sharpened. "You could be responsible for the part about my being after a wealthy husband, now that I think about it."

"I am not, however. Certain opinions I keep to myself." He stared at her moodily.

Daye ignored what she considered a veiled insult. "I'd like to know who *is* responsible. I'd like very much to set whoever it is straight and. . .and dish out a piece of my mind at the same time." Her hands clenched at her sides. "I won't have horrible lies circulated about me. I won't!"

"It was inevitable. When a young and beautiful woman suddenly appears on an island such as Anani it causes speculation. Particularly when she is a guest in the home of two wealthy men." His eyes were very cold.

Inevitable! Daye ran her hands distractedly through her hair. Perhaps he was right about that. But why must she be made the villain—or villainess—of the piece? "It isn't fair." Her voice was tremulous. "And what about Charles? What if he hears? He will be so upset."

"About your becoming Madame Chavot before the year ends? I think not," he said bitterly.

His bitterness hurt her but she had to agree that Charles would not be upset at the prospect of a marriage between Philippe and herself. "I really meant he would be upset at my being called a fortune hunter," she explained.

"Naturellement!" Philippe's broad shoulders raised in a shrug. He moved across the room. "May I offer you a drink?" he asked, proceeding toward the well-equipped liquor cabinet.

"No, thank you, I'll have some tea soon."

"Ah, tea. I have never cared for it." He strolled toward her, his drink in his hand. He had not changed since this morning, she noticed, and in his less than immaculate state, with his dark hair ruffled untidily, he seemed more vulnerable. In spite of herself, and the knowledge that he had no real liking or respect for her, a powerful surge of love rushed through her and she looked away hastily in case he read it in her eyes.

"Perhaps you don't care for anything predominantly British," she said spontaneously.

His glass was halfway to his lips, but he lowered it and gave her a cold glinting glance. "What would you like me to say to that, *mademoiselle*?"

Embarrassed, she replied, "Say absolutely nothing! It was a stupid remark for me to make, especially since I can see you're spoiling for an argument." She walked to the door, her head high, but something compelled her to turn and add, "Thank goodness, you won't be here tomorrow. And after that you will be too occupied with your... friend to enter into petty arguments with me." She did not wait to hear what he would say. She hurried to the haven of her bedroom and lay on the bed covers, her heart heavy, her eyes aching with tears she could not shed.

PHILIPPE AND AUDREY flew to Papeete early the next morning and were expected to return, accompanied by Melisse Montand, before darkness fell. But it was almost time for dinner when Charles received a message, via the radio set, that their plans were now changed.

"It appears, *mes enfants*," said Charles, "that Philippe has discovered unexpected business and Audrey wishes to stay with her friend who has been released from the hospital. As for Melisse," he shrugged, "she will be delighted to remain in Papeete for a few days."

Derek, who had been invited to dinner that evening, groaned. "A few days! Audrey, what have you done to me? Charles, I'll have to take my meals with you or starve." He grinned. "Unless you allow your adorable guest to come and cook for me."

Charles laughed heartily, and Daye said, "Charles is amused because I've told him I'm a dreadful cook. I really am, Derek."

"I don't mind. Who could care about the taste of food with you around?"

"Stop teasing, Derek, *mon ami*," Charles ordered. "Daye, *petite*, Derek is an excellent chef. Nevertheless, he is more than welcome at our table, *n'est-ce pas?*"

"Oh, I should think so." Daye smiled, keeping her tone light. Philippe would be away for a few days, she thought. Audrey would be staying with her friend and Melisse would stay with Philippe. Of course she would! Philippe had an apartment in Papeete, so it was only logical for Melisse to share it. Was it a one-bedroom apartment? Would they share a bed? She felt miserably angry with herself for these thoughts, but she seemed unable to do a thing about it. How would she ever bear the next few days, thinking of Philippe and Melisse together? How would she ever be able to bear the next few days not seeing him? The pain inside her was so intense she felt like crying out. If this was what it was like to be in love she could do without it, she told herself bitterly.

As it turned out, the next few days were easier to bear than Daye had expected. Each morning Charles gave her a riding lesson and afterward they swam in the island pool. Even this was easy to do as long as she did not allow her eyes to drift to that particular spot where she and Philippe had embraced. Her afternoons were taken up by Derek, and for this she was grateful. He took her sailing, which she loved, eased her into tennis, which she found rather difficult in the afternoon heat, walked with her in the damp coolness of a tropical valley where he acquainted her with more of the island's flora, and took her to his studio where she sat on a high-backed chair while he did some sketches of her. She had not as yet promised to sit for her portrait, but it seemed to be more or less taken for granted that she would, eventually. Philippe would be averse to this, of course, but Daye refused to worry about it. Anyway, she was certain he was wrong about his friend Derek. When he was sketching her, Derek's gaze was totally impersonal. She could have been a piece of pottery he was drawing, she told herself, amused. True, artists had been known to fall in love with their models, but it seemed doubtful Derek would follow their example.

Philippe and Audrey had been away for almost a week when Daye told Derek, "I've enjoyed myself these past few days."

"So have I." Derek was sketching her again but he paused to smile at her. "I've hardly been able to believe my luck, having you to myself every afternoon." He returned to his work, still talking. "Charles doesn't seem to have minded your running off with me, does he?"

"Minded? Why should he? Oh, I see, you mean we've left him alone. But I seldom see Charles in the afternoon. He rests, Derek—I thought you knew. Besides—" she raised her brows quizzically "—even the best of friends must spend some time apart, wouldn't you say?"

"The best of...? Hmm. Daye, my lovely, there's something I...no, turn your head just a little to the right. That does it!" He worked in silence, breaking it suddenly to ask, "You are fond of Charles, aren't you, Daye?"

"Oh, yes! In fact, Derek, I sometimes wonder if I could possibly care more if he were my own father."

Derek's hand stilled, and Daye found herself the object of a long, steady scrutiny. She was ready to ask what was wrong when he spoke, "You've moved your head, Daye. Put it back where it was, will you?"

She obeyed. "Derek, did you know Charles's daughter?"

"Claudette? Yes, I did. A lovely girl. Her death was a real tragedy. Poor Charles couldn't accept it, and we were all quite worried about him. Philippe in particular, naturally." Derek returned to his work once again. "To tell the truth, Charles hasn't been what you could call happy since the girl died. That is, not until these past couple of weeks or so. It's you, of course." He spoke almost absently. "You've filled a void. You're like a daughter to him."

"Yes, I really believe I am. Derek, did you know

that Claudette and I share a birthday, that she would be exactly my age had she lived?'' Daye laughed a little nervously. ''You know, I might not be here if it was not for that coincidence.''

''Really? It doesn't bear thinking about, my sweet.'' He grinned.

''No, it doesn't,'' she said seriously, her mind drifting back to the night she had met Charles. ''I was so unhappy and Charles was terrifically kind even before he knew it was my birthday. When he did find out, he said it was fate and began to talk about Claudette. Then I started telling him my problems, and here I am!'' She realized Derek was watching her, the grin still creasing his face. ''Oh, dear, I was rambling, wasn't I?''

''A bit. Oddly enough, though, I understood.'' He walked over to her and held out his hand. ''That's enough for today. Come on, let's go to the bungalow, and I'll make you a nice cold drink.''

As they walked the short distance that separated the studio and bungalow, the drone of an airplane's engine drifted on the breeze. The sound grew louder and Derek said, ''They're home, Daye.'' He stopped and looked up. ''There they are.''

Daye looked up, too, shading her eyes against the sun's glare. The small aircraft was obviously coming in to land. *Oh, God,* she thought suddenly, *what if Philippe crashed! What if he should be killed!* Her hand dropped to her side, and she closed her eyes tightly. . . waiting.

''Well, he's landed,'' Derek said, and she opened her eyes to find him looking at her oddly. ''Were you nervous?''

"No." It was not a lie; she had not been nervous, she'd been frightened to death. "The sun was so bright," she offered in explanation.

In the charming living room of the bungalow he shared with his sister, Derek made her a gin and tonic. Earlier this week Derek had introduced her to the drink, which happened to be his favorite, and Daye found its tangy taste pleasing. She sat curled in the corner of the comfortable flower-patterned sofa and sipped it, thinking how nice Derek was, how much fun to be with, and how she wished... how she fervently wished she could feel as relaxed as she had been such a short time ago. How could she though, knowing that soon she would see Philippe again? The past days had gone so quickly, yet now she felt as though she had not set eyes on Philippe for months.

Derek had come to sit beside her. "Looking forward to meeting the celebrated Melisse Montand?"

Daye gulped her drink. How could she, even briefly, have forgotten that Melisse would be with Philippe? "What is she like?" she queried, ignoring Derek's question.

He looked thoughtful. "Melisse is attractive, charming, generous and affectionate. I think you'll like her."

Daye very much doubted this. "Since she has so many wonderful attributes, how could I not?" She tried not to sound acerbic and had to restrain herself from adding cattily, "Denise doesn't like her."

Derek gave a short burst of laughter. "She is also temperamental and somewhat conceited. Does that make you feel better, Daye, my dear?"

She opened her mouth to protest, but instead she

raised her glass and quickly finished her drink. "May I have another, please, Derek?"

"False courage?" Derek's blue gaze was perceptive.

"Of course not! I'm thirsty, that's all." She avoided his eyes.

"If you are trying to quench your thirst, you won't do it this way. How about a plain tonic with lemon?"

"I like it with the gin." Daye felt impatient. "Oh, come on, Derek, I can have two drinks, can't I?"

"Certainly you can." Derek took her glass and went to replenish it. "Only don't drink this one so fast or you'll end up sick."

She knew he was right so she merely smiled at him. "Will Audrey be home soon, do you think?" she asked, after a moment or two.

"I imagine Philippe will drop her off shortly." He came back to give her her drink and once again sit beside her.

"Oh!" Daye had not expected this. "Will he come in with her?"

"He might if he knows we are here. Otherwise I doubt it. Why?" Derek looked amused. "Don't look so scared, Daye, you're decently, if scantily, clad—" his narrowed eyes took in her brief white shorts and red-and-white halter top "—and we're not up to any mischief, are we?"

"And if we were, I can assure you Philippe would blame me, not you." The words were out before she could prevent them.

"What makes you say that?"

She shrugged. "Oh. . .he thinks I'm some sort of femme fatale."

"You do have the right equipment to be one,"

Derek teased. "Tell me, my dear, did the big French brute warn you to keep your pretty hands away from his *bon ami*?"

"Not exactly. He said if I let you paint me you would fall for me." She knew the drink had loosened her tongue.

"I could do that anyway."

"That's what I told him." She looked at him anxiously. "But you won't, will you, Derek?"

He laughed. "I'll try not to. Look here, Daye, don't let Philippe upset you. I'm sure he doesn't mean to, he just—"

"Oh, but he does mean to!" she interrupted, unable to control her agitation. "You should hear the things he says, as if he hates me!" Daye took a swift gulp from her glass, her eyes watering as the liquid stung her throat. "But hate me or not, Philippe Chavot doesn't hesitate when it comes to kiss—" She pressed her fingers over her mouth. "Oh, dear, I'm giving away secrets."

Derek said calmly, "You're not much of a drinker, are you, sweet?" He pursed his lips, eyeing her contemplatively. "I had a feeling that was the way things were going. I'll have to have a talk with my pal, I can see."

"Oh, no, Derek, please!" Daye felt her panic rise. "I don't want him to know I've even mentioned him."

He nodded. "All right, I won't say anything. Not yet, anyway. Not unless things get out of hand." His expression was enigmatic. "It will do Philippe no harm to be kept in the dark for a change. I mean, about your confiding in me," he quickly explained when she looked puzzled. "Audrey may have gone to the house with Philippe and Melisse,'' he stated. ''If she did, and Charles mentions we're together, she'll probably wait there for us.''

Derek was correct in his assumption, they found, when they returned to the house almost an hour later. Daye had put off leaving the bungalow for as long as possible by persuading Derek to give her another drink and staying stubbornly curled up in the corner of the sofa. She had not uncurled until Derek said gently, ''The sun will go down in half an hour, Daye. Either we let Charles know you'll be staying here for dinner, or I take you home.''

Daye had almost grasped at the proffered straw, but it was no use putting off the inevitable for any longer. Philippe and the woman who was quite possibly his mistress had to be faced. With a sigh she got to her feet and was a little taken aback when the room seemed to tilt. She laughed rather foolishly and said, ''Come on then, Derek. I'll give you a race.''

''Oh, no, you won't!'' He caught her arm and held on to it. They had used bicycles today and had left them propped against Derek's studio. ''If you do anything silly, I'll make you walk,'' he threatened as they left the bungalow.

She did not do anything silly—at least not intentionally. But she knew she was not riding too steadily. In fact once or twice she almost ran into Derek's front wheel. Instead of taking this seriously she began to giggle and then to laugh, and before long Derek was laughing with her. They were still laughing when they went into the house and as they passed one of the tall, gilt-framed mirrors that hung in the hall, Daye stopped and stared at herself. She wore no makeup and her already tanned face was even more flushed from the warmth and the laughter. And her hair! "Oh, look at me," she cried woefully, trying to smooth her windblown hair. "What a sight I am, Derek."

"A lovely sight. You look like Nature Girl."

"Who's she?" Daye inquired innocently, and Derek laughed and kissed her on her neck, lifting up her hair to do so.

It was while his lips were still nuzzling her neck that Daye saw another reflection appear in the mirror, and she stared for what seemed endless moments, mesmerized by a pair of pure gray eyes. Then she swallowed. "Derek, stop it," she whispered. "Please!"

He lifted his head and saw Philippe reflected in the mirror. "Phil!" he turned to greet his friend, warmth in his eyes.

Philippe smiled but his eyes were cold. "It is late, is it not? *Mon père* was, I believe, becoming concerned." His eyes slid to Daye and deliberately moved over her.

She quivered for a moment, feeling naked and vulnerable. Then her spirit returned and she twirled slowly, seductively, as though modeling her brief outfit. "Well, have you seen enough?" she asked saucily.

"Naughty, naughty," Derek muttered, but Philippe simply stood there, his eyes fixed on Daye.

Then he said in a low, controlled voice, "Her eyes are huge. What has she been drinking, Derek?"

"Would you believe three *mild* gin and tonics?" Derek grinned.

"Don't tell him! You don't have to." Daye slid her hand through Derek's arm and gave Philippe a defiant look. But her courageous stand was not going to last much longer, she knew. Philippe was here, and all she really wanted at the moment was to walk into his arms. She turned her head away. "Let's go to find Charles and Audrey," she said, pulling on Derek's arm.

"They are in the salon with Melisse," Philippe said stiffly.

For a brief second she hesitated. "How nice. Take me to meet her, Derek."

"Would you not care to change your clothing first?" Philippe asked.

She spun to face him. "Why? Will my scant attire shock your lady friend?" She spoke tauntingly.

Philippe appeared to be struggling to keep his temper. "Nothing shocks Melisse," he said at last. "I was foolishly considering *your* possible discomfort." He strode past them, opening the salon's wide double door and standing aside waiting for them.

Daye gave his determined face one quick glance, hearing Derek say, "Philippe, old pal," before she hurried into the salon. Her eyes focused immediately on Charles, but as she went toward him she was conscious of Audrey and another woman, dressed in white, who sat beyond her line of vision.

Charles hugged her tightly then looked into her face. "You look sixteen with your windblown hair and wide eyes. You have enjoyed yourself, *petite*?"

"Yes, I have. Oh, Charles, I do hope you were not too worried.

"*Non, non, ma chère*. I knew Derek would guard you well."

"But Philippe said you were becoming concerned."

He tilted his head. "Did he? Ah! Perhaps it is he who was concerned." He spoke in a low voice.

Daye stiffened. Of course, Philippe would have been concerned. After all, she was with his *bon ami* and that *bon ami* must be protected against someone like her. She turned in Charles's arms and saw Philippe was watching. She was sorely tempted to wrinkle her nose at him but satisfied herself with a glower of defiance.

"Hello, Daye." Audrey's greeting was warm. "Has my baby brother behaved himself?"

"He most definitely has," Derek broke in. "Hello, sister mine. *Bonsoir*, Melisse. You're looking lovely as always."

"*Bonsoir*, Derek." The pleasant husky voice caused Daye to turn her head toward the sofa where the woman sat.

Although Melisse Montand was seated, Daye could see she was tall; she could also see the figure in the white linen dress was extremely well proportioned. She was possibly thirty or so, and though she was not exactly beautiful she was outstandingly attractive with flashing dark eyes, creamy complexion and full, shapely mouth. Her dark hair looked thick and lustrous and she wore it in a smooth style that covered her ears and was fastened low on her nape. She looked, Daye thought, more like a Spanish *señorita* than a French *mademoiselle*.

Charles performed the introduction and Melisse said, "I have been watching you and I am quite overwhelmed. What an exquisite face you have." She smiled, showing beautiful white teeth. "Sit here beside me, *mademoiselle*, or may I use your so unusual first name?'' Her English was excellent, her husky voice charming.

Daye sat down, supremely conscious of her brief shorts, her slender tanned legs against the blue velvet sofa. She wished now that she had gone upstairs to change and wondered how Philippe had guessed she would feel uncomfortable.

Melisse was speaking, leaning forward slightly, and a wave of perfume enveloped Daye. The scent was familiar and for an awful moment she almost burst into laughter. Melisse was wearing Golden Dreams. She had no idea why this should amuse her; perhaps those drinks she had taken had something to do with it. She was certain they were to blame for the headache she was now suffering. Unconsciously she put her fingers to her temples and massaged.

''You have a headache?'' Melisse sounded sympathetic.

Before Daye could answer, a voice said curtly, ''Drink this,'' and a glass was thrust at her. She gazed at it blankly before looking up to meet Philippe's totally unsympathetic expression. ''It is water,'' he said mockingly. ''I assume you must be thirsty.''

''She has a headache, *pauvre petite*,'' Melisse explained.

''Vraiment!''

Daye felt sure he was being sarcastic, and she got to her feet, ignoring the glass in his outstretched hand. ''If you will excuse me,'' she said to Melisse, ''I have some tablets in my room, and I need to change, anyway.'' She waved a vague hand at Charles, who was conversing with Audrey and Derek, and hastily left the room.

When she reached her suite, she took two headache tablets before running a bath. Terii was not around and Daye felt mildly annoyed because she could have used the girl's help this evening. As she stepped into her bath she reflected that Terii had been absent several times lately, and even when she was here she was inclined to be sullen. Was the girl upset about something or was she suffering from *fiu*, an ailment common among the Polynesians. It was not an illness, Daye knew. *Fiu* was merely a word for boredom or exhaustion or perhaps plain laziness, but when it struck, the victim found it impossible to work. "That is why we have a Chinese butler and a French cook," Charles had laughingly told her.

Daye hurried with her bath and then slipped into a short-sleeved silk dress in a pale lilac color. She had not had enough time to wash her hair, but when she had finished brushing it she was satisfied that it shone as though freshly shampooed. Critically she stared at her reflection in the mirror. Her eyes still looked overly large but since the effects of those gin and tonics had worn off it couldn't be that, she told herself. So it must be nervousness, excitement. Because Philippe had returned, because tonight she would experience the painful delight of being able to look at him.... She closed her eyes. But Melisse was here, too, and she would have to watch them together. Jealousy burned like hot coals inside her, and she despised herself for the sensation. Under other circumstances she could easily have grown to like Melisse Montand. As it was, she felt she hated her.

Presently Daye went downstairs, steeling herself for the evening ahead. The salon doors were evident-

ly ajar for she could hear voices. Among them was
Derek's, which meant he and Audrey would be staying for dinner, she happily reflected as she started
across the hall.

"Mademoiselle!"

Daye swung around, startled, and saw Paul beck-
oning to her from the half-open door of the cloak-
room. It was not far from the front door, and there
was no need for her to pass the salon to reach it.
"What is it, Paul?" she asked rather sharply when
she joined him.

"Mademoiselle, please, I wish to speak to you. In
private."

Uneasily she hesitated, but after a moment went
past him into the cloakroom. There was only a dim
light burning but she could see Paul looked distraught. Stifling her irritation she asked again,
"What is it?"

"I have had an argument—with *maman*." Paul
ran his hands through his hair. "It was most unpleasant. She knows, you see, that Melisse has arrived and
she has issued an ultimatum." His voice oozed
misery. "If I go to the guesthouse, if I speak to
Melisse when others are not present, she will persuade papa to leave Anani forever." He paused dramatically.

"Goodness." Daye gazed at him in helpless confusion. "That does seem a bit drastic, Paul, and I wish
I could help—"

"You can, *mademoiselle*, you can help me to see
Melisse, to play for her without *maman*'s knowledge."

"Oh, no, I couldn't!" Daye shook her head vehemently. "I can't be a party to such a thing, Paul.

Listen, I don't believe your mother would really ask your father to give up his work here and leave.''

"She would! You do not understand! Where Melisse is concerned, where my music is concerned, *maman* is... is obsessed!'' Paul's voice rose but immediately lowered. "*Mademoiselle*, I am young. If we leave Anani I will recover, I will find a way to go on with my music. But it would destroy papa if he were to leave. He has devoted so much of his life to the island, to the children he teaches.''

Daye moved restlessly. "Then perhaps you should do as your mother asks. As you've admitted, Paul, you're young and you'll find a way to carry on with your music. Next year you go away to school—your chance will probably come along then.''

He drew himself up stiffly. "You are heartless and cruel, *mademoiselle*. You tell me to submit to *maman*'s blackmail when you know how much my music means to me. Melisse can be of great help to me in this and—''

"But I can't!'' Daye broke in. "Really, Paul, it seems to me you must learn a little self-control.'' She bit her lip as Paul's expression registered tragic surprise. "Oh, dear, I'm sorry, Paul, but I.... Look here, couldn't Charles speak to your mother? Or Philippe—would he help in some way?''

"*Non*, they would not help. Not if it meant by losing the argument with *maman* they would also lose papa.'' Paul's mouth turned down at the corners. "What will Melisse think when I do not go to see her? She will expect me.'' He gave Daye a sidelong glance. "Melisse once suggested I leave Anani—go to Paris. There is a fine school there where I could study. If I did go, it would solve the problem, *n'est-ce pas?*''

"Do you mean leave without your parents' permission? It would be running away, Paul. Besides, where would you get the money to do this?"

He lowered his eyes and did not answer.

Daye suspected Melisse had offered him funds if he decided to leave, and anger against the woman flowed through her. "Don't do it, Paul. It isn't right," she said sharply.

He sighed. "I doubt I would have the courage. *Mademoiselle*, will you do me a favor, *s'il vous plaît*? Will you explain to Melisse the reason I cannot meet her?"

"All right, I'll do that," Daye promised. She could not entirely agree with Paul, and definitely she could not agree with Melisse. And yet she also felt a wave of anger toward Denise, who allowed her unreasonable hatred to cause her only son such misery.

CHAPTER TWELVE

THE EVENING was one of the worst Daye had ever spent. From the moment she entered the salon, her lilac dress swirling silkily about her legs, Philippe had looked at her with supreme indifference. Accustomed as she was to being the object of his attentions, which ran the gamut from anger to desire, his indifference came as a brutal shock. It caused a half-forgotten incident to creep to the surface of her mind, and for a few moments she was back in London, at some party or other where a young man had urged her to dance with him. "I've been staring at you all evening," he had said, "but you've looked right through me. I would rather you had looked at me as if you hated me than have you look so completely indifferent."

Daye knew, now, just exactly how the young man had felt. At the time, however, she had been merely bewildered by his words.

During dinner, when Derek began to discuss the sketches he had done of Daye and the fact that he wanted her to begin sitting very soon, she was sure Philippe's indifference would disappear. "All right, Derek," she agreed, "I'll be ready whenever you say. But since I don't intend going to Papeete, you will have to look through my wardrobe and tell me what to wear." She stole a hasty glance at Philippe, but he was apparently absorbed in his food, for he showed no reaction to her words.

"So you will paint the *petite Anglaise*, Derek?" Melisse looked interested. "Such a painting will bring you a small fortune, *mon ami*."

"But it won't be sold—not ever." Derek spoke with assurance. "One day, though, I might give it to Daye as a wedding present. Or to her husband, if I think he's worthy of her." He smiled at Daye.

"A gallant gesture." Charles applauded, and Audrey smiled too, while Philippe merely looked blank.

Dinner was almost at an end when Kao came in and spoke quietly to Philippe. The Frenchman nodded, a slow smile lighting his face. "Vairea and Mari now have a son," he announced.

Amid the pleased comments Melisse's laugh rang out clearly. "*Chéri*, you could not sound more proud if you were the new papa."

"Perhaps not." Philippe raised his glass. "To the son of Mari and Vairea."

They all raised their glasses and drank, then Charles said bluntly, "Mari is one year younger than yourself, Philippe, and he has four little ones. Four. And you, *mon fils*, have none."

"Which is fortunate, considering my unmarried state," Philippe answered dryly.

Everyone except Daye laughed, and Melisse added, her husky voice tinged with reproach, "And if Philippe were married, he and his wife might prefer to have no children."

There was a short silence. "That is ridiculous! Philippe is a Chavot. The Chavot men always desire children. And what woman does not possess the *na-*

turel urge to hold her own *bébé* in her arms?"
Charles sounded offended.

"Some do not." Melisse gave him a defiant look.
"Sometimes a wife may prefer a career." She lowered her dark lashes and stared down at her long,
shapely hands. "Sometimes she will be regretful and
wish for another chance."

The silence was longer this time, and Daye was certain they all wondered if Melisse was talking about
herself. Was this the reason she and Philippe had not
married? Because he wanted children and she did
not? Daye's heart sank. But now Melisse wanted another chance, the chance to be Philippe's wife, the
mother of his children. She stared down at the rich
custard-and-almond dessert she had been eating and
felt she might be ill if she took another mouthful.

Audrey said softly, "I wanted babies but after two
miscarriages I was told to give up trying."

"Why did you not adopt? Is it not the thing to do
if you cannot have a child of your own?" Melisse's
voice held a fractious note, but she turned at once to
Charles and laughed. "You wish so for grandchildren, *mon cher* Charles, and yet you are virile
enough to father *enfants* of your own."

"That is so," Charles agreed smugly. "But, *ma
chère* Melisse, I would have to be certain to take for
my wife a woman youthful enough to bear those
enfants."

Daye sipped her wine as she listened to the light
banter, but her gaze fell on Audrey and she noticed
how the woman flushed and bit her lip at Charles's
words. Surely Audrey did not think Charles was
serious. He wasn't the sort of man to marry some
giddy young woman. She smiled quickly as Audrey

glanced her way, and after a brief hesitation Audrey smiled back. "Is your friend feeling better?" Daye asked, aware she'd had no chance to talk to Audrey yet.

"Much better, thanks. In fact yesterday Philippe took her for a nice ride. Melisse and I went too, of course." Audrey looked at Derek, who sat beside Daye. "Has Philippe told you about the land we looked at?"

"There has been little time to even mention it, *ma chère* Audrey," Philippe spoke gently. He always spoke gently to Audrey, Daye thought.

"Land?" Charles's eyebrows rose.

"Land. On which to build a house, papa," Philippe spoke blandly. "I intended discussing it with you at some other time."

"A house for yourself?" Charles frowned. "For what reason? Do you not own a charming *appartement* in Papeete?"

"*Oui*. But it is not large and—" Philippe paused "—perhaps I wish to build a home of my own."

"Philippe, does this mean you are considering marriage?" Charles asked the question sharply.

Another silence, as if they were all awaiting his answer. Daye knew that *she* was.

"Is it necessary for me to be considering marriage, papa?" Philippe laughed easily. "Come, may I not build a home in Tahiti if I wish? Even if I never use it?"

"*Mais, certainement*. Although I feel it does not make sense."

"But, Charles," Melisse said placatingly, "you might, one day, wish to marry. And if you did Philippe would feel like an intruder."

Philippe said, "Melisse!" in an annoyed tone. Then, "Papa, I—"

"Enough!" Charles put up his hand. "We will speak no more on this subject tonight." He raised his wineglass and drained it. "Come, *mes amis*, let us adjourn to the salon."

But once there Melisse excused herself, claiming sudden exhaustion, and Philippe left with her, ostensibly to escort her to the guesthouse. Audrey and Derek left shortly after, but although Charles and Daye remained in the lounge for over an hour, Philippe did not reappear. Neither of them mentioned the fact, but when Daye kissed Charles good-night she knew he looked at her anxiously. Pride kept her smiling, made her say cheerfully, "See you after breakfast. Don't forget you promised me a much longer ride this time."

"I have not forgotten, *petite*, but since Melisse will undoubtedly join Philippe and myself, perhaps you would care to accompany us?"

Hastily Daye refused, using her inexperience as an excuse. The truth of it was she could not stand the thought of facing Philippe and Melisse in the early morning, after they had spent the night in each other's arms. She did not doubt this would happen, and as she climbed the stairs she tortured herself with the thought of the two of them together. At this moment, this very moment, they could be making love. Philippe could be murmuring to her—in French, of course—and Melisse would respond. . . .

Daye's insides felt racked and torn and she wanted to weep and continue weeping until Philippe was washed out of her system.

She felt that way frequently during the next three

days, for it seemed that Philippe and Melisse must be spending all their moments together. Neither put in an appearance until the evening, and while Charles explained this was not unusual as far as Melisse was concerned, he made no effort to explain his son's absence. Yet Daye was sure he knew, or suspected, exactly where Philippe was spending his time and exactly who he was with.

In spite of Philippe's constant company, Melisse did not appear to neglect her work. Frequently during the long hot days the sound of piano music could be heard, and once or twice Daye had lingered, just out of sight of the guesthouse, listening to a passionate rendition of a polonaise or sensitively played romantic prelude.

Daye had not yet delivered Paul's message; she considered it a private matter and preferred to wait until she could see Melisse alone. Actually, she was beginning to wonder if Melisse cared one way or another about Paul and his music, for she never heard the boy's name pass her lips and she was certain Melisse had made no attempt to contact him. Had the pianist's interest in Paul been a transitory thing? Was Denise all wrought up over nothing? Unless, of course, someone, Philippe perhaps, had suggested Melisse discontinue her efforts to help Paul.

Poor, poor Paul. Daye's heart bled to see him so unhappy. Each day at lunch he displayed little interest in his food and looked at her as if she were twisting a knife in his heart. Well, if he considered her to be cruel and heartless he would soon be over his infatuation for her, Daye concluded. Then she thought of Philippe and his subtle cruelties and wondered why she could not be as hopeful of her recovery from the emotional wounds he'd inflicted on her.

On the morning of the fourth day, Melisse had come into the hall where Daye was waiting for Charles. She was wearing smartly tailored riding breeches with a matching shirt, and she looked healthy, attractive and extremely sexy. "*Bonjour*, Daye," she greeted her. "You are going riding with Charles?"

Daye nodded, noting she'd reacted as she always did when Melisse was around. It was a strange sensation, almost as though she was fighting with herself not to like this woman. Then she remembered Paul's message and, before Charles could appear, quickly delivered it. Fully expecting Melisse to react somewhat indifferently, Daye was surprised when her full mouth tightened and her dark eyes flashed with anger. Quietly, almost viciously, she began to mutter in French and Daye noticed that she beat one clenched hand steadily against her thigh.

At last she seemed to remember Daye was standing there staring at her, for she said in English, "Denise is a bitch, is she not? She does not deserve a son such as Paul. *Pauvre petit*—he must be so upset. Small wonder that he did not come to me."

"What would Philippe have said if he had?" The words were out before she could stop herself.

"Philippe?" Melisse opened her dark eyes wide. "Philippe would not object. Unless, of course, he is aware of Denise's threat to remove Jean from Anani. He would not care to have Jean go away. None of the islanders would."

"Do you think Jean would actually leave?"

"Jean is an honorable and loyal man." Melisse

lowered her eyes and stared at her fingernails. "If Denise insisted, he would do so." She raised her eyes and looked steadily at Daye. Had they been standing closer Daye knew she could have felt intimidated by the woman's extra inches of height. "Jean would not object to my giving Paul the benefit of my experience. It is Denise who has...she is a bitter woman, a possessive wife and mother. She refuses to see that all I wish is what is best for Paul. For his future, his happiness. All she does see, all she believes, is that I am attempting to lure him from her side. Ridiculous, is it not?" Melisse smiled, but Daye sensed the anger in her. "Tell me, Daye, do you not consider it wicked of Denise to threaten her son, to give him such a choice?"

Daye, feeling trapped, avoided a direct answer. "I really can't believe Denise would ask Jean to leave Anani. Jean is her husband and she would know how much it would hurt him."

Melisse uttered a short, sharp laugh. "Perhaps it is Jean she wishes to hurt most of all." She spread her hands expressively. "But that is not my affair. It is Paul who is important; his talent must not be wasted." She spoke with grim determination. "You agree, do you not? The boy has confided in you, which means you are his friend."

"Yes, he has done that, and I do want to be his friend, but this is a difficult situation. To tell the truth, I sympathize with Paul, but I hate deceiving his parents."

Melisse gave her a long, thoughtful look. "Paul feels great affection for you, *n'est-ce pas?* He has fallen under your spell? One cannot blame him, for you are truly beautiful." The compliment was offered in a matter-of-fact tone, and she barely paused before saying, "I have learned Paul works here. It is so?"

Daye nodded. "With Monsieur Perrot. Are you going to see Paul?" She spoke tentatively.

"*Oui, ma chère.* I came here with that intention. Oh, do not be concerned. I'll be most careful. Denise will not find out."

"But Monsieur Perrot will be with Paul, I'm sure," Daye warned.

"Monsieur Perrot has known me since I first came to Anani. He will say nothing if I make the request." She made a movement as if to turn away, but instead she asked quickly, "You are free today? In the afternoon, perhaps?"

Taken by surprise Daye had to think. "I'm not sure. This might be the day I promised to sit for Derek."

Melisse shook her dark head. "It cannot be. Derek and Philippe have flown to Kahoa island. Something to do with one of the Chavot pineapple plantations, I believe." She spoke carelessly. "They will not be back until sunset. So, *ma chère*, you'll come to visit me? We'll talk and I'll make you a cup of excellent English tea." Not waiting for Daye to accept or refuse, Melisse flashed her charming smile and left Daye standing there, staring blankly after her.

ALTHOUGH MELISSE DID NOT APPEAR AT LUNCHTIME, it was more than evident that she had talked with Paul. There was an air of subdued excitement about him, and when he looked at Daye his eyes glowed with the old devotion. His appetite had returned, too, and while Daye felt relief because of this, she could not help wondering how Denise, his own mother, could have borne her son's unhappiness these past few days.

The guesthouse was just beyond the gardens and one used the path leading through an avenue of trees to reach it. Daye did so reluctantly and stood for a moment at the bottom of the steps that led to the veranda. It was a charming little house, painted white, with blue shutters and door and blue-painted veranda railings. Daye had never gone inside and she had no urge to do so now, since she knew this was more or less a love nest for Philippe and Melisse. But even as she stood hesitating, the blue door opened and Melisse stood behind the insect screen, looking out at her. "Welcome, Daye," she called. "I wondered if you had decided not to come."

Inside, the guesthouse lived up to its charming facade. The lounge was long, stretching from front to back and at each end was a wide window. One of these, at the far end, was a bay window and there an upright piano stood. Brightly colored rugs covered a polished wooden floor and the sofa and chairs were covered in flower-patterned chintz. Near the window at the front of the guesthouse, there was a round white table with two chairs. In the center of the table rested a bowl of crimson flowers and before each chair lay a lacy placemat. There was something about this that suggested intimacy, and Daye suddenly wanted desperately to leave.

But Melisse was urging her to sit down. "There is a tiny kitchen there." She waved a vague hand. "And through that door is the bedroom." She laughed charmingly. "The bed is not yet made and the room and bath are *so* untidy. Later I will send for someone to take care of this for me."

Daye sat in one of the small armchairs and looked about almost warily. There was nothing that she could see to indicate Philippe had ever been there, but why should there be when there was the bedroom and bathroom in which to leave personal belongings. Daye looked around to see Melisse watching her. "Er, do you do your own cooking, Melisse? I mean, you don't come to the house until dinner and I wondered. . . ." Daye's voice trailed to a stop.

"Cook? If necessary I can do so. But lunch is brought here by one of the maids and for *le petit déjeuner* I have coffee and croissants." Melisse moved over to her piano and stood there looking at Daye. "You would care for tea, Daye? Or is it too early to serve it?"

"A bit early, thank you."

They carried on a discontinuous conversation for a time, and Daye began to wonder why Melisse had invited her to come here. Then Melisse, who had not sat down since Daye arrived, suddenly seated herself at the piano and allowed her fingers to ripple the keys. Imagining she was about to play, Daye received a shock when the door to the bedroom opened, and Paul stepped warily into the room.

"Paul!" Daye stood up. "Oh, Paul, should you be here?" She turned to look at Melisse. "I think you should tell. . . ." She frowned, for Melisse did not look at all surprised to see the boy; she looked as did Paul, a trifle wary. "You knew, didn't you? You knew he was here?" Daye demanded. She looked from one to the other, a suspicion shooting into her mind. "Is that why you invited me here, Melisse? You think if Denise should turn up, she wouldn't mind so much if someone else was present?" Daye couldn't help a laugh. "I've met Paul's mother only once, and I can assure you my presence here would possibly make matters worse."

"*Maman* is wrong about you, *mademoiselle*," Paul spoke urgently, then subsided, looking as if he had said too much.

Daye had just time to wonder about this before Melisse rose and came toward her. "Do not be angry, Daye. I will admit I invited you here for a particular reason, but try not to be angry, *s'il vous plaît*." She moved to Paul and put her hand on his shoulder. "I hoped you would make certain Denise does not appear to surprise us."

"You see, *mademoiselle*," Paul said, before Daye could answer Melisse, "*Maman* has been twice to the office to see if I am actually there. If she does so today, Monsieur Perrot has promised to say that I am busy elsewhere. He will not lie, you understand, because I will be busy. The trouble is—" he bit his lip "—*maman* may be suspicious." Paul spread his hands in a gesture that seemed vaguely familiar and looked at Daye beseechingly.

"So what do you expect me to do? Lie in wait for your mother and...and knock her on the head, or something?" Daye felt angry.

"Come, come, *ma chère* Daye," Melisse soothed. "We will wish merely to have you sit beside the window where you can see the path. If Denise appears you warn us, and Paul will hide until she goes away. She will not remain long if she sees that you and I are having a friendly conversation."

"But it's deceitful! If I do it, I shall never be able to face Paul's parents again." Daye was distressed, partly because she meant what she had said, and partly because Paul had conspired with Melisse to persuade Daye into this deceit. And yet, deep inside her she knew she wanted to help Paul. If he was a true talent he should be given his chance. Daye ran her hands through her hair and with nervous fingers pushed it behind her ears.

"I beg of you, Daye; it's not so much to ask, is it?" This was Melisse pleading with her. It made Daye oddly ill at ease for she could not understand why the woman should be so determined she would humiliate herself by begging Daye's cooperation. Melisse, she was certain, was not the sort of woman who begged for anything. Of course, she was an artist and, as such, would deplore wasted talent. Besides which she had known Paul since he was a child, possibly since Denise and Jean first adopted him, and was most likely extremely fond of the boy. Daye was staring at Melisse and Melisse stared back. I'll help him no matter what happens, Melisse's dark eyes seemed to say.

Daye knew then that she had little choice in the matter. If Denise learned her son was defying her, Anani would probably lose its schoolmaster. The children would suffer in that case, along with the gentle Jean Dubois. Not to mention Charles, who would, Daye thought, be quite devastated if Jean should leave them. Daye drew in her breath and slowly expelled it. "All right, I'll help," she said in a soft voice. "But if you don't mind I'll sit out on the veranda. If she comes I'll let you know at once." She gazed at the two of them unsmilingly, but before either could speak she opened the door and went out.

It was not until she had curled into a large cane armchair that she had the feeling of having missed something. What was it? She racked her brain but whatever it was eluded her, and after a time when Paul—she thought it was Paul—began to play she allowed the elusive thought to slip completely away.

The afternoon passed pleasantly. Daye leaned her head against the back of the high chair, keeping her face turned toward the opening in the trees from which the path emerged. She enjoyed listening to the music, even if whoever was playing did frequently break off only to begin again and yet again. Melisse would talk with Paul between these breaks, and although Daye understood little of the French spoken she could tell Melisse was calling on a great deal of patience. This was rather odd, Daye noted, since she had considered Melisse to be a somewhat less than patient woman.

After a while she began to yawn as languor stole over her body. Her lashes drooped and the sound of Franz Liszt's "Un Sospiro" began to fade. But another sound hovered in the air, a sound that grew louder until it was practically overhead. An airplane! Were Philippe and Derek back already? Daye wondered if Melisse had heard and if she would now ask Paul and Daye to leave. But Melisse—for it now had to be Melisse—kept on playing, and presently Daye relaxed once again.

She came to slowly, aware that the piece now being played was something by Grieg and that someone was standing nearby, watching her. It was Philippe and she met his eyes drowsily before a sensation of almost devastating pleasure swept over her. "Oh, it *was* you, then," she said, smiling involuntarily.

He did not return her smile; he simply stood there looking at her in a way that made her insides tremble and her heart swell with love for him. "Oh, Philippe," she breathed, uncurling in one graceful movement and getting to her feet.

She would have gone to him had he not suddenly put out his hand. She subsided, sick with humiliation, her legs coming up against her chair. She wanted to go, run past him and get away, but he was near the steps, and she would have to brush past him too closely for comfort. So she stood there breathing heavily, her body shaking, until he dropped his arm and with his face set in firm lines walked past her and into the guesthouse.

Daye stood for some moments, willing herself to stop shaking and to move. There was no need for her to stay now. Philippe was here—let him handle everything. She walked down the steps and crossed to the path. When she reached the trees she stopped, unable to resist looking back.

Philippe had come outside again and was watching her. Even at this distance she could see his handsome face wore a bleak expression, but she was too distracted to wonder why or to even care that for the first time in days he had looked at her without indifference.

CHAPTER THIRTEEN

THAT EVENING, during dinner, Philippe asked casually, "You and Melisse will play chess as planned, papa?"

Charles nodded. "We are looking forward to it, are we not, Melisse?"

"I look forward to your surrender for a change, *mon cher* Charles." Melisse raised her wineglass, smiling.

Last evening, before she and Philippe left for the guesthouse, Melisse had challenged Charles to a game, and Daye learned the two of them often played when Melisse visited Anani. "She was taught by me when she was but a child," Charles had said, "and she has become a worthy opponent. Philippe, unfortunately, does not care for the game, but perhaps one day I can persuade you to learn, *petite*?"

Before Daye could answer Philippe had spoken. "Audrey plays chess, can you have forgotten, papa?" There had been a resentful note in his voice, as though he considered his father was neglecting Audrey. And if Charles was doing so, Daye reflected unhappily, it would mean another black mark against her in Philippe's book.

Now, remembering this, she stole a glance at Philippe's handsome face, lowering her lashes when she found his eyes were on her. If Charles and

Melisse played chess this evening what were she and Philippe expected to do? Quickly she decided to excuse herself early. Better not to see him at all than to know he sat near, his mind only on the woman who would later lie in his arms.

"There will be spearfishing on the reef tonight," Philippe said suddenly. "It is a feat Daye should not miss."

"That is so," Charles agreed. "However, there will be other nights of spearfishing."

"Since you and Melisse will be involved in your game, I considered taking Daye myself." There was no expression in his voice.

Daye's eyes flew toward him and she felt her color rise. Had she heard correctly? Had Philippe actually suggested he take her out? Then with immediate suspicion she wondered why. What was he up to? Lately he had behaved as though she did not exist, yet now he was asking for her company. Could it be that an evening spent watching his father and his mistress play chess was too boring to contemplate? Or was he in the mood for an argument? About this afternoon and the obvious fact that she had been helping Melisse and Paul, perhaps? Not that it really mattered. Whatever his reasons she knew she wanted to go with him, wanted desperately to go with him. But in spite of this she heard herself say politely, "Thank you, but I don't think I—"

"*Mais, oui*, it is an excellent idea!" Charles broke in enthusiastically. "Melisse and I will be too absorbed to even notice your absence. Do you not agree, *ma chère*?"

Melisse, Daye noticed, wore a petulant expression. Evidently she did not agree with Charles. However, after a moment she nodded, raising her wineglass to her lips and gazing speculatively at Daye over the rim. "Unless," she murmured, lowering the glass and staring into it, "Daye does not wish to go with Philippe."

"Of course she wishes to go." Charles's tone was unusually sharp.

"Shall we allow Daye to answer for herself?" Philippe spoke smoothly, and when Daye glanced at him she found his clear eyes watching her intently. "Would you care to watch the ancient art of fishing by torchlight—with me, *mademoiselle*?" he questioned softly.

"Yes." The word was out before she realized it.

Philippe merely inclined his head. It was Charles who said, "*Bon*, it is settled then! Come, let us not linger here too long; Daye and Philippe must change into more suitable clothing, while you and I, Melisse, keep our appointment with the chessboard. Ah!" he smiled broadly. "This promises to be a memorable evening for us all, *n'est-ce pas?*"

His words came to her a little later when, after changing into "suitable" clothing—slacks and a lightweight sweater—she reached the stairs to see that Philippe was waiting in the hall below. He, too, had changed, and was wearing blue denim slacks and shirt with white canvas shoes. For a moment or two she stood still, watching him as he paced the tiled floor with that familiar indolent grace. He was smoking, and although this was not unusual, she thought he smoked in a nervous manner. Immediately she dismissed the thought; Philippe was not the sort of man to be affected by nerves. She took a deep breath. It was she who was nervous.

She felt as if she had never before gone out with a man.

Philippe looked up, and she hastily composed her features and descended the stairs. He watched her without smiling, his clear gray gaze drifting over her contemplatively as if he wondered what lay beneath the pale blue clothing she wore. And, of course, he did know. She fought the emotions this knowledge provoked and gave him a faint, indifferent smile.

During the drive to the beach they carried on a polite, rather meaningless conversation, while Daye sat stiffly beside him, her slender fingers twisting together in her lap. Philippe drove expertly, handling the hills and curves with casual composure though at a speed Daye considered somewhat reckless. Philippe might not be a nervous type, Daye reflected, but he was definitely acting like a man with something on his mind. Could it have anything to do with her, and why he had suggested this outing? She fervently hoped it was nothing unpleasant.

When they arrived at the beach several small fires were burning and the women of the village, both old and young, were gathered there, as well as children, many of whom were curled fast asleep on woven mats. "When the men fish at night the women build fires to guide them through the lagoon," Philippe explained when she looked questioningly up at him. "It is no longer a necessity for them to do so, of course; the men now have lamps and torches to guide their way." He smiled at her, his face disquietingly attractive in the firelight. "It is a custom that was begun a very long time ago, and on Anani the natives are superstitious about the old ways."

Shaken by his smile and the unexpected clasp of his

hand over her own, Daye walked beside him toward the women. Brilliant smiles and cheerful voices greeted their approach and Daye recognized some of the faces, among them the elderly Repeta and Terii. Terii had not been at the house today at all, but Daye was no longer bothered by the girl's unreliability. In the three weeks since her arrival on Anani she had learned to communicate quite well with the rest of Charles's staff. She smiled at Terii, who acknowledged it with the curiously stiff little smile she had proffered of late. As usual Daye felt puzzled, but when the girl sidled up to Philippe, her smile an open invitation, it was all suddenly clear. Terii was in love with Philippe. It was in her dark eyes as she looked at him, in the way she said his name, the softness of her voice as she spoke to him in his own language. And when Philippe laughed and pulled teasingly at her long hair, she flung Daye an almost vindictive look that plainly indicated jealousy. Terii was jealous because she thought Philippe was interested in her. Daye recalled now that Terii's coolness had begun the day Philippe came to her room while she slept. Was she also jealous of Melisse, Philippe's "much good friend"? Poor Terii. Daye was as sorry for her as she was for Paul. And for herself, she silently added.

"There is Vairea. She will expect you to admire her son," Philippe said softly, and Daye saw Vairea sitting beside one of the fires, unabashedly breast-feeding her new baby.

He was a handsome, husky infant, and as Daye knelt down beside Vairea she felt a surge of some unfamiliar emotion. He was sucking with greedy enjoyment, his plump dark face intense, his eyes blissfully closed. Daye tentatively stroked his silky black hair and then the soft baby cheek. "He is so beautiful," she told Vairea, and as if she understood the woman gently but firmly removed him from her breast and handed him to Daye.

"Oh!" Daye breathed the word and laughed softly, cuddling the baby close. Unbidden tears rose to her eyes and spilled onto her cheeks. She had never held an infant this small and it filled her with a strange new wonder.

Then as someone touched her cheek she looked up, smiling, to see that Philippe was squatting beside her, an unfathomable expression in his eyes. "Why do you weep?" he asked shortly.

She blinked. "I'm not. Not really crying, I mean. It's just that I've never held a little baby before."

His eyes narrowed. "And when you hold your own *enfant*, will you weep?" Slowly his fingers brushed away the dampness on her cheeks.

"Probably." Daye tried to smile, not to let him see how his touch, his words affected her. She looked down at the baby and thought of how it would feel to have a child who belonged to her and Philippe. The knowledge that this would never become reality sent a coldness spreading through her heart.

She raised her eyes to find Philippe still watching her, and for a moment she thought desire flared in his eyes. But his hand left her cheek and he said in a curt voice, "Come, Daye, or you will miss what you really came here to see."

The coldness was still there. Only the baby in her arms was warm. Reluctantly she gave him back to his mother and got quickly to her feet. Philippe took her arm and silently they crossed the beach to the jetty.

There were several motorboats as well as two
launches tethered there, and Philippe swung Daye
into one of the motorboats before leaping agilely to
join her. Moments later they were cutting through
the still waters of the lagoon toward the light-
spattered reef, where, as they drew nearer, Daye
could see figures moving about and the slim shapes
of canoes beached on the coral.

But when they were still some distance away
Philippe cut the engine. "This is close enough," he
said. "The water is shallow and there are rocks as
sharp as any knife."

She could not suppress a shiver, both at his words
and at the relentless roar of the ocean breaking
against the rocks.

"It's all rather intimidating, isn't it?" She spoke
shakily.

"You are not afraid?" Before she could answer he
added reassuringly, "There is no need for you to
have fear. I shall not allow you to come to harm."
He uttered a mirthless laugh. "If I did, I would never
dare return to *mon père*."

So he had to let her know he held no personal interest in her safety! Daye said nothing, but she turned
her head and stared fixedly at the reef.

"If you would agree, you and I could return
tomorrow during daylight. You would find it very
beautiful and not at all intimidating."

Daye turned back to him once again, but the lights
on the reef were not bright enough to show his expression. "I . . . beg your pardon?" she said faintly.

"The water here is extremely clear and one is able
to see shoals of colorful fish and the more magical
colors of the coral. You would enjoy it, I think." He

spoke almost indifferently, but Daye sensed he was waiting, with some interest, for her answer.

She could not give him one, however. Her thoughts wrestled confusingly. You and I, he had said, which seemed to indicate the two of them—alone. But what about Melisse? The woman had not seemed particularly pleased about this evening's little outing; how ever would she react if there should be another one tomorrow? Did Philippe not care about Melisse's feelings? Was it possible he was growing tired of her? She tried to remember if Philippe had behaved differently toward Melisse and suddenly realized that he had never yet behaved like a lover toward the woman. He treated her with courtesy, friendship and affection but not as if he was her lover. And, come to think of it, despite her obvious disapproval this evening, Melisse did not behave as if she was in love with Philippe.

Which meant nothing really. When a couple had known each other, possibly as lovers, for so many years, they would be beyond public displays of affection and warm glances. It was when they were alone, in bed, that they would—

A startled gasp escaped her as lights, harsh and bright, flared into the darkness. The interruption cut off that last tormenting mental picture and showed her Philippe's face, his eyes regarding her steadily. "How bright the lights are," she said, longing for the comfortable darkness to return.

"Even this ancient art has added a modern convenience," he stated with mild cynicism. "Long ago, the natives used crude torches that they made from palm leaves."

She looked at the reef and then at her companion.

"Have you ever tried what they are about to do?"

He laughed in amusement. "*Oui*, I have attempted it several times. I cannot pretend I was particularly successful, however." He reached across the small space dividing them. "Watch now," he commanded, taking one of her hands and holding it tightly.

Although the warm clasp of his hand was inordinately distracting, Daye obediently turned her head toward the reef. Drums had started a rapid tattoo, and as she watched, lithe dark figures, dressed only in loincloths, began to run swiftly along the coral. Each man carried a fiercely glowing torch in one hand and a pronged spear in the other, the latter being used to strike out in all directions at huge gleaming fish that appeared either hypnotized or bedazzled by the brightness of the torch lights. Once caught on the spear prongs the fish were speedily transferred to the sack each man carried on his back. When the sack bulged the fish were unceremoniously tossed into the waiting canoes. Daye could see them heaped there, gills flapping, silver bodies feebly twitching. She tried not to look at them. The only thing she was enjoying about this evening was being here with Philippe. Almost as if he knew the line her thoughts had taken, Philippe said, "It will not continue for long. The men catch only the amount of fish needed." His hand tightened over hers. "Do you wish me to take you back, Daye?"

Quite suddenly, from across the lagoon, the women's voices rose in singularly sweet harmony. The drummers on the reef paused then, only to begin again, their rhythm changing to a hauntingly sensuous accompaniment. This, combined with the roar and tang of the sea and the drifting scent of night-blooming flowers, created an atmosphere that was primitive, paganlike—as if, Daye thought, they had gone back in time to the days when there was no "civilized" way of living—and loving. She sat there in the uncanny torchlit darkness, unable to answer Philippe—unable, it seemed, even to shake her head. Yet her blood was flowing too hotly through her veins, her heart was pounding, her mind overflowing with tantalizing thoughts. As if he, too, was affected, Philippe reached for her other hand, and she saw his lips move, forming her name.

How long they sat there she had no clear idea. She only knew her unmoving body strained toward him, and she longed for him to take her in his arms and make love to her until the stars dropped from the heavens.

She came down to earth when the voices and the drums ceased, and the glitter of the lights on the reef dimmed to mere flickers.

"It is all over." Philippe spoke in an abrupt tone as he let go of her hands and turned to start the motor.

To Daye the words held a double meaning. It was all over, she thought, the spearfishing, the magic, the emotions she had sensed in Philippe as he held her hands. She felt chilled, the unsatisfied longing to be in his arms leaving her with an aching sensation of loss. Soon the evening would be over, at least for her. But for Philippe would it be just beginning? Would he again leave with Melisse and spend the night with her in the guesthouse?

At the jetty Philippe tethered the boat before reaching to lift Daye out. His nearness was a delicious torment, and only innate pride prevented her from clinging to him, letting him know how she felt about him. But still it was difficult to let her hands slide from his broad shoulders with apparent indifference.

The village women were still gathered around their fires and, as they had done earlier, they called out greetings as Daye and Philippe approached. This time, however, Philippe merely raised his hand in acknowledgment before taking Daye's arm and walking determinedly past them. "If we are here when the men return we will find it difficult to leave at all," he said, explaining his reason for not lingering.

So he could not get this outing over fast enough! Obviously he wanted to get back to Melisse as soon as possible. Dejectedly she wondered again why he had invited her to see the spearfishing, and why, oh, why, had he suggested another outing tomorrow? But he had not pressed her for an answer to that suggestion—which meant he had most likely changed his mind.

She was wrong, as it turned out. Scarcely had they begun the return journey when Philippe asked, "You will go with me tomorrow?"

"Tomorrow?" She hoped she sounded as though she had forgotten all about it.

He flicked her a sidelong glance. "To see the lagoon. You have forgotten?" He seemed irritated.

"Oh, yes, the lagoon." She was tempted to ask in a cool sarcastic tone if Melisse would mind his taking her. Instead she said evasively, "I ride and swim with Charles in the morning."

"That is understood." It was he who spoke with cool sarcasm. "So it will be in the afternoon, *naturellement*."

She wanted to say, yes, yes, yes, but she kept her self-control. "All right, I . . . oh!" She put her fingers to her mouth. "I forgot. Tomorrow I promised to sit for Derek."

He muttered under his breath; the car gathered speed. Daye could see by the set of his mouth in profile that he was not at all pleased. Neither of them said anything, but the silence was alive with unspoken thoughts and emotions. It seemed to go on endlessly until something exploded in Daye's head and she asked tremulously, "Why did you take me out tonight?"

She heard the intake of his breath.

"I assumed you would find it interesting."

"The spearfishing?"

"What else?" Again he flashed her a quick glance.

"I don't really know that I believe you." Daye turned her head to stare at the unrecognizable objects flashing past. "You've never before cared whether or not I'd be interested in anything."

The car swerved slightly. "Have I not? Tell me, Daye, do you believe I intended making love to you tonight?"

His bluntness surprised her. "Of course not. In the village that day you made it clear. . . ." She hesitated. "I wouldn't have gone with you if I'd thought that," she added stiffly. But she knew she lied. And she wondered, deep in her heart, if she had not suspected this was his intention—even hoped that it was. She gave a ragged little sigh. "Well, thank you for taking me, anyway. I enjoyed it very much."

He laughed. "*Non*, you did not! I noticed your withdrawal when the fish were speared."

She looked at him in surprise. "I didn't like that part," she admitted. "I'm squeamish, I expect."

"Some would claim you are tenderhearted."

Daye could have sworn he had stressed that first adjective. "But you wouldn't?" she asked spontaneously.

He stared straight ahead without answering and presently turned the car into the long drive that led to the house. Near a lighted side entrance he parked, switching off the engine and headlamps. Immediately he said, "What would you say if I told you I did intend making love to you tonight?"

Her mouth felt dry, but she tried to speak lightly. "What changed your mind?"

He drummed his long fingers on the steering wheel. "Perhaps the idea of taking you beneath the trees held no appeal."

She gasped in sudden anger. "You flatter yourself that I'd have let you go that far, Philippe Chavot." Jerking the car door open she slid out, making for the house with blind urgency, knowing only that she needed to get inside, to get to Charles, before he caught up to her.

But it was not to be. At the door he forestalled her, pushing her back against the wall and pinning her there with his body. Apprehensively she stared up at him, her head resting against the cool stone. "Don't, Philippe," she whispered, stiffening her body and her self-control.

"Oui, ma chérie," he whispered back, his face lowering toward her own. She caught a glimpse of the arrogant confidence in his expression before his head blotted out the light.

Daye kept very still as he kissed her, her arms

hanging straight at her sides, her body rigid. The silent battle she was fighting was incredibly difficult, for every nerve in her body struggled frantically to respond. But she refused to give in to temptation, and when at last Philippe raised his head to frown at her in puzzlement, she knew she had won.

He continued to frown at her for what seemed a very long time. Then he gave his usual shrug and moved away from her. "Congratulations, *mademoiselle*," he said with soft mockery. He offered her a slight bow before going over to open the door, holding it until she pressed herself away from the wall and went past him into the house.

Daye would much rather have gone directly to her suite, but had she done so Charles would have suspected something was amiss. Sensing more than actually hearing that Philippe was close behind her, she made her way to the salon where Charles and Melisse, their game apparently at an end, sat arguing amiably. Fixing a smile on her face, Daye asked brightly, "Well, who won?"

Charles tapped his forefinger against his chest, his expression smug.

"Philippe *mon cher*, come and give comfort to the loser." Melisse spoke woefully, raising her attractive face to Philippe, who laughed, bending at once to kiss her full red mouth.

It was the first time Daye had actually seen him embrace Melisse and she was shocked by the raw pain that pierced her. It was followed by anger so intense she wanted, for a ghastly moment, to turn on Philippe and scratch and claw at him like a cat. Quickly she sat down, her legs weak, her body suddenly cold. What if she and Philippe *had* made love this evening? Would he still have spent the night with Melisse? She knew a frantic urge to get away from everyone, especially to get away from this room; she felt she could not possibly remain here until Philippe took his mistress to the guesthouse.

She suffered through an interminable half hour before she could excuse herself and escape upstairs. There she spent over two hours pacing aimlessly, her mind in complete turmoil, before crawling into bed to fall into an uneasy sleep.

SHE AWOKE SUDDENLY, with the overwhelming impression that she was not alone in the room. Too drowsy to be exactly frightened, she rolled onto her side to switch on the bedside lamp, her eyes moving automatically to the door. Philippe, dressed only in his denim trousers, was leaning indolently against the jamb, his eyes narrowed, his lips curved in a mocking little smile. Bewildered, she stared at him. "What are you doing here, Philippe?"

"Did you not expect me?" One eyebrow quirked upward.

"Expect you?" Daye swallowed. "Of course I didn't expect you. Please...get out of here, Philippe."

He shook his dark head. "*Non, mon amour*, I do not intend to leave. At least, not until the morning."

"The morning?" Daye's heart began to palpitate. "Philippe, you can't!" She swung her legs to the floor, looking frantically about for her dressing gown. It was over the back of a chair—on the other side of the bed. She had the feeling if she moved to fetch it he would stop her. "What...what do you want?"

"A foolish question, *ma chère*. You know quite well what I want." He straightened, as though to move toward her, then swayed slightly and put his hand on the doorjamb to steady himself.

For a moment Daye was puzzled, but enlightenment dawned and she blurted accusingly, "You've been drinking, Philippe."

He shrugged. "A little wine, that is all—I am not drunk." He gave her a wicked look. "The same cannot be said for *mon ami* Derek. It is doubtful he will be able to work on your portrait tomorrow."

Daye ran her tongue over her dry lips. "You were with Derek? I thought you were with...." Just in time she stopped.

"I was with Derek," he agreed, "and also with Mari and the other men." He straightened again, this time remaining steady. "Daye, *mon ange, ma belle*, let us not waste time talking." He took a step or two toward her.

She thrust out her hands. "Don't come any closer! I don't want you here. Why...why aren't you with your mistress?"

His dark brows raised. "My mistress? And which mistress is that, may I ask?"

"So you have more than one on Anani, do you?" She spoke with reckless sarcasm.

His lashes flickered, shading his eyes. "Do you believe I would be foolish enough to allow my mistresses close to one another?" He gave her a smile that seemed to reach across the room to touch her. "Come, *ma petite belle*, what is it you are speaking about? Who is it you believe to be my mistress?" His voice coaxed her, his eyes, suddenly alert, roamed boldly over her.

Her pale green nightdress was short and sheer. All she wore beneath it was a pair of tiny panties. He had seen her in less, but the knowledge did not ease the sensation of total vulnerability that consumed her. She wrapped her bare arms about herself, staring at him defiantly. "I'm sure Melisse wouldn't care to know where you are at this minute."

"Melisse?" He frowned. "Melisse would...ah, I see. You believe Melisse to be my mistress." A smile touched his mouth. "You are mistaken, Daye, she is not my mistress."

She wanted desperately to believe him but she dared not. "Oh, go away!" she whispered urgently.

Instead he came very close, open admiration and desire in his eyes. *"Comme tu es belle,"* he murmured huskily. Daye, *ma chérie, le bon Dieu* knows I have tried to resist you, to put you from my mind, but I cannot. What am I to do? I shall go mad if I am denied you for much longer."

She began to tremble. "No, you won't. You will go to Melisse and she...she'll give you what you want."

"She cannot. Only you can do that." He put out his hand but did not touch her. "Only you, Daye."

She backed away until she touched the wall. "I don't believe you. How can I, when every night you go with Melisse and...and you don't come back." Her voice quavered in betrayal.

Philippe's hand fell to his side. "This distresses you?" He sounded surprised.

"Of course not!" Daye wrapped her arms even more tightly about herself. "I just...I just....." She stopped, staring at him wretchedly.

He muttered under his breath and came to her

quickly. With a deliberate movement he took her wrists and gently forced her arms downward, all the while holding her eyes with his own. "If it distresses you, tell me, Daye." He spoke urgently. "It is something I must know."

She shook her head, pressing her lips together.

He took her in his arms, lifting her up against him so that she felt the warmth of his body penetrating her flimsy attire. *"Petite,"* he murmured hoarsely. "So small and beautiful. *Embrasse-moi. Chérie*, put your arms around me."

The wine on his breath must be intoxicating her, Daye thought wildly, as she obeyed him without question, locking her hands behind his neck and eagerly meeting his waiting mouth. They kissed... and kissed again and again, their lips clinging with a passion as hot and primitive as the tropical night. Philippe's arms were hard and strong. He held her in a strong embrace, straining her slim body against him. This was where she wanted to be, and she did not care if he ever let her go. She closed her eyes and gave herself up to the warm, sweet desire flooding her being.

Slowly, and with evident reluctance, Philippe's mouth left hers and he set her on her feet. She opened her eyes, swaying unsteadily, her arms still tightly clinging so that he had to bend toward her. His face was still close, and Daye could see it glistening damply, could see his eyes burning fiercely between the black lashes. She wanted to speak his name, but could not. Her breath shuddered through her lungs and escaped her parted lips and she could only gaze up at him, mutely beseeching. Philippe must have found something in her face that satisfied him—what it could be she did not know—for he smiled. "I knew I was not mistaken. Tonight, on the lagoon, you felt as I did." His strong fingers pushed into her long hair, twisting the silky strands into wild disorder. "Ah, how I wanted you," he said thickly. "But I could not be satisfied with a stolen hour beneath the palms. I want to hold you throughout the night, *ma belle chérie*. When I awaken, it is your face I wish to see before anything else." His hands moved to gently cup her face. "*Mon amour*, I am desperate for you. So desperate, I do not care who will be hurt if you become mine. Do you understand?"

Daye nodded, not really understanding but totally uncaring. She was remembering the way he had said *mon amour*. His love! He had not said it with teasing mockery this time, but with a passionate tenderness. Oh, if only he truly meant it! If only he loved her! But no, he was only desperate to possess her body, and the tenderly spoken words were all part of the game. Yet she would not let this knowledge come between them. Her love for him was rich and warm inside her, and she wanted to become his no matter what the consequences.

Still unable to speak, she turned her face so that her lips pressed into the palm of his right hand. *I love you, love you,* she silently told him, and as though he had heard, a tremor ran through him.

He turned her head, gazing down at her for an endless moment. Then without a word he gathered her against him. His kiss was fiery and seductive, his lips moving with soft persistence over hers until they parted. And as he had done once before, he ran his tongue tantalizingly between them, stroking over them until this time her own tongue wandered, driven to meet his. At once he groaned, his body shaking noticeably, his kiss deepening into total possessiveness.

Daye's own body was shaking, attuned to his, inflamed by a raging excitement that left her unable to think. Acting purely by instinct, she pressed closer, moving her hips enticingly, her excitement growing in intensity as Philippe stiffened, his hands slipping down her spine to hold her against him. Making a low tortured sound, he released her mouth and muttered against it, "You are driving me mad, *chérie*." Almost impatiently he loosened his arms and held her a little away from him. Then, with his burning gaze devouring her, he slid her nightdress up over her trembling body and let it fall to the floor.

But there was no impatience in the way he touched her. He did so deliberately and with concentration, his hands moving in light torment as they molded her from breast to thigh. Over and over he shaped her body, until her blood seared her veins and her senses whirled with wild ecstatic desire. The potent sexual needs he had brought to life that day beside the pool could not begin to compare to what she felt now. "Love me, love me."

She heard the words echoing through her brain, and when he whispered, *"Oui, mon amour,"* and took her mouth with devastating sensuality, she knew she must have cried the words aloud.

He lifted her into his arms and laid her on the bed. Weak with desire, she watched him remove his denims, and when he came to her and slipped her brief panties over her hips she could barely move to help him. Yet she came alive when he lay beside her, unhesitatingly going into his arms and fitting her body to his. Their mouths joined, moist and hot. Their bodies writhed together, legs tangling in such a shattering intimacy that Daye, bedazzled as she was, suddenly knew how inevitable was their coming together. She tensed, more apprehensive than afraid.

Perhaps sensing this, Philippe stopped kissing her and raised himself, leaning on his forearm to look down at her. "I wish to give you pleasure, *chérie*," he whispered thickly, and proceeded to fondle her breasts with possessive fingers. "Does this please you? Or this?" He bent his head, his parted lips following his hand, grazing lightly, titillating her, sending thrills, like small electric shocks, darting to her nerve ends. When she thought she could endure no more, she gasped, her hands moving restlessly over the dark head at her breast. Philippe lifted his mouth just enough to say, "Tell me I please you. Let me hear you say it." His tone was quietly passionate.

"Yes." It was barely a whisper. "You please me, Philippe." But as his hand slid over her, seeking to explore more intimately, she uttered a sharp cry, her stomach muscles contracting, her senses flaming. "No!" she cried. "Don't!" Yet her body was accepting his sensuous touch, wanting these new delights to last forever.

"*Chérie.*" Philippe suddenly pulled her very close and began to mutter in French. He sounded strange, incoherent, and when he at last spoke in English she still could scarcely understand. "Please me, *mon amour*. Touch me, hold me." His breath came harshly and Daye obeyed, moving her hands lovingly over his virile body. His skin was damp with perspiration, his pulses pounded heavily. She knew this emotion was for her, knew Philippe was out of control. But so was she, her mind accepting nothing but the exquisite pleasure she was experiencing.

"This is torture!" Philippe spoke against her mouth. "*Chérie*, I can wait no longer." His body moved over hers, his hands slid beneath her. Daye felt no fear at all, the need for satisfaction surpassing all emotions. Only as she instinctively moved her body to accommodate him did she feel a vague anxiety because she might not be able to please him. . . .

"Philippe."

The voice was soft, yet it penetrated the passionate drumming of her heart. She tensed, her fingers ceased their convulsive movements against his back, her eyes opened very wide. Philippe's face was just above her own, his forehead beaded with perspiration, his eyes heavy lidded with desire. He stared down at her, perplexity flitting over his face. "*Chérie*, what is wrong? It is too late to change your mind," he muttered thickly.

Daye gazed up at him mutely, her arms sliding away from his body. As she did so she heard his name spoken once again, and this time he heard it, too.

He went quite still, his dark brows drawing together in a deep frown. Slowly he turned his head and Daye heard the oath he uttered as he rolled away from her, pulling up the sheet to cover her nakedness.

He appeared unconcerned by his own lack of clothing. Sitting on the edge of the bed with his back to Daye, he lashed out at Terii in French, the words sounding bitter and furious. The Polynesian girl listened, her dark eyes scarcely blinking, her full mouth shaped into a sullen pout. She waited, not moving, until Philippe stopped berating her, then said placidly, "But Philippe, you tell me to wait in your room, and I do. I wait long time while you drink with men." Terii cast a suddenly angry look at Daye. "You did not say you go first to her." She pointed an accusing finger.

It took a stunned moment or two for Terii's words to sink in, and when they did Daye felt she wanted to die. A low moan escaped her and she rolled onto her side, covering her face with her hands.

"*Mon Dieu!* Daye, do not listen to her, I beg of you. The girl lies!" Philippe spoke in a harsh tone that became even harsher as he switched to French, evidently lashing out at Terii again. While he was doing so, Daye slipped hastily out of bed, tugging the sheet with her and wrapping it around her. Philippe, she noticed almost indifferently, had somehow retrieved his denims and was standing, fastening the belt. He turned swiftly to look at her, his handsome face strained and somehow pale despite his tan. "Daye, listen to me, *s'il te plaît*. It is not how you think. Terii will explain, she will admit the truth or I...." He broke off, striding toward Terii, who had edged her way to the door. He looked so threatening Daye thought he was going to strike the girl, but he grabbed her arm and pulled her roughly over to where Daye stood. "Tell *mademoiselle* you lied. Tell her I did not ask you to wait for me." He spoke between his teeth.

Terii lowered her eyes. "*Très bien*, Philippe." She looked up a glint of malice in her eyes. "Philippe did not ask me to wait, miss." The words were mouthed without expression, like an obedient child. Then she turned to Philippe and smiled eagerly. "Did I say properly, Philippe?"

"Too properly, as well you know." Philippe let go of Terii's arm and stared broodingly at Daye. She stared back almost blindly, the sheet clutched around her body. She felt chilled to the bone and very sick; what was even worse, she felt betrayed. Something of these feelings must have shown for Philippe said quietly, "You are pale, *chérie*, will you not sit down?"

He attempted to take her arm but she stepped back giving him a wild look. "Don't touch me! Just get out. And take Terii with you." She uttered a short laugh. "But of course you would do that without my telling you."

His mouth tightened. "She will leave; I will not. We have much to discuss."

"We have nothing to discuss. Not ever. So will you both please go?"

He did not move, but he spoke to Terii and after shooting a venomous glance at Daye, the girl moved gracefully to the door. No sooner had she reached it she turned back to say softly, "She is angry, Philippe. You will need Terii now?"

Still he did not move. "If I see you again tonight, *ma fille*, I swear I will break your neck." He sounded as if he meant it and Terii must have thought so, too, for she made a hurried exit, the sound of the door closing behind her seeming loud in the silence.

Philippe broke it to say, "You cannot truly believe what you are thinking, Daye. Surely you must understand Terii imagines herself to be in love with me. Unfortunately she also imagines I will become hers if she eliminates her competition." He smiled faintly.

Daye did not answer. She was wondering if she could reach the bathroom and lock the door before Philippe became aware of her intentions.

"*Chérie*, ask yourself how the girl knew we were together. Would she come in here on chance? *Non*, of course she would not. Obviously she was spying; she has done so before."

Daye's chin went up. "On you and who else? Melisse? Or do you have other women here on Anani? Besides the two I know about, of course." Pain injected a quavering huskiness into her voice. "Do they line up for you, Philippe? Is your sexual appetite so insatiable that you...." She stopped as he moved forward, an angry glimmer in his eyes. "If you so much as touch me I'll scream the house down," she told him in panic.

He put up his hands in a placating gesture. "*Très bien, chérie*, I will not touch you. You are upset, *naturellement*; I, too, am upset. But if you will listen to me I am certain you will understand."

"Will I? Would you understand if you were in my place?"

He shrugged. "I should attempt to do so. At least, I should listen to your explanation."

She gasped, hurt and frustration making her abnormally angry. "How dare you say that! How dare you lie! Starting with that night in Paris you've accused me of all sorts of things and you've never listened to me or tried to understand. Well, have you?" she demanded.

"Evidently not." He shifted his bare feet restlessly. "I have been unreasonable, Daye, and I will, I promise, try to make amends. But, *chérie*, it is the present that is important. This situation between us must be resolved. I do not believe I can tolerate it much longer.''

"You mean you want me back in that bed?" Her tone was scornful.

He sighed. "That is not what I meant. However, I cannot deny it is what I would like. *Chérie—*" his voice deepened "—has tonight meant nothing? Has it not proven we belong together?"

"We? You mean you and I...and Melisse and Terii, perhaps? Anyone else, Philippe?" Her voice held hysteria and she wondered if she was going to break down.

Philippe's face darkened, but he spoke calmly. "Have you finished, *chérie*?"

"I don't know. And stop calling me *chérie*. You haven't the right."

"That is true."

Misery welled up inside her and the cold sickness returned. She took two steps in the direction of the bathroom but the trailing ends of the sheet hampered her. "Please, please, leave me alone," she pleaded, feeling the color leave her cheeks.

He ignored her obvious distress. "Give me the right, Daye. Go with me to Tahiti. We can live in my *appartement* until a house can be built for us there."

She ignored the sudden leap of her heart. "So you are still trying to get me to leave Anani, are you?"

She saw his hands clench. "And you are trying to make me angry, *n'est-ce pas?*" He sighed again. "We cannot make our home on Anani, as well you know. It will be difficult enough for *mon père* to accept, but he will recover much faster if we are out of sight."

Daye knew what he meant. Charles would not ap-

prove if she became Philippe's mistress; consequently, they would not be able to stay on Anani. But the
problem would never come up. She had no intention
of becoming his mistress. Unshed tears burned her
eyes. She loved him, wanted him desperately, and she
might have been able to forget his association with
Melisse. But Terii—that child-woman who waited
while he made love to someone else. Oh, God! If he
asked her to marry him she would have to refuse
because she would never be able to trust him.

Bracing herself, she met his eyes. "No, thank you.
I prefer to stay here with Charles."

His eyes sparked fire. "In spite of all that has happened between us?"

Daye hesitated. "What has happened? I mean,
Terii interrupted before. . . ."

"Oui." He looked grim. "Had she not done so we
would still be in each other's arms. And tomorrow
you would willingly have agreed to leave Anani with
me." He raked a hand through his already untidy
hair. "*Mon Dieu*, I could throttle her!"

"I expect you could."

"Such a cold little voice." Philippe's eyes narrowed and he came close, looking down at her.
"Such a cold, beautiful face. Ah, *mon amour*, will
you not believe me when I say there will never be
another woman in my life if I can have you?"

If she could believe that she would go with him
anywhere. But of course she could not. She lowered
her eyes, unable to look at him without weeping. "I
don't feel well, Philippe, so would you please go?"

"*Chérie*, listen *s'il te plaît*," he sounded almost
desperate. "I have never made love to that misguided
girl—somehow I must convince you. And Melisse is

not...Daye, look at me." He grasped her chin and forced her face upward. Daye saw that he looked absolutely sincere and wondered if he could possibly be telling the truth. "I confess to you that once, long ago, Melisse and I were lovers, but not now, *chérie*, not for years." He looked at her intently.

She knew she needed to think about that—think about it when she was alone. If she could only be alone.... "Thank you for telling me," she said distantly.

His expression clouded with anger, and he let go of her chin and strode deliberately to the door. "Another maid will be found for you if you require one." He paused to look back at her.

"I don't. Thank you, anyway."

"Très bien." He inclined his head with a slightly mocking smile. *"Bonsoir*, Daye. I trust you will sleep more peacefully than I."

For what was left of the night Daye lay awake, her mind ravaged, her body a mass of tormented nerves. She had felt so relieved when Philippe at last left her alone, but as she lay there she knew if he returned she would not send him away again.

SOON AFTER THE FIRST SLIVER OF LIGHT APPEARED in the sky, she got up and slipped into a swimsuit. If she swam until she was exhausted she might be able to find relief in sleep, she told herself. Quietly she left her suite, her eyes going instinctively to Philippe's door. Would he ride as usual this morning? Was he even now stirring awake? Or had he, too, not slept at all? As she had done so often during the past hours, she remembered his expression when he said there would never be another woman in his life if he could have her. Had he truly meant it? Had he told the truth about Terii and Melisse? Exhausted and vulnerable, she felt more inclined to believe him. Longingly she gazed at his door, wishing she had the courage to go to him. Oh, if only it would open and Philippe would appear.

And open it did. But even as her heart leaped expectantly she saw the voluptuous young figure in the red-and-white pareu. "Terii," she whispered, feeling as if her lifeblood had suddenly drained away.

Terii closed Philippe's door quietly. "He still asleep," she said defiantly. "I much tired now. I go home to village."

Daye's lips parted, but she uttered no sound as Terii moved swiftly past her and disappeared around a bend in the hall. So Terii had waited for Philippe after all, and he had not sent her away. He had gone to his rooms needing a woman, and as angry as he was with Terii he had not hesitated to use her. Unless he had never been as angry as he had appeared. Perhaps it had all been an act, a lie. Philippe wanted her, desired her, she was sure of that. Perhaps when he felt this way about a woman he was unscrupulous about the way he won her over.

Oh, God! And only minutes ago she was wondering if she could have misjudged him, had actually begun to convince herself that she had done so. Because she wanted to, of course. Loving him, she needed desperately to believe in him. Lethargically she went back inside her suite and stood beside the sitting-room window watching the glorious morning unfold. She so loved it here on Anani; already it was home. But now she would have to prepare herself mentally for eventual departure. There was, she knew, no possible way she could endure seeing Philippe each day, knowing what he was; knowing, too, that she would always be fighting a battle with herself to stay out of his arms.

CHAPTER FOURTEEN

APPARENTLY SHOCKED by Daye's wan face and shadowed eyes, Charles readily accepted her explanation
of a "feminine problem" and insisted she return to
bed. Daye needed no second bidding, too unhappy
and numb with fatigue to feel guilty about lying to
him. She spent the rest of the day behind her securely
bolted door, opening it only to accept a lunch tray
from Suzy, a message from Derek cancelling—as
Philippe had predicted—her sitting and later in the
afternoon to admit a sympathetic Charles. After he
had gone, Daye gazed critically at her reflection in
the dressing-table mirror and told herself it was no
wonder Charles had suggested she have her dinner in
bed this evening.

It was as she listlessly drew a brush through the
tangles of her hair that she heard a door open, and
even as she swung around, remembering she had not
bolted the sitting-room door when Charles left,
Philippe was striding into her bedroom. Evidently
dressed for dinner, he wore the gray, that suited
him so well. Daye's eyes moved to his face, noticing his somewhat drawn appearance, the tight set
of his mouth. "Your door has been locked the entire day. To keep me out, I presume?" He spoke
curtly.

Daye nodded.

He sighed heavily. "Come, Daye, you are aware that we must talk."

She turned back to the mirror, still not answering. As she resumed brushing her hair, she could see Philippe's reflection in the glass and noticed he watched the action, his expression fascinated. Quickly she lowered her arm and he gave a start, his eyes meeting hers. There was no mistaking the flames of desire burning there, and Daye tensed, moving quickly away from him. "Please, will you go and leave me alone?" she asked dully.

"Have I not left you alone all day? Have I demanded to see you?"

"You couldn't very well. Charles wouldn't like—"

"As to that," he interrupted irritably, "I believe it is time *mon père* learned what is between us."

"There is nothing between us but a few kisses," Daye said stonily. "And I assure you that's all there ever will be now."

"You are so certain?" Philippe came to her, his hand reaching out to stroke her hair. "*Ma petite belle.* My lovely English girl. *Chérie,* I will come to you later tonight and we will talk. I shall explain about that foolish girl and all will be well between us."

After what she had seen this morning? Daye wanted to laugh and cry simultaneously. But she could not tell him what she knew, could not bear to see his face, hear him attempting to explain *that*. Bitter with misery, she pushed his hand away and said with exasperation, "Don't touch me! It makes me feel *sick*. Sick and humiliated. Oh, God, how I regret last night! Oh!" A shocked gasp escaped her as he raised his hand as if to strike her, then let it fall.

The following silence was absolute. They stared at each other—Philippe with total disbelief in his expression. She was remembering the only time a man had slapped her. Sam Milo had done so when she'd discovered those dreadful photographs and had become hysterical. Her flesh crawled, and when Philippe gently moved toward her she drew back with a nervous cry. "Go away, Philippe, I don't want you here."

"You cannot mean that."

"I do mean that, Philippe." Daye's back was to him and she did not turn before going into the bathroom and closing the door.

It was some time before she heard the door to the hall close, and only then did she give way to the tears burning in her eyes.

DURING THE NEXT TWO WEEKS she often wept, but always at night in the seclusion of her room and always because the preceding hours in Philippe's company had stirred her emotions to an unstable pitch. And yet, although the end to each evening was painfully inevitable, Daye would not have missed them. Despite the things she had said to Philippe—all lies, of course—she needed to be near him, to see him, hear his voice. It was an obsessive need, and she knew if she did not get away from Anani soon she might, in a weak moment, give her feelings away.

Before this happened she must, of course, leave. But although she had written to tell Reg of her decision, she had so far been unable to summon the courage to tell Charles, who seemed to be taking it for granted she would make Anani her home. He knew how much she loved it here, knew she had no obligation or desire to return to England to live, knew her so well, in fact, that there was nothing she could tell him—except the truth. And that she would avoid if it were at all possible.

While the evenings had been difficult these two weeks, the days, except for a few instances, had passed with considerable ease. Daye kept herself occupied, still spending each morning with Charles and the afternoons either posing for Derek—in the turquoise chiffon evening gown he had decided upon—or sitting on the guesthouse veranda while Melisse tutored Paul. Usually, when she was posing, Audrey would come to the studio and the two of them would talk while Derek worked. These were pleasant hours for Daye who found she could for a little while forget the heartache that tormented her. Except for one afternoon when the cause of her heartache unexpectedly turned up at the studio. Audrey greeted him with her usual warmth, Derek with a vague, "Hello, old man." Daye herself kept silent, but when he deliberately addressed her she felt compelled to acknowledge him with at least a brief nod. He stood watching her moodily until her skin crawled with nervous awareness.

It was Audrey who finally broke the tension by suggesting to Philippe he go with her to the bungalow for a cool drink. He acquiesced with a nonchalant shrug, and Daye turned her head to watch through the window as he and Audrey walked away from the studio.

"It never ceases to amaze me how blind people can be," Derek said suddenly. When she shot him a surprised look, he added, "For instance, it's perfectly obvious to me that Daye Hollister is crazy about

Philippe Chavot, but nobody else, including the man himself, seems aware of it."

"And I hope he never does become aware of it," Daye said, deciding there was no point in embarrassing herself with denials. "It would give him too much of an advantage, I think. Besides," she gave Derek an overly bright smile, "I plan to get over this little infatuation as quickly as possible."

Derek said no more but merely looked at her enigmatically and returned to his canvas. Automatically resuming her pose, Daye asked herself if Derek could be wrong when he declared nobody else was aware of her feelings for Philippe. She had wondered sometimes if Charles suspected, and there was the rumor Paul had told her about. Only that was a nasty rumor that suggested she was after a wealthy husband, not that she was in love with Philippe.

Without moving her head she looked toward Derek. "There's a rumor about Philippe and me, though. That I want to marry him for his money, I mean."

"Is there?" Derek shot her a curious look. "Well, I can tell you honestly I've never heard that rumor. Now stop frowning, my dear girl, you'll get lines in your forehead."

After a short silence Daye asked apprehensively, "You won't tell Philippe or anyone, will you, Derek?"

"You know damned well I won't," he answered mildly, and Daye expelled a shaky sigh of relief.

Philippe had not come to the studio again but only yesterday, while sitting on the guesthouse veranda, she had suddenly noticed him standing in the shadow of the trees. He was watching her steadily, and it was as if he emitted some sort of magnetism that drew her gaze in return. But when he began to stroll indolently across the grass toward the house, she jumped hastily to her feet and went inside, knowing she could not possibly handle being alone with him.

Presently when Philippe, too, entered the house, she told herself she would not stay here if he intended to remain. But when he settled himself in an arm-chair, her body refused to comply with her mind's wishes and she stopped there, sitting not far from him, trying desperately to concentrate on the music and Melisse and Paul, as though Philippe Chavot were miles away.

When Paul had to leave Daye went with him, but Philippe stayed with Melisse. Would they make love? Of course they would she thought as, blind with jeal-ousy, she walked along the path beside Paul. Philippe had lied about Terii so it stood to reason he had lied when he said he was not Melisse's lover. Unable to stop herself, she said to Paul, "Philippe doesn't appear to mind these assignations. Or is it that he ignores them to please Melisse?"

"It is, perhaps, both of those reasons. Philippe will not actually assist us, but I am certain he feels *maman* is unreasonable. He is sympathetic, you understand?" Paul was very serious. "Then, too, it is natural that he would wish to please Melisse. She is dear to him. They would, I believe, have married had not Melisse given herself to her career." He laughed sheepishly. "That is what I have heard. It may not be correct. Still, it seems possible, do you not agree?"

"Quite possible." Jealousy mingled with a sudden sharp anger, and she blurted, "You wouldn't have heard whether or not they are lovers at the present time, I suppose?''

She was ashamed as soon as the words were uttered. It was not the sort of question one asked a young boy. But when she looked up at Paul she noticed he was only slightly embarrassed.

"*Maman* claims they are," he said, "but since *maman* does not like Melisse...." He left the rest unsaid, and Daye took the opportunity to quickly change the subject.

TODAY PHILIPPE AND DEREK had flown to Tahiti on business and Audrey had accompanied them. She had suggested Daye take the trip, too, but although she would have enjoyed it, Daye had refused. Last night she had made up her mind that today, after their swim, she would tell Charles she had decided to leave Anani.

But it had not worked out as she had planned. Ironically, Melisse had chosen this particular morning to go swimming, and afterward she had returned to the house with them and was even now sitting on the terrace in her beach robe drinking a preluncheon sherry. Daye, who had slipped upstairs to change out of her swimsuit, could not help feeling somewhat frustrated. If Melisse had not turned up to swim with them the dreaded emotional scene with Charles would now be over. Frustration was washed away by a wave of depression. It would be over, and Charles would not smile and talk cheerfully during lunch. He would be dreadfully unhappy and so would she, but at least she would have no excuse for prolonging her stay.

It was Melisse who suggested that Paul play for

them after lunch. Charles, Daye noticed, gave a quick frown, but agreed nevertheless that it would be delightful so long as Monsieur Perrot could do without Paul for a while. Monsieur Perrot could, it appeared. Daye reflected he had been able to do so rather frequently, of late. It was obvious the elderly Frenchman nurtured a soft spot for Melisse and was prepared to do a great deal to please her. Paul, of course, was on cloud nine, his dark eyes glowing as he glanced from one to the other and came to rest on Daye. The smile he gave her was warm with affection where it had once been shyly adoring. So it appeared that Paul was recovering from his infatuation, she mused, possibly because of Melisse's attention and encouragement. Which was all to the good, but what would Paul do when Melisse left, as she had indicated she would be doing in ten more days? Would he turn again to Daye, embarrassing her with his attentions? Ten days. But by then she would most likely be gone from here, so she need not concern herself about it.

As he had done before, Charles listened to Paul for half an hour then went upstairs to rest. Afterward, Paul resumed playing, and now Melisse would interrupt to offer advice. At one point the two dark heads were close together, their profiles clearly defined, and as she had before, Daye received the impression that she had missed something of importance. Then like the sudden flaring of a light in darkness she knew what it was. Melisse and Paul looked alike. They had the same dark hair and eyes, the same nose in profile, the same...no, not the same mouth. Paul's mouth, his smile, although attractive, was not at all like Melisse's. Daye chewed her lip, unable to tear her eyes from the two at the piano. Really, they were alike enough to be related. Was it possible they were? After all, Paul was adopted. Perhaps a member of Melisse's family was his mother. . . or his father; perhaps his talent for music was inherited through this particular side of her family.

Daye bit down rather hard on her lip but scarcely noticed the pain. Melisse had one arm around Paul's shoulders, and she was looking into his face as she talked to him softly. In her expression was something almost possessively fond. An older sister might look that way. . . or a mother. But this was ridiculous! She was allowing her imagination to run wild simply because there was a resemblance, and because Paul was adopted. Besides, Melisse was not old enough to be the mother of a seventeen-year-old. . . .

The two at the piano were posed like statues, their wide dark eyes riveted on something, or someone, near the door. She followed their gaze, her heart giving an uneasy jolt when she saw who was standing there.

It was Denise Dubois, Paul's mother. Her slim body was strained, her fair skin flushed and her blue eyes sharp with fury. Slowly she advanced into the room, her eyes never leaving the frozen figures of her son and Melisse. Evidently she had not yet noticed Daye, but when she did she stopped moving and said in a strange high voice, "So you too take part in this plot to rob me of *mon fils, petite poule*?"

Paul sputtered, *"Maman!"* in a shocked tone.

Indignantly Daye got to her feet. "I've no idea what *poule* means, so I can't very well take offense, but I can and do take offense at your accusation. There is no plot, Mrs. Dubois; no one wants to take your son from you." Daye sighed, her temper fading. "Oh, this is so silly! Paul was merely playing for us. I don't think there is anything wrong in that."

"I do not care what *you* think!" Denise exclaimed angrily. She spun to face Melisse and Paul, who had risen to his feet. Whatever it was she said to them in French, it must have been outrageous, for Melisse's nostrils flared angrily and Paul's darkly tanned face appeared to pale. Several times he made an attempt to interrupt his mother but she raved on and on, her body shaking, her small-boned hands fluttering in agitation.

It was Melisse who finally managed to get in a few words, her voice snapping like a whip. But those few words were enough to cause Denise to cover her face with her hands and begin to weep. As responsible as Denise was for this horrible, embarrassing scene, Daye could not help feeling compassion for her. She was, however, considerably more sorry for Paul, who looked as if his world had come to an end.

To give the boy credit, he made an obvious effort to control himself, then he went to his mother and tried to put his arms around her. But she pushed him away, sobbing and talking at the same time. After a few more futile attempts Paul gave up, and with distress showing plainly on his young face, he hurriedly made an exit.

"Paul!" Melisse called his name and made an instinctive movement to follow him.

"Let him go, Melisse." Daye spoke with sharp authority, surprising herself as well as Melisse who raised one eyebrow, coolly quizzical. Nevertheless she did not follow Paul but instead seated herself gracefully on the piano stool. She did not even glance at Denise, who was still quietly sobbing.

Daye felt compelled to say something. "Mrs. Dubois, can I get you anything? Water, perhaps, or a little brandy?"

Denise shuddered and rubbed her hands over her eyes. Then she took a trembling breath and glared fiercely at Daye. "You can get me nothing! You are as bad as that one!" She pointed a quivering finger at Melisse. "She claims she wishes to teach him his music, but it is not so. She wishes to take him from me, take Paul from me, when he is mine, mine! And you!" she swung the pointing finger to Daye. "What do you want of *mon fils*? A youthful lover?"

Daye's mouth fell open. "What? You don't know what you're saying!"

"Do I not? I say you wish for a youthful lover. It is to be expected that Charles cannot satisfy you."

For a moment Daye did not quite understand. "What are you saying? Charles...oh, God!" She felt a sickening wave of shock. "How...how dare you! How dare you suggest Charles and I are...are lovers."

But Denise only laughed derisively, and after flinging Melisse a look of pure hatred, walked swiftly from the room.

For some time after Denise had disappeared through the doorway, Daye stood very still, seeing nothing. Then she looked at Melisse, who was staring down at the piano keys, and said unsteadily, "What she said about Charles and me...it isn't true."

"*Pardon?*" Melisse looked up. "Ah, I see. Do not fret, *ma chère*, I am certain only Denise believes such a thing." Melisse spoke absently.

Daye was not consoled. "But why should she believe it? Because I'm staying here?" She paused, remembering Philippe had said something about her presence in the home of two wealthy men causing speculation. "It's horrible! It's an insult to Charles as well as to me," she protested.

Melisse idly picked out notes on the piano keyboard. "What can it matter? It is known that you and Charles intend to marry quite soon." She gave Daye a guilty look. "That I should not have said."

Daye wondered if she was having a rather weird dream. "It's known that Charles and I will marry?" She spoke with difficulty.

"Ah, but I am sorry, Daye. You and Charles hoped it was a secret, *n'est-ce pas?* You wished to make the announcement and surprise everyone?" Melisse flashed a warm, understanding smile. "How could it be a secret when it is so obvious that Charles adores you? Besides, did he not give himself away to Philippe some weeks ago?"

"You mean that Charles told Philippe we were going to marry?" Oh, yes, she must be dreaming, Daye thought distractedly.

"Perhaps he did not use those exact words." Melisse shrugged. "Let me see.... *Mais, oui!* When Philippe returned home a few weeks ago, Charles told him you were expected to arrive. At first Philippe was certain his papa was playing the matchmaker—as he has often threatened—by bringing a young woman to be a guest in his home, but Charles made it most clear that you were coming to Anani to be with him, and that he hoped you would make the island your permanent home."

"And from *that* Philippe deduced I was to marry Charles?" Daye questioned incredulously.

"There were, I think, other indications," Melisse explained. "Charles had gone to great expense to decorate and furnish Claudette's suite for his *petite Anglaise*. He also, most mysteriously, refused to discuss you, and finally—" Melisse paused dramatically "—and finally, *ma chère* Daye, Charles did something he had not done for years. He shaved off his beard. To look more youthful, hmm? When Philippe met you he assumed, most naturally, that his papa was in love, and that you, so young and beautiful, could be interested in an older man only for his wealth."

"Philippe told you all this?" Daye was curious.

"*Mais, oui*, when we were in Papeete recently." Melisse's smile was reminiscent. "After an evening of dining and dancing, plus a little too much wine, Philippe was in a confiding mood. Ah, *pauvre chérie*, the idea of a stepmama younger even than himself is not at all pleasing, I think. And then, of course, there is the matter of small brothers and sisters." Melisse spoke with a hint of mischief. "A small *garçon* with black curls and a *petite fille* with golden hair and green eyes, *n'est-ce pas?*"

Daye experienced a moment or two of blank incomprehension before realization flooded her. Philippe must have told Melisse what his father had said that night...how long ago? Charles had been speaking teasingly of the grandchildren he desired and hinting, Daye was sure, at the possibility of a marriage between Philippe and herself. Afterward, she had assumed this was the reason Philippe looked so utterly infuriated, but all the while he was incensed because he thought Charles was referring to children he himself would father. Little brothers and sisters for Philippe Chavot. A spurt of foolish laughter escaped her, and when Melisse looked questioning she said, "I can't help it, Melisse. You see, I really didn't know what Philippe was thinking, what everyone was thinking. I've been such a fool. And...and so has Philippe. He should have questioned his father a bit more before jumping to conclusions."

Melisse looked rather bored. "It is possible that Philippe did not wish to upset his papa with so many questions. Since Charles's heart attack, he has been most protective. Overly so, I think."

"Since what?" Daye gasped, stunned. "Heart attack? Charles?"

"*Mais, oui.* Did you not know of this?"

"No! No, I didn't. When did it happen?"

"It has been three years, more perhaps. Do not look so concerned *ma chère*—it was a minor attack, I assure you. Charles was told he must limit his activities, business and otherwise, and this he has done."

Daye was scarcely reassured. "That's why he rests every afternoon without fail? Why he will swim and walk but won't play tennis?"

"It is a strenuous game, particularly in this heat. I wonder...." Melisse paused, looking down at the piano keys once more. Then she said softly, "Philippe worries, perhaps, that such a youthful wife will be a strain on his papa's health. He would, I think, prefer someone such as Audrey for whom he has always had a tender spot in his heart." Melisse smiled quickly at Daye. "However, I have noticed you and Charles when you are together, and I am certain your affection for each other will give you much happiness." Her fingers skimmed swiftly over the keys, producing a sound similar to the tinkling of crystal bells. "Still, one cannot help but wonder if you will find life difficult in the future. Charles is handsome and so *charmant*, it is true, but he is very much your senior." She stopped playing and turned her head to give Daye a direct look. "And Philippe is a beautiful, virile male animal, *n'est-ce pas?*"

Daye had listened to all of this, not knowing whether to be amused or indignant, and was about to tell Melisse there was absolutely nothing romantic in the relationship she had with Charles. Now she hesitated, saying after a moment's thought, "You think I might be tempted, is that it?"

"You are human, are you not?" Melisse laughed lightly. "As is Philippe. No matter how he resents you I am certain he will eventually be tempted. That is, of course, if he remains on Anani. If he is sensible he will live in Papeete. Already he has an *appartement* there and speaks of one day building a house. Who can tell—" she laughed again "—I might decide to share it with him."

Daye wondered if Melisse was warning her off, letting her know she shared an intimate relationship with Philippe, but at the moment she could not have cared less. There was too much to think about as it was—so much that she doubted her ability to deal with it. Later on she would have to try to sort it all out. She pushed back her long hair, her hands shaking. Melisse should be told the truth about Charles and herself. Everyone should be told—Philippe in particular. She wondered what he would say when he knew. He would be relieved, of course. He might even apologize for ever thinking that she was after his father's wealth. She was not too indignant about this now. In his shoes, she might have thought exactly the same.

But was it necessary that he go so far to protect Charles from her feminine wiles? Had it been necessary to make love to her? Oh, God! A heart-searing pain forced tears to her eyes. It was obvious, now, that his latest plea for her to become his mistress was, as it was on her first evening on Anani, an attempt to separate her from Charles. But on that first evening, although unaware that Philippe thought she was romantically involved with his father, she had at least guessed what he was up to. Since then she had become convinced that he truly desired her, wanted her for his mistress.

But he had not. He had never wanted her for more than the time it would take to assuage his passion. His plan, she was certain, had been to make her submit to him, to persuade her to leave Anani and live with him until he was satisfied that her relationship with Charles was irrevocably severed. And then he would callously send her away....

Daye moved restlessly to the French window and stared out at the sunlit gardens beyond the terrace. She could hear Melisse playing something exquisitely beautiful and rather sad. It was here in this room that Paul had asked her if she was to become Madame Chavot and she had thought he meant Philippe's wife. Philippe had heard Paul, of course. He had heard and thought her marriage to his father was imminent. The next day he had left for Papeete to fetch Melisse, and while there he not only confided in Melisse but perhaps brooded and plotted. When he returned he treated her with cold sarcasm because she and Derek were late in returning to the house and because she was slightly high after the gin and tonics. But after that, he had resorted to the indifference that had so upset her. All part of his plan, of course. Nothing like indifference to spark someone's interest. And then, when the opportunity presented itself, he had so cleverly offered to show her the spearfishing, knowing, she did not doubt, the effect the native drums, the singing, the entire sensuous pagan atmosphere would have on her. He had known she expected him to make love to her but, again so cleverly, he had not attempted to do so until they were back at the house. Her lack of response to his kiss must have surprised him, yet he was experienced enough to understand the effort she'd had to make to resist... experienced enough to know that later, when he returned, she would give in.

Daye clenched her hands at her sides, a desire for revenge momentarily obliterating all other emotions. How she would like to punish him! But she could, if only in a small way, by letting him continue to believe she intended marrying his father.

"You are distressed, are you not?" Melisse's voice interrupted Daye's thoughts. "Is it because you have discovered your romance is not a secret, or because of the scene caused by Denise?"

Daye walked slowly toward her. "Both, I expect. I...would appreciate it if you didn't let on to Charles that you know... about us."

"*Très bien*. But if he does not make the announcement soon he is bound to learn it is no secret."

Daye nodded, feeling guilty.

"As for this affair with Denise, you must not permit it to upset you. I shall make certain you are not blamed." Melisse spoke soothingly, the strains of a suitably soothing melody drifting from beneath her trained fingers.

Daye stifled a somewhat hysterical urge to laugh and said, "I'm not worried about being blamed for anything. But I don't like the feeling I have that I've helped to cause trouble." She frowned as a thought suddenly occurred to her. "Melisse, what if Denise persuades Jean to leave Anani now?"

Melisse kept on playing. "There will be no point in her doing so."

"What do you mean?" Daye moved closer to the piano and stood facing Melisse. "You mean you won't see Paul again? That is, you won't go against Denise by—"

"Do not be foolish, Daye!" Melisse interrupted scornfully. "The boy has great talent. I will not permit that creature to destroy him."

Again Daye frowned. "That *woman* has rights, Melisse. She is Paul's mother."

Melisse's full lips parted, as if she were about to answer, but instead she pressed them together again, curving them in a faint enigmatic smile. With an abruptness that was startling, she switched from the soothing lullaby to a rousing "Polonaise" and Daye stood there listening, wondering if Chopin himself could have looked more triumphant when he played his composition.

CHAPTER FIFTEEN

"PHILIPPE WILL NOT RETURN UNTIL TOMORROW, and Melisse has decided to dine alone in the guesthouse...which means, *mon enfant*, that you and I will have only each other for company this evening," Charles said, as Daye walked into the salon. "You will not find this boring, I trust?"

"You know very well I'll love it. A quiet evening with you is all I need at the moment." Daye meant this sincerely, yet, during dinner, her eyes fell on Philippe's empty chair and an almost demoralizing loneliness pervaded her being. It would be easier once she left the island, she told herself, for in England there would be nothing to remind her of him, no empty chair, no tang of cigarette smoke or that particular brand of after-shave he fancied. And there would be no clear gray eyes to watch her or heart-shaking smile to confuse her emotions, no charmingly accented voice to seduce her.... Daye's senses reeled and she had to force herself to concentrate on what Charles was saying.

Frequently, as they ate and made small talk, Daye felt Charles was looking at her curiously, but it was not until they were settled with their coffee in the homely sitting room that he softly stated, "You are troubled and unhappy, *ma chère* Daye. Do you not wish to confide in me?"

She had not intended doing so, but later she thought she must have subconsciously wanted to, for with barely a hesitation she spilled out everything that had happened in the afternoon. And to top it all, she ended by breathlessly blurting, "Charles, I've got to tell you. I'm going back to England."

Charles had listened without comment, his expression inscrutable. But as she uttered the last words a shadow crossed his face and he seemed as if he would protest. When he spoke, however, it was to tell her she must not blame herself in any way for the scene with Denise, that it was a situation that had been brewing for some time and that he would do his best to settle it once and for all. Then after a short pause he said mildly, "Last week, my cousin Henri asked when I would announce my betrothal to you. *Ma chère*, I was completely surprised, quite shaken in fact, although I have since then realized I should not have been. Philippe's attitude, his subtle remarks about your youth, the disapproving glances he bestowed upon you and me when we laughed and teased each other should have told me what he was thinking." Charles shook his handsome head regretfully. "It is true, *petite*, in the beginning I refused to discuss you at length. I did not believe it to be necessary. After all, you were coming to my island to see me, *n'est-ce pas?* And as for my beard—" he laughed with amusement "—although I do recall saying, merely to tease, that I had removed it to please you, the truth is I had debated doing so for some time. Ever since a certain lady very spiritedly accused me of hiding behind it." Again he laughed. "We were having a small disagreement at the time."

"Audrey?" When Charles nodded, Daye felt she

ought to encourage this line of conversation. Instead she heard herself saying crossly, "I agree that Philippe could have misunderstood at first, but later on, seeing us together, he should have known our relationship was platonic."

"Could our conversations have misled him? You have already mentioned that he misunderstood when we spoke of children; could there not have been other occasions when he did so?" Charles's expression was rueful. "And frankly, *mon enfant*, have we not openly demonstrated our affection for one another?"

"It never occurred to me that we shouldn't," Daye said defensively. "No, Charles, I think Philippe's been incredibly blind to be deceived this long. And really, you'd think he would have said something to us if our supposed romance upset him so." Daye stopped, looking at Charles anxiously. "Oh, dear, I *am* sorry. I know Philippe wouldn't say anything because of your heart. I'm not upsetting you, am I? If I am, you must tell me."

"Be calm, *ma chère*, be calm. My heart is not so delicate that it can accept only the pleasantries life has to offer. Philippe is...you must try to understand that Philippe's concern is perhaps overdone because he has lost so many loved ones. He lost his mother when he was but a youth, his beloved grandparents, and then his sister. Philippe dearly loved Claudette, *ma chère*. When I became ill he feared, I suppose, that I too would be lost to him." Charles spoke gently. "Can you understand this?"

She could certainly understand. She felt guilty now because she had once thought Philippe too cold and hard of heart to be affected by the death of loved ones. She lowered her eyes, staring carefully at her fingernails. "I suppose I've been dreadfully blind, too, in many ways. I mean, I've totally misunderstood things Philippe has said to me," she admitted. "Why, the day I met Père Martin and Philippe asked if I was becoming a Catholic to please you, I didn't even know what he really meant."

"He assumed you were preparing for our marriage."

Daye looked up. "Yes, I see that now." She forced a smile. "I suppose you could say there has been a lack of communication between Philippe and me." Except when we kissed, she added silently. He might have been acting a part, but when he kissed me we *communicated*.

"But soon now the truth will be known, *ma chère*," Charles said soothingly.

"I suppose so. I do wish, though, he hadn't thought it necessary to tell so many people what he suspected."

"How can you be certain Philippe did this? He told Melisse, it is true, but the others?" Charles's smile was faintly reproving. "Rumors begin and are spread, and one seldom discovers the true source." His smile faded and he asked somberly, "Audrey does not believe we are to be married?"

"I don't know for sure, but I would expect she does. And Derek, too, or at least he did. I remember now he was a bit surprised when I told him I cared for you as I would a father."

"Ah! He would, then, have told this to his sister." Charles sounded relieved.

"I hope so." Daye chewed her lower lip. Perhaps he had told Philippe also, she mused, aware now that her plan to punish him for a while longer had never stood a chance. She could only pray now that if Derek had spoken to Philippe, he had also remembered his promise. Oh, God! Her humiliation would be unbearable if Philippe found out that she loved him.

Charles's voice probed her thoughts. "Despite our close friendship we have kept our secrets, *n'est-ce pas?*" And when she raised questioning brows, "I have not told you that once I seriously considered asking Audrey to be my wife."

"Oh, Charles! Why didn't you, then?"

"I presented myself with many reasons, but in the end I decided Audrey deserved more than fondness and loyalty from her husband. You see, *ma chère*, I do not love Audrey—at least, not in the way I loved my wife, Claudine. If she accepted me in marriage she would be cheated, do you not agree?"

"No, I don't think so. In any case, Charles, you ought to have let Audrey decide. After all, she might not be able to love you as she loved her husband."

He chuckled. "How properly I am put in my place." He rose and came to sit beside her. "But it is two other people I wish to speak of now. Two people who were, I believe, fated to belong to each other from the moment they met. In Paris, was it not? In a hotel anteroom where the girl was given a fur coat for her birthday?"

Daye's eyes widened. "You know the Frenchman was Philippe?"

He nodded, reaching for her hand. "I suspected when you told me about him, although I said nothing. But after we parted, I returned to my suite intending to question Philippe, and if he was the man you spoke of, to demand he apologize. Philippe, however, did not return until almost four o'clock in the morning and he was, unfortunately, very drunk. As I assisted him to bed he did a great deal of angry mumbling and I learned about a so beautiful golden girl who sold her body to any man who could afford her. When he awoke several hours later it was quite apparent that he did not remember talking to me about you, and after some consideration, I decided not to tell him.'' Charles squeezed her hand and sighed. ''I decided to leave it to fate. If you came to Anani it would mean you and Philippe were destined to meet again. And when you did—ah! You would, of course, fall in love and marry. You would give me beautiful grandchildren and fill my heart with joy.''

Daye tried to smile but failed. ''How romantic you are, Charles. Now if this were a film or a novel it would end as you described. Only it isn't a book or a film, it's real life, and it isn't going to end happily for us all.'' Daye's voice thickened and she fought to keep her tears at bay.

Charles's grip on her hand tightened. ''You love Philippe, do you not? That is why you are unhappy? But, *ma petite*, I do not understand why you are unhappy. Surely you must know Philippe returns your love.''

She gave him a disturbed look. ''Why do you say that?''

''Because it is true. Surely you do not think Philippe objects to our marriage only out of concern for me? He does not want us to marry because he desires you for himself.''

''You can't know that for certain.''

"*Non, non*, that I admit. But, *ma chère*, it is so obvious. Have I not noticed the way he looks at you?"

"Disapprovingly, you said," she made herself speak carelessly.

"That is the way he looks at the two of us when we are together, *ma chère*. Come, do not pretend to misunderstand my meaning."

There was a silence while Daye struggled with the emotions rampaging inside her. If Charles should be right and Philippe did care for her, it could mean that he had wanted her to go away with him because he truly desired her for himself. It could mean he had no intention of leaving her when he considered he had broken up the relationship between Charles and herself. That awful evening when he lost his temper... he'd said it was time his father learned what was between them. Had he intended to confess all because he loved her?

She was swept by an incredulous, joyful hope that this was true; but then a picture of Terii leaving Philippe's room crept insidiously into her mind. Despair washed away all other sensations and she gave an audible shiver. It would make no difference if he did love her. Any man who could make love to one woman while another waited was incapable of deep, true and *faithful* devotion, and she wanted no part of him.

"You tremble, Daye." Charles moved closer and put a comforting arm around her. "I will speak to Philippe the moment he returns."

"No, no, no! Don't! Please, Charles, I would be so humiliated."

"I meant, of course, to merely inform him that we are not romantically involved. I must ease his mind, *petite.*'' He settled her head gently on his shoulder. ''You must promise not to speak of leaving Anani for at least a little while longer. After all,'' he chuckled softly, ''you would not wish to distress a man with a condition of the heart, would you, *ma chère*?''

''Oh, Charles, you're not playing fair, are you?'' Daye's voice was muffled. She would not speak of leaving again, she thought, she would just go. She would somehow arrange for a launch to fetch her, or she could ask Derek to help. No, she would not involve him, it was not fair to do that. Wait! Very soon they would all go to Papeete to celebrate Audrey's birthday and would stay there for two or three days. This would be the chance she needed to leave. She could catch a flight, any flight she could get that would take her out of Tahiti, and with care and luck no one would know until she was well on her way. Of course, she could not take all her clothes, a matter of little importance anyway. She doubted she would ever be able to look at her things again without remembering when she had worn them on Anani.

THE NEXT MORNING, neither she nor Charles mentioned the previous evening's conversation. But it was on her mind constantly, as was her decision to leave. While they rode and swam and sat drinking chocolate on the terrace, she thought that soon she would no longer do these things, that soon she would be in England where the wind was cold and the autumn sky frequently gray with rain clouds. Still, she would see Reg again. Dear Reg. She wondered what his reaction had been when he received her letter telling him she would be returning to England sooner than expected. Surprise? Delight? Oh, yes, she was sure he would be delighted. The letter she had received only a week ago had been filled with declarations of how much he missed her. If she married Reg she could be certain of his love and faithfulness. *If* she married Reg. Well, why not? She could never love him the way she loved Philippe, but love him she did. Yet even as she considered this, part of her rejected the thought of lying in his arms, allowing him to make intimate love to her. Oh, could she? After Philippe could she ever allow another man's hands to caress her body, his lips to kiss her with drowning passion? The surge of blood pounding through her veins made her feel faint, and it was only the sound of Charles's voice that kept her from collapsing into a shattered heap and weeping.

Only Monsieur Perrot joined Charles and herself for luncheon. Philippe had not yet returned from Tahiti; Melisse had not put in an appearance all morning, and Paul, Monsieur Perrot said, had decided to have his meal at home. Denise's orders, Daye wondered, or had Paul lied and gone to see Melisse? Would he do such a thing after that awful scene yesterday? One thing was certain, she told herself, disinterestedly spearing a piece of fish, she would never become involved with helping either of them again.

When Charles went upstairs soon after lunch, Daye wandered through the perfumed gardens, her heart heavy with sadness. She was so deep in thought that she did not notice she had moved in the direction of the guesthouse until it was suddenly there, ahead of her. Not wishing to have Melisse notice her and perhaps come out to call to her, Daye turned to go back through the trees. But even as she did so she saw the door opening and hesitated.

It was not Melisse who came out, however, it was Paul. He had seen her, for he walked hurriedly across the clearing toward her, one hand slightly raised as if begging her to wait. When he reached her he stopped, an embarrassed expression crossing his handsome young face. "You do not look pleased, *mademoiselle*," he said in a low voice.

"I'm not." Daye shook her head and turned away.

"*Mademoiselle*, wait, *s'il vous plaît*." Paul moved to her side, putting his hand on her arm. "I am going to Paris."

She stared at him. "Paris?"

"*Oui.* Do you recall I told you once that I might do this?" Paul took a deep breath. "I am pleased that you are here as I would not wish to leave without bidding you *adieu*."

"But... when are you going?"

He gave her an evasive glance. "I am not certain. As soon as arrangements can be made."

"Oh, Paul, don't do this!" Daye spoke impulsively, taking his hand in both her own. "Your parents don't know, do they?"

"*Non, non!* No one knows but you. And of course Melisse." His long black lashes flickered. "*Mademoiselle*, you must promise to tell no one of this."

"Paul, I—"

"Mademoiselle Daye, it is better for us all if I do this. I will have the life I wish to lead and papa will be able to remain on Anani. Already he and *maman* argue about this, so you see I must go." His eyes were beseeching. "You must give me your promise."

"Paul, tell your parents how you feel and I'm sure—"

"I have! Papa is furious because I have upset *maman* and will not listen. *Mademoiselle*, I beg of you! Your promise."

"All right, I promise." Daye spoke reluctantly. "Oh, Paul, where will you live? What will you do for money?" As if she didn't know, she thought angrily.

"Melisse has a house in Paris. I will live there." Evidently embarrassed, he ignored the question concerning money.

Daye gripped his hand tightly. "Paul don't do this! You are wrong! Your poor parents will be heartbroken. Oh...oh, damn it, Paul, Melisse has no right to encourage you to do this."

He stared at her, his eyes bright. "She has the right. She is my natural mother."

Daye was scarcely surprised. "I see. Did *she* tell you so?"

"*Oui.* I suspected it because of something she said to *maman* yesterday, and when I asked she admitted she was." His tone changed, became defensive. "She was my age when I was born—so young and already planning a career. She could not keep me, so she allowed my...the Dubois to adopt me. This she regretted later. I feel—" Paul lifted his chin defiantly "—I have a duty toward her. She *is* my natural mother."

"You have no duty to her, Paul." Daye tried to speak calmly. "You do have a duty to your parents, though. They raised you, taught you, loved you. It was Denise who. .who fed you, changed your diapers, took care of you when you were ill, did the thousand things that need to be done to raise a child properly. You know, Paul, I feel very sorry for her. No wonder she's been unreasonable, knowing Melisse was always hovering in the background trying to get you away from her.''

Paul pulled his hand from her grasp. ''You side with *maman*, and it is she who declared you were to marry Monsieur Chavot for his wealth. And yesterday she called you a *poule*. It is not a nice word as she meant it.'' He sounded distressed.

Daye frowned. ''Because your mother has been nasty to me, it doesn't mean I should take sides against her. Besides, she's in the right. I know she's been unreasonable about your music, Paul, but don't you think it's because she was afraid? Afraid because you had so much in common with Melisse?''

His expression showed confusion. ''But what of my career? Always she will oppose it. Sooner or later I would have to go my own way.''

''Let it be later, then. Next year you'll go away to school, and your mother will have time to get used to it. Who knows, Paul, she might change if you. . . if you show her you love her and appreciate all she has done for you.'' Daye clasped her hands in unconscious appeal. ''If you go away now, desert your parents for Melisse, you'll cause a rift that you won't be able to mend. You and Melisse could never come back to Anani, now could you? You might never see your parents again.''

''I had not thought of it,'' he muttered.

And Melisse would never mention it, Daye silently declared. Aloud she said, ''In less than two weeks Melisse will leave for her concert tour. When she has gone, your parents will calm down and you can discuss this properly."

He was silent for so long Daye was certain she had won, but then he gave a small, hopeless shrug. "It is no use, *mademoiselle*, I would give much to please you, but what you ask of me is impossible." He snatched her hand and raised it to his lips. *"Au revoir, ma chère mademoiselle."*

As he walked stiffly away from her, Daye tried one last time. "Paul, if you do this, I'll have no respect for you." She thought he hesitated, but then decided she was mistaken. Impotently she watched his tall, slender form disappear into the trees. She felt so angry she wanted to lash out at something or someone and almost involuntarily she swung around and marched to the guesthouse.

Melisse was seated in an armchair, an open book on her lap, when Daye walked into the room. "You have storm signals in your eyes, Daye," she said placidly. "You have spoken to Paul, hmm? And you do not agree that he should leave Anani."

"No, I don't. Melisse, this isn't my business—"

"No, it is not," Melisse cut in.

"But I'll say it anyway. You are entirely wrong to encourage Paul. Aside from the moral issue, you could get yourself into trouble. Paul's under age."

"His...the Dubois would not press charges against me." Melisse smiled. "They would not want a scandal."

Daye swallowed. "I can hardly believe anyone could be so cold-blooded, so hardhearted."

Melisse's eyes lowered. "You call me such names because I wish to give my son what he desires?" Her eyes raised. "You know he is mine?"

"I know you gave him life, Melisse. And then you gave him away," Daye said coldly.

A flicker of emotion crossed the woman's attractive face. "I was seventeen when Paul was born; there was no possibility of marriage or of keeping him. The Dubois had been married only a year but they knew Denise was barren." A mocking little smile touched her lips as she uttered the old-fashioned word. "Jean pleaded for the *enfant*, and I could see no reason why he should not take him. She rose gracefully and began to walk up and down the room. "You think I was foolish giving the *enfant* to a family with whom I was acquainted?"

"It wasn't too sensible. I mean, you knew you might see him when you visited Anani."

"True. But I intended returning to my studies in Paris, which meant I would not visit Anani too often." Melisse paused beside the piano and drummed her fingers on the polished surface. "It did not occur to me that I would become so interested in the child."

Daye tried to curb her curiosity and failed. "Didn't your parents object to your giving up your baby?"

"Mama was dead. Papa had remarried and was living in Versailles. Paul was born in a private hospital in Queensland." Melisse spoke abruptly.

"And what about the baby's father?"

"Did he object to my giving up the child?" Melisse gave an amused laugh. "*Mais, non*, he was most delighted."

"Oh." *What an awful man,* Daye thought. "Did he help you, er, financially?"

Melisse shrugged. "Charles made all arrangements

and paid all the bills. He was most generous, *n'est-ce pas?*"

Daye turned away, staring almost blindly about the room. Why had Charles done so? Because Melisse was a family friend or for another more personal reason? Philippe had admitted he and Melisse had had an affair, could it have ended in her becoming pregnant? Was Paul Philippe's son? But if he was, surely Philippe would have married Melisse, or, if she had refused him, at least given the boy his name and a home in his father's house. Of course, seventeen years ago Philippe himself would have been only eighteen. Perhaps he and Melisse had not told Charles who was the child's father. . . .

"Will you tell Denise and Jean about Paul's intentions?" Melisse spoke sharply.

Daye turned her head. "What? Oh. No, I promised Paul I would tell no one. I wish I hadn't, though. Someone should stop him." Daye decided to make an effort. "Melisse, you can. Tell him you've changed your mind about helping him. Please. I'm afraid Paul will regret it if he leaves his parents."

"How can he possibly have any regrets? He will study music, which he loves, and I will be with him as frequently as my schedule allows." Melisse moved to seat herself at the piano. "You will excuse me, *ma chère* Daye, I must practice."

"At least think about it, Melisse." Daye's temper, which had cooled, threatened to boil again. "Think about Paul and what he will be giving up."

Melisse did not answer. Instead she picked up a stack of sheet music and began to look through it. Daye gave an exasperated sigh and went to the door. She had opened it when Melisse said, "Would you not like to know the name of Paul's father, Daye?''

Daye stood quite still. Then she answered, "No, thank you,'' and went out, closing the door firmly behind her.

THAT EVENING there was to be a dinner party attended by three couples Daye had not yet met. Derek and Audrey would be present, too, which meant there would be twelve of them in all. Daye felt inordinately relieved about this. She could not hope to be unaware of Philippe, but at least the presence of several others would be distracting.

She dressed in a cocktail-length gown of cream silk jersey. It was long sleeved but with a wide neckline that left most of her shoulders revealed and dipped in a low V at the back. It was a dress she had worn before, but tonight she felt she did it more justice because of her deepening tan. This was as deep a tan as she could permit, she told herself. It would not suit her to become too brown and besides it would ruin her skin. But that was something she would not need to worry about much longer. In England her tan would quickly fade.

She stifled a sigh and pulled tentatively at the curls dangling in front of each ear. When Suzy came up with her afternoon tea, Daye had, with the help of the French language book Audrey had given her, asked the girl if she could help her put up her hair. Suzy proved to be surprisingly deft and the resulting hairstyle was attractive and suited Daye very well. Having Suzy helping her reminded Daye of Terii, and she wondered, as she had frequently wondered these past two weeks, if Terii was still in the house. She had never noticed her, so if she was she obviously stayed somewhere in the servants' quarters. Except perhaps at night when she would creep upstairs to join Philippe in his bed. If he wasn't in Melisse's bed, that is....

"Oh, stop it!" Daye said aloud. "You're being masochistic, *mademoiselle*." She swung away from her mirror and made her way swiftly toward the door.

She opened it just as Philippe was passing and she stopped, standing in the doorway staring at him. She was aware that he had returned from Tahiti. Late this afternoon she had heard the drone of the plane's engine. But coming upon him so suddenly was a surprise and a thousand nerves sent shock waves sizzling through her body. Her legs weakened, her face felt stiff, and she clutched the doorknob as if it was a life support.

Philippe spoke first. "*Bonsoir*, Daye." His eyes did not move from her face.

From somewhere she found her voice. "Hello, Philippe. How are you?" Such an inane question to ask, she silently scoffed.

"As far as my physical health is concerned, I am well." His tone was wry. "And you?"

I'm sick, sick with love for you, she had the urge to cry. But she said coolly, "Quite well, thank you," and stepped into the hall, pulling the door shut behind her.

He did not move. "You are most beautiful," he said quietly, without smiling.

Her eyes roamed over him, noticing how the white evening jacket he wore contrasted boldly with his bronzed skin and made his hair appear even darker. "So are you." The whispered statement was involuntary and no sooner was it out she was regretting it. Oh, God! He would think she was being flirtatious.

But all he said, was, *"Merci."* Then he took her arm in a gentle, quite impersonal grip and led her through the hallways to the main stairs. Neither of them spoke, which did not help Daye's nerves in the least. As they descended the stairs, however, the doorbell chimed, and Kao answered it to admit Audrey and Derek. Daye's little cry of pleasure and relief was instinctive, and Derek crossed the hall quickly, reaching up to span her waist and swing her away from Philippe. "Hello, you marvelous creature," he laughed, kissing her briefly. "I love your hair—it does things for your already perfect features." He grinned over her shoulder. "What do you think, Philippe?"

"It does not matter how her hair is styled; she could not be other than beautiful." Philippe spoke with soft intensity.

There was an awkward silence that was at last broken when Audrey said briskly, "What a superb compliment." She gave Derek a gentle push. "Go away, you two men. Daye, dear, come to the cloak-room with me, will you?"

Daye followed, feeling bemused. Philippe had not spoken as if he merely offered a compliment, he had spoken as if. . . as if what? As if he was in love? There she was, imagining things again. Of course he did not love her. And even if he did, had she not decided she wanted no part of his kind of love?

There was a small lounge behind the cloakroom where female guests could relax or freshen their makeup. Audrey went straight inside, turning abruptly to face Daye as she closely followed. "I hope you won't be shocked or annoyed, Daye, but I've got to ask. Are you and Charles going to get married?"

Daye saw the anxiety in the woman's attractive face and flashed a quick smile. "No, definitely not, Audrey."

Audrey sighed. "Derek was right, then. Oh, my dear! Do you know.... Daye, you didn't seem surprised at my question. Have you known all along what we were thinking?"

"Only since yesterday. Audrey, I'm so sorry! If only I'd known before. Have you been awfully unhappy?"

Audrey laughed tremulously. "So you know how I feel about Charles? Well, my dear, it isn't your fault if I've been unhappy. Heavens, do you know how horribly jealous of you I've been? And yet I've never been able to dislike you." She gave Daye an affectionate hug. "Oh, Daye, when I think of how I dashed to the waterfront that morning. But I simply had to see you. Philippe had telephoned in a rage, and said his father didn't have a chance, that no man would if you decided you wanted him. Lord, now I've done it!" Audrey shook her head ruefully. "Don't blame Philippe, Daye. He was really concerned about Charles."

"Yes, I know. And it was all for nothing, wasn't it?" Daye lowered her eyes. "Did Derek tell Philippe... what he told you?"

"No, he didn't. And he asked me not to until I'd spoken to you first. Daye, why don't you tell Philippe?"

"Charles will, I expect. He might have already done so."

"I shouldn't think Philippe had time to see Charles before changing. After we landed we all went to the bungalow and Philippe didn't leave till an hour ago." Audrey gave a startled gasp. "Charles! Oh, Daye, does Charles know what fools we've been?"

"Yes. Only he doesn't think anyone was foolish. It was a misunderstanding, that's all." Daye wished the same could be said about the Melisse-Philippe-Terii affair. But that was a wish that could never come true. She smiled with false brightness at Audrey. "We'd better join the others before they send out a search party."

Daye had hoped to be less disturbed by Philippe's presence this evening, but although the dinner party was a lively affair and she was drawn constantly into conversations, she was more than ever aware of him. There was no need to ask herself why. Charles had suggested Philippe loved her, and persist as she might in telling herself it did not matter one way or another, she was keyed up, reading more into Philippe's long, steady appraisals than was good for her equilibrium.

By the time the party began to break up, Daye was so discomposed she had no clear idea of what anyone was talking about. Automatically she accompanied the others into the spacious hall, and just as automatically she smiled and joined in the *bonsoirs, adieux* and good-nights, as the three couples she had met only that evening left together. Then Audrey was yawning and telling them she was more than ready for bed, and Derek was kissing Daye's cheek and telling her to come to lunch so that he could get in an extra hour's work on the portrait.

Daye nodded, forcing a smile to her stiff lips, and

Charles, who was standing beside her, said, "Ah, the portrait! I cannot wait to set eyes on it."

"Not until it's finished, Charles." Derek grinned.

"You have not changed your mind?" Charles sounded hopeful.

"About letting you have it?" Derek stopped grinning and added seriously, "I can only say that I've definitely decided to give it to Daye for a wedding present." His blue eyes slid from one to the other of them, and as though unaware of the awkward silence that prevailed, he continued, "Pity she won't marry me, then I could keep my masterpiece for myself, couldn't I?" He took his sister's arm. "Come on, old girl. Philippe, shall we walk with you and Melisse to the guesthouse?"

In spite of herself, Daye glanced toward Philippe. He met her gaze at once, his eyes bleak. Then he turned his head to give Derek a slight smile. "You will not mind escorting Melisse, *mon ami*? There is something I must do." So saying, he turned and strode to the stairs. He took them two at a time, and it was not until he was out of sight that anyone moved.

But Philippe's quick departure was not mentioned, and after a few last-minute words concerning Audrey's birthday and the trip to Tahiti, Charles and Daye were finally alone. They went upstairs together and parted in the hall. Daye felt tired now, too tired to think. Perhaps tonight she would not lie awake, her mind filled with thoughts and pictures of Philippe, her body restless with aching, burning desire.

She opened her door, her hand reaching automatically to the wall switch. Even as she pressed it to flood the room with light she smelled cigarette smoke and knew she was not alone.

CHAPTER SIXTEEN

HE WAS STANDING in front of the window, facing the door, and as Daye stared at him he put out his hand. "I am here to speak to you, that is all."

"No!" Blindly she turned to leave.

"I swear I will not touch you, but keep the door open if you will feel safer." Philippe spoke with controlled savagery.

Slowly Daye faced him. "Couldn't you have waited until morning?"

"By then I could be a raving lunatic." Philippe moved a few steps and bent to push his cigarette into a small china ashtray. When he straightened, his expression was grim. "For two weeks I have waited for some indication that you were prepared to listen to my explanation concerning Terii. But you have remained cool and distant." He spoke accusingly.

"Is that what you came to say?" Cool and distant? She must be a better actress than she thought, Daye told herself.

Philippe shook his head. "When Derek spoke of presenting you with your portrait for a wedding gift, I confess I was taken by surprise. I had almost convinced myself that you and *mon père* had decided against marrying. Your relationship has of late seemed somewhat different."

"The relationship between Charles and me hasn't changed," Daye assured him.

Philippe stood in silence, not taking his eyes from her face. Daye watched him in return, becoming so absorbed that she was taken by surprise when he spoke. "Must it be *mon père* that you marry? Why not become my wife, Daye?"

"What?"

"I am asking you to be my wife. I, too, am wealthy. I can give you furs, jewels, whatever you wish. We can travel." Philippe's expression seemed almost anxious. "The world holds many wonders that I would enjoy showing you."

Daye felt strangely light-headed, and she grasped the edge of the open door for support. *His wife,* she thought. *His wife.* Philippe was offering her marriage. But she could guess why. "Before this I was invited to become only a mistress," she heard herself say.

"Had you gone away with me I should have asked you to become my wife. Daye, *will* you marry me?"

"Why?"

He looked disconcerted. "Why does one usually propose?"

"Because one is in love, I would think." Daye's mouth felt dry, her body strangely numb. "But in your case that doesn't apply, so perhaps you'd give me your reason."

"You do not believe I am in love with you?" He spoke carefully.

"I believe you are willing to sacrifice yourself to save your father from the witch's wiles," she retorted.

"It would be no sacrifice. What man would not be honored to have you for his wife?" He gave her a crooked little smile. "Come, *ma belle*, you are very aware of the fact that I desire you."

"Desire! There's a lot more to marriage than sex." Her tone was scornful.

"But sex plays a most important role, would you not agree?"

"In your case it would." Daye felt unreasonably irritated. "As far as I'm concerned, it would play a very minor role."

Philippe's narrowed eyes slid over her. "I find that difficult to believe. Have you forgotten the passion you have shared with me?" His laugh was low and husky. "*Ma belle* Daye, if you were married to me you would soon consider the physical side of marriage to be most enjoyably important." He seemed about to move toward her but evidently changed his mind. "I am not a clumsy lover, Daye. I would give you nights to remember."

The jealous question, *As you do all your lady loves?* sprang to her mind, but she merely said indifferently, "Yes, I suppose you would."

She saw him frown. "Have you and *mon père* made love?"

The question shocked and horrified her. *"No!"*

"Then you are perhaps unaware that a man of his age...ah!" He nodded thoughtfully. "This is why you insist sex is of minor importance in a marriage."

Daye drew in a shuddering breath. "You are quite wrong," she said distractedly.

"Am I?" He smiled slowly. "Marry me, Daye."

She gave him a wild look, then shut her eyes. "You would take me away from your father?"

"Without hesitation."

She opened her eyes and met his. "You've been so careful of his health so far, I'm surprised you're not afraid such a shock could harm him."

"It can harm him no more than could marriage to a *jeune fille* such as yourself. A marriage that could end with your leaving him for a younger man." His tone suddenly was harsh and cold.

She felt a pain somewhere in the region of her heart. "So you admit you want to marry me to save your father?"

"I admit no such thing. While I would do my utmost to prevent *mon père* from marrying any twenty-two-year-old woman, I would not go so far as to ask her to be my wife." Philippe's tone was still harsh, and he moved restlessly to the window where he turned and continued, "You must have known how I have always wanted you. From the first moment I saw you in that hotel in Paris, I wanted you for my own. I spoke to you as I did because I was angry. Afterward I regretted it, but...." He shrugged. "When I saw you in Papeete I felt an urgent need to know you, that is why I was so persistent. Subconsciously, perhaps, I sensed you and the Paris girl were one and the same." His eyes glittered angrily. "*Mon Dieu!* Do you know I spent half the night searching Papeete's hotels and nightclubs for Gloria Day? Do you know how I felt when I found her to be Mademoiselle Hollister, the English girl my father loved?"

Daye badly wanted to ask if he was telling her he loved her, but she was afraid to. If he said yes, she might end up in his arms, and his arms were a trap into which she dared not venture. Summoning up her paltry defenses, she said unsteadily, "There's no point in your saying any more, Philippe. I won't marry you."

"Now I will ask why.."

Daye moved away from the door to stand with her hand resting on the back of a nearby chair. "I'm afraid I don't trust you, Philippe."

His face darkened. "Because once, years ago, I had an affair with Melisse? Because of that foolish girl, Terii? You refuse to believe that she lied? *Mon Dieu!*" He gestured savagely and moved toward her. Daye flinched, her hand tightening on the chair, and Philippe stopped with a groan. "Daye, I am not going to touch you, but you must know that I ache to do so. These past weeks have been hellish—seeing you, wanting to take you in my arms. Marry me, *chérie*, marry me. I swear you will never have cause to regret it."

She gazed at him, her emotions in turmoil. Oh, how she wanted to fling herself into his arms and cry, *yes, yes, I'll marry you*. Wanted to so urgently that she had to cling tightly to the chair, willing herself to remain where she was. For there was Terii, always she would remember that he had satisfied his need with the Polynesian girl while she, Daye, lay sleepless with misery and longing. And now there was Paul. Paul who might be his son. Daye felt a tight ball of pain form in her throat. For all she knew, he could have fathered other children. He had traveled, had obviously known many women intimately. Raw jealousy caught at her and she lowered her eyes in case he should read what she was feeling. Marry him? Even if he said he loved her, she would not marry him. How could she, when each time he was away from her she would be in agony, wondering what woman he held in his arms?

She shook her head wildly. "I can't! I can't marry you!"

She heard the door close and raised her eyes expecting him to be gone. But he was still there and his eyes held a dangerous glint as slowly he walked toward her.

Daye backed away. "You promised you wouldn't touch me," she cried in panic.

"You mean you trusted *me* to keep my word?" he mocked, still advancing.

Daye backed into a table and stopped. Fear washed over her as Philippe came close, so close there was scarcely space between them.

"Don't, Philippe!" She hardly recognized her own voice. "I'll never forgive you."

"That is a chance I must take." He bent his dark head and she felt his breath on her cheeks. He unexpectedly lifted her into his arms. "If tonight we should make a child together, would you then consider becoming my wife?" There was an emotional quality to his voice.

Disturbed, Daye gazed into his eyes, and for a long moment she was filled with a yearning so intense her entire body ached intolerably. Oh, how she loved him! Wanted him! But as he strode with her into the bedroom, she struggled, knowing she could not allow him to take her. "Please, Philippe," she begged, "don't do this!"

He paused near the bed, his face devilish in the dimness. "Do you value this gown? If you do, then I suggest you do not struggle when I remove it," he said thickly.

Her heart lurched at the thought of his hands on her body. But she closed her mind to it and said urgently, "I'm not going to marry Charles. I never was. He and I are friends, that's all. Only friends, Philippe."

He was suddenly still. "You say this hoping I will let you go, *n'est-ce pas?*"

"Yes. Yes! But it happens to be the truth, Philippe. I only learned yesterday what you have thought all this time. I . . . your father is going to speak to you about it." Daye did not move in his arms, but she added, "Put me down, please, Philippe. I'm not going to rush out of here."

He set her on her feet and she moved away to switch on a lamp. "So you see, you were wrong about me. I'm not a fortune hunter after a wealthy husband, and Charles, poor dear, never intended to be more than a fatherly companion to me." Daye felt tears on her cheeks and wondered absently why she was crying. "All you had to do was talk to your father. So simple, really." She faced him, not caring if he saw her tears. "Charles believes we made it easy for you to misunderstand our relationship. If we did, then I'm sorry to have caused you to be worried."

He seemed to be looking right through her. "If this is true, then it is I who should apologize." He took out his cigarettes and as he lit one Daye saw that his hands were shaking. "I was, of course, blinded by my own guilt and confusion because he appeared to have what I so desperately wanted."

Daye swung sharply away and said, "There's no need for you to pretend any longer, Philippe. Your father doesn't need saving." She went to the dressing table and began to pull the pins from her hair. "I'm going to leave Anani, you know. I've promised Charles to think it over, but I've already made up my mind." She spoke conversationally, willing her voice not to quaver.

He was silent for so long Daye shifted her position slightly to see if he was reflected in the mirror. He was not, and she was startled when he spoke from the doorway. "Why are you leaving?" His voice sounded odd.

"Oh... several reasons," she answered airily, picking up her brush and stroking it through her hair. "Well, to tell the truth I will most likely go back to England and get married. To Reg. Remember Reg? I haven't mentioned this to Charles as yet, so I would appreciate it if you didn't."

Again he was silent, and when she felt composed enough to steal a glance at him, she was shocked by his expression. He took a step forward, and the hairbrush fell from her fingers.

"At this moment I believe I could kill you," he snarled. Then making an obvious effort to control himself he asked, "When will you leave?"

"I'm not sure. A week or two, perhaps." Daye whispered the words.

He subjected her to a long steady scrutiny from eyes still bearing small flames of anger. But he said nothing, and presently he left. Left her to wonder if he did perhaps care for her, and if she was a fool not to snatch at happiness even if it was not meant to last.

WHEN DAYE RETURNED FROM DEREK'S STUDIO the following afternoon, she came upon Philippe and Jean standing in the hall, talking quietly. Philippe's handsome face looked grim, and Jean, Daye noticed uneasily, looked pale and strained. She had just time to wonder if Jean was breaking the news that his family was leaving Anani when both men noticed her. "Paul cannot be found," Philippe said shortly. "Apparently he has not been here all day, nor has he been at home."

"Oh. What about his friends or—" Daye glanced tentatively at Jean "—Melisse?"

Philippe and Jean shook their heads at the same time and Jean said, "He has not been seen the entire day. This morning, very early, we heard him leave, but this he does—to ride or swim—so we were not concerned." Anxiously he looked quickly at Philippe and muttered something in French.

Philippe put his hand on Jean's shoulder and murmured back. Then he gave Daye a brief glance. "We are going to search for Paul before it grows dark. You will excuse us?"

"Wait!" Daye said, as the two men started to move away. "Did I . . . you know I don't understand very much French, but did I understand Jean to say Paul has had an accident?"

"We have to face that possibility. He did not ride any of the horses today, but he could have gone swimming." Philippe stopped.

"What are you thinking—that he might have drowned? Oh, dear! I wonder if . . . ." Daye hesitated, irresolute, then, unable to bear Jean's distraught expression, "I think Paul might have left the island."

Jean gave her a puzzled look, but Philippe scowled. "What is this you say?"

"He told me he was going to leave, but I didn't expect he would go quite so soon."

"You knew this yet told no one?" Philippe's voice was as chilly as his eyes.

"I promised," Daye answered defensively. "The only reason I said something now is because I can't let Denise and Jean worry unnecessarily. I suppose Denise is dreadfully upset?" she finished miserably.

"*Naturellement.* Fortunately Père Martin is on the island and will go to her." Philippe pushed his hands through his dark hair. "You know where the boy has gone, *n'est-ce pas?*"

"Yes, I know. But I can't tell you that. It would really be breaking my promise."

He gave her an exasperated look, but instead of trying to persuade her he asked, "Melisse knows of this, does she not?"

Daye had no intention of defending Melisse who was responsible for Paul's defection. "Yes, she knows."

Jean gave a despairing exclamation and began to walk quickly toward the door. Philippe favored Daye with one last brief glance and followed. Left alone, Daye wandered into the salon thinking angrily that Paul might have had the decency to leave his parents a note. If she had not known he intended leaving, there would have been a frantic search and Denise and Jean would have gone through hell imagining something terrible had befallen him.

She was still in the salon when Philippe returned half an hour later and said Melisse refused to tell where Paul had gone. "Even Père Martin could not persuade her," he muttered disgustedly. "Stubborn woman, I would like very much to choke it out of her." He sighed. "Daye, you must tell me where Paul has gone so that I can go to bring him back."

"You can't force him to come back," she protested. "It isn't your job. Leave that to his father. To Jean," she added, suddenly remembering that Philippe might be Paul's natural father.

Philippe looked as if he might tell her to mind her own business, but he merely frowned and said, "He would resent me less."

"He would probably resent anyone who tried to force him to return home." Momentarily her mind wandered as she watched Philippe. He was wearing a white knit shirt and khaki-colored Levi's and looked virile as well as excitingly attractive. Her eyelashes flickered as she realized he was gazing back at her. What was she talking about? Oh, yes! "You know, I don't believe Paul was really happy about leaving Anani," she continued. "Perhaps, given a little time, he'll return of his own accord."

"And he may be too proud to admit his mistake. Tell me this, Daye, has Paul gone to Australia?" When she shook her head he went on thoughtfully, "He would not remain in Tahiti, of course, so where.... Melisse has a home in Paris. Has she sent him there?"

Daye said rather distractedly, "Paul is going to study music. He's obsessed with having a career, becoming a famous pianist, and Melisse will give him the chance to do that. I asked him not to go, but still I can understand how he feels."

"Melisse has convinced Paul he will become a famous pianist?" Philippe spoke sharply.

"Well, I gathered as much."

He muttered in French and said, "Melisse knows this will be most unlikely. Paul has talent but he will never become a virtuoso." He gestured angrily. "Always she has used the word encouragement where Paul is concerned. I did not know she was deliberately deceiving him.''

Daye felt shocked. "But that's wicked of her! To do that to her own son. . . .''

Philippe's brows quirked, but he did not ask how she knew Paul was Melisse's son. "I am afraid her belated maternal instincts have caused her to behave irrationally.'' His tone was grim, and Daye sensed he was not excusing the woman. "So, Daye, it *is* Paris?''

She nodded.

"Merci." His smile was faint but it gave her heart a jolt. "I will inform Jean and Denise, and early tomorrow I will go to find Paul.''

"It's a long way. You will miss Audrey's party.''

"She will understand. It might be possible to have Paul detained at some point of the journey, but this would humiliate as well as alienate him.'' His eyes held hers but she read nothing in his expression. "Which gown will you wear?''

The suddenness of the question confused her. "Gown? Oh. For the party, you mean? I don't know. Why do you ask?''

"Because I am a fool!'' He raked his hair once again, leaving it boyishly disheveled. "You still intend to leave for England—to marry this Reg?'' he questioned roughly.

"Yes.''

For what seemed an age, he studied her broodingly. Then he gave a shrug and strode to the door. But when he reached it he turned and, his tone still rough, asked, "You will not leave before I return from Paris?''

"I don't expect so." It was a lie, of course. If she left from Tahiti as she intended she would definitely be gone before he returned. Which meant, since he would fly away early tomorrow morning, she would not see him again after tonight. She tried to be resigned, telling herself she had known this moment was inevitable. But long after Philippe had left her, she stood in the salon feeling devastated by misery. The last time. Tonight was the last time she would see Philippe....

ALTHOUGH PHILIPPE FLEW TO PAPEETE the next morning as planned, by late afternoon he had returned to Anani...and Paul was with him.

Daye had suffered through an emotional, tension-filled evening, a tearful, sleepless night and shockingly unhappy day, and when Charles came to her suite to give her this news she at once began to cry. "There, *mon enfant*, it is over. You are most relieved, *n'est-ce pas?*" Charles said warmly, patting her eyes with a large white handkerchief. "And it appears that you must take credit for Paul's return. Apparently, when the moment arrived for the boy to board *l'avion*, he recalled your words and was unable to go because he was so ashamed. He spent a most unhappy night at the airport, and this morning was attempting to gather the courage to contact his parents when he saw Philippe. So, *ma chère*, you should feel most proud and pleased."

"Oh, I am pleased, believe me," Daye said tremulously, seeing no reason to tell Charles her relieved tears, her pleasure, were mainly due to the fact that Philippe had come back and she would see him for just a little while longer.

THE NEXT MORNING they journeyed to Tahiti by launch, and from Papeete's harbor rode in the cream-and-maroon automobile in which Daye had driven almost six weeks ago. Charles, Melisse, Audrey and herself were driven to a large, very modern hotel but Philippe and Derek continued on to Philippe's apartment where they would stay. Arrangements were made to meet that evening, which gave them plenty of time to do some shopping, Charles said, adding teasingly that he intended purchasing some delightful lingerie for Audrey's present. Audrey blushed, which was unusual for her, and said if he did she would consider it tantamount to a marriage proposal. Then she blushed even more and blurted that she was really only teasing.

But Daye noticed Charles was thoughtful, and she wondered if he could be considering adding a ring to the gold bracelet she knew he planned to buy for Audrey.

The telephone was the first thing Daye saw when she entered her hotel room, but she was suddenly reluctant to phone the airport as planned. Why not enjoy the rest of this day without the knowledge of a particular flight time hanging over her head? Tomorrow she would make arrangements or perhaps even later tonight. Flights to England left in the early morning hours, she knew. When she returned here after Audrey's party she might find out if a flight was leaving and if a seat was available. The thought made her appallingly miserable. Tomorrow morning, before dawn broke, she could be high above the Pacific. Flying away from Philippe. . . .

Shortly after their arrival, Daye and Audrey left to roam the Vaima shopping center. Melisse declined the invitation to join them and Daye sensed, although Melisse was coolly polite to her, that she was provoked because Daye had been instrumental in Paul's decision to return home. Had the boy been brought back kicking and screaming, so to speak, Melisse probably would not have minded nearly so much.

She and Audrey had a marvelous time buying new gowns to wear for the evening. Audrey's was a beautiful shade of green, in a style more sophisticated than she was accustomed to and that she bought because Daye insisted it suited her perfectly. Daye's gown was midnight blue, a slender strapless sheath with a top layer of gossamer-sheer chiffon.

For Audrey's birthday, Daye purchased a gold filigree brooch, and for Charles she lovingly chose a small, exquisitely carved horse. When she was no longer on Anani he could look at it and remember their companionable morning rides, she thought, sadness filling her heart and casting a cloud over the enjoyable afternoon.

That evening Daye arranged her hair to hang long and straight over her back and held away from her face and forehead by the narrow silver band she had bought in a fashionable boutique. Small, pear-shaped silver earrings dangled from her ears, and around her neck she wore a slender silver chain. Almost curiously she viewed her reflection in the tall mirror, taking in the slender curved body in the midnight-blue gown, the golden sheen of her complexion, the glowing dark green eyes and platinum-streaked hair. Strange, but nothing of the burning misery that racked her insides showed on her face.

Presently Audrey came to her room and the two of

them went downstairs to the private lounge where
cocktails and hors d'oeuvres would be served and
Audrey would receive her gifts. They found the
others already assembled, and Charles and Derek at
once detached themselves from the small group and
came toward them. Then a slight, dark-haired
woman approached and kissed Audrey warmly. She
was, Daye learned, Polly Hammond, Audrey's
friend who had just recently been so ill. Polly was an
Australian as was her husband, Neil. Neil was rotund
and merry faced; he was also a natural comic and
before long had them all laughing at his amusing
jokes and anecdotes.

But although she listened and laughed with the
others, Daye was only partially conscious of partici-
pating. The greater portion of her mind was taken up
by Philippe. Every time she glanced up at him, which
to her increasing dismay was quite often, she found
his eyes were on her, and she began to feel as if an in-
visible wire stretched between them, a wire that was
inexorably tightening, drawing them ever closer. Yet
neither of them had actually moved toward the other.
Daye still sat in the chair to which Derek had led her,
and Philippe still leaned indolently against the small
bar to which he had strolled soon after her arrival.
Melisse, looking her usual attractive self in an off-
white, heavy silk gown, was sitting nearby, but even
when Philippe spoke to her, his gaze roamed to Daye
and lingered....

When Audrey had opened and exclaimed over her
gifts, Derek took them upstairs to her room. After he
returned, they all went in to dinner where Audrey,
looking radiant with happiness, was seated at
Charles's right. He had not added a ring to his gift,

but when Audrey slid the beautiful gold bracelet over her wrist and kissed him for it, Daye had noticed his expression and thought it might not be too long before he produced the ring. Now, as she gazed at them across the large round table, she remembered she would not be with them if this event ever took place. She would, naturally, be invited to the wedding, but she would not accept.

Her sigh was involuntary, and from his seat beside his sister Derek gave her a quizzical look. Daye hurriedly smiled, then frowned as it occurred to her that she had somehow expected Derek to sit beside her at dinner. Neil Hammond was on her right, and on her left.... A surge of heat rushed to her face and she turned her head cautiously.

Philippe's clear gray eyes gleamed. "Will it spoil your appetite to have me sitting beside you?"

Recovering quickly, she shrugged. "Not unless you watch me the whole time and make me nervous."

He smiled. "I apologize if I make you nervous, but it is difficult not to watch you." His smile faded, and he leaned forward in his chair. "Do you know, Daye, that each time I see you I tell myself it is impossible for you to look more beautiful. Yet always you surprise me." His voice was soft but intense, and as she gazed speechlessly into his eyes, he added even more softly, "Later we will dance together."

Daye caught her breath. He might just as well have said, "Later I will hold you in my arms," because that was what he meant. She turned her head away, feeling threatened. Dance with him? Let him hold her in the seductive warmth of his arms? The very thought of it reduced her nervous system to a shambles, and feverishly she began to plan the excuses she would offer to avoid him. Then quite suddenly she was annoyed, partly because he had upset her, partly because he had taken it for granted she would dance with him. Swinging her head to look at him, she said in a patronizing tone, "Well, we'll have to see if I have a dance to spare, won't we?"

His hand shot out to cover hers, and she felt a quiver of apprehension at the glint of anger in his eyes. But then his hand slid away, and he showed his strong white teeth in a mockery of a smile. "Do not anger me, *petite belle*. Tonight, it is doubtful I could control myself."

He did not speak to her after that, at least not during dinner. Daye said nothing to him either, nor did she look at him. But throughout the lengthy meal she felt his eyes on her and, consequently, her appetite disappeared. However, nervousness caused her to drink more wine than she was accustomed to, and by the time they were ready to leave for the nightclub, she was feeling distinctly disoriented. When she stood up the heady sensation became just plain dizziness, and she gripped the edge of the table for support. She was vaguely berating herself for being so stupid, when Philippe said in her ear, "I expected this. Had you eaten more, the wine would not affect you so."

Daye had to overcome the urge to slap his face. "Well, since you were obviously watching me, why didn't you offer your advice before it was too late?"

"Would you have taken it?"

"No," she admitted.

"So." He moved his shoulders in a slight shrug then took her arm. "Come."

"No," she snapped, "I want to walk by myself. Good heavens, I'm only a bit. . .a bit unsteady." She tried to tug her arm free but he held on grimly. "I'll make a scene," she threatened.

He laughed. "It would appear you already have. *Mon ami* Derek is coming to your rescue." His hand left her arm and he said, as Derek reached them, "She is yours for just a little while, *mon ami.*" Then he strode away to join Melisse, who was waiting, a thoughtful frown creasing her brow.

Derek looked thoughtful, too. "Why don't you put the poor devil out of his misery?" he asked enigmatically, laughing when she gave him a startled glance. "I meant nothing shocking, my dear. I just meant. . .oh, forget it for now. We'll talk about it some other time."

But there would not be another time, Daye thought, as she and Derek followed the others. Because she would go away tomorrow, she would definitely go tomorrow.

The nightclub was crowded when they arrived, but a large table had been reserved quite near the dance floor. There was an excellent orchestra, complete with male and female singers, and Derek at once twirled Daye into a sensuous tango. Derek was quite an expert at dancing and since Daye was no longer feeling the effects of the wine, she thoroughly enjoyed the experience. After the tango the orchestra swung neatly into another dance number, and when Derek raised his eyebrows, Daye nodded, her steps moving in time to the music. She was flushed and out of breath when they got back to the table, and she thought if Philippe should ask her to dance when the music began again, she could always say she was worn out.

But to her relief the lights were suddenly dimmed and a master of ceremonies appeared to announce the beginning of the floor show. This featured a guitar-playing girl singer, a group of Polynesians who performed several intricate native dances, and a famous, very amusing comedian. It was a most entertaining show, and Daye enjoyed it despite the ever-present awareness of Philippe, who sat just inside her line of vision. She did not once look at him directly, but she knew whenever he moved his head to look her way and was glad of the dimness that protected all expression.

When the show ended and the lights brightened, she tensed automatically, bracing herself for the moment when the orchestra would resume playing. Philippe would waste no time, she was certain. He would get to his feet in that deceptively lazy manner and would be at her side in seconds. And she could not possibly refuse him—not with everyone looking on.

The waiter hovered at her shoulder, offering champagne. With a smile she refused, then immediately wished she had accepted because the orchestra had begun to play, and she needed something to give her courage. Sheer panic took hold of her. Philippe was rising, looking at her with smoldering determination. Then he was moving around the table, and she knew he was coming for her.

Daye murmured, "Please excuse me, everybody," and was on her feet, making her way with blind haste toward the foyer. Once there, she fled across the thick red carpet, seeking the safety of the ladies' lounge. The door opened as she reached it, and she collided with a woman who was on her way out.

"I'm awfully sorry," she apologized breathlessly, and without actually glancing at the woman, began to slip past her.

"Gloria?"

Daye paused, her heart skipping a beat. Then she slowly turned around.

The woman was tall and slim, with elaborately styled platinum hair and a large-featured, yet attractive face. She wore glasses with jeweled rims behind which shrewd blue eyes glittered. "Gloria!" she said again. "My God, it *is* you!"

"Hello, Esther." Daye spoke huskily.

Esther Sullivan, Max Lucan's personal secretary, gave Daye a brief hard hug. "Well, thanks be to the heavens!" she declared. "We only arrived yesterday, but Max is in a foul mood because he wasn't able to find you immediately. You know Max—Mister Impatience himself." Esther looked at Daye closely. "You look tremendous, naturally, my dear, but so different. Your image has—"

"Please!" Daye put out an unsteady hand. "You're here with Max?"

The woman nodded. "Robert is here, too. You remember Max's valet?"

"How did Max know I was here?" Daye bit her lip. "Reg didn't tell him!"

"Not Reg. He wouldn't tell Max a thing. But Max has his methods of finding out what he wants to know. He bribes people. Porters, charwomen, whoever it takes. It's a simple matter to read a postmark on a letter and report to Max." Esther shrugged. "Don't imagine I agree with him totally, dear, but there you are. Anyway, you didn't really think Max would give up without a fight, did you?"

Daye gazed at her numbly, but before she could answer an arrogant male voice called out, "Esther, we're leaving," and Daye saw Max Lucan's thickset form heading briskly for the exit. But he did not reach it, for Esther called his name and he hesitated, looking bad-temperedly across the wide foyer.

"Look who I've found, Max," Esther said playfully, before Daye could prevent her.

Max stared. "Gloria!" Rapidly he covered the space between them. "Gloria, we've been looking everywhere for you." Max took her hands, holding them tightly as his dark eyes roved over her face. "You look different. Different, but *gorgeous*. God, how I've missed you!" He bent his head toward her, and Daye moved hers just in time so that his mouth came to rest on her cheek.

She tolerated his embrace briefly before easing herself away. "Hello, Max, how are you?"

"That isn't much of a welcome, Gloria," Max chided. His tone was mild but Daye sensed his displeasure. "I've come a hell of a long way just to see you."

She refrained from saying I didn't ask you to come, and forced a smile. "That's very nice of you, Max."

He pursed his rather full lips. "My polite little Gloria." The lips stretched into a tight smile. "Why did you run away, little girl? If a holiday in Tahiti was what you wanted, why didn't you say so? You know I'd give you anything your heart desired."

Daye felt uncomfortable. "I'm sure you know it wasn't just a holiday I wanted, Max."

"Hmm. Well, we won't discuss that now." He spoke impatiently. "We'll go to my hotel and have supper, and then we'll talk."

"I'm afraid I can't. I'm here with friends, Max, and I really should be getting back to them."

"You must be joking! I haven't traveled thousands of miles just to let you get away from me so easily." Without looking at Esther, he told her arrogantly, "Esther, go and find out who Gloria's friends are and tell them she's going with us."

"Max, I am not going with you," Daye protested, wishing she felt less intimidated by him.

"Of course you are!" Max threw a powerful arm about her shoulders and propelled her toward the exit. "We have a lot to talk about, little girl."

"No, we haven't." Daye twisted away from him. "Max, please understand. I...I won't come back to work for you—that's final!"

He caught hold of her arm before she could leave. "Now, what makes you think I want you to work for me again, Gloria? I want to talk about you and me in a more personal sense." His voice lowered and he bent his head toward her. "You know I've always wanted you, Gloria. Not just to be Lucan's television Dream Girl either. I want you for my wife."

"Please, Max, you know I don't...don't love you. I can't marry you." Daye was embarrassed and dismayed. "But I've told you this before, haven't I? You...you didn't think I would change my mind?"

Max frowned darkly. "Why not? I've a lot to offer a woman. She would live in the lap of luxury, married to me."

Daye sighed. "Oh, please, Max, don't talk about it anymore. Really, I must join my friends—"

"Not until we've had our talk," Max insisted, then, apparently losing patience, he snapped, "Damn it to hell, Gloria, you will listen to me!"

"Not unless she wishes to." There was menace in the softly spoken words.

Distracted as she was, Daye had not noticed Philippe approaching. But he was there, only a few feet away, his handsome face an expressionless mask from which his eyes blazed dangerously. He was staring at Max, and it seemed to Daye he waited for the exact moment to spring. And although she knew his silent aggression was not directed at her, Daye could not suppress a shiver. At once Philippe's gaze moved to her and she saw the lines of his face gradually soften, and his eyes flicker with a different flame. Then he smiled, and in that moment she was consumed by a sweet, wondrous joy, because she saw he did indeed love her, and that in spite of all he had done, his love was all she truly wanted. "Philippe!" She spoke his name with spontaneous pleasure.

His smile faded and he said urgently, "Daye, you're unharmed?"

Before she could answer Max exploded, "Unharmed? What in God's name do you think I've been doing to her?" His grasp on Daye's arm tightened cruelly. "Who is this fellow, Gloria?" He was holding her left arm, and with a jerk he raised it to stare at her hand. "No ring. God, for a minute I thought you'd got yourself married."

All at once Philippe was very close. "Before you say more, you will release *mademoiselle*." He spoke politely. "If you do not, I swear by *le bon Dieu*, I will break your arm."

Esther said nervously, "Max, let's go. We can see Gloria another time."

Max ignored her. "Don't threaten me," he said to Philippe, but his tone lacked conviction, and he ap-

peared to be sizing up Philippe. The Frenchman
stood half a head taller and his lean yet broad-
shouldered form looked fit and powerful. Max, too,
was powerful, but although Daye sensed he would be
a formidable opponent in a fistfight, he was obviously reluctant to pit himself against Philippe. "Who *is*
this Frenchman?" he demanded again, his eyes moving to Daye.

"Release *mademoiselle* immediately!" Philippe's
tone was no longer polite and Daye was not surprised
when Max obeyed. Still, he looked so viciously furious she felt strangely afraid. Then Philippe held out
his hand, and as she put her own into it, the fear was
washed away by a glorious sensation of well-being.
"Come," he said simply, his eyes glinting at her from
beneath his lashes.

"Wait a minute!" Max ordered. "Don't I know
you?" He spoke to Philippe who merely gazed at him
with cold disdain. "You look familiar," Max went
on. "I know we've met somewhere. Look here," the
tight smile appeared once more, "why don't we all go
into the lounge bar and have something to drink?"

"Merci, *monsieur*, but I think not." Philippe inclined his head toward Esther, who, Daye saw, was
staring at him admiringly. "*Bonsoir, madame.*
Come, Daye, *mon père* will become concerned if we
do not return soon."

Max's smile faded. "Damn it Gloria, does this
Frenchman have the right to tell you what to do?"

Daye raised her eyes to meet Philippe's. "Yes, he
does," she answered without hesitation, and Philippe
took a very deep breath, giving her a look that made
her knees weak. With difficulty she tore her gaze
away and smiled at Esther. "It was nice to see you

again, Esther. Will you remember me to everyone when you get back to London? And, Max—" Daye smiled at him, too, aware that she no longer felt nervous and intimidated "—I'm sorry that you came all this way for nothing."

Max made one last effort. "Gloria, we have to have a talk. Where do you live? I'll come to see you tomorrow."

"That would be most unwise," Philippe stated coldly.

"I see." Max's eyes slid from Philippe to Daye. "You are living with this fellow, Gloria?"

Philippe muttered something beneath his breath but Daye laughed and said recklessly, "As a matter of fact, I am."

Max glared impatiently, then with an angry movement turned and strode to the exit. Once there he stopped, looking back over his shoulder. "This isn't the end of it, little girl. I'll have you yet, by fair means or foul." Having uttered the threat he rudely pushed his way past a group of people who were attempting to enter and disappeared from sight. After a moment Esther murmured a hasty goodbye and followed him.

"An unpleasant man," Philippe said. "And yet I can feel sympathy for him." He smiled at her look of surprise. "Because he is in love with you, and you do not even like him." Then his eyes narrowed and he asked grimly, "His threat has not caused you to be afraid?"

She shook her head, wanting to tell him she would never be afraid if he was by her side. "But I'm glad you arrived when you did." Her lashes flickered under his steady gaze. "Had you come to look for me?"

"I followed when you ran from me, and I watched until it occurred to me you were having a small difficulty."

"I'm very grateful."

"It is not gratitude I want from you, Daye." Quite unexpectedly Philippe raised the hand he was holding and pressed the palm against his mouth. "You allowed him to think we were living together as lovers." He spoke huskily.

"Yes."

"In the hope that he would become discouraged?"

"I don't believe I was thinking of that." She lowered her eyes because he seemed to be trying to read her mind.

"You have changed your mind about returning to England—and to your Reg?"

She nodded, still not looking at him.

"Because of the so unpleasant Max?" There was underlying urgency in the question.

"No, not because of Max." Daye met his eyes, loving him so much she was certain he could read it in her expression.

And perhaps he did, for his lips curved in a triumphant smile before he quietly told her, "Tomorrow we will go somewhere to be alone."

"Yes." Daye knew that by agreeing, the bridges she had begun to burn when Philippe appeared to rescue her from Max were now totally destroyed. She would not look back, nor would she look ahead. As each day arrived she would live it, and perhaps if she was lucky, she would never have cause for regret.

CHAPTER SEVENTEEN

IT WAS LATE WHEN THE PARTY ENDED, but Daye was wide awake before eight o'clock, swinging herself out of bed and twirling ecstatically about the room. Never had she felt so happy, she told herself. Never! Pausing before the mirror she crossed her arms over her breast and watched a dreamy smile touch her mouth. Last evening, after the incident with Max, Philippe had taken her back to join the others. At least, he had started to do so, but before they reached their table the orchestra began to play a slow sweet melody and Philippe had drawn her unresisting body into his arms. They had not actually danced, only moved slowly, their bodies close together, and presently Philippe had gently pressed her head against his chest and then rested his face on her hair. They stayed that way, like lovers in an embrace, and to Daye it did not matter at all who saw them.

Apparently it did not matter to Philippe either, for as one dreamy dance moved into another he held her even closer, so close she could almost feel the passion growing in him. And somehow this emotion was transferred to her, so that her body began to ache with desire, and she wished he would take her to some isolated spot where they could make love until the ache went away. Yet, contrarily, she was not disappointed when he at last led her toward their table.

She was, in fact, relieved that he was not taking immediate advantage of her unconcealed response to him.

Only Charles, Audrey and Melisse were seated at the table when they reached it. The Hammonds were dancing, and Derek had gone to speak to some friends elsewhere in the room. Audrey smiled at them both, betraying no sign of having noticed their intimate behavior on the dance floor. Charles's delight, however, was conspicuous. He said nothing, but happiness glowed in his eyes and his smile showed satisfaction. Melisse, Daye noticed, looked them over in a cool, speculative manner that held mild irritation but, so far as she could tell, no jealousy. So Philippe must have told the truth about Melisse and himself. If they were, or had recently been lovers, she would surely be furious with jealousy.

For the remainder of the evening Daye was only half-conscious of what went on around her. Philippe seemed to be the sole occupant of her mind, his face the only face she clearly saw, his voice the only voice she actually heard. She was far too obsessively in love with him, and while it was now quite obvious that Philippe returned her feelings, she was sure it was to a lesser degree. Still, when he asked her again to marry him—as she was certain he would—she would say yes. And she would have to pray he cared enough to be able to resist the temptations other women might offer. If he did not—well, she would have to cross each bridge as she reached it. The unease that attacked her mind was quickly dispersed. Now, she felt it was foolish of her to remember Terii and assume, because of what had happened that night, that Philippe could never be faithful to one woman.

Daye had no regrets when Charles suggested they retire for the evening. Now she needed to be alone, away from Philippe's distracting presence, so that she could think, and dream, about the future. . . .

THE TELEPHONE SHRILLED. Quickly Daye went to answer it, her heart thudding because it might be Philippe calling her. But Max's voice came over the wire, a voice that sounded almost too smooth and controlled. "Good morning, Gloria, my dear. How are you?"

Bluntly she asked, "How did you know I was here?"

"Never mind, little girl. Is your Frenchman there with you?"

Daye hesitated. "Not at the moment."

Max laughed. "I thought not. If you are living with him it's not here in Tahiti. In fact, you really aren't *living* with him as I meant at all, are you, Gloria?"

She swallowed. "Max, I don't have to—"

"His name is Philippe Chavot and you live on his father's island," Max went on as though she had not spoken. "They belong to an old, very aristocratic French family, and they are loaded with money—and pride. They are very proud, Gloria." Max paused significantly. "Now let me see, little girl. Ah, yes, I also know the names and occupations of the others you were with last night. Shall I run them off for you?"

"Max, I don't see the point of all this."

"Don't you? Ah, well, Gloria, maybe I'm just trying to show you I can find out what I want when I want to. That you won't get away from me unless I want you to.'' He paused again, deliberately. ''Now, when can we talk?''

''Never. I told you—''

''And I told you, by fair means or foul, I'll have you back.'' Max's tone was harsh with anger. ''I'm warning you, Gloria.''

''You don't frighten me,'' Daye said. ''Now don't phone me again, Max.'' Firmly she replaced the receiver, shaking badly in spite of her brave words.

When a knock sounded on the door an hour later, she was afraid it might be Max in person. But when she flung it open, steeling herself for the sight of Max's angry black eyes, she saw instead Philippe's clear gray ones. Her heart leaped with relief and delight, and she uttered his name on a breathless note.

Philippe smiled, a soul-stirring flash of pure white in the dark tan of his handsome face. He was wearing a cream-and-brown-striped shirt and cream slacks, and she almost said, ''Philippe, you look so beautiful, and I love you terribly.'' But she merely smiled back at him, suddenly pleased that she had worn blue because she knew it was her best color.

Philippe did not move to enter her room. *''Bonjour, mademoiselle.* I am not too early?'' The lightness of his tone belied the intent, almost hungry, way his eyes searched her face.

''No. Come in.'' Daye was all at once absurdly shy.

He did so, standing just inside the room with the door still open. ''I want to kiss you,'' he said thickly, ''but if I begin I will not stop and if we were interrupted. . . .''

Her throat was so tight she barely managed to say, "Yes, I know."

Philippe kept his eyes on her as he said, "I have a message for you from Derek."

"Oh?"

"I am to tell you he will try to have your portrait finished in time."

"In time? Oh!" Daye felt warmth flood her cheeks, and she could say no more.

"I took the liberty of telling him I did not believe it would be." He gave her a slow, warm smile. "I asked Derek to make our excuses to the others."

She nodded. "I'll just get my handbag." She went toward the table where it lay, then paused. "Where are we going?"

"I thought you would first like to see the land I have purchased."

"That would be nice." She did not pick up her handbag before turning to face him. "Philippe, I... would it be possible to go to...Anani?"

Surprise flashed across his face. "Do you mean today? You and I?"

"Yes." Daye bit her lip.

"There is something wrong, Daye?" He looked concerned.

"No, nothing's wrong. I just...suddenly wished I...we were there." Embarrassment flooded her. "Oh, please forget it, Philippe. It was a silly idea."

"*Au contraire*, it is a splendid idea." Philippe moved a few steps then stopped. "I can think of nowhere else I would care to be...with you." His tone was husky. "I shall arrange for one of the company boats to be readied for us."

Daye gave a nervous little laugh. "Do you think the others will mind or think it . . . well, odd?"

He did not smile. "Does it really matter, *chérie*?"

"No, no, it doesn't," she admitted honestly.

Now, he did smile. "*Bon!* I will use the telephone now, if I may." He strolled to the bedside table to lift the receiver and speak in rapid French while Daye watched and listened, loving the sound of his voice, and thinking that she would really have to learn to speak his language. When at last he replaced the receiver, he wore a slight frown. "It appears we will not be able to leave as early as I hoped. The company launches are in use, but one will be returned in two hours."

"That's all right. We shall have time to see the land you've bought. You are going to build a house on it, aren't you?"

"That depends." Philippe came toward her, gray eyes gleaming. "If the lady I intend to marry prefers Anani, I shall build my house there."

His meaning was clear. Daye felt no shyness, only the most superb happiness as she said, "I'm certain the lady would much prefer Anani."

As it turned out, it was after two o'clock when Philippe guided the small, sleek blue-and-white craft away from Papeete's harbor. Daye sat in the cockpit and watched him, her eyes taking in the tanned, muscular forearms covered with fine dark hair, the broad shoulders beneath the striped shirt, the dark hair twisting into absurd curls on the back of his neck. She watched, loving him so intensely she felt dangerously close to tears. Then, as he turned his head to smile at her, she was beset by pure, wanton desire. Never had she known a man intimately, yet instinctively she knew her body needed him. And tonight—she closed her eyes—tonight she knew she would lie in his arms, their naked bodies would touch, their hands would wander freely. And this time...this time she would truly give herself to him.

Her eyes flew open, and she rose almost involuntarily and went to stand beside him. At once he slipped an arm about her waist and they stood there, not speaking, for a long time.

Philippe was the first to break the silence. "Do you truly believe me to be a womanizer, Daye?"

Daye was taken aback by the suddenness of the question. "I was awfully upset when I called you that." She sent him a swift upward glance.

"Ah. So you did not mean it?" His expression was quizzical.

Daye looked out at the endless miles of turquoise ocean. She did not want to admit she had meant what she said, nor did she want to lie. But most of all she did not want to even consider whether or not her opinion had changed. So she remained silent and presently Philippe's arm tightened and he said wryly, "Your silence is your answer, *chérie*. What can I say? How may I convince you I am not such a man?"

Daye raised her face to smile at him. "Philippe, it doesn't matter. Honestly. I don't...I'm not going to think about Melisse and—"

"Melisse?" he broke in swiftly. "You still cannot believe we are lovers!" He gave an abrupt laugh. "*Chérie*, our affair began twelve years ago and lasted little more than two months. We found we cared for each other more as *amis* than as lovers."

Twelve years! If Philippe spoke the truth then Paul could not be his son. But still she had to make certain. "You and Melisse had known each other for years, though, hadn't you?"

"That is true. But it was not until we met unexpectedly while on skiing holidays, that we decided to, er, experiment." His smile was rather mocking. "There is something on your mind, *n'est-ce pas?*"

Daye sighed. "Oh, Philippe, I'm sorry. I thought you might be Paul's father."

"Do not apologize, *chérie*. You are not the only one who has considered this possible." He gazed intently into her face. "The pleasure of having a son or daughter is yet to be mine." As if he could not help himself he let go of the wheel and turned her into his arms. His kiss was long and filled with the promise of passion. "I have told myself I must be patient," he said, staring straight ahead. "However, it is not at all easy."

Daye knew just what he meant. Her mouth tingled from that one tantalizing kiss and wanted much, much more. But she stood silently beside him, casting frequent, somewhat furtive, glances at his superb profile, and thinking how very much she loved him. Tonight she would tell him so, and perhaps he would tell her. . . .

He caught her glance and smiled, but his tone was serious when he said, "Since Melisse involved you in her affairs, I am surprised she did not offer to tell you the name of Paul's father."

"In a way, she did. I . . . didn't want to know." *In case she said it was you,* she silently told him.

"Oh? But I want you to know. It is Jean Dubois."

Daye's lips parted. "Jean is really Paul's father?"

"Oui."

Comprehension dawned. "That's why Melisse said

the baby's father was delighted that she gave him up. And that's why Denise hates Melisse so much, why she behaves as she does to Paul. Oh, Philippe. Didn't she know about her husband and Melisse when she accepted the baby?''

"Denise knew only that Melisse was the *enfant*'s mama. It was not until two years ago that she learned of Jean's involvement.''

"How dreadful for her!" Daye spoke from the heart.

"*Oui*. I am afraid she did not take such news well.''

"I should think not! How ever did she find out after all this while?''

Philippe's expression was grim. "Melisse. Apparently she became angry when Denise refused to allow her to take Paul on tour with her. She insisted afterward it had not been her intention to disclose Jean's paternity, but it is possible she hoped Denise would relinquish Paul if she learned he was her own husband's *enfant d'amour*.''

"It was wrong of Melisse to do what she did." Daye could not help the note of distaste in her voice.

"I agree, *ma petite*. As it was wrong of Jean to be unfaithful, and then not to confess to his wife what he had done. Denise should have been told and given the chance to decide whether or not she wanted the *enfant*.''

Daye was silent for a few moments. "How could such a thing happen?" she asked then. "I mean, Melisse was only seventeen when Paul was born.''

"Melisse had been attracted to Jean since she was thirteen years old. Jean had not encouraged her, however, but when Melisse came to Anani for her school holiday the year she was sixteen, Denise, unfortunately, was away, visiting an ailing *grand-mère*. Jean was, I suppose, lonely and vulnerable. Still, it does not excuse him.''

''You believe a man should be faithful to his wife?'' Daye asked swiftly.

''*Oui.* As should a wife be to her husband.''

As I will be to you, she told him silently. Aloud she said, ''Somehow I had the impression you were not entirely sympathetic toward Denise.''

''She has my sympathy but not my respect. She has forgiven Jean, yet she holds his mistake above his head. And toward Paul she has behaved without intelligence and understanding.'' He looked down at Daye, his stern expression softening. ''And one evening she unwisely sharpened her frustrated claws on you, *chérie.* I did not like that at all.''

Daye knew he must be referring to the night he had deliberately upset Denise by mentioning Melisse. And later, when Derek told her Philippe had done so because Denise had embarrassed her, she had scoffed disbelievingly. ''You were unkind to her,'' she chided gently.

''*Mais, oui.*'' He shrugged.

''Poor Denise. Perhaps she thought I, too, was a threat. That I'd lead Paul astray.'' Daye met Philippe's eyes. ''Someone else more or less accused me of that,'' she stated, raising an eyebrow at him.

''I was jealous. Even of that boy.'' He spoke simply, reaching to touch her cheek before turning back to the controls. After a moment, Daye heard him mutter under his breath and it seemed to her the launch picked up speed.

But she placed no importance on this. It was in her

mind now to clear up all that was between them. So she touched his arm and said tentatively, "Philippe— about Terii...."

"Terii?" He gave her a distracted frown.

"Yes. It won't make any difference. I mean, I won't change my mind about us. But I...I have to tell you I know about her. I know that when you left me that night, you...you slept with her." There, it was out! And she felt intensely relieved.

"*Mon Dieu!* What is this?" Philippe stared at her in amazement.

Daye tried to smile. "Philippe, I saw her leaving your room very early. She said you were still asleep and that she was...tired. It was obvious that you had...." She stopped, puzzled by the look on his face.

"Terii was in my suite? Daye, *mon amour*, if she was, she was there alone. When I left you I was angry. Frustrated! I felt the need to talk to someone...." He shook his dark head as though remembering. "Audrey appeared to be the wisest choice, so I walked to the bungalow and thoughtlessly roused her. She made coffee and we talked until daybreak. After leaving her, I went to the pool to swim." He bent his head unexpectedly and kissed her hard. "Daye, I did not go to my suite until it was time to change for my morning ride with papa. I did not even catch a glimpse of Terii."

Daye stared at him speechlessly.

"I speak the truth," Philippe assured her. "Audrey will confirm it, and I am certain you know Audrey will not lie." His arm slid around her, pulling her against him. "*Mon amour*, say that you believe me."

"I believe you. Oh, Philippe, I'm so sorry. And I'm so angry because I've made myself miserable over nothing." Daye leaned against him, her head buried against his heart. She had misjudged him. There was no reason now to think he would be unfaithful to her. No reason to think she would ever be anything but happy with him.

"Had I known this I would have dragged the girl to you to confess," she heard Philippe say grimly. "Ah, Daye, *ma chérie*, we have been fools, *n'est-ce pas?* But no more...." He stopped so unexpectedly that Daye looked up in surprise.

Philippe was staring ahead, his expression full of anxiety. "What's wrong?" she asked.

"It was predicted there would be a storm, but I was certain we would be safely home before it reached this area." His tone was harsh, and he released her suddenly. "Go below and put on a life jacket. You will find them in the lockers beneath the bunks."

Daye followed his eyes, seeing for the first time the ominous gathering of dark clouds in the distance, the haze that covered the sun. Then she turned to obey him and find the life jackets. Returning with two she donned one, fumbling a little with the straps. "Now you, Philippe," she said, when she had succeeded.

He did not look at her, but kept his eyes on the horizon. "Presently," he muttered.

"Now, Philippe!" she commanded. And when he turned to flash an arrogant scowl, "If you don't put it on, I shall take mine off."

His expression lightened. *"Très bien, ma petite."* He began to shrug into the jacket, keeping one hand on the wheel. Daye helped him fasten the straps, enjoying the small intimacy. When she had finished, yet was still close to him, he dropped a kiss on her nose and said, "Go below, Daye. You will become wet and uncomfortable here."

But she stubbornly shook her head and stood at his side, watching with half-fearful fascination as menacing black clouds hurtled through the sky, obliterating the sun and plunging the world about them into gray, purple-toned dimness. Then, with terrifying suddenness, a brilliant flash of lightning split the gloom and the crash of thunder mingled with the savage howl of the wind. Spears of rain pelted down, drenching them in seconds, and as the launch rose and fell, captured and released by the gaping jaws of massive waves, water poured over the already soaked decks and spilled into the cockpit.

Turning, a cry of fear escaping her, Daye was thrown off balance and fell sprawling. But Philippe was there at once, lifting her to her feet and half carrying her back to the controls. "Keep down!" he shouted in her ear. "Hold on to my legs." And she slid down, obeying him, her mind almost blank with fright. They were going to die. Just as they were on the verge of finding happiness together, she and Philippe were going to die. And *she* had suggested returning to Anani....

She huddled there for what seemed an eternity before shame overcame fear and sent her to her feet. Then she immediately wished she had stayed where she was, for through a thick curtain of rain she saw jagged points of dark rock and knew they were headed toward a reef. "Keep down!" she heard Philippe shout savagely, and when she turned her head she saw that he looked savage, too, with his wet hair plastered against his head and his lips drawn back against his strong white teeth. His clear eyes glittered with a reckless light, and she knew he was determined to find a break in the reef and get them to the safety of the island beyond.

But it was not possible. In this storm he would never find it, and they would be dashed against those rocks.... Nausea welled up in her stomach, and she moved away from Philippe, trying frantically not to be sick. Again she was thrown off balance, and this time, as she fell, she struck her head and saw a myriad of dazzling lights. Darkness followed, blotting out all thought, but it must have been brief, for when she dazedly got to her feet, Philippe was still at the wheel, fighting to keep control of the boat. Somehow she managed to reach him, only to slide down again, shivering in distress. Her head ached abominably, her stomach heaved. And now she was attacked by another fear, the fear that somehow she would survive this nightmare, and Philippe would not. "Oh, God," she prayed, "don't let that happen. If you take him, take me, too."

Another age seemed to pass as she crouched there. Then, miraculously, the launch appeared steadier, the howling gusts of wind and piercing rain less forceful. Was the storm abating she wondered, or were they... could they have made it through the reef into the lagoon? Even as she asked herself this, the engines stopped and Philippe bent down to her. "We are safe, *chérie*," he said near her ear. "*Le bon Dieu* has brought us safely through the reef. I must leave you now to anchor the launch and when the lagoon is calmer we will use the dinghy to reach the shore."

He rose and left her, and she was infinitely relieved

because she needed to be very sick. Somehow she got to the rail and clung to it, violently retching, totally unaware of the passage of time. She was in a vague, dreamlike state when Philippe's arms went around her, when his voice told her something about islanders, canoes and a village. Then she felt as if she were spinning around and around like a top before everything went sickeningly black.

DAYE WOKE UP SLOWLY, aware of soft voices and movement. Gradually her half-opened eyes focused and she realized she was lying on some sort of bed, and that someone was leaning over her. Philippe. "Hello," she murmured and raised a lethargic hand, wanting to touch his face. He took it in one of his, holding it tightly against his chest. His eyes were narrowed, his mouth a thin straight line. "What's the matter, my darling Philippe?" she whispered anxiously.

He made a soft groaning sound and began to speak in French. Daye did not stop him, sensing he needed, for some reason, to express himself in his own language at this time. Then her befuddled brain began to clear and she knew why. "I'm all right," she insisted. "Truly, I am. Goodness, what a fool I was to faint like that."

He raised her hand to his lips. "You were unconscious for almost thirty minutes. *Mon Dieu*, I thought I would lose you!" Philippe sounded greatly agitated.

"You won't lose me so easily." Daye smiled. "Let me sit up, Philippe." And when he had raised her, "Ouch! My head hurts! It must be the bump I...."

"You are hurt? This is why you faint! *Chérie*, when did this happen?"

"You were busily trying to get us into the lagoon." Daye touched his face, as she had so often wanted to do. "Oh, Philippe, do you know that I love you?" How wonderful it was to say it!

"I prayed that you did, *mon coeur, mon ange*. Ah, but I have known such torture because of you, such jealousy! I have hated *you* for the way I felt, and I have hated even *mon père* because I thought you were to belong to him. And Derek, my *bon ami*, I have hated him also." Philippe's voice shook and his hands, when he drew her to him, were shaking, too. But he hesitated, with his mouth inches from hers and whispered, "*Mon amour*, I forget, we are not alone. And you are not dressed."

His hands were warm on the bare skin of her back, and looking down she saw she was indeed not dressed. "The women removed your wet clothes," Philippe told her, his voice unsteady as he pulled up the thin blanket that covered her lower limbs. Then he turned his head and said something in Tahitian, and two young women came forward. One carried some brightly colored cloth, the other a very modern plastic mug. The cloth turned out to be a muumuu, which was deftly slipped over Daye's head; the mug contained coffee, sweet and milky, which Daye rather liked, although she was unable to take more than a few swallows. Really, she did not feel at all well, she thought. Her head hurt and there was still that nausea. She closed her eyes and leaned back again, but when she heard Philippe's urgent voice she opened them and tried to smile. "I'm just tired, that's all," she explained.

He did not look convinced. "The chief of this village owns a radio set. I will attempt to contact the *docteur* in Papeete."

"Philippe, no! Wait until we get to Anani."

"*Chérie*, we will not reach Anani until tomorrow. As you must hear, the storm is not yet ended, and soon it grows dark. Even if the *docteur* cannot reach us, he can advise, *n'est-ce pas?*" His lean, strong fingers probed beneath her hair. "Where is the pain, *ma petite?*"

Daye indicated a spot at the back of her head, wincing as Philippe's fingers located it. "It does not appear to be a large bruise, and the skin is only slightly broken," he said thoughtfully. "But there is still the risk of concussion, so you will remain here until we leave for Anani." He bent to give her a lingering kiss. "Ah, *mon amour*, this is not at all how I planned to spend this evening."

"Nor I," Daye said miserably.

"So? Our plans were, perhaps, similar?"

"I'm sure of it."

He sighed and stood up. His clothes looked crumpled, as if they had dried on his body, his dark hair was ruffled untidily, his strongly boned face bore signs of strain and anxiety. Yet he looked arrogantly male and incredibly sexy, and despite her disposition Daye felt excitement. "You will come back, won't you?" she whispered,

"*Naturellement*. And then, *chérie*, I will send the women away so that I can steal a few kisses in private." He smiled, but she saw the small flames of desire light his eyes and knew he wanted more than kisses.

After he had gone, ducking his head to get through

the doorway, the two women who were hovering in the background glided forward to sit on the floor near the bed. They stared at Daye with the same friendly curiosity to which she had been subjected on Anani, so she was not embarrassed. Contentedly she nestled her aching head into the surprisingly soft pillow and listened to the storm still raging outside. Strange to feel so safe and secure, she thought, her eyes drowsily taking in her surroundings, in a house that was apparently constructed of wooden planks and plaited palm leaves. Her gaze roved farther, noticing the floor was covered with woven mats, and that there was another iron bedstead complete with a rather thin mattress. There was also a wooden table, two cane chairs, and an oil stove. Rough shelves contained what appeared to be cooking utensils and on the floor beside the door stood a four-legged contraption Daye recognized as a coconut grater. An odor of damp foliage had drifted into the house and mingled with the smells of fruit and fish. Yet Daye did not find it unpleasant despite her squeamish stomach. To whom did the house belong, she wondered, and then thought how generous was the Polynesian nature that a family would relinquish their home for a stranger's comfort....

When she awoke this time she knew the storm was over, and that it was quite late. The two women had vanished she noticed as she sat up, but Philippe was stretched out on the other bed. At first she thought he was asleep, but then his black lashes raised, and his clear eyes met her own. He rose and came to sit on her bed. "How do you feel now, *chérie*? Unfortunately I was not able to contact the *docteur*, but the storm is over, and I will attempt to do so once again.''

"There's no need. Don't go, Philippe, I feel better, really.'' But did she, Daye asked herself. The moment she had sat up her head had begun to swim, and the nausea had returned. But she tried not to think about it because Philippe was here and she was so glad to see him.

"Are you hungry?'' He put his hands on her shoulders, caressing them through the thin cotton material.

She shuddered. "Oh, no. But I'll have a drink of water, please.'' And when Philippe crossed the room to fetch it she asked, "Whose house is this, Philippe?''

"It belongs to the chief's son.'' Philippe came back with the water and watched as she slowly sipped it. "It was given to us to share. You do not mind, *chérie*?''

Mind? When she had expected, wanted to share his bed? Mutely she held out the mug of water, and when he had set it on the floor beside the bed she held out her arms. He wore no shirt and she could feel his smooth bare skin beneath her hands. "Oh, Philippe,'' she whispered. "I love you so.''

He made a soft, hoarse sound deep in his throat and began to kiss her—ardent, aggressively demanding kisses that bruised her mouth and caused her head to reel. Kisses she was unable to respond to for he was taking all he wanted, drawing out her very soul. And between the kisses he murmured to her in French—soft, beautifully seductive words that fired her passion even though she did not understand him, fired her passion even though she could do nothing but lie weak and trembling in his arms.

Then at last, when she began to feel she might drift into unconsciousness, he seemed to come to his senses. Raising his head he gazed into her face with eyes that were strangely blank. *"Mon Dieu!"* he breathed in a tortured voice. "I must be mad. Forgive me, *mon amour*, I lost control." Gently he smoothed back her tousled hair. "Your eyes are huge and you look faint and afraid. Do not be afraid, *chérie*, I will not persuade you to make love when you are so unwell."

"But I want to. Philippe, I want to!" She drew away from him and began to slide the native gown up over her body. "Help me to take this off, Philippe."

He did so gently and without haste.

"Now hold me," she whispered. "Make love to me, Philippe."

"Chérie, how can I remember to be gentle when you tempt me so?" Philippe's voice was unsteady, as were his hands when they caressed her body. "I do not want to handle you roughly." His voice was thick. "The first time for us must be tender as well as enjoyable."

The first time! It would be the very first time for her. Reminded of it, Daye was suddenly apprehensive. More apprehensive than she had been that night in her room. Because now it was even more terribly important that she know how to give him pleasure. She shivered under the seduction of his hands, feeling her own passion rising to fever pitch. "I want to please you, Philippe," she managed to say huskily, "but I don't know what to do. So will you tell me and...and be patient?"

"Patient?" He eased her back on the pillow, his body half covering hers. "Have I not been patient, *chérie*?" His mouth touched hers in gentle, seductive kisses.

"You...you don't know what I mean. Philippe I...I've never made love before."

He straightened, his eyes curiously watchful. "What are you saying?"

"I know you think I've had lovers, but I haven't. Does it matter very much, Philippe? I mean, I shall do my best to...to please you." Daye bit her lip anxiously. "I know you would prefer me to be experienced...."

His fingers covered her mouth. "Hush, *chérie*, hush. How can you believe I would prefer you, the woman I love above all else, to be experienced?" His fingers traced the outline of her lips. "You are untouched." There was amazement in his voice. "*Chérie*, I am almost afraid."

"Don't be. Oh, darling—" she sat up, winding her arms around his neck "—I'm so glad I waited for you." Her lips touched his cheek, and at once he wrapped her in his arms. Loving arms. He loved her above all else. At last she had heard the words she wanted to hear. "Philippe, lie down with me. Darling, I'm tired of dreaming of this."

He laughed again, unsteadily. "*Mon coeur*, you are shameless. Ah, but I love you. And I need you so much I can scarcely bear the pain." He eased her back, bending his head to trail his lips over her breasts and flat stomach.

Every nerve inside her reacted, and she moved her body feverishly. "Please, Philippe," she whispered, and with a low groan he let her go and stood up.

A sudden pain burst in her head and she cried out. Philippe was at once bending over her. "What is it, *chérie*?"

"My head—" she tried to rise "—it hurts dreadfully."

Philippe was again pressing her back on the pillow. "*Chérie*, I must attempt to contact the *docteur*."

Daye opened her eyes. "In the morning, Philippe. Stay with me now." Weak tears filled her eyes.

"*Très bien, ma chérie,*" Philippe said soothingly, but she saw he looked worried. "I will stay but in the other bed. You must rest."

"I'm sorry. So sorry to spoil everything."

It was a drowsy murmur, and from a long way off she heard him answer, "Do not apologize. My love for you, *ma chérie*, is stronger than any desire."

THOSE WORDS were the first thing she remembered in the morning, but even as she lay there, relishing them, Philippe was bending over her, his face and voice filled with anxiety. "I feel marvelous," she told him, and drank some coffee and ate half a banana to prove it. But as she dressed in her own clothes, she knew she was not entirely herself and felt relieved when she learned he had left her while she was asleep and contacted the doctor who would visit her on Anani this afternoon. "You know, Philippe, Anani really ought to have its own doctor," she suggested, thinking that if she and Philippe had children she would want a doctor close at hand in case of emergencies.

"Anani's doctor passed away less than a year ago. We will have one again, do not fear." He spoke as if he had read her mind.

Wondering if he thought her presumptuous, she quickly changed the subject. "I'm glad you let Charles know we were safe."

"No more than I. He was already arranging to search for us." Philippe was watching her closely, a slight smile on his lips. "Are you prepared to meet the chief and his people, *chérie*? This we must do before we leave for Anani."

She nodded, and they went outside to where the chief waited. He was a massively fat middle-aged man and he wore red Bermuda-type shorts, a wildly colored shirt and blue-and-white peaked captain's hat. He sat in a huge cane armchair surrounded by his wife and family and what appeared to be about a hundred or so of his people. He beamed good-naturedly at Daye and Philippe and began to talk. Philippe talked back, laughing at times and turning to Daye to translate what was being said. Everyone else laughed or giggled while the children simply stared, particularly at Daye, in wide-eyed innocent curiosity. After what seemed a long time, two pretty young girls draped garlands of white blossoms around their visitors' necks, and then they all trooped to the lagoon where the islanders stood and watched as Daye and Philippe were rowed out to the launch.

The lagoon was still and clear as crystal; the ocean, as they sped toward Anani, deeply blue with only the merest ripple. Daye inhaled the scent of the flowers around her neck and wondered what she had done to deserve such happiness. Philippe loved her, she would become his wife. They would live together on beautiful Anani and raise adorable, dearly loved children. Her heart full, she glanced up to meet his warm caressing gaze and was unexpectedly overcome by panic. If something happened to separate them now she would never, never get over it.

Turning away, she stared blindly into space. Panic subsided into an oddly resigned premonition of impending disaster. Involuntarily she moved nearer to Philippe, relishing the comforting warmth of his body as he drew her close to his side. She remained there, frightened and depressed, hardly noticing when at last Anani came into sight.

It was not until they were gliding toward the jetty and she saw their own islanders waiting to greet them, that her fear and depression eased. And when Philippe lifted her from the boat and kissed her, saying, "Now they know you are truly my woman," she felt wonderfully happy again, and threw her arms around him and kissed him with fervent passion.

She was still happy, if extremely tired, when they reached the house and Philippe insisted she go upstairs to rest. "You will have your lunch in bed," he commanded. "And you will remain there until the *docteur* has examined you." He led her gently toward the stairs, pausing when Kao came into the hall and spoke to him. "It appears a special messenger from Papeete has delivered letters for us both," he told Daye when Kao had finished speaking. "Kao has left them in our sitting rooms."

As they climbed the stairs, Daye felt again that curious sensation of fear. "I wonder who the letters are from," she said nervously.

"Perhaps from Derek, to wish us an enjoyable time together." He smiled.

"Oh, yes, perhaps." But Daye did not think so.

They stopped at her door. "I will not come in. Not

until the *docteur* has made certain you are well."
Philippe kissed her, a gentle kiss that turned into a
soul-shattering passionate demand. *"Mon amour,"*
he whispered, when at last he raised his head, "I do
not know how much longer I can tolerate this."

"Nor I. Philippe, come in now, please!" Daye felt
almost fearfully desperate. "Come in now before...." Before what, she wondered? Before she
lost him?

"Do not tempt me, *chérie*. I will not come to you
until the *docteur* has seen you, until I am assured you
are well." He opened her door and she went inside.
Then the door closed and Daye was alone.

Her eyes went at once to the little writing desk. A
white envelope lay there, shockingly ominous, although she had not the least idea why. Slowly she
went to pick it up staring at the typewritten words:
Miss Daye Hollister, c/o Charles Chavot, Anani
Island. Her fingers shook as she tore it open, and
when she saw the bold, dark handwriting her heart
plummeted and she remembered her earlier premonition.

Dear Gloria (Or should I call you Daye?),
    Saw your friends at dinner last evening. Intro-
duced myself, but found them uncooperative
when I asked where you were. But later on, the
pianist woman came over to my table and we
had a nice chat. What have you done to her, little girl? She seems to have it in for you. Anyway,
she told me you and the Frenchman had gone
back to the island—Anani, isn't it?
    I'm not pleased with you, Gloria, and I don't
like your damn Frenchman. So I've sent the ar-

rogant snob a little present that will shock him
down to his aristocratic toes. I've let him know
I've got the rest of the set in my possession, and
that I will publish them if he doesn't tell you to
pack your cases and leave. I think he will do this,
Gloria. He won't want to be involved with a girl
who used to pose for naughty pictures.

By the time you get this I'll probably be on my
way to Hawaii. I'll wait there for you at the
Hilton.

Sorry about this, Gloria, but as I see it you'll
be more than ready to come back to me when
your Frenchman throws you out.

Max

The letter fell from Daye's nerveless fingers. Oh,
dear God, those dreadful photographs had come
back to haunt her. To ruin her life, perhaps, because
when Philippe saw.... Daye sank into the desk
chair, her legs weak, her heart thumping brutally.
She'd had no idea Max possessed a set. Only a few
had been sold, and then Reg had destroyed the others
as well as the negatives. Her hands shook as she
pushed back her hair. What was she to do? Philippe
would never understand; he would think she had
posed in that horrible way, because Sam Milo had
been very clever. No one looking at those photographs would guess that Daye Hollister's head was
superimposed on another woman's sexy body. Daye
clasped her hands, willing herself to stay calm, to
stop thinking so negatively. Of course Philippe
would understand. He loved her, and because he
loved her he would listen to her explanation, and
then he would believe her. That night in Paris she had

told Charles about the photographs, and he had believed her. But Philippe would see the photograph first, before she could explain....

Daye started in fright as a knock sounded on the door. Philippe! He was here! He had seen the photo!

Somehow she got to her feet. "Come in." Her voice sounded hoarse to her ears.

The door opened, and she felt faint with relief when Suzy entered and came toward her, a small white card in her outstretched hand. Daye accepted it mechanically, seeing as if through a mist the words: May I speak with you? Denise Dubois.

Denise. Oh, she could not possibly see Denise now! Yet as if she had no will she found herself nodding in acquiescence. Then after Suzy had gone she wondered why she had been so stupid. She must go to Philippe. Perhaps he had not seen the photograph yet.... Her door suddenly crashed open and she saw Philippe standing there, the photograph gripped in one shaking hand.

He looked terrifyingly angry. There was an odd pallor to his tanned face, his nostrils flared, his eyes held a dangerous gleam. The beautiful, sensuous mouth was parted, and Daye heard his breathing, raw and harsh in the silent room. A tiny whimper escaped her. He looked angry, yes, but he also looked tortured, and her heart felt as if it were bleeding for him. Pleadingly, she put out her hands. "Philippe, don't look like that! Please, darling, you don't understand."

"Do I not?" His voice rasped. He stared at her, then raised the photograph and stared at it. "How can I not understand? The pose, my innocent one, is most explicit."

A sob rose in her throat. "It isn't me, Philippe. Please listen; it isn't me!"

"So? It is, perhaps, Gloria Day. You have what is called a dual personality?" Philippe's voice was calm, too calm. "One is the chaste Daye Hollister, the other Gloria Day, the tramp. It was Gloria whom I met in Paris, *n'est-ce pas?* And here on Anani you have become Daye, who teases and torments but manages never to give. What excuse would you have found to use had I accepted your so recent invitation? Illness again? Ah, *oui*, you would, perhaps, have fainted in my arms." With a swift, savage movement, he kicked the door shut and advanced toward her. "Last night I lay awake, so obsessed with anxiety for your well-being that even my physical need for you seemed unimportant." Philippe spoke between his teeth, his voice no longer calm. "But this morning, to my infinite relief, *ma belle chérie* seemed recovered, and I allowed myself to dream of tonight, when I would hold her tenderly and make our coming together pure delight. Ah, yes, our coming together." Philippe uttered a short, bitter laugh. "I was nervous, unsure, do you realize that, *ma chère?* After all, was not *ma belle chérie* an inexperienced young woman who must be handled with particular care?" He glanced again at the photograph, drawing in a harsh breath. "No innocent would pose in such a manner." His tone was scornful. "No woman, innocent or not, would do so unless she were completely immoral."

"Philippe, please!" Daye begged. But he gave her a look of such fury she fell silent, tears rising quickly to her eyes.

He kept staring at her. "That is why I feel half-demented at this moment. It is not your lack of innocence I abhor but your lack of morality.'' He closed his eyes tightly, but before she could speak he opened them again, and she saw they were dark with despair. ''I was mad for you,'' he muttered. ''Mad. And for you it has been a game, *n'est-ce pas?* Torture the poor besotted fool with the promise of your body, but make certain, even to feigning illness, that he never learns its secrets.''

''Oh, Philippe, you don't know what you're saying.'' Tears trickled slowly over her cheeks. ''I've never intentionally denied you. I've wanted you more than I can say. Remember the night Terii interrupted? I . . . you had almost. . . .''

''Taken you?'' He laughed. ''Perhaps even you can have a weak moment.'' Unexpectedly, he thrust the photograph in front of her eyes. ''Did you pose for this in a weak moment?''

Horrified, Daye stared at the photograph, seeing the curvaceous, nude body in its shamefully suggestive pose. And above it, the fair young face with long, silkily light hair. Her own face.

''But it isn't me!'' she cried frantically. ''The head is mine, yes, but not the body. Oh, can't you tell, Philippe?'' Even as she asked she knew it was useless. The girl who had posed, although slightly plumper, had a body remarkably like her own.

His eyes were cold now. ''What I saw of your body, I saw in the heat of passion. It is naturally difficult to recall each detail, but I do not doubt the body is the same.'' Philippe pushed away the hand Daye had impulsively laid on his arm. ''Your explanation is quite unbelievable—a ridiculous lie.'' He suddenly flung the photograph aside. ''This is why you wished to return to Anani, *n'est-ce pas?* Max Lucan is aware of your . . . character, and you hoped to escape him." Again, the bitter laugh rang out. "You would do well to return to this Max, *petite Anglaise.* He must truly adore you if he can ignore what you are. I, most definitely, cannot."

Daye felt as if he had struck her. Oh, God, what was she to do? She was going to lose him. But she must not lose him! Life would be nothing without him. If only he would listen to her, let her explain! Fear made her desperate, shattering her pride. If he would not listen, she would make him *feel*. With a low cry she flung herself at him, winding her arms about his neck and pressing her mouth into his throat. "Hold me, darling," she murmured passionately. "Hold me! Make love to me! Make love to me *now*."

She could feel his body tensing, feel the quick upsurge of his desire. Then his hands were slipping over her, pulling her hips closer against him. *"Mon Dieu, mon Dieu!"* he whispered hoarsely. "I need you, *chérie*. I want you!" He began to mutter feverishly in French, and when Daye raised her face he took her lips as though he would devour them.

Thank God, she was not going to lose him! Relief and joy mingled with her own passion as she urgently returned his kisses . . . bruising kisses that hurt her soft mouth. Then she felt his hands beneath her shirt, fingers fumbling with the catch of her bra, and turned her head so that his hungry mouth rested on her cheek. "Darling," she breathlessly whispered, "let me do that. Let me undress for you."

Philippe's hands stilled, then fell away. Daye stepped back a pace or two and quickly pulled the blue knit shirt over her head. Her bra was next and as she met his eyes without shame, she undid the waist-band of her slacks and removed them. Only her brief panties were left and, still without shame, she stepped out of them and stood before him, a triumphant Eve.

Philippe stared silently at her, his narrowed eyes traveling over her body. Daye, too, was silent, her senses alert as she waited for him to take her in his arms. Why was he taking so long to do so? She had not expected him to have such self-control. Anxiety pricked her. Surely he would not reject her. Oh, no, he would not do that. Not Philippe.

"If you attempt to deny me. . . ." Philippe said suddenly.

"I won't." Daye's voice shook with relief. "I want you very much, Philippe."

"So. Has the game ended for you, *ma chère*?" Philippe's eyes had not left her body, but now they did and Daye's heart sank as she saw the icy indifference in their depths. "I do not doubt you are most accomplished in the art of pleasing as well as teasing a man, but the offer of your. . . wanton body is refused." His voice was like a lash, whipping her. "I admit I am a male who enjoys sexual pleasures, but I am most particular with whom I enjoy them." His eyes flicked contemptuously over her before he strode to the door. Without turning he said, "I cannot compel you to leave Anani, but if you decide to remain then I will go." He turned his head, and Daye flinched at the bitter dislike etched on his face. "I pray I will not have to set eyes on you again." The door opened and closed, and Philippe was gone.

Unable to immediately assimilate what had happened, Daye stared blankly at the closed door. She stared for an indeterminate time until the nagging ache in her heart swelled into almost intolerable pain. She began to tremble then and sickness curdled her insides. Lethargically she moved to her bedroom and like a mechanical doll removed a dressing gown from the wardrobe and put it on. As she did so her eyes fell on the bed, and in her mind's eye she saw herself there with Philippe, their bodies entwined. They would be there now...but he had not wanted her. His love had not been strong enough to withstand the shock of that photograph. He had not loved her enough to listen to her explanation and so he had left her....

Daye heard the tap on the door and for a moment thought Philippe had come back. Yet there was no eagerness in her as she went to the sitting room. And when Suzy entered, followed by Denise Dubois, she felt no disappointment and only the faintest surprise.

Suzy said something in French and glided away, leaving Denise standing there. "When you did not come downstairs I thought, perhaps, you expected to receive me here." In spite of the dullness of her mind, Daye knew Denise was nervous.

"Sit down, won't you?" she said politely. And when Denise perched on the edge of a chair. "Did you...? Oh, yes, you wanted to speak to me."

"*Oui, mademoiselle.* I wish to apologize for the so terrible things I said to you. I have wished to do this since Paul returned to us, and when I learned you were no longer in Tahiti, I knew I must approach you at once." Denise spoke swiftly, her accent pronounced.

"Oh. Well, there is no need to apologize, Madame

Dubois." Daye tried to sound sincere but heard the words coming out flatly.

"You are most generous, *mademoiselle*." Denise looked miserable. "I can excuse myself only by saying I was. . .desolate."

As I am now, Daye thought, sinking wearily onto the sofa. "I hope everything will be all right now," she made herself say.

"I am hopeful, also." Denise clasped her small hands together. "Is *mademoiselle* aware that Jean is Paul's true papa?"

Daye nodded, not knowing. . .or caring. . .if she should have lied.

Denise did not appear to mind. "Paul was shocked when he was told, and at first he was angry because I, his mama, had been wronged. But I assured him I am no longer resentful, and now he is so very happy." Tears glistened in her blue eyes. "I am happy. Oh, I have been a fool!"

Daye ran her tongue over her dry lips. "It isn't easy to behave rationally when you receive a. . .a shock." Her eyes suddenly fell on her discarded clothing: slacks, shirt, bra and panties. At least she had kept her sandals on. A bubble of laughter rose in her throat and she swallowed hastily. Had Denise noticed the clothes? Daye found she cared little one way or another. She blinked, focusing her eyes on Denise's face. "I mean, it must have shocked you to. . .to learn your husband was. . . ." She stopped. Why was she rambling on like this? Why was she so dizzy?

"Are you unwell, *mademoiselle*?" Denise's voice sounded far off.

"Hmm?" Daye dragged herself back from wherever she had drifted. "No, I'm all right. Er, what about Paul's music, *madame*?"

"We have agreed he will attend a college of music in Australia. It was wrong of me to keep him from something he loves." She gave a tiny smile. "Strange, is it not, that Paul is no longer certain he will make a career of music? Perhaps, he says, he will find he is not talented enough."

According to Philippe he was not talented enough. But Daye said nothing. Apparently Paul would be able to accept this if it turned out to be true. "I'm so pleased you are happy," she told Denise, knowing she meant this. Yet she could not inject sincerity into her voice or any feeling of pleasure into her heart.

"You have had much to do with this. Had you not spoken to Paul as you did, he would have gone to Paris and, who can tell, we might have lost him."

"Oh, no, I don't think so. Paul is a sensible boy, and he loves you." Daye forced her stiff lips into a smile.

"*Mademoiselle*, I wish you to know I will do anything for you. I am so very grateful." Denise hesitated. "You *are* unwell, *n'est-ce pas?*"

"I had a little accident," Daye admitted. "The doctor is coming...." She did not want to see the doctor or anyone else. All she wanted to do was leave, go home. Home to England. "*Madame*... Denise, do you know anyone here who will take me to Tahiti? I...I must catch a plane."

"You are leaving?" Denise sounded surprised.

"Yes...yes, I'm leaving today. Do you know anyone?"

"*Oui*. But will Philippe not—"

"Please!" Daye rose unsteadily. "You...you said

you would do anything, and although I hate to...to take you at your word I....'' She put her hand to her forehead. "Could you help me pack a few things and...and then find someone to take me away. At once. I must go at once." Her voice sounded strange to her ears.

"Très bien." Denise's voice was low. "You will return to Anani, will you not?"

"No." Daye managed to get to her feet. "I won't be coming back." Her voice held a peculiar calm and now she even felt it. She could think about leaving Anani, of never seeing Philippe again without the slightest hint of pain.

CHAPTER EIGHTEEN

"WELL, MISS HOLLISTER, the doctor tells me you are leaving us tomorrow." Sister Brady's plump figure paused at the foot of the narrow hospital bed.

"Yes." Daye smiled. "After almost four weeks, I expect you'll be pleased to get rid of me."

"Now, you know better than that. You've been an ideal patient. Too ideal if you ask me. No complaints, no temperament, no tears. Well, I don't mind when my patients have a little cry now and then; it's quite normal, really." Sister Brady took an inquisitive look at Daye's breakfast tray. "Dear, dear, you didn't finish again. What a naughty girl!"

"You just said I was the ideal patient," Daye reminded her.

Sister Brady laughed heartily. "Now, now, no cheek, my girl." She started to move away, then hesitated. "Who will come to fetch you tomorrow?"

"The taxi driver."

"Oh, rubbish! That isn't a nice way to go home from hospital, with no friend to keep you company. Now, why don't you telephone someone today? And don't try to tell me you haven't any friends because I won't believe you. You're a nice girl as well as a very pretty one, so you're bound to have friends of both sexes."

It wasn't the first time Sister Brady had said this or

tried to persuade Daye to let someone know she was in hospital. In fact, she had begun to harp on the latter by the end of Daye's first week as a patient. Daye was able to sit up then, the blinding headaches and nausea having subsided and the periods of wakefulness becoming more prolonged. "When you were admitted, you said you didn't want anyone notified. But I'm sure you've changed your mind now, haven't you, dear?"

But Daye had not changed her mind. She had no desire to see anyone, not even Reg. She did not want to talk to people or answer questions. Once she had asked the attending doctor if she could pay for a private room, but he had told her none was available. And although she suspected he had lied, not wanting her to shut herself away from the noise and bustle of the patient-filled ward, she had not argued. It was not really important, after all. She was learning to shut out the noise, and she was not compelled to join in the other patients' conversations. At that time, as the days of the second week slipped by, she felt very little physical pain and mentally, none at all. It was as if the concussion she had suffered had effectively blocked out the things it would be painful to remember. And then she had come down with the flu that was rampant in London, and after another week in bed she had suddenly found the doors of her mind opening, allowing the painful thoughts and memories to come crowding back. The past few days, as she recuperated, she often wondered how she could go on living, feeling as she did. Yet she was unable to cry. She, who had so often wept her heart out, was unable to shed even a few meager tears.

Sister's voice penetrated Daye's thoughts. "What

about the lady who looks after your house? Aren't you going to telephone her to get it ready for you? You'll have to keep warm, you know, and have food in the pantry.''

"You are kind to worry about me, sister, but I'll be all right. I thought I would go to a hotel for a few days, until I'm well enough to drive myself to the country.''

"A hotel!" Sister Brady looked exasperated. "Well, what more can I say? I'm not your keeper, and I can't force you to be sensible and let *somebody* know.''

After she had stalked off, Daye got out of bed and slipped into her dressing gown. It was red, a color Daye seldom wore, but it was warm and comfortable, if not exactly stylish. There had been nothing warm enough in her luggage, so when she was first able to get up, one of the young student nurses had offered to buy one for her. The girl had shopped at Marks & Spencer, bringing back most of the money Daye had given her. It seemed a long time since she had worn anything from Marks & Spencer, Daye thought, her mind drifting vaguely to the luxurious quilted dressing gowns in storage somewhere in London.

She thought of them now, and of the other warm clothing she would need, as she walked to the nearest window and stared out at the gray world beyond. It was sleeting, and the roads and pavements looked slippery even from this distance. She would have to leave the hospital in only a lightweight jacket and summer shoes. The very thought was chilling. Which month was it now? November? Or perhaps it was already December. Soon it would be Christmas, the season she had always loved. This year she had expected to spend Christmas on a sun-drenched tropical island with Charles and Audrey and Derek and.... Pain pierced her, and she stifled a moan, pressing her head against the cold windowpane.

But he was there, and she could not rid herself of him. He was there with his clear eyes looking into her soul, and his beautiful mouth hovering above her own. And she could hear his voice, that fascinating French-accented voice speaking soft words of love. And then the voice was speaking harshly, and the eyes were filled with contempt. Daye shivered, the tightness in her chest unbearable. How long ago was it? A lifetime... or only yesterday?

She wanted to move from the window because she was chilled. But she was riveted there while her mind forced her back to that last day in Anani, forced her to remember how she had felt when Philippe left her, rejected her. But afterward leaving the house with Denise, how had she felt then? She must have been numb, dazed, because the memory of the trip to Papeete in the boat that belonged to Denise's friend was extremely vague. As was the ride to the airport in a taxi, her good fortune in acquiring a seat on a 747 to Los Angeles, her booking in at the nearest hotel to wait until the early hours when the flight left. And on the flight itself she had slept, neither eating nor drinking and had only wakened at the insistence of the stewardess who wanted her to adjust her seat belt before landing.

On the flight from Los Angeles to London she had slept again, drinking only a little tea before they landed. Her headache was back, blindingly so, and she hardly managed to get herself through customs. Then as the porter trundled her luggage toward the exit she had quite suddenly slipped into an abyss of darkness. When she came to, she was here in the hospital, a white-coated doctor bending over her....

"Miss Hollister." It was Sister Brady again. Another lecture, Daye thought wearily, but the woman had only come to tell her the doctor had prescribed vitamin tablets. "To perk you up, dear. You must remember to take them twice a day when you leave here."

When she left here. That would be tomorrow. All of a sudden, Daye knew she did not want to leave here alone, could not face the anonymity of a hotel room. She would telephone Reg, ask him to make sure her cottage was made ready, ask him to come to get her. Dear Reg. Of course, she should have let him know she was here. Reg would not have upset her with questions, and he would never have told anyone she was in England if she had asked him not to. Daye felt relieved and a little happier. Sister Brady would be relieved and happy, too, she told herself, as she went to tell the woman of her decision.

Reg was the first visitor to enter the ward that afternoon. He carried an enormous bunch of hothouse flowers and his thin face was lit by a broad smile. Without looking at them, Daye was aware of the other patients' curiosity as Reg dropped the flowers on the bed and took her in his arms. "Lord, but I'm glad to see you," he whispered, kissing her on both cheeks and then, warmly on the mouth.

Presently he leaned back, looking at her intently. Over the phone he had said little, listening to her hasty explanation of where she was and why and then telling her simply that he was coming to see her.

Now, he said, "I found out almost three weeks ago that you'd left the islands and come back to England. But I wasn't worried, not at first. I thought you'd gone off somewhere to be alone and that soon I'd hear from you."

"I'm sorry, Reg." Daye put her hand to his cheek. "But who. . .? How did you know I had left Anani? Did Charles tell you?"

He looked at her thoughtfully. "We've been in touch. He's very worried about you."

"Yes, he would be." Daye felt vaguely sorry for causing Charles worry. She smiled at Reg. "You look well, darling."

"You don't." He spoke bluntly. "You're too thin and your remaining tan doesn't hide the fact that you're ghastly pale. Damn it! How the hell did you get concussion anyway? Did. . . ." He paused, his generous mouth tightening. "How did it happen?"

"I fell on a boat. It was during a storm." Daye spoke woodenly. "But it was this silly flu that really set me back. Fancy catching flu while you're in hospital."

Reg caught at her hands and Daye realized she was twisting them together. "You're unhappy," he said. "This trip to paradise was a bloody fizzle."

Her mouth opened to voice a denial. But she only said, "I don't want to talk about that."

"You might not want to but you're going to. I know you, Daye. Something is all bottled up inside you, and it wants to be let out. Come on, luv, tell me about it." Reg leaned closer. "Tell me about Philippe."

The sound of his name sent a shock tingling through Daye's body. "No!" she moaned, closing her eyes.

"Daye, you aren't going to faint on me?" There was panic in Reg's voice.

Daye opened her eyes and stared at him wildly. "How do you know about him? Did Charles. . . ."

"No. Well, that's only partly true." Reg massaged her fingers. "You've gone icy cold."

"Yes." Daye felt it was an understatement.

"I don't want to hurt you, but there are things I must say. And putting them off won't do any good. Can you get up and go with me to the waiting lounge or somewhere?"

She nodded, and Reg helped her into her dressing gown, and they left the ward and went down the corridor to the lounge. There were, fortunately, only two people there, both men, both apparently absorbed in magazines. Reg led Daye to a sofa as far away from the others as possible, and they sat quietly for a time before he asked softly, "You're all torn up because of this Philippe, aren't you? What did he do to you, Daye?"

"Nothing."

"That's a lie." Reg spoke calmly. "You're in love with him, aren't you?"

Daye shivered. "I feel nothing for him. If I did I'd hate him, not love him."

Reg heaved a sigh. "Damn it, your eyes are like green stones with no shine or warmth. I can't bear to see you like this. I'd rather you got angry or had screaming hysterics; at least you'd look alive." He turned her to face him. "I know all about it. I just wanted you to tell me voluntarily."

Daye's throat was suddenly tight and she swallowed with difficulty. "What do you know?"

"That Max sent a certain photograph as well as a

nasty, insinuating letter to Philippe Chavot. And that Philippe Chavot then treated you like dirt.''

The tightness in her throat made her voice husky. "How do you know about...what happened?"

Reg gently smoothed back her hair. "Daye, Philippe came to see me about...oh, I'd say it was almost three weeks ago now. He told me himself what he'd said and done to you. No, listen!" he ordered sharply, as she tried to interrupt. "He apparently regretted it at once, but he left the house and went riding until he'd cooled off. When he got back to the house a couple of hours later, he was told you'd gone with...what's her name? Denise? He said he didn't try to see you then because he knew you'd be upset and would need some time to get over what had happened. Then the next day he discovered you'd left the island." A slight smile touched Reg's mouth. "He found a letter from Max in your room and thought you'd gone to Hawaii to be with Max. So he went to look for you there." Reg's smile stretched into a satisfied grin. "He threatened Max with dire consequences if he ever went near you or if he did anything to hurt you again, he'd probably kill him. And if you think Philippe bragged about it to me, you're wrong. Esther gave out the info when she telephoned a couple of days ago."

Something kindled inside Daye. It felt rather like anger. Strange, but it seemed an aeon since she had felt anger. "That's practically funny," she said tightly. "He hurt me more than Max ever did. The photograph wouldn't have mattered if he had shown me he cared enough to let me explain. I didn't expect him to ignore it; I knew he would be upset, but I didn't think he would...." Daye's voice had risen, and she lowered it. "I want to go back to the ward now," she said, getting unsteadily to her feet.

"Not for a minute." Reg pulled her onto his lap. "Be a good girl and don't make a fuss. Those two chaps over there are ready to punch my nose." She sat in stiff silence as he continued. "I admit he was wrong, your Philippe. And no one knows it more than he. And, God help me, Daye, I think he was asking me to bash his face in. I mean, he would have sat there and let me do it." Reg's voice shook slightly.

"I doubt that," Daye scoffed.

"You didn't see his face, luv."

Daye stared fixedly at the incredibly bad reproduction of John Constable's *Hay-Wain* that hung on the wall. "He's most likely ashamed," she stated flatly. "Ashamed because he knows now I was telling the truth about the photograph."

"And how did he find that out, Daye?"

"From Charles, I suppose."

"And he traveled to Hawaii and then to England just to say he was sorry?"

Daye shrugged. "Well, I...he...he has a lot of money and traveling means nothing to him." But she frowned, staring into Reg's face almost warily.

"Philippe didn't tell his father about the photograph. The day after you left he spoke to Charles for a few minutes and in some roundabout way got himself off to Hawaii. I've been in touch with Charles as I said. He's worried about you, but he thinks you and his son had an argument. A lovers' quarrel." Reg gave her a rueful smile.

She felt an unreasoning irritation. "Then *you* told Philippe about the photo."

"Yes... yes, I did. I told him the photos were composites. C'mon, Daye, please.... Knowing how much he loves you, how could I in all fairness not tell him the truth? He knows he reacted badly but he came after you anyway. Now you can't imagine how he feels, luv. He's sure you'll never forgive him."

Daye rose to her feet so swiftly she swayed. "What you're saying is he came after me still thinking I posed for that photo."

"That's enough, you silly girl." Reg rose, too, and tucked her hand under his arm. "Come on, let's get you back to the ward. You could do with a rest."

They strolled slowly along the corridor, and because she could not help herself, she asked, "Have you seen him since then?"

"Just once; a week ago. But we keep in touch. He wanted to find you himself."

Daye looked quickly up at him. "Where is he now?"

"I don't know exactly, but two days ago he phoned to say he was driving to Skye. Flora Evans was one of the first people I told him about, and although he's telephoned her twice and she's assured him you're not there, he apparently decided she might be fibbing, or that you might have turned up there in the meantime. Pathetic isn't it, to think of that big strong man chasing all over the place, driving himself crazy?" Reg spoke flippantly, but he did not smile.

Daye tried desperately not to think of it. "You sound as if you're sorry for him," she said accusingly.

"Is that so strange? He may be rich and good-looking, but he's the most unhappy man I've ever laid eyes on.'' They had reached the ward and paused before going inside. ''You know,'' Reg went on thoughtfully, ''I've watched no end of chaps go overboard for you these past few years, but this time it's different. Do you suppose it's because you're as much in love as the fellow is?''

She lowered her head. ''He doesn't love me,'' she said bitterly.

''Yes, he does.''

''No!'' Daye shook her head violently. ''And I don't love him. How could I after. . . after the things he said?'' She raised her eyes to give him a stricken look. ''He acted as though I were a. . . a slut. And when I. . . when I *offered* myself he. . . .'' She choked on the words.

Reg put his arms around her. ''There, darling, don't get so upset. Remember he's a human being. He was angry and disillusioned. And as jealous as hell, too.''

''*You* wouldn't have behaved as he did,'' she muttered against his chest.

''Perhaps not. But then I'm Reg Parker, not Philippe Chavot.'' He let her go, looking down at her with his attractive grin. ''You know, I've loved you for years; you've spoiled me for other women. Yet when we're apart I'm happy enough, and I can live a normal life. Frankly, I don't think your Frenchman can do that.''

''He can. He's very strong willed.'' Her voice was strained.

''Except where you're concerned, I'd say.'' Reg pushed open the ward door. ''Have a nice rest, and I'll see you tomorrow.''

Again she clutched his arm. ''You won't tell him

where I am, where I'm going? Please, Reg, I'm not... I'm not ready.''

It was true; she was not ready. Yet when the long day was over and only a dim light burned in the ward, Daye lay awake, her heart heavy with pain, her body restless with longing. And at last she wept, not even ceasing when the sympathetic young night nurse came to comfort her.

REG DROVE HER HOME the next day and stayed overnight, sleeping in one of the two upstairs bedrooms while Daye chose to sleep in the downstairs room that had been converted into a bed-sitter for her mother. Originally the dining room, it was light and pleasant with French windows that opened onto the back garden. It was decorated in yellow with touches of green, and Daye had furnished it with beautiful cherry wood and a double bed with gleaming brass bedstead. Most of her mother's personal belongings were packed away, but Daye thought she might unpack some of them—her books and one or two pieces of china—and arrange them as her mother had done. She mentioned this to Reg as they sat over the breakfast Mrs. Brown from the village had cooked for them, but he gave her an exasperated look and said, "Stop trying to tell yourself you're staying here, Daye."

"What do you mean?" Her voice faltered. "I... I'm going to live here."

Reg popped sausage into his mouth and chewed slowly. "So that's what you'll tell Philippe when he comes for you?"

Daye felt her cheeks whiten. "When he comes...? Reg, I've said I'm not ready. You haven't...you didn't...?"

"Tell him where you'd be? No, luv, I haven't spoken to him since he left for Skye."

"But you mean to tell him when he phones?" She put down her knife and fork, her hands shaking. "Oh, Reg!"

"I won't tell him where you are if you don't want me to. But I won't lie if he asks if I've heard from you. Look here, Daye, the chap's been here twice already; it isn't unreasonable to suppose he'll come again."

"Then I'll go somewhere else."

"No, you won't. Stop being a fool, luv, you know you have to see him sometime."

Reg took a gulp of tea and stood up. "I've got to be off now. I'll phone in a couple of days." He bent to kiss her. "Take care of yourself; eat well and keep nice and warm. And for God's sake, my dear, start admitting to yourself that you want to forgive the man. That you have to, because your life will be miserable without him."

Of course it wouldn't be, she silently insisted, yet the next three days were spent in an agony of suspense, waiting for the telephone or doorbell to ring. And whenever an automobile entered the quiet lane that curved past the house, she would fly to the window, watching anxiously until it went by. Then she would sigh. . .with relief, she always told herself, ignoring another little voice that whispered her sigh was actually one of disappointment.

Reg telephoned on the third day, but although she waited expectantly he did not mention Philippe. Daye did not mention him either, yet when she hung up the receiver she covered her face with her hands and sobbed in bitter frustration, because she had so badly wanted to.

Daye had been home almost a week before she spoke to Reg again, and by this time she was wretchedly certain that Philippe had changed his mind and decided he did not love her enough to continue to chase around a strange country in search of her. He had gone home to Anani, she thought despairingly, and of course Reg suspected—perhaps even knew for certain—and was afraid to phone to tell her in case she went to pieces. Oh, God! Here she was, more than ready to see Philippe again, and now...now he would never come to her.

She was huddled miserably by the fire, contemplating a future that yawned emptily, when she decided she had to phone Reg, hear the worst from his lips. And afterward she would take a long hot bath, put on that comfortable red dressing gown and drink several glasses of wine while she watched television. Slowly she spun the dial and waited for Reg's voice. When it came she said quickly, "Philippe went to Skye about nine days ago, didn't he? Has he...? Hasn't he telephoned you since then?"

"Well, luv, as a matter of fact he hasn't phoned." Reg spoke casually.

"Why? I mean...Reg, has he gone away? Are you not telling me in case I get upset?"

"Now, I'm sure he hasn't done that," Reg soothed. "You know the weather up north has been rotten. One snowstorm after another."

Her heart dropped. "Oh, dear heaven! Could he have had an accident?"

"No, no, I would've heard. He had my address

with him, you see." Reg paused. "Look, my dear, can I phone back? I, er, I've got someone here."

"Oh. A woman?" She spoke lightly, and when he did not answer said a quick good-night and hung up. She felt oddly hurt. Reg had never been short with her before. Did he have a woman in his flat with him or was he reluctant to talk to her because he *did* know something she did not? Did he want time to think of a way to tell her? Daye walked dazedly upstairs to the bathroom and turned on the taps. Somehow she knew, and thanked God for it, that Philippe had not met with an accident. When Reg phoned back, he would tell her Philippe was no longer in this country.

It was eight o'clock before she came downstairs again and went to look out of the sitting-room window before drawing the curtains. It had begun to snow, huge flakes that drifted slowly from the night sky. So beautiful, she thought, and tears brimmed quickly in her eyes. But before they fell, she brushed them determinedly away and went to pour herself a glass of wine.

She had finished her second glass and was half-heartedly watching a rather noisy detective play on television when the doorbell buzzed. Her heart gave a little jerk of alarm, and her eyes flew to the clock. Ten minutes past nine. Who on earth could it be? Then she knew. It was Reg. He could not say what he had to over the phone, so he had come to see her. Glad she had drunk the courage-giving wine, she got to her feet, switched off the television, and went to open the door.

"*Bonsoir, mademoiselle,*" said the man who stood there.

He was wearing a sheepskin jacket with the collar

turned up, but his head was bare and his dark hair was ruffled and flaked with snow. His eyes were brilliant and some indefinable emotion lurked in their depths as he gazed at her. "Will you allow me to come inside?" he asked huskily.

Daye said nothing. Like an automaton she stepped back, opening the door wider. Was she dreaming or drunk, she wondered, as he passed her and stood in the hall, filling it with his presence. Then he spoke again, still in that husky voice. "You will catch a cold." Gently he removed her hand from the door-knob and closed the door.

It was the touch of his hand that proved he was real. He was truly here, in her house! He had not gone back to Anani. Afraid he would see the incredible joy that was pouring into her, she lowered her eyes. "How did you know I was here?" she asked in a low voice.

"I was with Reg when you telephoned. I have been at his flat since I returned from Scotland three nights ago." Philippe spoke in an odd, shaky tone and when she looked at him Daye saw he was indeed shaken. "I was mad with impatience," he went on, "but Reg assured me you would telephone soon and that it would mean you wished to see me."

"Reg said that?" Her voice was faint. She should, she thought, be annoyed with Reg for allowing her to suffer these past few days, and for taking so much for granted. But she was not in the least annoyed. "What if I hadn't telephoned when I did?" she could not help asking.

"My patience was almost at an end. Tomorrow, I think, I would have come and begged you not to send me away." Philippe's tone was still oddly emotional.

"Daye, you have been ill, in the hospital. You had the concussion and I accused you of...." He paused, his expression somber.

Daye forced herself to remember the amenities. "Won't you take off your coat and...and come in and sit down."

"Merci." Philippe removed his heavy jacket and draped it over the nearby coatrack. He was wearing a thick white sweater with a roll neck and Daye thought that he must feel the cold after being used to warmer climates. It occurred to her then that he did not look well. He seemed thinner, tired looking, his dark face bore signs of strain. She struggled with an overwhelming desire to put her arms around him and soothe away the strain.... Turning swiftly she led the way into the sitting room and indicated the large armchair opposite the sofa.

But Philippe did not sit down at once. "You are recovered now?" he asked, frowning. "But you are too slender and pale. Do you not eat?"

"I'm not hungry very often." She sat down on the sofa and stared into the fire. "You are thinner, too, and you look tired. Our English climate must not agree with you."

"It is not the climate," he said thickly. "Daye, I have thought I would go mad. I have thought, at times, I would never see you again."

She dared not look at him. "I'm sorry you've chased about so much. Was the weather in Scotland awful?" She spoke rapidly, nervously. "Did you see Miss Evans then? Is she well? I really must—"

"Daye, *mon amour*, stop!" Philippe cut in urgently. "I cannot stand it. Let me hold you for just one moment. I promise...for only one moment."

Panic rushed through her and she glanced up at him, shaking her head vigorously.

He moved a few steps away then stopped. When he looked at her again she saw his eyes were bleak.

"How do I begin?" he asked. "What can I say to excuse myself for my behavior. Shall I say that I was so suddenly dashed from heaven into hell that I lost my mind?" He walked restlessly to the center of the room then back again. "It would be the truth, but I am a man, not a boy and should have more control over my emotions." He spoke grimly, his face so drawn his cheekbones were more than usually prominent. "It seems impossible, now, that I could have treated you as I did. That I could have left you there, looking at me with such anguished eyes. *Mon Dieu!*" Philippe rubbed the back of his neck distractedly. "Daye, will you believe I am inundated by shame?"

Daye said nothing. She huddled farther into the corner of the sofa, playing nervously with a button on her dressing gown.

"So you find it difficult to believe?" Philippe spoke rather bitterly. "Then you will find it even more difficult to believe that when my senses returned that day I knew I did not care about your past. That I loved you more than my life and would do so forever. I went to Hawaii, blind with fury and ready to kill Max. I warned him that if he ever... ever...did anything to harm you again he would not live to....." His voice broke suddenly. "What a fool I have been." He strode to the fireplace and stared down into the flames as he said quietly, "Always I shall live with the knowledge that I failed you. My immediate reaction when I saw the photograph should have been to destroy it." He turned his head, meeting her eyes.

A silence fell, during which they simply gazed at each other. Then Daye heard herself say, "No, I don't think you could have done that. Not many men could. It must have been a terrible shock and...." She paused. Was she really saying this, and what was more, meaning it? Was she really understanding what he had gone through when his eyes fell on that dreadful photograph? A sudden, dizzying emotion overcame her, and the horror of that scene in her bedroom began to fade. "You are only human," she whispered.

Philippe was staring at her uncertainly. "Dare I hope you have forgiven me?" He raised his arms, then let them fall again to his sides. "Dare I hope you still care for me, that you will marry me?" His tone was uncertain, too.

Daye bit her lip. "So you do believe I cared for you?"

Philippe sighed. *"Oui, mon amour."*

She quickly stood up. "Can I offer you something? A...a glass of wine?" She motioned vaguely toward the sideboard.

"You can offer me your love. And your forgiveness." He spoke softly, not moving from where he stood.

"The two seem to go together. If I love you, then I must forgive you. And, Philippe—" a sob caught in her throat "—I love you very much."

As the confession left her lips he moved, and she was caught in his arms and held so tightly she could scarcely breathe. *"Mon amour, mon coeur,* I have longed for this moment for weeks. Life has been hell, wanting to see your face, hear your voice, hold you in my arms." His voice was hoarse, muffled against her hair. "*Chérie*, I promise, I swear by all the saints I will never hurt you again. Never!"

Urgently his lips roamed her face, touching everywhere but her waiting mouth. And when Daye could no longer stand it she pressed her fingers against his neck and whispered, "Kiss me properly, Philippe. Oh, kiss me! I love you so!"

He met her lips, kissing her with a devastating passion that was somehow free of demand. It was as if he was giving, not taking, telling her over and over again that he loved her. Daye was shaken, almost humbled by the intensity of the love he was offering, and presently she wept, her body trembling in his arms.

Philippe lifted his head. "Why do you weep, *ma belle chérie*? Are you not happy?" His voice was low and anxious.

"Oh, yes! *So* happy, my love." Daye rested her head on his chest and gave a satisfied sigh. "You're mine, aren't you? All mine for always?"

He laughed softly. "I am yours, *mon ange*, and you belong to me." He held her away from him, his clear eyes intent. "You will marry me as soon as possible, *n'est-ce pas?* Before we go home to Anani?"

Home to Anani! With Philippe as her husband. She looked exultantly into his face. "Oh, yes! Yes!" Her laugh rang out happily. "Won't Charles be pleased!"

"He will," Philippe agreed, then caught her close again. "*Ah, chérie, je t'aime, je t'adore.*" His lips found hers and this time his kisses were different, taking as well as giving, and filled with a longing and need he made no attempt to control. Nor did Daye try to hide her own need, her desire for more than kisses and caressing hands. Eagerly she helped him unbutton her dressing gown, delighting in the touch of his hands moving in urgent possessiveness over her body. "You are going to stay here with me, aren't you?" she asked in a passionate whisper.

He kissed her again, a sensuous, lingering kiss, his hard body trembling as much as her own. And when he raised his head at last, he asked in a husky, uneven voice, "As your guest, *mon coeur*, or as your lover?"

"As my lover," she whispered, smiling up at him joyfully, longingly.

Passion darkened his eyes, and as he kissed her yet again he swept her up into the protective embrace of his arms. "Let us go now," he murmured invitingly, drawn by the soft light of the bedroom. "We have waited too long for Paradise."

What readers say
about SUPERROMANCE

"Bravo! Your SUPERROMANCE [is]... super!"
R.V.,* Montgomery, Illinois

"I am impatiently awaiting
the next SUPERROMANCE."
J.D., Sandusky, Ohio

"Delightful... great."
C.B., Fort Wayne, Indiana

"Terrific love stories. Just
keep them coming!"
M.G., Toronto, Ontario

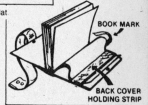